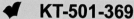

KT-501-369

WITHDRAWN FROM
BROMLEY LIBRARIES

 To renew, find us online at:
https://prism.librarymanagementcloud.co.uk/bromley
Please note: Items from the adult library may also
accrue overdue charges when borrowed on
children's tickets.

In partnership with

Bromley

BETTER
the feel good²

Bromley Libraries

30128 80487 732 5

Also by Jadesola James

Redeemed by His New York Cinderella

Carina Press

The Sweetest Charade

Also by Kelly Hunter

Claimed by a King miniseries

Shock Heir for the Crown Prince
Convenient Bride for the King
Untouched Queen by Royal Command
Pregnant in the King's Palace

Discover more at millsandboon.co.uk.

MILLS & BOON

THE ROYAL BABY
HE MUST CLAIM

JADESOLA JAMES

RETURN OF
THE OUTBACK
BILLIONAIRE

KELLY HUNTER

MILLS & BOON

All rights reserved including the right of reproduction
in whole or in part in any form. This edition is published
by arrangement with Harlequin Enterprises ULC.

This is a work of fiction. Names, characters, places, locations
and incidents are purely fictional and bear no relationship to
any real life individuals, living or dead, or to any actual places,
business establishments, locations, events or incidents.
Any resemblance is entirely coincidental.

This book is sold subject to the condition that it shall not,
by way of trade or otherwise, be lent, resold, hired out
or otherwise circulated without the prior consent of the publisher
in any form of binding or cover other than that in which it is published
and without a similar condition including this condition
being imposed on the subsequent purchaser.

® and TM are trademarks owned and used by the trademark owner
and/or its licensee. Trademarks marked with ® are registered with the
United Kingdom Patent Office and/or the Office for Harmonisation
in the Internal Market and in other countries.

First Published in Great Britain 2022
by Mills & Boon, an imprint of HarperCollins*Publishers* Ltd,
1 London Bridge Street, London, SE1 9GF

www.harpercollins.co.uk

HarperCollins*Publishers*
1st Floor, Watermarque Building,
Ringsend Road, Dublin 4, Ireland

The Royal Baby He Must Claim © 2022 Jadesola James

Return of the Outback Billionaire © 2022 Kelly Hunter

ISBN: 978-0-263-30074-1

03/22

MIX
Paper from
responsible sources
FSC C007454

This book is produced from independently certified FSC™ paper
to ensure responsible forest management.
For more information visit www.harpercollins.co.uk/green.

Printed and Bound in Spain using 100% Renewable Electricity
at CPI Black Print, Barcelona

THE ROYAL BABY
HE MUST CLAIM

JADESOLA JAMES

MILLS & BOON

CHAPTER ONE

"TARGETS IDENTIFIED," SAID Kemi Obatola's little sister, Tobi, gleefully, not twenty minutes after they'd entered Café Abuja. The nineteen-year-old was fairly dancing in the rhinestone-studded heels she wore that night. She looked ready to burst with self-satisfaction and excitement.

Though the sisters were like twins when it came to face and figure, with cheeks that *would* look round no matter how much contouring they did, deep amber-hued skin and brown eyes as round as their faces, personality wise they were completely different. Kemi was quiet, ladylike, with a manner that verged on timid, hammered into her by her late mother and the string of stepmothers that followed her. Tobi, on the other hand, was a veritable firecracker, and Kemi had her hands full ensuring the girl stayed out of trouble.

Tonight was one of the nights she'd be working overtime.

"Tobi," Kemi said wearily. It had been only an hour since they had left their hotel, and Kemi's head was already pounding; her sister usually had that effect on her. "One drink. That's all. And we go back."

"I've been at you all week to come out with me," Tobi said smugly and flashed the hostess in the front of the restaurant and nightclub a sweet smile. "There's no way

I'm going to let you drag me home after an hour!" Kemi nearly lost her footing as Tobi threw an arm round her shoulders, leaning heavily on her. "Just look at this place. It's a perfect night, *biko*. We're out, Kemi. We did it— we escaped!"

Kemi was half-sick from a mixture of adrenaline and dread, but she couldn't help the tiny spark of excitement that blossomed in the middle of her chest.

We escaped. When was the last time she'd been out like this? And Tobi had a knack for making everything seem so *magical*. Dressing hurriedly in their luxury hotel room in finery they'd purchased that day—dresses and shoes for dancing and being danced with. Champagne and cakes. Bribing mean-faced security guards to help them.

The girls had accompanied their father, the Oba of Gbale, to Abuja, where he was making a presentation along with several other local kings and chiefs, speaking on the progress of female education and the vast and varied achievements of young women all over the country. It was a rare trip—their father was known for his conservatism as much as he was for his iron-fisted control of his household, and Kemi could not remember a time they'd been permitted to go this far away from home. Even in this modern age, when their fellow countrywomen traveled worldwide and excelled in every career under the sun, their father seemed to be stuck in an age that was long gone, and his daughters normally had no choice but to go along with his wishes.

"We're practically locked down in a cult," Tobi declared passionately. And it was true. Security at the palace monitored their every move; they had no access to money, transportation or any resource not approved by the king. Running away was not an option; where would two spoiled princesses who'd been kept under lock and key since childhood *go*? They'd end up dead or worse, and their father reminded them of that at every turn, regaling them with tales of women raped and robbed and stolen away from the streets when they were foolish enough to venture out without protection.

"Nigeria isn't what it used to be," he'd declare, and he'd look at Kemi then, his eyes clouding with worry. But he wasn't a total jailer: they technically had everything they might want. Money, gifts, the finest food to be found, extensive wardrobes. They just weren't free—not really.

And really, Kemi couldn't blame him, not after everything she'd put him through.

Tobi was determined, as usual, to wriggle out from her father's restrictions, and the "educational" trip had been the perfect opportunity. After a week of demurely sitting at the older man's side at the summit and visiting Abuja's finest stores under the escort of her father's security team, Tobi had finally persuaded Kemi to sneak out with her—by blackmailing her.

"If you don't come with me, I'll go by myself," she threatened.

"Tobi!" The idea of her little sister being set loose upon the Abujan party scene alone was more horrifying than the idea of going out. So Tobi had bribed their father's security team with items from their bulging jewel boxes for safe and unrestricted passage from the hotel.

Now, her father's security guard was parked some distance away, waiting for his signal to bring them back to the hotel. Kemi hated being out in the open, so exposed. The only thing that kept her calm was that here, in this great city, no one would know who they were. They'd fit right in with the multitude of girls crowding the entryway in tight, fashionable dresses, looking to drink, to dance, to flirt, to get their hearts broken.

She hoped.

Tobi had chosen well; the dimly lit nightclub was one

of the newest, hottest places featured in the society papers, and goodness knew Tobi kept up with her society papers. Despite the hum of air-conditioning and several industrial fans, the interior of the room was muggy and warm, and a faint sheen of perspiration broke out on Kemi's skin within moments of entering. She could see the charm of the place, however. Medium-size round tables littered the space, creating nooks for intimate mingling, and leather booths lined the walls, shrouded by lush greenery that looked so real Kemi itched to touch it. It smelled of cigars and alcohol, smoky grilled meat and the mingled perfumes of thousands of women who had been there. A dance floor that stretched out to an enormous covered patio featured an elevated stage with a live band playing a throbbing, pulsating juju beat that set toes tapping just as soon as they entered the space. Tobi had never looked prettier; her large eyes gleamed with fun, and her full lips pursed speculatively.

"It's beautiful," Kemi admitted, raising a hand to tuck her braids behind her ears. She loved music, loved to dance, and the rhythm was sliding warm and seductive over her skin. She swayed, just a little bit, and Tobi saw this and grinned.

"The bar," she decided, and navigated Kemi firmly toward the large marble-topped edifice that took up the center of the room. Men and women hung out there, eating off small tin plates, drinking, gossiping, sizing up the crowd. It was the single men and the ones who hung out in pairs that worried Kemi. They looked assessing. Speculative. Hungry.

Wolves.

Tobi adjusted her cleavage, then asked for two gin and tonics from the bartender, a slim fellow dressed all in black with crooked but bone-white teeth.

"I got enough from the guard for two rounds," she

whispered to her sister, extracting a small bundle of bills from her minuscule handbag. Kemi's stomach knotted. While this part of Abuja was posh enough to be considered relatively safe, it was still well after dark—and this was still a city they didn't know. It made them vulnerable in ways Tobi likely wouldn't think about. Kemi tucked her own handbag as tight to her side as she could manage and winced when a large, friendly-looking man in a suit just a hair too tight bumped into her, muttered an apology, did a double take and grinned.

"*How* now—"

"Keep walking," Kemi snapped, a little more nastily than she wanted to; nervousness had given her an edge. The man lifted his brows but did walk away, and Tobi managed to pull up her slack jaw.

"Kemi! He could have bought us drinks!"

"He was being a creep," Kemi muttered, even though it wasn't true. Their glasses came just in time, and Kemi took a long sip, though she really didn't like the taste of gin.

Tobi scowled and smoothed her face out with some effort, then reached out and cupped Kemi's cheek in her hand. "No moralizing," she said. "I am determined to have some fun, and you're going to be the one to do it with me."

"Tobi—"

"No." Her sister shook her head. "Stop being a martyr, Kemi. Whatever happened in the past, Dad's behavior is outrageous and you know it."

Kemi felt her skin grow hot. Neither of them had alluded to her past that night, but it had hung over both of them like a cloud, context that neither wanted to admit to. Kemi reached over absentmindedly and massaged the length of her arm.

The scar tissue there stretched from the elbow all the way to her shoulder and still hurt badly sometimes, even though the bullet fragments had long been removed from where they'd embedded in her skin, muscle, bone. Surgeries had left her with use of her arm, but a limb that still, despite its repair, ached sometimes, as if reminding her what she'd gone through. She'd spent years learning to write and navigate with her left. Even now, it felt awkward, and that awkwardness felt as if it'd penetrated every area of her life, as if she was consistently doing everything slightly wrong.

Her sister's quick eye caught the gesture. "Does your arm feel all right?"

Kemi nodded. Tobi continued to chatter away, something about getting them a table and Kemi taking an aspirin for any pain, but she was fading out, her mind anchoring to a memory, pushing out light, sound, everything else in that moment.

Three bullets.

She'd never forget the number, and she'd caught them on a night much like this one. She'd been wearing a dress quite similar to the one Tobi wore tonight and out on a balmy evening during the rainy season, much like this one. There had been music, and handsome men, and a nightclub, and she'd been as daring as Tobi was that night, scaling the palace wall and meeting her friends. She hadn't realized what was going on until there was a semiautomatic pressed to the small of her back—

No. She exhaled, and quickly, bringing herself back to reality with a whoosh. Tobi was peering into her face, looking so worried that Kemi managed a rather sickly smile. She swayed slightly on her heels, then managed to lift her chin and look her sister in the eye.

"Oluwatobi Temitope Olufunmilayo Oluwadara Obatola," she said sternly, "you *will* behave."

Her sister actually stepped back and looked cowed for

a minute, then she laughed and wrapped her plump arms round Kemi's waist.

"I will," she promised and planted a kiss on Kemi's cheek, then reached up to tuck one of her sister's long braids behind her ear, speaking a little more gently now. "We're going to dance, and we're going to drink, and we're going to find some gorgeous bachelors to buy us cocktails and the best rice and chicken in this neighborhood—"

"Bachelors? I can bet that three-quarters of the men here are married."

Tobi ignored her, then took her hand and drew her toward the patio, where the band had segued into a playful highlife beat. "This music is about sixty years old," she said disdainfully, "but I picked this place because I know you like it. Dance with me, sister."

Kemi went—at least dancing would get them away from the men at the bar—and in the first few moments, she found herself relaxing. She did so love traditional music—the starts and the stops, the playful ways the drums interacted with each other. The bandleader winked at her. He was a middle-aged man with a fine baritone that he navigated skillfully, making it an instrument of sorts. A soft, rainy breeze from the showers earlier that day washed over them through the mesh walls of the patio, and the lead singer's voice was deep and rich, caressing the familiar words of one of her father's favorite songs.

"I told you this was a good idea!" her sister shouted into her ear, and Kemi felt her lips curving up, despite herself. She settled into a rhythm of her own, hips and waist swaying gently to the beat, working in harmony to twist themselves round the music. She could feel people bump against her, as warm and as damp as she was, and just as carried away, laughing, showing each other up. She sighed and threw her head back, feeling her long braids skimming the small of her back. When was the last time she'd let herself *relax*?

She hated to admit it, but perhaps Tobi was right.

Luke Ibru *loathed* social events of any kind, but he liked money, so here he was.

"You'll *love* this place," his longest-standing and highest-paying client, Jide Abalorin, said cheerfully. Jide had flown in from his home in Las Vegas that week to outline a new security plan for one of the many nuclear plants he oversaw in the United States, making the sole condition of renewing his multimillion-dollar contract with Ibru Enterprises one night out on the town. "Don't you think you'll enjoy it, Luke? Dinner? Drinks? Maybe even get you a date?"

"Nothing could be worse" was Luke's crushing response. Jide had laughed in his face.

"Do you know what nickname they've given you at my firm, Luke?" Jide paused for effect. "'That sad bastard.'"

"Good," Luke had said at the time. He didn't care what people thought of him—had he applied for the position of Father Christmas? Did his business depend on being *nice*?

Jide prevailed upon him, though, and Luke had spent three hours—*three!*—sitting in a crowded booth at an absolutely tacky nightclub, drinking whiskey that tasted as if it'd been distilled in a boot and eating grilled *suya* that was deplorably underdone, and would quite possibly give them dysen—

"I can't deal with you anymore," Jide said exasperatedly and left him to join the crowd of women mingling on the dance floor, resembling well-dressed butterflies in their bright dresses. Luke wasn't sorry; he knew it would be a failed experiment. He finished his watered whiskey with all the satisfaction of a grump who has successfully spoiled someone else's mood, then he approached the dance floor in an attempt to corral Jide. He'd completed the three hours he'd promised his friend; it was nearly ten, and he was ready to go. He walked to the edge of the dance floor, scanned it for Jide. The man, he noted with astonishment, seemed to be engaged in some sort of dance that resembled the flopping death of a sea bass removed from water. The man was thirty-four, for goodness' sake. Had he no sense of decorum?

Before his divorce Luke had been married for so long that he'd nearly forgotten how to notice women, beautiful or not, and he definitely hadn't stepped foot on a dance floor. To Luke, nightclubs were networking places for clients who wanted some fun before flying back to their home countries. A little flirtation was a necessary evil, sometimes, if his guests were inclined in that direction, but he certainly never sought out female company himself.

Nothing had changed since his divorce and all the unpleasantness that had followed. In fact, he'd never been less interested in pursuing anything romantic, whether casual or otherwise.

Then, just at the corner of his vision, a young woman caught his eye.

She was dancing in the midst of the throng, and unlike the others round her, she was so completely lost in the music, utterly unaware of the flirtations and gyrations that went on around her. Her concentration was on the stage alone, on the highlife now shaking the floor, and when her eyes were open, they were fixed solely on the band. He watched her deftly avoid one, two, three men who attempted to come up behind her and dance—not nastily, but with a shy, almost diffident shake of the head, followed by a touch on the arm and pointing at the band. Some men lingered for a few moments, trying to start up conversation, but they quickly moved on when it became clear she was completely enraptured with the music.

Luke told himself that he was looking because he'd never seen such a young woman so taken by a common nightclub band, but a more visceral part of him was attracted to more than that. Despite full curves that would have rivaled any Nollywood actress, long, well-defined legs topped by full, soft thighs and breasts that he told himself he would *not* stare at, she made the minidress of soft gold she wore look almost demure. That was it. She looked so out of place—it was impossible not to notice her.

Classy. A virtue, he thought, that was severely lacking in some of the women he encountered on the nightclub set.

His attention was distracted when he was prodded by Jide, who gave him a drunk but mischievous grin. He'd seen, and he approved. "I found a friend," he said cheerfully, indicating a busty young woman who was making her way to the coat check. "Looks like you did, too— Well done, man. We're going to—well. Find somewhere a bit *quieter.* Have fun after I leave, eh, *oga?*"

Disgusted and embarrassed by his own lack of professionalism, Luke shook his head. "I'm not—"

"The hell you were," Jide said cheerfully. His eyes were bright, interested. "You have to go and talk to her! This is the first time I've ever seen you even look at a girl since—"

"That's enough," Luke said sharply. There were some things that even Jide didn't get to bring up.

To his surprise, his friend threw an arm around him—he must be very drunk even to dare, Luke thought irritably—and spoke just a fraction more quietly.

"I know it still hurts like hell, Luke," he said. "It won't always, I swear. But you've got to try. You'll never be able to move forward if you don't make an *effort.*"

Luke's jaw felt tight. If it were anyone but Jide, he'd curse him out without a thought, but Jide had been there through everything, and—

"Please, man, for me," Jide said, and the happy-go-lucky drunk was, for the briefest of minutes, very, very sober. He clapped Luke on the shoulder, hard. "Do something that makes you happy, for once."

With that, he was gone, and Luke was left wordless on the edge of the dance floor, mouth as dry as if he hadn't had a single drop, his heart thudding dully in his ears.

Do something that makes you happy. Jide was assuming that there was something left, after everything he'd lost. Talking to a girl who looked like the ink was barely dry on her university diploma would do nothing to assuage the damage that he suspected would follow him for the rest of his life.

More importantly, he had no desire to change.

But still—

He must be more tired than he thought. And that, he told himself, was why his eyes still lingered on her.

A song ended, and she was approached again, this time by a stout gentleman with a beard, a shirt that was far too shiny and a determined look on his face. He was not as easily put off as the others; he used his wide shoulders to block her, leaning in. She stepped back once, twice, three times; when she was against the railing of the patio, nowhere else to go, the man started talking, gesturing earnestly. He saw the young woman begin to glance round the room, a trapped look in her eyes. Her companion pointed to the bar, then walked rapidly toward it. He was getting drinks for them, it looked like. Best-case scenario, he was attempting to get her drunk, and worst case... Well. He hoped the young woman knew better than to take drinks from aggressive strangers.

And that, he told himself, was why he found himself heading back to the edge of the dance floor, as if propelled by some unseen force.

CHAPTER TWO

"YOU CAN SAY you're with me, if you want."

Kemi was so distracted by the suitor she'd been trying to get rid of that the voice didn't register at first, but then the speaker said it again. His voice was very quiet, but deep, rich and so strong it stood out from the sea of laughter and conversation on the crowded patio. She turned left, then right—and then she saw him.

Kemi registered a hazy impression first, of a tall, thin man in a tailored suit that skimmed impressively over lean muscle. A snowy shirt was open at the neck, contrasting with the rich brown tints of his skin, so much deeper than hers, smooth and perfect. His face was half-hidden in shadow, but her heart fluttered—and not from panic, either.

"I—" Kemi found herself moving closer to him, still swaying gently to the beat. The band had segued into a grave rendition of an old Ebenezer Obey song; the lead singer was crooning, softly, of love and commitment and not listening to detractors that kept lovers apart. The man who had spoken to her tilted his head, as if sizing her up. She could not tell what assessment he was making; despite his pleasant tone, his eyes were veiled. Unreadable.

She hesitated. Did he want to…dance? He wasn't moving; he was like stone.

"I know," he said, "that you are perfectly capable of

taking care of yourself. But I'd be happy to say you're here with me, if you like." He spoke with an odd note of reluctance in his voice that didn't match the curiosity that was sparking through the blankness of his expression. His fine-featured face was sober as a judge, almost grave— but she'd *intrigued* him.

She felt her skin flush hot.

There was something very familiar about the handsome stranger, something familiar enough, at least, to make Kemi nod her head. Had she seen him at one of her father's events, perhaps, or was he one of the minor celebrities on Nigeria's social circuit that her sister was so obsessed with?

Tobi. She glanced sharply round and exhaled in relief when she saw her little sister engaged in what looked to be lively conversation with a girl of her age at a standing table. She could also see her "friend" headed back in their direction, with an alarmingly pink-hued drink in his hands and a determined look on his round, bearded face.

"Thank you," she said to her rescuer.

"Dance?" he said casually, and Kemi, a lump suddenly taking up all the room in her throat, nodded.

His hands settled at the curve of her waist, and Kemi felt her whole body tighten involuntarily. Not from nervousness, as she expected, but from a shock of awareness that surprised her more than anything else. She had brothers, and a father, of course, but she'd never been so hyperaware of maleness in all her life. It was all heat, a spicy scent with no identifiable source, the overwhelming feeling of being smaller. Softer.

He bent his head, and she felt the slow, gentle warmth of his mouth at her ear.

"Just do what you did before," he said. "I'll follow."

Kemi swallowed. So he'd been watching her. The thought gave her more of a thrill than she cared to admit.

She didn't even have to tell her body to move; dancing with him was as easy as with herself. He moved easily, coaxing her through the rises and falls of the rhythm; his grip at her waist and lower back was not tight. He didn't press against her, but it was impossible to have no contact; her breasts brushed against the wall of his chest, and her body responded so readily she had to bite back a sound.

She *ached*.

His hands hadn't wandered, not even a bit, but she ached, low in her gut, where desire—it couldn't have been anything else—was beginning to stir. She hadn't felt this level of intensity since—

Since never, really.

His eyes were closed; he was humming his own bass line under his breath, once that matched the lightness of her steps. She bit her lower lip, and hard; his voice did something to her, too, *there*—

Get a hold of yourself!

"I'm Kemi," she said. She hated how breathless she sounded, but she needed to say something.

"Kemi, finest dancer in Abuja." His voice was wry and matter-of-fact. "I never dance. You have powers, apparently."

"Oh." Kemi felt her face grow hot again. Was he making fun of her? He hadn't volunteered his name. She'd never been very good at flirting, never had the opportunity to, but she wanted to prolong this conversation for some reason. "I— Thank you."

"You would have been fine. I should thank you for giving me the opportunity." His voice was unhurried, unbothered, but there was nothing lazy in it; the timbre caressed her as languidly as the hands at her waist did. "Can you understand what he's saying?" he added, nodding at the band leader.

Oh. He wasn't Yoruba, then, despite the fine features.

She cleared her throat, wondering where he was from but too shy to ask. "It's a love song," she said, and her lips stuck on the words.

"I guessed."

Kemi turned her head so she could hear better, then took a breath and rested her hand on her companion's chest. If he recognized it as an opportunity to draw her close, he did not take it, and Kemi felt strangely disappointed. "He's telling her," she said, after licking her lips, "that his love isn't a lie, no matter what others say."

"Go on." His voice rumbled low; his eyes had darkened with interest. In her or in the song, she had no idea.

"He's saying…he only has eyes for her. That others are beautiful, yes, they are—but only she matters." Her skin flushed hot as she said the next bit. "When they're together, when she moves beneath him—her skin, her eyes, her face—"

"Mmm." The single syllable, like a caress, ran lightning hot, razor-sharp, to the part of her that was genuinely, completely, undoubtedly aroused. Inexplicably so. Kemi pressed her thighs together, forcing herself to keep talking.

"And now—he is hers until the end of time. They fit. They're—meant to be."

As she'd been translating, she'd been drawing closer, like one pulled to the heat of an open fire during Harmattan chills. She did not know how to articulate it, but she wanted this man to draw her close. Nothing too wild— they were in public, after all, and he was a stranger. But this was the first time Kemi had ever felt such complete, undeniable attraction. To anybody.

"Do you believe him?" His fingers were dancing at the small of her back now, and Kemi felt slightly faint. She opened her mouth to answer, having no idea what she'd say, but the song ended with a flourish of drumming, and the lead singer was calling out that they were taking a break and guests were welcome to say hello at the bar.

They stayed together for another few seconds, just a lingering moment, and then the man pulled back, bent to kiss her cheek. The skin of his mouth was soft and warm, and Kemi felt her eyes fluttering closed. She wanted to ask him to stay, to talk to him about more love songs, to figure out why he looked so familiar. She wanted to know why the simple pressure of his fingers at her waist had left her trembling, wanted to know if the skin of his chest and shoulders was as smooth as that of his hands, and she wanted to know why, suddenly, for the first time this week, she wanted to be somewhere besides the security of her hotel room.

Magical. Tobi had claimed the evening would be this, for both of them, and then this stranger had shown up. A prince stumbling on a dancing princess, on an enchanted evening. Perhaps Tobi had been right. Perhaps—

Don't be silly!

Kemi had never felt so utterly unsure of what to do as she was at that moment. What did women do in these situations? Tobi with her quick wit and bright disposition would know exactly what to say; Kemi felt completely dull in comparison. She said nothing, only smiled, just a little.

He peered into her eyes, for a moment, as if he were looking for something. Kemi caught her breath, wondered if he'd find it, or be disappointed.

"Thank you, Kemi," he said and inclined his head. Then he turned and walked away.

Kemi.

He'd not only looked, he'd danced with her. Kissed her. On the cheek, yes, but the memory of the full softness of her mouth… It was an enchantment, had drawn him in despite himself.

Stop it.

Perfume still lingered on his fingertips, hung round his head and shoulders, a soft, gentle cloud of fragrance. More than that, her face still lingered in his mind. It'd been a lovely face. Sweet. Soft. Her body, though his hands had barely skimmed it, was much of the same. He'd danced with a woman for the first time in—how long? Certainly it had been before his marriage.

He couldn't even blame this on drink. He'd had a single glass of watered whiskey with Jide, and he hadn't even finished it. Every bit of intoxication he felt had come from the young woman herself.

Go home, he told himself. He had no business being in this corner of Abuja at this time of night, dancing with beautiful girls and flirting in a way he hadn't realized he still knew how to do. It was more than flirting as well; even now, from that relatively innocent contact, his body tightened in a way it hadn't since…since—

He forced the thought out of his mind.

His quiet apartment at the Abuja Standard Hotel awaited him, and he could not wait to retire there, to shower off the stickiness of the evening. When he walked outside, hands shoved deep into his pockets, he glanced around with very little curiosity, until he heard a woman talking.

"Oluwatobi! Tobi? Where are you?"

Her voice was frantic, panicked, and Luke knew that it was Kemi. He wasn't sure why he was so certain; he couldn't even understand what she was saying, as she was now speaking Yoruba so fast he hadn't a hope of picking out even a word. But her voice stood out from the din outside the door; it was soft and sweet, even in its urgency. It matched the face.

His eyes caught up with his brain a moment later, and there she was, illuminated by the watery light streaming from the club entrance, shaking her mobile as if she were angry with it. She peered into the darkness beyond the nightclub, past the lamps that illuminated the parking lot, a decidedly frightened look on her face.

She muttered something under her breath and squinted down at her phone again.

"Are you all right?" Luke asked. The words left his mouth with absolutely no permission from him; he couldn't have stopped them even if he wanted to.

The woman looked up, clearly startled at his address, and Luke felt a violent lurch deep in his stomach when her eyes met his. They were brown and as dark as they'd been on the dance floor, beautifully shaped, and accentuated by long, wispy lashes that were currently quite damp.

"I can't find my sister," she said.

Her sister. He hadn't noticed her with anyone inside, but then again, he hadn't had eyes for anyone but her while she swayed on the patio. He stepped a little closer and saw her tense, then stopped for that very reason. "Is she in danger?"

"She ran away!" Frustration twisted her lovely face into something both angry and worried. "She was talking with a group of college students and went off with them— She's only nineteen—"

"College students?" The danger was greatly lessened then; at least it hadn't been with a man. "And it was a group?"

Kemi nodded, and her cheek deflated as she bit the inside of it, shifting nervously from leg to leg. "We're visiting—"

"Lagos?" he guessed.

"No, Badagry. It's impossible to keep track of her. She's very impulsive—"

"Right." Sounded about right for a teenager. "I'm Luke," he said after a beat.

"Luke?" That seemed to catch her attention, and she finally looked away from her phone and peered into his face. "Luke Ibru?"

"Yes," he said, taken aback.

"I— You're one of the speakers at the summit, aren't you? I saw you yesterday. Onstage." The frustration in her voice had been replaced by fascination, and he saw her straighten up, superciliously tugging the hemline of her dress down before extending her hand. "The security expert. You spoke on safety for women in the modern world. When you came up to me earlier, I thought you looked familiar—"

So he had. He was surprised at her quick recognition of him, in this dark and smoky club, and took her hand wordlessly. It was small and soft and trembled just a little bit. This arm was scarred, he realized belatedly, and released her, not sure if it would hurt. There was a faint flush, tinting the soft brown of her skin with the stain of wine.

"It was wonderful."

"Thank you," he said carefully looking down at her face. Was she a student, perhaps? She looked older than that, though. Mature, and not just in body. She had the face of someone whose life experience had sobered her. She was peering down at her phone again, a worried look on her face, speaking half to herself. "My father is going to kill her."

Kemi was absentmindedly tugging down her dress— and yes, he was looking again, remembering the way the soft fleshiness of her thighs had looked in the light, her skirt shifting over a shapely backside as she danced. Close up, the bare skin looked butter-soft and a little fairer than the skin of her face, as if it didn't see much sun. He cleared his throat and opened his mouth, wondering why the hell he was still there, but their conversation was cut off by the sound of an engine revving. Both turned in time to see a bright red convertible, top down, with a group of young people spilling out the sides, screaming along with a pop song blasting out of the speakers, shaking bottles and laughing uproariously. The driver was a young man in a bright green sequined cap, who was navigating his vehicle with a young woman's arms looped round his neck. She twisted his head toward her and kissed him full on the mouth, making the other occupants of the car scream with laughter and mock applause.

Again, the exclamation from Kemi's lips was something he could not understand, but he understood the look on her face, as well as the way she raced forward, screaming so loud the veins stood out on her neck. "Tobi!"

That was her sister, he presumed. He had no time to react, though, because the driver of the car, thrown off completely by the passionate embrace he was locked in, veered sharply to the right. Kemi and Luke both leaped aside nimbly, and the car was gone, taillights dancing in the night.

"I think she may have ditched you," Luke said.

CHAPTER THREE

I'm safe!!!!!! Don't worry. David said he will follow. At party outside Abuja University. Call car, go home and get some rest. I put money in your purse.

"I HOPE THEY all get arrested," Kemi said with a vehemence that was quite unlike her.

Luke stifled a laugh into a cough. "That isn't very nice, big sister."

Kemi felt heat rush up to her ears. It'd been barely twenty minutes since Tobi had ditched her to attend the off-campus party with students she'd met in the nightclub; at least she'd had the sense to have their driver follow. In Kemi's anger, she'd also managed to divulge every single detail of the evening to the virtual stranger standing next to her, and though he still wasn't smiling, he was looking highly amused.

Luke Ibru. Even looking at him now made her skin tingle. She'd seen him not forty-eight hours previous, speaking on Nigeria's responsibility to provide security for its citizens.

Kemi and Tobi were basically at the summit for show: her father liked flaunting his daughters to the adoring throng of educators that had gathered for the summit. They would never know, Kemi thought darkly, that neither she nor her sister had ever been to school, not in person.

He'd employed tutors for them, followed by online university. The result of his vigilance had been one daughter who barely opened her mouth in public settings and another who couldn't keep it shut.

The first night of the summit, Kemi had sat quietly beside her dozing sister, prodding her at intervals and listening to the speeches of the young women who mounted the podium and shook hands with her father and the other dignitaries present. They came from a variety of backgrounds—some were doctors, some scientists, some artists, some writers. Some had studied abroad; some had stayed within Nigeria. All had made contributions that made a significant impact on the world, had done good things. Important things. Things for a better Nigeria, and a better Africa.

The speeches had made Kemi's heart ache with dull longing. She'd done nothing in her twenty-five years, she thought, but sit in her father's house, eat the finest food, languish away in her gilded palace. If she were braver, or smarter, or more clever, she'd have been able to break away, but—

You can't blame him. Your own foolishness is the reason your life is like this.

She'd always longed for something more, and if she did not know exactly what, she knew she wanted the opportunity to strike out on her own, to discover what that might be. However, her guilt at the trouble she'd caused everyone had held her fast. She'd already proven she couldn't be trusted and could not protect herself. Her father had been forced because of her recklessness to pay a price for his daughter's life. She could not put him, or her family, through that again. And so she remained in her father's house, a virtual prisoner, and she'd locked poor Tobi in with her.

Luke's gentle bass voice broke through her thoughts.

"Will you be all right to get home then, Kemi? I can arrange a ride for you."

He'd been handsome on the stage—so handsome it was almost unreal, with his designer suit, carefully styled hair and eyes that seemed to penetrate the audience, find her where she sat wide-eyed and listening intently. He'd talked passionately of fear, of the legacy that violence had left behind, of the fact that it was unconscionable to live in a modern state where young women feared to go out, to socialize, to go to school, to live.

On the dance floor, she'd felt the intensity of his gaze, knew their attraction was mutual. His eyes had flickered over her bare thighs and up to her chest. Kemi was accustomed to being looked at, especially at the events her father hosted at the palace, which were breeding grounds for men of high society, both young and old. Still, no man, not then and not now, had gotten close enough to even kiss her, talk less of anything more, and certainly none had never elicited a bodily reaction from her the way Luke Ibru had. She'd been startled out of her worry for Tobi when her belly tightened and her skin flushed hot and—

He wasn't scary.

Since her abduction, Kemi had treated men with a mixture of indifference and, yes, a little bit of fear. Although her captors had been relatively gentle with her, she knew that her position and her father's prompt response to their demands were mostly to credit for that. Men, *strange* men, could be brutes. You never could know what lurked behind their facades, and she'd avoided any intimate interactions since the incident, taking her father's overprotectiveness as an excuse to shield herself.

Luke, in only a brief conversation, had scaled that wall, peered over it to see the girl within. Also, damn it, she couldn't stop blushing. Being attracted to a stranger you'd seen at an event from far away was all well and good.

You could fantasize all you wanted, like a teenager with a poster on a wall. Having him standing in front of her, close enough to touch, was a different matter.

She'd googled him after the summit, of course. He was a Delta State native who'd designed high-level security systems for years in Russia, America and the UK, and his clients supposedly included the CIA, KGB and MI6. His brain, magazines hailed, was a "feat of human engineering."

Those extraordinary eyes stood out piercingly from the shadows of his narrow face in every publication Kemi read, and he topped more than a few eligible-bachelor lists. He'd returned to Nigeria after years abroad, using his skills to design security systems for senior officials, government buildings, schools, universities and other places in the country that needed to stay safe.

Security. Perhaps that was what Kemi had sensed in those few moments they'd spoken. He was solid. Immovable. He possessed a confidence that went far beyond any sense of danger, and maybe she was attracted to that because she wanted those qualities so badly in herself.

She swallowed hard, and when she did speak, the words that came out of her mouth surprised her. "Might I—buy you something to drink?"

Luke's heavy brows lifted, and she forced herself to focus on something just above his left shoulder so she wouldn't blush again.

"I actually am just leaving," he said slowly.

Oh. Embarrassed, Kemi took a step back. "I'm sorry, I shouldn't have assumed…"

"…but perhaps you'd like to come with me?" The corners of his mouth tipped up. It wasn't quite a smile, but that was the closest she supposed she'd ever get from him. The gesture made something deep in her chest turn over. There was an attraction, but this was something else entirely, almost involuntary, almost primal, something that made Kemi emerge from her self-imposed shell and push the interaction.

"I don't know..." she faltered. In a strange city? This was stupid, at best.

Luke's face gentled; again, Kemi had that vague feeling he was reading her mind. "I'll arrange for a taxi," he said, "and while I'm in Abuja I live in a public hotel just a street away from the bar I have in mind. You will be quite safe."

There was no accusation in his tone; he barely seemed to care which way she answered, and it was this that made up her mind, speaking over the pounding in her chest. What if God, or fate, or the universe, or whatever it was, had arranged for this one small window of opportunity for her to do something exciting, something completely out of character—and with a man she admired so much? Would she take it, or would she turn away, retreat back into the shell that she'd added layers to by the year?

There was a glimmer in those dark eyes that made her tummy quiver. She took a step back, released the lip she didn't even realize she'd been biting.

"I will come," she said, so rapidly the words nearly ran into each other.

"I've never seen someone so excited about a garden bar before," Luke teased.

The swanky Maitma's Gana street was far behind them, and they were now in Jabi, where street stalls had been fired up since dusk and the mingled smells of smoky meats from dozens of red-hot grills hung heavy in the warm, damp air. The open-air bars would have been filled with men drinking ice-cold beer after work hours ago; now they had cleared out for the party crowd and people who lived in the neighborhood who were hungry, bored and eager to mingle. It was that magical hour when night cloaked the streets with a warm and welcome darkness. The heat of the day was gone, and the air fairly crackled with life. Kemi's blood warmed; a flush roamed from her face to a place low in her belly. She instinctively moved closer to Luke, who smiled that grave smile that did not reach his eyes.

Kemi felt as if she was in one of those dreams where awareness is heightened, where you can speak, and move, and choose what you want to do, but your surroundings are nothing like you'd have in real life. Luke hadn't said a word since they left the party. Now she reached out, allowed her fingers to skim his hand, and he took it, squeezed it once.

She instantly felt better.

"Is it safe?" Kemi whispered when she saw the crowd.

Luke glanced at his watch. "It is. It's not late enough yet for crime to be an issue—see? Neighborhood people are out with their children still. And this bar is one of the posher ones—it's attached to a restaurant, with a rooftop. I'll get us a table there. You're safe."

He had a way of stating exactly what would reassure her, she thought.

"And I'm with Nigeria's top security man," she said with a note of laughter in her voice. She looked up at him from beneath her lashes, and he cleared his throat, spoke quickly.

"'Point and kill,'" he said, indicating where fat, meaty catfish wriggled in their tanks. A young woman in jeans, a loose white shirt and a hot-pink hijab studded with rhinestones commandeered the area. "I thought a girl from Badagry might appreciate seafood. And after that…" His voice trailed off. "My place isn't far from here. Maybe a drink?"

Kemi felt her eyes go round. If he was saying what she thought he was—

And she wasn't horrified, she found. Not at all. In fact, she shifted a little closer to him, avoiding a raucous group of young men that walked by, jostling them, talking, joking loudly. He placed a hand on her waist, and she did not protest when he drew her close. In fact, she took a breath and then eased herself against him.

"Thank you," she said, so soft even she barely heard it.

Anticipation was building low in her gut, the sort of nervousness that churns the belly and makes color burn hot beneath skin.

Anticipation for what? What, exactly, was she doing here? Kemi was innocent in many ways, but she wasn't naive; she knew exactly what an invitation such as Luke's probably meant. However, her attraction to him had startled her with its intensity, and that was enough to propel her forward, to make her want to explore it. What if she never felt like that again, about anyone?

She'd been convinced after her kidnapping that some vital part of her had been broken, a part that wanted human contact. Her brief encounter with Luke at Café Abuja had made it roar back to life, and she could not abandon that.

Luke cleared his throat, and she peered up at him, a little shyly.

"We can talk in a moment, over dinner, I think," Luke said quietly, against her ear, and there it was again, that desire roiling slow and heady over her. She exhaled and let her body fully relax. The warmth of his palm burned against her skin. "Are you hungry?"

She nodded dumbly.

"Good. I am." His eyes lingered on her mouth, and— oh, he wasn't talking about food, was he? Kemi raised a hand to her throat, feeling a little faint.

Foolhardy wasn't the word. And yet, curiously, Kemi felt no fear. Perhaps it was because she was so unschooled in these things, but the sixth sense that had been her hallmark since her abduction years before was nowhere to be found. She felt none of the stomach-tightening anxiety, the prickles of fear on her scalp, the metallic taste in her mouth that usually came when she was in a situation she felt she could not control. Luke Ibru devoured her with those stormy, smoke-filled eyes, and she followed him. Willingly.

The Hausa restaurateur wielded her wooden stick with accuracy, and Luke ordered both pepper soup and grilled catfish, along with the *suya*. When they climbed the steps to the rooftop, Kemi was surprised to find it completely deserted.

"A few naira in the right hand can do anything," Luke said dryly.

The fish arrived, roasted to perfection and nested in a bed of spicy, savory chili sauce, garnished by candy-sweet plantains fried golden brown. The soup was a marvel of flavors as well; bitter *utazi*, smoky-sweet crayfish and enough pepper to make the tongue tingle, to break dampness out on skin.

It was all delicately seasoned and fragrant, but Kemi couldn't manage more than a few bites; her stomach knotted tight round each mouthful. She wished he would just say something. Anything. Yet, all he was doing was looking at her calmly, meticulously separating bones from his fish.

Kemi waited for him to initiate conversation, but he didn't; Luke was engrossed with the food on his plate, and she was left feeling oddly bereft. Had she imagined their connection while they danced? And if she had, why did she ache to be close to him, still? Those few moments they'd shared, pressed together in Café Abuja, and the all-too-brief feeling of his leanness pressed against her...

Kemi dropped her fork and stood abruptly, and Luke stared up at her, those dark eyes soft as they rested on her face.

"Are you all right?"

No! She wasn't! She was suddenly hot and cold and shaky all at once, and could hardly keep her body from trembling. Kemi turned, pressed her hands to her cheeks, wishing she could cool them by will—her entire body felt too hot, although the rain-washed air was mild for this time of year.

"It's warm out here," she said through lips that tingled with warmth from chili pepper and curry. She walked past him to the edge of the roof, peered out over the city. They were high enough so she could see Abuja glittering in all directions, hear the mingling sounds of the city, of cars and lorries and faint music and the hum of the enormous generators that would ensure partygoers could eat, drink and make merry in perfect comfort.

She felt rather than saw Luke come up behind her, and she spoke without turning around, feeling she should say something to explain her jitters. "I was—injured when I was a teenager. A kidnapping. I was shot. My arm."

He was silent, but then—thank God, thank God—she could feel him close to her back, lips once again hovering round her ear. Kemi took a deep breath and exhaled, leaning back against him. She was working purely on instinct now; she would not know what to do with the desire she felt even if he'd asked her. So, she talked. It brought up some semblance of intimacy, anyway.

Hold me. Touch me.

"I sneaked out to go to a party with my classmates," she said, "and I got caught up with a group of armed robbers. I came out of it all right," she continued, through lips that felt very stiff. "But—what you said at the summit— I loved it, Luke. It's not about systems, or gadgets, or manpower. Society everywhere needs to change so that women don't need that to be safe, so they're not afraid of even the most normal things—"

Her voice broke a little, and she paused to swallow. Something in him must have heard what her body cried out for; his arms slipped round her, cradling her close. When he spoke there was a husk in his voice that she was grateful to hear; she wasn't the only one affected by his nearness.

"Kemi. When I said dinner, I truly didn't mean more than that," he said, and there was no reproach in his voice, only kindness that pulled her to him even more. Aside from freedom from the confines of the palace, she'd never wanted anything more than to have this tall stranger with the angular planes of an ancient brass carving kiss her until she couldn't think anymore.

"Kemi?"

She sighed again, letting her head loll down to his shoulder, peering up through the mesh at the night sky, and Luke's hands were finally skimming the cradle of her hips, resting there as if they belonged. There was a gentle pressure, and he was turning her around, and she was looking up into that dark, narrow face, as inscrutable as it'd been when she first arrived. But she knew better. She'd seen the little flashes of desire at the nightclub, when she'd pressed the full curves of her body into his leanness downstairs, and now, when her breath quickened and her breasts were swelling, full and soft, against the wall that was his chest.

Kemi wordlessly stood on her toes, slipped her good arm behind his head, but it was he who bent, closed the inches between their lips and kissed her.

Luke had no business doing this. And yet, he couldn't stop.

Kemi was absolutely decadent, every last bit of her. There was simply no other word. Kissing her was a pleasurable assault on every sense he had, and she yielded so readily, parting her lips, tongue sliding slow and hot over his, that heat spread, slow and sexy and sure, over every part of his body. Things he'd sworn he'd forgotten were coming back in vivid detail. The scent of a woman's skin. The soft noises she made, deep in her throat, when she wanted more. The musky sweetness of her arousal, and the way the curves of her body were made for his hands. Not to mention the quiet vulnerability she'd shown him in those moments... She'd been hurt, he knew, and badly. Even someone who hadn't seen her arm or heard her speak of safety would know that. That alone should make him run in the other direction.

Still, here he was, sliding his hands down the length of her as if they'd been destined to do this from the beginning.

Luke did not think Kemi a skilled seductress; she'd been too uncertain for that, too unschooled in the games that usually characterized encounters like this one. However, everything Luke knew had been learned by observation, not by experience. He'd met his wife in school, stayed with her through his university years and married her. He had never been tempted by anyone else; when he was young and idealistic, love was more than enough for him. Afterward, when he'd lost her, the thought of a woman, a stranger, was most unappealing. Why would he throw his dignity away on a cheap gilt imitation of the fine thing he'd ruined?

Regardless of reason—this was as uncharacteristic for Luke as he suspected it was for Kemi—he was older, bigger, stronger. He had the upper hand.

If this was going to stop, it would have to be from him.

Kemi whimpered soft against his lips, a sound that crumbled any headway he was making in resolving this. Her small hands slid beneath his jacket, eager to touch him; they skimmed his waist once or twice, then slid back up.

Luke was not as restrained. His fingers dipped to trace the skin that swelled full and warm above her bodice, watching as her breasts strained, lifted; the fact that they were so restricted by her dress made the sight all the more arresting. His other hand slid over the generous curve of her bottom, cupping, stroking. Kemi gasped into his mouth and adjusted her hips; he had to swallow the curse that wanted to escape. The center of her was now pressed to where he throbbed for her—soft, yielding and so warm. Her head tilted back, and he lowered his mouth, dropping one soft kiss to where her pulse raced in her throat.

"Luke, please," she gritted out.

He very carefully kept his eyes on her face; her breasts were threatening to escape the bodice of her gown, and if he looked, he might end up just taking her here, after all.

Enough.

It took every bit of self-control Luke had, but he took a full step back, wrenching his body away from Kemi's. Even through his shirt, his body burned from her touch.

"Kemi," he said, and managed to speak sternly.

Her eyes looked overbright, unfocused.

"I think it's time to take you home."

Kemi had crept forward into the light; her arms were wrapped round herself. Her eyes were still dark with want, her full mouth kiss-swollen. Wet.

Beautiful.

"I don't want to go yet," she said, and her voice trembled slightly.

Luke pressed his lips together against the soft curse that wanted to escape. He could still feel her in his arms, how yielding and soft she'd been. The way she'd trembled, whispered things he could not understand against his skin. They'd only embraced for a few minutes, but he still felt her touch now, as palpably as if she'd spent the entire night in his arms. How could she feel so familiar already, when he'd only kissed her for the first time tonight?

"You didn't ask me if I wanted to stay." Her voice was so quiet he could barely hear her. The party was still going strong below; he could hear indecipherable voices talking and laughing, the sound of the DJ spinning tunes.

"I'm not in the habit of manhandling strange women on rooftops," he said bluntly. "And you don't seem to be the type of woman who likes being manhandled. It'd be a tryst at best. I don't do trysts. And especially not with women who—" Even as he said the words, he was surprised by them, by the depth of wanting this. Luke hadn't wanted anyone for so long that his reaction to Kemi was utterly unexpected. He wanted to know why this was, and desperately, but he didn't have time. Not to explore her, not to ask her questions, not to know anything about her.

Her lips curved up a little, gleaming full and soft in the darkness. He saw her head dip.

Silence hung between them for a moment, then Luke sighed.

"You kissed me," she said, finally.

"That I did," he admitted, and he did not move when Kemi took a step toward him. The dim lighting of the roof illuminated her in eerie half shadows; the smell of lilies was intoxicating, hanging heavy and sweet in the humid air.

"I know you asked me to go," she said after a moment, very softly. "But you don't get to speak for me. I—I don't want to leave."

She stood on her toes then, leaned in and pressed those full, soft lips to his with only the smallest bit of hesitation.

To his body it was as if he and Kemi had never had those brief moments of separation; he was instantly hard again, blood throbbing between his legs. Kemi sighed as if she knew it, canting her body soft and full against his own; her arm lifted, twined round his neck, and she kissed him again, wriggling against him.

"You feel so good," she breathed against the skin at the corner of his mouth, and it took all the willpower inside Luke to capture her wrist between his fingers. It was as round and soft as the rest of her, and she looked up at him, lips parted, an expression of trust on her face that wrenched somewhere deep in his gut.

The last woman who'd looked at him like that had been his wife, and that had turned out worse than either of them could have ever imagined. He'd loved her, but love wasn't enough to prevent him from spoiling both their lives, from ushering in the kind of devastation that had torn them apart forever. Love hadn't been enough; it never was. If he was to do this with Kemi Obatola— here, and now—he'd have to make a few things clear.

Strength came to his voice as he lifted his chin, felt his back go ramrod straight. "Tonight. That's it."

She looked up at him. Those lovely, heavily lashed eyes were cloudy with want; he felt his own response surge strong, a hint of pleasure to come that he fought back. He'd always been a fool for lovely eyes, and he could read everything in hers. "Tonight," he repeated, and his voice was a little softer this time. He gave in to impulse and cupped the smoothness of her silk-soft cheek, running a thumb over the curve of it, down to where her lips parted and her breath hitched. She was so gloriously responsive and had not the sort of dissembling that would make her hide it. He'd be able to bring her to pleasure quickly, he sensed. Intensely.

"That's all that I can give you." His fingers traced down to the hollow where her pulse beat wildly in her throat, then farther down, over the warmed silk that was her décolletage, pausing to dip between the fullness of her breasts. Perhaps it was unfair to give her this choice while his hands roamed her body, hot and slow, but he couldn't help it.

"Luke—" Her voice trembled already.

"Let me speak." His voice was gentle but allowed no disagreement, and he lowered his mouth to first kiss the soft shell of her ear, then hover over it as he spoke.

"You don't have to leave—I won't send you away." It'd be stupid to deny his interest, when he was harder than he'd ever been in his life and pressed against the soft fullness of her hip. "But tomorrow, you'll go back to Badagry, and that'll be it. You have to promise me, Kemi. Or I'll take you downstairs and put you in a car right now." How was the curve of her neck so warm, so fragrant? The scent of lilies was gone; it had been replaced with something clean, and sweet, and womanly, something that crept across his skin, held him fast. He nipped at the tender skin, soothed it with his tongue; he felt her buckle, then sag against the wall of his chest.

"All right," she gasped. "I'll do anything you say. Just—"

"Come here," he said roughly, and he did not have to pull her to him, for Kemi lunged forward, soft and yielding and so eager, and he kissed her again.

He could not say what it was—perhaps the eager slide of her tongue on his, allowing the plunder of her honey-sweet, wine-tinged mouth, or perhaps the way she melted back into the concrete wall behind them, seemingly too overcome to stand. Whatever it was, it unleashed something in him that he'd thought was long dead and buried. He slid his hands down to grip the fullness of her hips, anchored his abdomen close to hers, to let her feel him—all of him. He would take her back to his room, undress her slowly, feast his eyes on those magnificent breasts and that soft, warm, yielding body, take his time.

He had only a brief period in which to get this maddening, utterly fascinating woman out of his system, and he planned to make the best of it.

CHAPTER FOUR

IF HER FATHER, the king, had any inkling that his daughter was now in a massive gold-plated four-poster bed in the most opulent hotel suite she'd ever seen, and with a man she'd just met, he'd likely faint, Kemi thought a little ruefully, then pushed the thought away. Her father was the last person she wanted to think of at this moment when her body ached so *badly*. She felt a wild wanting now that far surpassed anything she'd ever known. It burned on her skin, warmed her cheeks, kindled a low flame deep in her belly. The want outweighed the guilt.

One night.

Despite her relative inexperience, she wasn't afraid. There was something in the quick, slender, dark-eyed man's face that pleased her ever so much. Luke reminded her of those old rock structures Nigeria was famous for— craggy, rough and impenetrable, but occasionally, light and sweet water trickled from the cracks. She lowered her lashes, and then—finally—Luke was kissing her.

He kissed the way he did everything else, with a studied deliberateness that left no room for anything but carefully curated control. She was so engrossed in the kiss she did not notice his fingers on her back, did not notice the smooth slide of the zipper until she felt cool air tickle her spine. Her stomach leaped.

I'm really doing this.

Luke's fingers paused.

"It's all right," he said.

Perhaps he was saying it to give her an out, to let her leave if she wanted, but Kemi instead took it as a reassurance that she wouldn't regret this. She cleared her throat, dropped her hands to her sides. The boning inside her party dress released her breasts from the confines they'd been in all night. She hadn't worn a bra; it was one of the benefits of having everything custom-made by the palace tailor. They rested heavy and hot on the wall of her chest for one shy moment. Her fleshy, full-busted figure likely would have been more fashionable sixty years ago, and it had never been scrutinized this closely by any man.

She took a breath before lifting her eyes to Luke's. She wanted him to look at her, wanted her body to please him.

Luke's eyes dilated to a smoky hue that stopped the breath in her throat. Her body seemed to answer of its own accord; she lifted her shoulders proudly, arched her back, thrusting her breasts forward in a way so brazen even she was shocked. She saw his eyes flicker over her injured arm with curiosity, but they quickly went back to her breasts, to the full, dark nipples that had distended nearly to the point of pain.

"Lean back," Luke said, his voice thick. "Take your dress off, completely."

Kemi lifted her chin. Her body had been taken over, it seemed, by some wanton, quick-acting woman who had seized control of her brain, her speech. "You do it."

He laughed a little raggedly. "You don't want me to rip it."

Again, a thrill went through her, rippling in a light-ning-hot path that made her nipples throb, made that soft, secret place between her thighs ache so badly it stole her breath. Luke was in front of her in a moment, watching the subtle bounce of her chest as she scooted backward to the mound of pillows on his bed, catching his fingers in the sides of the dress and yanking down.

Kemi didn't have time to dwell on her nakedness, for soon Luke was stretched out beside her. Not on top of her, not pinning her down, but looking at her with an expression that was so oddly gentle that she blushed.

He reached out and cupped one of her breasts, balancing the heavy weight of it in his palm. She inhaled, tried hard not to squirm when his thumb moved whisper-soft over the jutting nipple. It was as if he sensed her inexperience; everything about the way he touched her was deliberate. Slow. Measured.

"Beautiful" was all he said, and then he drew her to him. She wanted to ask him what he liked, what he wanted her to do. She wanted to ask him why he was still fully dressed. But his mouth had moved to her neck and he was kissing it, tenderly, and she hadn't any idea how sensitive a spot that was until now—

Luke pinched her nipple gently, and the sound of her ragged breath broke the silence in the room. She closed her eyes tight; she did not want to see his face when he looked at hers, see the naked wanting there. He'd shifted to the other breast now and was kneading, circling her nipples, stroking back and forth, his mouth never leaving her neck. He was breathing things half in English and half in a language she didn't understand, filthy and low—

"Luke—" she gasped out, but that was all she could say, because the sensitized tip of her left breast was captured in the warm wetness of his mouth, and he sucked *hard*—

Kemi cried out. She couldn't help it. The throbbing between her legs had intensified to the breaking point, and pleasure overtook her in waves, drawing her body taut, manifesting in the sort of shuddering release that she'd never felt, not with another person. Luke's slim fingers dropped between her thighs, easing them open, coaxing the rest of her climax from her with quick, skillful fingers. Kemi was gone, swept away by want, by sensation; she clapped her hand over her mouth, squirmed away from him, half turned over, reached for a pillow to hold to her face.

He'd barely *touched* her.

She fought to breathe, concentrating hard on the rustling sounds he made; there was low laughter, as well.

"Kemi."

She didn't look back; his hands settled on her hips, down to her bottom, squeezing appreciatively, and that deliciously achy feeling was back. It heightened when he swore softly, following her curves with his hands. "Kemi."

She still could not speak, but she scooted half-shyly back against him. She wanted to roll over and face him, to stroke his face and press her lips to the hollows of his cheeks and touch him as a lover would. But he was a stranger, and she didn't know how to do this.

Not to mention that turning round, in a way, felt like visiting a point of no return.

"Kemi?" His voice rumbled low in her ear. "We don't have to do anything else, you know. It's all right."

She squeezed her eyes shut. *It's all right.* She swallowed and half rolled, and there he was, face hovering close to hers. The lust had tempered into something else— a gentleness that was fast becoming familiar, and more than a little curiosity.

"I haven't done this before," she blurted out. It was dreadful, she knew, but she could not baldly go into this, cool as ice cream. Her sister, Tobi, would be able to, but she'd never had Tobi's devil-may-care attitude about anything. She was too careful. Too terrified.

His brows lifted. "You've never gone off with a man at a party?" he teased. "Neither have I."

"No. I've never gone off with a man at all." She bit her lip, closed her eyes briefly. She hoped that she would not have to explain herself further and thought she heard Luke sigh.

His eyes shuttered, but that easy half smile never left his face. "Well, you have to get it over with at some point," he said lightly.

Oh. Kemi felt a dullness in her chest, a stab of disappointment that was quite unexpected. She didn't know what she was expecting. A declaration of love, perhaps? Or for him to beg her not to share this moment of intimacy with him, to give it to someone else? He was a virtual stranger. She would be a fool to expect anything more from him.

She was a fool to be doing this, and with this person. Impulsiveness had never been her strong suit. No wonder she was bungling this up so badly. She felt a puff of air-conditioned air waft down from the wall unit and shivered a little, though it wasn't just from the cold. Luke's heavy brows came together, and he peered down into her face.

"Terrible attempt at a joke. I'm sorry if that sounded insensitive," he said gravely. He followed up his words with gentle kisses on the corner of her mouth, her shoulders, that tender spot just south of her ear that made her shiver every time he touched it.

She nodded. She couldn't speak. Odd quivers were back, weakening her limbs.

"What I was rather awkwardly trying to say is that it isn't an issue for me, but..." He paused again, and seemed to consider his next words carefully. "This can stop here," he said. "It's—it may be more important to you than you realized."

Kemi was shaking her head even before he finished. This was not the time to tell Luke about the wild longing that made her body coil tight, or the need she had to do something that was all for herself, for once. "I want to."

"What do you want?" His voice had lowered to a husk, and Kemi swallowed hard as he pulled back, drew his shirt over his head. His undressing revealed miles of gleaming skin, the flat, muscled abdomen and—him, jutting proudly from between lean, muscled thighs.

"You are beautiful," she murmured, and he laughed without smiling.

"I should be saying that to you." He tilted his head. He was very clearly aroused, but the stillness of his body indicated none of the wild wanting she felt. "What do you want?"

Could she even say it? She wanted his mouth on her breasts again, wanted him to kiss them, bite them, make her feel as good as he had only moments ago. She wanted him to touch her where she could feel slickness between her thighs. She wanted to part her legs, wanted—

"I'd like to kiss you," she said, and quietly. She— There was no way she could ask for anything else.

"Have at it, then." His laughter was low, pulsed deep in his throat, and it warmed her like nothing else could have.

Luke tried his best to feel nothing.

He succeeded at first, by concentrating solely on the physical. She was beautiful, and her body was soft, pliable. Warm. She was quite possibly the most responsive woman he'd ever touched; only a few minutes of stroking her full breasts and she'd shattered in his arms and arched, pressing her wetness to his mouth, writhing in a way he knew would haunt his dreams for days to come.

His body, despite his indifference, responded to her with a decisiveness that made him smile inwardly. After four years of self-imposed celibacy, what kind of witchcraft had this virgin used on him? Kemi, who could barely look at his face as she cupped the hard length of him in those small, soft hands, who pressed her face in the innermost recesses of the soft down pillows to muffle her cries, who flushed deep beneath the amber-brown tints of her skin as he kissed every inch of it?

He concentrated on giving her pleasure, and he succeeded. He brought her to release once more with his mouth, reveling in her honeyed sweetness; he'd forgotten that heady musk, the pleasurable tang of a woman on his tongue. He held her fast until she could take it no more, pushed away his head with feeble entreaties. His duty tonight was to ensure that when the real love of Kemi's life came along, she'd have no bad experiences to sully the sweetness that clung to her, along with that ever-present scent of lilies.

He kissed her, let her taste herself on his tongue, told her in her ear in Edo and in English precisely what she tasted like, how much he liked it, how he would dream of her breasts and smooth skin and lovely eyes for days to come. And to his surprise—he felt himself meaning every word he said. They flowed off his tongue, smooth as silk and sweet as honey, because he meant them.

She did not say much, aside from little sighs and whimpers; when he finally sheathed himself and settled between the soft haven of her thighs, he looked upon her, thinking of how lovely she was. Something in him was drawn to her, besides desire. Perhaps it was the fact that he'd recognized himself in her, in those early days when love was enough, when his insides were not as barren as the desert that surrounded the oil fields that had contributed to his fortune. Loss and grief had left him dry.

He'd seen loneliness in Kemi's eyes before he'd kissed her. Maybe that was why he was so drawn to her.

When he finally slipped his hands beneath her hips, teasing her entrance gently, she reached up over her head.

Her breasts moved enticingly with every breath she took, but his focus was on her face. He'd never seen anyone look so soft, so open.

"It's all right," she said, and he bent to muffle her small cry of pain when he penetrated her. She locked him in with her legs at the small of his back; he paused, wanting to give her time to adjust to his size, but she shook her head.

"Do it," she husked.

"Not until I know you're all right."

To his surprise, she shifted, drew him in deeper, reached up with her good arm and held his shoulder, tight.

"I thought it'd be terrible," she whispered. "I thought I wouldn't like it. But this is wonderful, and you—"

Locked together as they were, he could not avoid the intensity that flushed her skin, drew her face taut—and a pressure began to build in his chest, one that shocked him so thoroughly he nearly pulled out of her altogether. It tightened his throat so he could not speak, but he didn't need to; she slid her hand up, rested it on the side of his cheek.

"So good," she sighed, and he instinctively began to move.

Kemi cried out, and yes—he felt it, deep inside his bones, resounding through him as if he'd been the one to make the sound. He gritted his teeth, then muffled it by leaning forward, pressing his lips to hers, dampening every expression. Pleasure crashed into shock; both mingled together. Something about Kemi had reached out and taken his reticence by the throat and dragged it away from where he wielded it like a shield, dragging it down to this soft, white bed where she arched beneath him, whimpering and gasping and crying out all at once, making his heart ache all the more with every thrust—

When his breath vented on a groan himself, it was so

foreign-sounding to him it startled him, and he froze inwardly. His fingers dropped down instinctively, gently skimming that little bundle of nerves between her legs, doing what he needed to do to end this, and quickly.

Kemi's body tightened against his, even as he found release, and his last coherent thought was that he was in trouble.

No trouble, he told himself sternly. There would only be trouble if this continued, and he'd made it clear this was just tonight. Even as he cradled her in his arms, he planned his escape.

They would never see each other again.

CHAPTER FIVE

PREGNANT.

Kemi found out exactly six weeks later, in a whirlwind twenty-four hours that involved bribing a maid to buy her a test from the pharmacy. It made sense, she thought, with a feeling of growing horror, the moment she knew for sure. In the weeks since Kemi returned home, she'd found herself a little abstracted and more than a little spacey. She often found herself daydreaming, staring out of windows to the waves crashing on the rocks below, eroding pale sand. Her body was very much back in the palace, back in the gilded cage that was her childhood home, but her mind was still with Luke.

The very thought of what she'd done with him horrified her as much as it tantalized her; she'd had crushes since she was a girl, of course, but none of them had manifested in anything like this, and she'd never felt about any one of them the way she felt about Luke.

Nights were the worst. Kemi lay in her soft, white bed that smelled sweetly of lavender water and eucalyptus oil. She would close her eyes and relive the feel of warm breath on the side of her cheek and her neck, feel gentle hands tracing loving patterns in her skin, before drifting into sleep. She awoke from vivid dreams with a rapidly beating heart and flushed skin, her body reduced to a dull throb between her thighs. She would rise on unsteady legs, drink cool water, turn on the air and allow it to waft over her heated, sweat-dampened skin. Frustrated. Still wanting. She avoided Tobi; she avoided everyone. She attempted to shake off her melancholy, buried herself in reading, in volunteering to appear at charity events at local schools. But the sun would always eventually go down, and memories of Luke would be waiting for her.

She couldn't love him, she thought; that would be absurd. She'd known him less than a weekend. However, his gentleness with her on that single night had planted something deep within her, something that blossomed a little more with every memory. She lost her appetite; she grew pensive. Tired. Quiet.

And then she'd missed her period.

Stupid, stupid, stupid! How could she have been so *stupid*? This was the same heady impulsiveness that had nearly gotten her killed years ago, an impulsiveness that she thought she'd buried under a decade of self-imposed rigidity. And how had it happened? Luke had used a condom, she remembered. He'd mentioned a tear at the end of their evening, which had rather soaked the whole encounter with cold water. But Tobi had managed to procure emergency contraceptive from one of the maids, and she'd taken it. Still—

Panicked, Kemi reached out to Luke in the only way she knew—a public email attached to his website. She knew that it was very unlikely he read it and cringed at the thought of a secretary knowing her business.

This is Kemi Obatola. We met a few weeks ago. Please call me. It's important.

There was no reply.

Three days later, she sent a second message.

Luke, I have something important to tell you regarding our evening at Café Abuja.

Nothing. Finally, on the third try and second week, desperately—

I'm pregnant.

He would not know the weight behind those two words, of the fear that sluiced through her body every time she saw a calendar and watched the missing days turn from weeks, to a month, to six weeks, to two months. Her father would know soon, and when he did…

Kemi choked back a sob. She'd done it again, ruined her life because of some stupid, selfish impulse. At least, she thought, rubbing her eyes, no one had nearly died this time. Instead, there had been Luke, and an evening of lovemaking she'd remember for the rest of her life. He'd seen her, seen what she wanted. He'd taken her seriously. He'd shown her she didn't have to be afraid, and for the first time in years, she'd felt worthy enough to take what she wanted.

It would do no good to linger over him in her mind. Having feelings for him was a serious error; he'd warned her, hadn't he? He had nothing to offer her, and no doubt she would have to navigate this pregnancy alone.

When Luke received the first message, and the second, he dismissed both with ease. Over the years Luke had developed a talent for ignoring unpleasantries for the sake of his own self-preservation, and Kemi's reaching out to him was certainly unpleasant. What was she about?

He'd clearly stated the terms of their night together, and though his body pulsed with pleasure at the memory of how he'd had his way with her, of the way her body had tensed with unbridled passion, a passion she'd never before had for any man—

He'd taken her virginity, that heated night when she'd tasted like wine and spice and the control he'd wielded for years had crumbled. He'd whispered things into her skin he'd never before said to any woman. She'd shattered in his arms. And now— I'm pregnant.

There were no demands in the message, no threats, no ultimatums, only a quiet desperation that struck him at the center of his heart. Luke swore furiously, then pressed a hand to his mouth. He stared at the screen until his vision blurred, as if he expected the letters to separate and perhaps—hopefully—turn into something else. Anything else.

They didn't. She was pregnant.

He couldn't even disregard this as a trick—he knew it had been a possibility, however remote. When it was all over, when she'd ceased trembling in his arms, he'd kissed and caressed her and finally, when they separated and he'd seen to the thin latex he'd sheathed himself with—

The tear had been small, but it'd been there. He'd gone to Kemi, her eyes still soft and dreamy from their union, and he'd told her.

"You might want to get emergency contraception," he'd said. It was the first thing he'd said to her after leaving the bed, and his customary crispness had returned. Kemi had shrunk away from him a little, and a bit of the light had left her eyes. He'd ignored the way his stomach twisted at that, and instead offered to send her the drug by courier the next morning. She'd lifted her soft chin, shaken her head.

"I'll take care of it," she'd said, and the situation was so absolutely uncomfortable, he hadn't insisted.

He was cursing himself for not insisting now. He knew instinctively that the shy young woman would not be capable of the duplicity necessary to bring him to this deliberately, but still—

Kemi Obatola. He had a name, at least, and an email address. He knew she lived just outside Badagry and was a woman of some means. He knew she had a sister, and he'd seen the marks on her arm. Kidnapped, she'd told him. Bullet wounds.

He also knew in his heart that this was not a matter of extortion. Aside from Kemi's obvious inexperience, she'd been as eager to leave his room that night as he'd been to have her gone. She wasn't poor, either; her hair, clothes and elegance all were markers of someone of higher class.

Nigeria was a huge country, but he had enough to go on. He would find this elusive Kemi Obatola, find out exactly who she was and, hopefully, solve this problem *quickly*. He took a breath, rubbed a hand over his eyes, then began to laugh. *Laugh.*

He'd been in this situation before; he'd gotten a woman pregnant when he wasn't supposed to, and the tragedy that had resulted had left him destitute emotionally, if not financially. Memory was reaching out with icy fingers to grip him by the throat, to bog him down. But he could not allow memory, no matter how painful, to keep him from thinking objectively. She was pregnant. And if she was planning to keep the baby—

Luke coughed hard to keep the nausea from rising in his throat. A *baby*. A child. His child. He forced the rising panic down with much effort and drew deep breaths.

It took a moment for calm to return, but it did, and he reached for his phone. He would get to the bottom of this, and quickly, find out who the hell she was—

and make a decision on what he was to do. As his panic faded, logic returned.

The summit. She'd been there, and there was a list of guests. Thoughts of her gentleness that night and the pregnancy that resulted had obscured his thinking.

All he had to do was check that list.

Sleepiness was the only symptom of pregnancy that Kemi had, and it was severe. She blamed it on a mild bout of malaria and spent much of her time holed up in her room, AC blasting and covers pulled over her head. Despite her exhaustion, it took sleep a long time to come; whenever she closed her eyes, she replayed her utterly disappointing lack of communication from Luke over and over. Not one word—not a call, not a response, not anything.

Perhaps it was all those hormones that she'd read about in her impassioned late-night searches on the internet about pregnancy and childbirth, but all of a sudden she wanted to cry. She'd been locked up for ages because of one stupid decision, and now, she was pregnant because of another.

Kemi was no romantic. Growing up in the midst of political intrigue with a father with multiple wives had ensured that. But, somewhere in the innermost recesses of her heart, she wished for something different. Maybe not necessarily wild and passionate love, the type in a romance novel or in one of the Nollywood movies she loved, but at least of partnership. Someone who loved her, who appreciated her and would be a good parent to whatever children they had. Now, Kemi wondered if the only thing she was good at was making poor decisions. She squeezed her eyes shut a little harder. Her faux illness would only buy her a few days; she would have to emerge, to tell her father everything. She felt sick inside at the very thought.

It was two days later, during one of her many naps, that

she was awoken by the sound of a lorry rumbling outside the palace gates. She blinked a little sleepily, wondering what it was. The driver, who clearly was disgruntled at the lack of speed with which the gateman attended to him, began honking his horn obnoxiously.

Kemi threw her covers off and slid out of bed. She crossed to the window that faced the main entrance of the palace and threw aside the blackout curtains, streaming the room with the white-hot light of early afternoon. From her tower room on the third floor of the palace, she could see Yusef, the gateman, marching over to the lorry, looking flustered. The driver was gesturing, talking so loudly that Kemi could hear his voice, if not words.

As they argued, Kemi heard another rumble; another truck was pulling up, this one bigger than the first one, the size of a truck that normally transported animals. She squinted through the security bars, straining to see. It made a groaning noise as the driver hit the brakes and killed the engine; the bright red door opened, and a second driver joined the fray. It was when a third lorry pulled up, stirring up enough dust to choke the entire neighborhood, that poor Yusef was overcome and began to shout. Loudly.

Kemi hurriedly pulled on a dressing gown and slippers, then ran downstairs. Aside from the house girls, no one was home—her father and her brothers were attending a function that morning, and Tobi had gone shopping under the careful watch of a maid. Disheveled, confused, but finally completely awake, Kemi burst into the compound and through the gate.

"What in God's name is all of this about?" she demanded, then choked and fought back a wave of nausea. The smell of petrol was absolutely unbearable; it burned hot in her lungs. "Who are you people? We expect no deliveries today."

The first driver barely glanced at her; in her dishabille

he must have assumed her a maid. "My *oga*'s name is Luke Ibru," he said condescendingly. "He's sending gifts to His Highness, the Oba of Gbale, in celebration of his marriage to Princess Kemi Obatola."

The floor seemed to shift under Kemi's feet. "*Marriage?*"

She could see now that the back of the first lorry was piled high with tubers of yam, rough and brown and smelling vaguely of earth and dust, yam enough to feed an entire village.

"The second lorry has fabrics, and the third wine," the driver continued, a little self-importantly. "The rest is coming, and if your gateman could so *kindly* let us in—"

Kemi was no longer listening to him; her heart still hammered with shock, and her mouth was dry, for she recognized the car now coming down the king's private road slowly, majestically, imperiously. It stopped half a meter behind the last lorry, and Luke emerged from the owner's corner. The driver got out, hurried to the boot and produced a flat box of mahogany wood, which he tucked in his employer's hands, then stepped back.

Luke peered over to where Kemi stood, and she took a step back, hand flying to her throat.

"Hello," he said gravely. "Princess."

The word cracked between them like a shot; his eyes shone so fiercely that she stepped back.

Luke navigated the space between them with his usual slow, easy steps. When he reached her, his eyes flickered over her; Kemi's skin burned as if his gaze had penetrated her dressing gown. She wrapped her arms round herself protectively; he held out the box, a gleam of challenge in his eyes.

"It's for you," he said quietly. "Your wedding set. Open it."

When Kemi didn't move, Luke bent and placed the box

on the gateman's stool, then opened it with a creak and stepped back. Kemi stifled a gasp—just barely.

On a bed of soft red velvet lay two necklaces—if these fantastic pieces of jewelry could be called such a paltry name. The first was made of three heavy strings of coral, rendered in a mixture of traditional orange-red beads, smooth as glass, intertwined with delicate chains of beaten gold. The second was a string of emeralds set in gold, each larger than her thumbnail, arranged in a pattern that would make a collar that encircled her neck, spread over her shoulders.

Jewels, really. She couldn't misrepresent them by calling them mere jewelry.

Dumbly she looked up at him; his eyes were burning with a heat that she felt deep in her chest.

"I had to do some digging to find you, and I got quite a surprise when I did," he said. "A king's daughter?"

She swallowed. "He isn't a very important king."

Luke's full mouth twitched once, and he turned his head to Yusef. "See these men inside and make space for these things in the compound!" he ordered. The man did so, and Kemi and Luke were left alone.

She didn't move. Perhaps she was frozen with shock.

Luke reached out impulsively, pressed the back of his fingers to her cheek. Despite the heat of the day, it felt unnaturally cool. Her eyes looked heavy, as if she'd just been roused from deep sleep, but she straightened, pulled her shoulders back.

Princess. The title fit her, he thought. She held her head as if she wore an invisible crown. When he'd discovered her true identity after scanning the list of guests at the summit, he hadn't been surprised. Her father, the *oba* of a tiny seaside village called Gbale, just a stone's throw outside Badagry, too small to even be included on a map, but a thriving fishing community. The man had a reputation for being stern and was also infamously religious—he'd lost a young wife early on, Luke learned, and he'd turned to God as a result. He had only two daughters, both of whom were active members of the local church community, and according to local whispers, he was very, very strict with them. No outings alone. No school. Most residents of the town had never seen the girls, except for church and for formal occasions.

These findings had explained some things rather than muddled them. The fact that she'd been clearly well-off, for that matter, and the fact that she'd initially been so shy.

Thinking it a silent assent, Luke reached into the box, lifted the emerald necklace. It was just as hefty as the jeweler had promised, and even more exquisite than it'd been, displayed in its case in Lagos.

"Move the fabric from your shoulders," he commanded. He was suddenly impatient to see it on her, to dress his princess, to drape her in jewels.

His princess. Did he think, then—

Luke pushed the thought from his mind. As if in a trance, Kemi lifted a trembling hand and moved her long gold-studded braids from her shoulders; Luke fastened the necklace, perhaps lingering a little longer than was necessary on the softness of her skin, then took a step back.

"Extraordinary," he breathed, and it was not of the necklace he spoke. Dark color flushed beneath the soft browns of Kemi's skin.

She'd never looked more beautiful.

The green absorbed the light from the sun, lighting up the fine tints of her round shoulders and neck, making her skin glow with health and vitality. Her lips were parted; her lashes were full and soft. She made a sensuous picture of fertility, of beauty, clutching her garments to herself modestly and looking up at him as if she wasn't sure who he was.

"Luke," she managed.

Luke's first emotion was of surprise; he had not expected this near-violent surge of want. He could not help it, however, any more than he could help breathing; he stepped forward till their bodies nearly touched, cupped her cheek in his hand, inhaled that subtly sweet scent of hers. "You're warm," he said.

"I just got out of bed." Her voice wavered just a fraction. She signed and softened against him, her breasts warm and unfettered beneath her dressing gown, and then—

When she pulled back, he blinked, thinking the driver had come back, but the blazing in her eyes told him otherwise.

"Kemi—"

"You have," she spat out, "the most audacity of any man I've ever—"

She was *angry*? Luke's brows lifted high. He'd expected surprise from her, of course, but not anger. "What?"

"You show up here," Kemi said accusingly, "unannounced, after I told you I was pregnant—"

"I was working on all this!"

"No calls, no acknowledgment of my many messages—"

"I am here now, aren't I?"

Kemi threw her hands skyward and stalked toward the gate, speaking Yoruba rapidly. He could only understand a few words, but he could definitely guess at the rest.

He stared for a moment before following. "Kemi."

She'd already reached the gate, and turned, her eyes flashing in frustration. "What?"

"Are you going to tell me what is upsetting you, or do you prefer to shout?"

That was the wrong thing to say. Kemi took a step forward, and for one thrilling moment Luke wondered if she was going to shove him. This furious creature was so different from the demure young woman he'd taken to bed weeks ago that he was quite amazed.

"I," she said, with clear and decided elocution, "am not going to marry you."

This Luke had prepared for, although he hadn't thought she'd respond with so much vehemence. "Why ever not?"

Kemi gaped. "Because—I don't love you. And you don't love me. You don't even have the courtesy to reply when I try to speak to you. And you're arrogant, and you're—"

"You let me touch you, just now."

He certainly hadn't expected to say that, and Kemi clearly wasn't expecting to hear it from him, either; she took a full step back and folded her arms round herself in a gesture he was finding increasingly irritating. "What?"

"You let me put jewelry on you," he said mildly. "And touch you rather intimately on a private street. Which, at least in my estimation, means you don't find me as repulsive a partner as you claim, at least in the physical sense. Why wouldn't you marry me?"

"Why would I?" she floundered.

"Come inside and I'll tell you."

Her eyes flashed again, and he was struck by the wariness in them, the tiredness. She looked older than when he'd last seen her, not because her skin was slack or less vibrant, but because she looked beaten down. Unsure. "You must be very sure of yourself, inviting me into my own home."

"The home of my future father-in-law," Luke said, and

immediately apologized. "All right—I was an ass for that one. Please, Kemi. It's warm out here."

She stood shaking with what he assumed was rage, but good sense prevailed, and she turned and walked toward the house, head held high. She did not look to see if he was behind her, and when they were finally seated in the small receiving room off the front hall, she did not look at him while she called a house girl to bring water, tea. The studied princess was back, cool, dignified, remote, but he'd already uncovered the fire beneath the coolness, and it no longer satisfied him. He wanted her, the fire, the anger; this aloof remoteness was no longer enough. That realization was a new one, but he had no time to dwell on it.

"I can't marry you," she said again.

"You won't marry me," he corrected. She'd forgotten she was still wearing the wedding necklace. Even paired as ludicrously as it was with that heinous dressing gown, she was radiant. Suddenly, irrationally, he wanted her to marry him, very much. "And why wouldn't you?"

"I already told you. I don't—"

"Would it help if I told you that I wasn't keen to marry you, either?"

He saw surprise enter those dark brown eyes, but he did not let her react before continuing. "I was clear that I could offer you nothing after what happened, Kemi, and you became pregnant, nonetheless—"

"You're acting as if it was my fault!"

"I didn't even ask you to take a paternity test, although we will carry that out when the child is born." Luke spoke slowly, deliberately; he didn't look at her face. Every time he did, he seemed to stop. "Despite the fact that you didn't take my advice and use emergency contraceptive after the fact—"

"I did! Did you think I wouldn't?" She was near tears.

"I got it at a local pharmacy. You know drugs in those places aren't reliable—"

"—that is immaterial now." Luke lifted his shoulders. "You're pregnant. You are the daughter of a prominent man, a prominent man who has a reputation for his conservative views—"

"Do you think I'd have slept with you if I *knew*?"

Luke sighed. Ruminating over the past was useless; he should know. He did it often enough. "I'll speak plainly. I am not willing to lose my reputation over a bastard, or over a king who chooses to badmouth me once he finds I've impregnated his daughter."

He heard Kemi gasp but steamrolled on—he'd finish what he came to begin, damn it. "You can divorce me after a week if you wish, Kemi Obatola, but we will marry."

There was none of the heat that had characterized their kiss outside only moments ago. Luke felt as if he was encased in ice, as if he was incapable of feeling anything but the logic, the cool practicality, that he was exhibiting now. "Come, Kemi," he finished, and his mouth curved up slightly. "You aren't a child, or a blushing college student. You're certainly not a virgin anymore—"

"You are cruel," she burst out.

"I am *truthful*," he snapped. "And I'll always be that, Kemi. Whoever I am, I will always be honest with you. Tell me this—would you rather marry me, and be mistress of your own house, and potentially become your own woman, or would you rather bear your child in this prison—yes, it is a prison, isn't it?"

Kemi had gone ashen to the lips. She stared at him, unblinking; her hand had traveled to rest on her abdomen, and she was trembling.

"Oh, you hid it well," he said flatly, "but I researched you very carefully, my dear." He began ticking off on his fingers. "You don't travel unless it's with your father.

You didn't do your national youth service. You don't even leave the *compound* without permission, and according to your gateman and the employees my people questioned, the answer is usually no."

Tears were pooling in Kemi's eyes, but he ignored them and went on.

"You didn't go away to university—at least not in person—you have no friends except that sister of yours, no access to money—"

"Are you here to make fun of me, then?" Kemi demanded.

He stood, drew his jacket closed, buttoned it.

"I did not come here to distress you," he said gently. "You are an intelligent and beautiful woman, Kemi. Use me. *Use* this. Take your freedom."

He did not allow her to answer; instead, he turned to leave the room. Kemi might not like it, but she was as practical as he was, steel wrapped in silk. She would see she had no choice, and she would agree. And being honest, part of him was glad to be able to play this part in her liberation. It would be a redemption of sorts for him.

Goodness knew he could do nothing else for her.

CHAPTER SIX

TAKE YOUR FREEDOM.

Kemi had been so focused on Luke, on his maddening inaccessibility, she'd completely forgotten about herself in the process.

Take your freedom!

She'd slept with him, yes. She'd given the magnate something she couldn't repeat—her first experience in a man's bed. She'd found it arousing in more ways than one. Not just sexually, but he'd woken something in her that she'd not allowed to breathe, to thrive, for years. The kidnapper's bullets had made her force it down, choke off its air. It was as if her brief encounters with Luke Ibru had pried a lid off, letting in sunshine, fresh air, nutrients, and it was growing.

Whom could she become, as Kemi Ibru?

Kemi spent the rest of the afternoon nervous as a cat, starting at small noises, feeling a vague nausea that she wasn't sure had anything to do with the baby growing beneath her ribs. She paced her room; she snapped at and fought with Tobi; she locked her door and tried on the wedding necklaces, one after the other, with trembling fingers. She remembered the way he looked at her, eyes lingering on her breasts in that absolutely inadequate dressing gown, and desire pooled low in her belly. She wanted this, and if she was honest, her freedom was only a part of it. Perhaps if she could get this cold, enigmatic father of her child alone, in the most intimate of situations…

She splashed cold water against the heat suffusing her face. *Again.*

Her own father hadn't said one word of dissent and hadn't answered any questions. Perhaps the extravagance of the bridal gift, combined with his daughter's wan face, told him more than he wanted to know. He'd only reacted when Kemi told him quietly that she wanted to marry soon. Very soon.

"You're a king's daughter," he said, sharply. "Invitations alone will need a month to go out—"

"Baba, I—" She'd rested a hand on her abdomen, unable to say the words out loud. Her father's face in that moment had been a study—disbelief chased anger, followed by something she could not define.

"How—"

Kemi closed her eyes. She could not confess without implicating Tobi, and would not. "Baba—"

"Did he hurt you?" the king said, almost roughly.

Kemi shook her head. The look on her father's face… "No," she said, then cleared her throat, forcing out the next words. "Quite the opposite."

Her father sat motionless for a full minute, not a muscle moving in his face, and when he spoke, Kemi knew that he was washing his hands of her. He told Kemi shortly that if she wanted to marry soon, a small, quiet wedding was not even to be considered; the diplomatic and social advantages this wedding would bring were nonnegotiable.

"I'll give you three weeks."

Trembling, Kemi lowered herself in a small curtsy, whispering her thanks, and left the room.

She showered and dressed; then, stomach still fluttering with nervousness, she called Luke's mobile.

"Hello?"

Right on cue, her stomach twisted with knots. "I'd like to speak to you."

"Fine. I'll pick you up," he said easily.

"My father…"

"Wants to get you married. I'm Nigeria's top security person, Kemi. You will be safe with me and he knows it."

"Right."

Twenty minutes later, Kemi sat with Luke in the back of the massive Mercedes, hands twisting the skirt of her dress in her lap. She might as well have been a part of the car; Luke gave her a polite half smile, then looked out the window. "Are you hungry?"

She shook her head. She wouldn't be, not until they resolved this. "If we marry—"

Luke looked at her, a glint in his eye. He'd been expecting this. "You have terms."

"Yes." Finally, something this hard-hearted business-man would be able to understand. She took a breath. "I'll marry you and play up our big love story—that's fine." As she spoke, Luke's hands went to where her hands were knotted in her skirt, freed them.

"Relax," he said gently and peered down into her face. "I'm not a monster, Kemi. I want to help you. Just let me know what you want."

She let out a short laugh. Help her? She didn't even know where to begin. "I've never done anything like this—"

"You say that a lot to me," he said dryly.

"Don't make fun of me!"

"I'm not." His lips twitched. "Marriage is a merger, Kemi, nothing else, and our marriage more so than most. We'll reassess in a year or so and see where we are. If there are no more mutual benefits…"

Kemi waited breathlessly for the end of the sentence,

but it did not come, and she restrained herself with some effort from grabbing her skirt again. "You'll divorce me."

"We'll divorce each other," he corrected and turned his mild eyes on her. "We've both gotten ourselves into a fix, Kemi. I don't intend to hold you to this permanently."

"Divorce?" She could hardly believe it. In barely a week she'd become not only a bride, but a future divorcée.

"Yes. It's quite painless when done correctly."

She gaped. "You're divorced?"

"Indeed, I am." He paused, wondering if he should share the next bit, then forged forward and did it anyway. "I haven't been—dating. Or anything. Not for at least four years. You don't have to worry about any…rivals. I have no interest whatsoever in any romantic pursuits."

Kemi did look at him then, and surprise colored her features before she shuttered them again.

"I'm glad that you found out your equipment still works."

Luke actually recoiled; then, to his surprise, he began to laugh.

Kemi leaned backward, eyeing him suspiciously; that only made him laugh harder. He reached out and took one of her hands, turning it over in his. The slide of butter-soft, warm skin on his brought back memory of the way they'd felt on his body, exploring with an eagerness that belied shyness, fear, inexperience. Kemi was frowning, but she wasn't pulling away; in fact, the look in her eyes had softened.

"Thank you, Kemi," Luke said simply, and he kissed her there, just a whisper of contact where her blood pulsed in her wrist. He felt her body tense slightly and relax, as if she'd let out a sigh. He took a moment to allow that sweet, clean scent of her to engulf his senses, then raised his head.

Kemi's eyes were soft—just as soft as they'd been when

he'd held her close, thrusting deep within her only weeks before—and wet. Not with tears, but with the type of emotion that only comes from that sort of deep connection that is more than mere chance. *Spiritual*, for lack of a better word.

Too bad it wouldn't last.

He had never been able to give any woman anything except pain.

For the remainder of their time in the car, Luke marched her through the terms of their deal with all the detached exactness of a military officer. He spoke of clothing allowances, of allowances for the baby, of a driver, a maid, a security team for her own use, of the society events she'd be expected to host, and to attend…

When he asked her if there were any questions, Kemi blinked. "Um—"

"Were you listening?"

"It was a lot of information," she said defensively. Was she marrying a man, after all, or a sergeant-major?

Luke sighed through his nose. "Any questions?"

She chewed her lip, then tentatively stepped out on the territory she'd been eyeing with trepidation. "Your ex-wife…?"

"She's not on the invite list, if you're worried," he said dryly. "She lives in Enugwu with her new husband, whom she flaunts rather tackily on social media. A senator, with the most impressive beer belly. She's better off—he spoils her abominably."

"Well," Kemi gasped. "Did you knock her up as well?"

At that jibe, the change in Luke was extraordinary; his entire body stiffened, and his bourbon-dark eyes narrowed to slits in his face. When he spoke, however, his voice was still very carefully under control. "I've given you this information as a courtesy, so you don't find it out from some gossiping woman in the toilet. That does not mean it's up for discussion. Under any circumstance, and certainly not through any ill-thought-out attempts at humor."

He was angry. So Luke Ibru could show emotion, though it wasn't close to what she'd been looking for. She swallowed hard and leaned back against the leather seat of the car.

"It was rude of me," she conceded quietly, after a moment. "And yes—I will marry you." It was the only sensible thing to do.

Luke cleared his throat. The fierce expression was gone, and he rubbed a hand over his head.

"Why don't you let me say what I have in mind, then?"

She nodded. Anything would be better than sitting her in uncomfortable silence.

"I live part-time in the Seychelles. It's quiet, away from the bustle of Nigeria. I propose we go there after the wedding, for a few months, and then to America to have the baby."

Of course he'd want his child born there; most rich men did—and kings, for that matter. There or Canada. She nodded wordlessly. Seychelles. America. Two places she'd read about, seen on television or in films, but never visited, never thought she could visit, until perhaps when her father had gone to sleep with the kings before him.

"You want your child to be a Yankee, then?" She couldn't stop making idiotic jokes, she supposed.

"You know it makes it easier." His voice was crisp. "We'll work on getting you a passport, too."

"You're a citizen?"

"Not by birth. My ex-wife was."

The elusive ex-wife. Kemi bit the inside of her cheek. She wondered wildly what sort of woman it must have taken to capture the enigmatic businessman's attention, and wondered whether her birth status had anything to do with it. He frowned as if he knew what she'd been thinking, per usual. "It wasn't a visa marriage, Kemi."

Her face burned. "I would never—"

"You were. Now let me finish." Luke took a breath as if to steady himself, then spread his fingers wide. "After you have the baby, I'll file for you, and you'll stay."

"In America?"

He lifted his shoulders. "I say the States because they have fine university programs."

"I *have* a degree." She cleared her throat. "In education."

He smiled. "You don't have the in-person experience. Trust me, you'll want to do uni in person, and a master's will serve you well. You can go all the way up to doctorate, if you want. I'll get you an apartment, a car, a maid, an au pair for the baby—you'll be able to have the life you want."

This was too much for Kemi's rather limited imagination; the possibilities were rising in her chest, cutting off her air. She lifted a hand to her throat. "And you?"

"I'll visit. I won't be a stranger to the baby. Once we can file for you—say two, three years—we can talk about formal separation."

So cold. So clinical. What the hell was she getting herself into?

She swallowed. "What happens now?" Kemi picked up the rest of her ginger ale, sipped it again.

"We have a wedding to plan," Luke said, and his voice had returned to its usual dryness. "You have your jewelry already, and your ring will be sent from South Africa by the week's end. I'd prefer to have this done as quickly as we can, if that is agreeable to you."

Kemi bit the inside of her cheek hard enough to draw blood and nodded. It had to be agreeable to her; she had no other choice.

"Oh—" he said, as if the next words were an afterthought. "We need to pick a house."

"A house?"

"Yes. I have one there, but it's the one I shared with my ex-wife before I divorced. It's on the market." He cleared his throat. "I've got my eye on two. There's one on Eden Island, which is pretty secluded and away from the main town. Houses there are small, but I will purchase three, renovate them into one. Then there's one on Victoria Island, in Mahe—the main hub. Busier. Noisier, but closer to everything. Then there's—"

"You expect me to pick from *here*?" Kemi's head was beginning to spin.

"Yes. I'll have the agent send you the links and pictures. Just correspond with him, tell him which one you prefer."

"Without seeing it in person?"

Luke was beginning to look impatient. "I trust him impeccably, Kemi. And if you don't like the place in person, we'll swap it out for another one. You're pregnant. I'm not dragging you round resorts until we can find a home, like some demented tourist."

"Some demented tour—" Kemi simply stared at him, not knowing whether to laugh or to open the car door and make a break for it. She was leaving her father's house, yes, but there had been moments today when Luke made her wonder if she shouldn't stay with the devil she knew. He typed busily away at his tablet, then handed it to her. "Swipe."

The beauty of the estates on the screen took her breath away; king's daughter or no, she'd never seen anything like them. Green, rolling hills served as backgrounds for stunning homes that arched up to reach the sky. The first overlooked a rocky beach with glass-clear water and a sky that rivaled it in blue.

"I thought you might like the water, being from here," Luke said from over her shoulder.

The second was a series of small, elegant houses that were interconnected by floral-lined glass passages. An infinity pool served as a front lawn, and even in the photos the water looked cool and inviting.

"Pretty, but hell to maintain," Luke posited.

Kemi swallowed. "Aren't I supposed to be choosing?" It was a joke, but her voice came out a bit more wavery than she'd intended. This was so overwhelming. She touched the button on the tablet's screen, turned it off. "I'll do the rest later. I'm tired." She looked up at him through heavy lids. "Will you take me home now, please?" she asked.

Luke nodded, then, to her surprise, he leaned in, looked into her eyes. His own were soft and cool, and Kemi felt those familiar stirrings of desire, deep down. It was funny, how the body could still be so aroused when the mind was so conflicted. She could not tell Luke that, however; even the thought was anathema to her.

"It will be fine," he said, with so much confidence that she almost believed him. There it was again—that sense of safety, despite the uncertainty of everything else.

CHAPTER SEVEN

IT WAS SURPRISINGLY easy to play the role of ecstatic bride in front of a crowd, and Kemi did it to perfection. Her father spared no expense in celebrating her wedding to one of the wealthiest men in Nigeria, and there certainly had never been an event of its magnitude in the sleepy old town of Gbale. The traditional wedding, of course, would be held first. She and Luke had both agreed that the church wedding should be smaller, more private and held after their child was born. The traditional wedding was enough trouble, really—and as a representation of Yoruba culture, would be more than enough to satisfy her father and his societal obligations.

Early on her traditional wedding day, Luke came to the palace, flanked by a band of men playing talking drums as well as his groomsmen, dressed identically in tailored tunics and pants, hats perched jauntily on their heads, beads encircling their necks, swinging walking canes and calling out for the king to let them in. Kemi and Tobi peered down at them from the balcony overlooking the palace walls, laughing at the theater; the king's representatives met them at the door, and all the men lowered themselves to the ground in obeisance, fanning crisp hundred-dollar bills out as an appeal, asking amid loud joking, laugher and singing to be let in.

Kemi's gown was absolutely ridiculous in its opulence;

in between her newly pregnancy-inflated bosom and hips, she could barely breathe. It was skintight, low-cut, studded with beading and peacock feathers, and still somehow staggeringly chic. She carried an enormous fan of peacock feathers, which she waved grandly at the guests, the lack of her husband's family noticeable. Luke was an only child, and his mother, he confided, had died a long time ago. His father did not live in Nigeria, and she did not push for more details.

The ceremony itself was long, elaborate, drawn out—a state occasion, almost. There were speeches and blessings by nearly every clergyman of importance in the area and formal recognition of dignitaries, some of whom had traveled internationally to attend, despite the short notice. There was a massive celebration lunch, on crowded tables groaning under the weight of soft pounded yam and spicy, nutty soups, hearty with meat and fresh vegetables. There was not one but several cakes, glossy with frosting, and wine flowed like water. When the celebration was winding down, a fleet of armored vehicles arrived to bear the new bride to the chartered jet they were to take to the Seychelles.

"I'll miss you," Tobi whispered once she had brought her sister the peacock-feather wrap she'd wear over her gown. She reached up and adjusted the stiff gold headdress on Kemi's head, then bent and kissed her cheek.

"I'll miss you, too," she whispered and wrapped her arms round Tobi's shoulders, tightening as if she'd never let them go. The girls had spent their last night together only hours before, Kemi sitting on a low stool at her sister's feet as Tobi put the finishing touches on her braids. Kemi had eschewed one of the many hairdressers at her disposal in favor of Tobi, whose nimble fingers and graceful hands had swiftly parted her sister's hair into what seemed like thousands of thin, silky braids over three days. The final result was a marvel—yards and yards of dark hair interwoven with tiny glass and gold beads that twinkled at the barest hint of light.

"It will last for at least two months if you're good about wrapping it at night," Tobi had said briskly once the last bead was attached, after the ends of the extensions had been sealed in hot water to which she'd added a few drops of lavender oil. "I'm sure you can find someone to fix it for you over there."

"Not as well as you would," Kemi said softly, and the two girls held each other for several moments, overcome by the emotion of it all. Tobi, of course, knew the secret of the child that grew beneath her sister's ribs; she'd shared it with her the night Luke arrived. After the initial shock, Tobi had taken the whole thing in her stride.

"It's not quite the thing," she said, "to marry someone like this. But there's nothing that has ever been normal about us, sister. And if you think he can make you happy… God willing, you will have a healthy baby, but things happen. Do this for yourself. And if it doesn't work out, *come home.*"

In her heart of hearts, Kemi knew that would never happen. That single, near-enchanted evening she'd spent in Luke Ibru's arms had sparked a chain of events that she knew would change her life forever. And now—

"Kemi?"

It was time to stop reminiscing. Kemi arranged her face into a smile and turned around to face her husband— her husband!

Luke looked marvelous, and her heart gave a little skip to see it. The slim, tailored dashiki and pants, in the same emerald green as her dress, suited Luke quite well, skimming his narrow, muscled frame. The green of the tunic made the deep tints of his skin glow, as did the tiny gold stud in one ear. Did he wear that normally? She hadn't even noticed he had a piercing. He hitched a brow, and she felt her cheeks flush again.

What was wrong with her? She couldn't even blame this on drink; she'd had only half a glass of sparkling apple juice, thanks to her condition. They had barely interacted during the event, which was fairly easy to do; traditional Nigerian weddings were so jam-packed with activity that actual interaction by the bride and groom could easily take a back seat. Luke's large hand fastened round the handle of her bag, and his other dropped to the small of her back.

"Our plane is waiting," Luke said quietly.

Kemi's heart felt as if it was lodged in her throat. Wordlessly she moved back and slipped her hand into Luke's; he turned it over, looked at the slim gold ring on one finger. He'd shown Kemi dozens, but in the end she'd only wanted a gold band. She did not, she thought, want to return an opulent ring once this was all over. She didn't want any personal gifts that would be difficult to part with, that she couldn't afford herself.

"Simple," he said, and his voice was dry. "It suits you."

Kemi nodded; she had no energy for wordplay. For a moment, just for a moment, she allowed herself to sag against her husband's side, and to her surprise he smiled gently down at her.

"You'll be able to rest soon" was all he said. "Let's go."

There was barely time for Kemi to say goodbye to her family or even to change her dress. They'd be flying out of Lagos, of course, and traffic was always unpredictable. They eased themselves into the back of the waiting limousine—dated, she thought, but worthy of their type of occasion—and finally, for the first time in days, they were alone, separated from the silent, deferential driver by a partition. Luke did not say anything. He fiddled with his phone as if he meant to turn it on, then looked out the window, instead.

They were now in the middle of one of Lagos's famous traffic jams, and she could see people in their cars talking, laughing, arguing, dancing. None seemed to have the sort of choking awkwardness that had hung over the two of them since they'd left.

She picked one of the costly beads off her skirt, then reached up to where the emerald necklace lay heavy on her neck and shoulders. She really should have insisted on changing before leaving instead of staying in this ridiculous outfit. Despite the air-conditioned interior, her hands were sweaty, as was much of her body—a side effect of pregnancy, she'd heard, and not one she was particularly fond of. Her fingers slipped on the clasp once, twice—she swore under her breath, and then Luke was there, next to her, his fingers gentle on the back of her neck.

"It's a delicate clasp. Let me help you," he said, and the feeling of his breath on the back of her neck did absolutely nothing to cool her down. She picked up the ridiculous peacock fan from where it lay on the floor of the car and began circulating air as quickly as she could. Her damned dress was far too tight, as well; she should have never let her stepmother talk her into this sexpot style, should have gone with the traditional, roomy *iro* and *buba* instead—

"Kemi."

She squeezed her eyes shut, concentrated on breathing. Tears were beginning to sting behind her lids; she forced her attention to the movement of her diaphragm. In. Out. In. Out. The interior of the car was receding, light, then dark; it was taking on that wavy shape round the edges that she knew heralded unconsciousness. She'd fainted only once, as a child after playing hard in the summer heat, and she remembered the feeling of breathlessness, the complete loss of control. She wasn't there quite yet, but in a moment—

She heard Luke's voice, risen high and sharp with concern, and there was a metallic, sour taste in her mouth. She tried to answer him, but all she could get past the lump in her throat was a gasp. She heard Luke swear, violently, shout something at the driver, and then, thank goodness, there was a violent tug, and she felt her body expand, fill with precious, blessed air as her dress opened in the back. She gulped, then sucked in more air, and then, hot and humiliated, began to cry.

"Breathe," Luke commanded. His voice was much less alarmed, almost brisk. "Breathe, darling. With me, all right, Kemi? Breathe."

She obeyed him, inhaling, exhaling, the buzzing behind her eyes reducing a little with each exhalation. Luke's hands were inside her dress, on her bare skin, pushing the material away. His hand brushed the side of her breast, bared by the boning and cups built directly into the dress, and she batted his hand away feebly.

"I assure you, that's the last thing on my mind," Luke said dryly, and Kemi found the strength to shift away from him, turn so that she could face him head-on and lift her chin. It would wobble despite her best efforts, and tears were running down her face, but at least he wasn't touching her.

"Thank you," she said. "I can handle it from here."

"I doubt that's the case," he said, and his voice was a little rough, but still gentle in a way it hadn't been before.

"My dress was too tight," Kemi said, but she knew that wasn't the only reason she'd had a meltdown. It was the sudden, overwhelming knowledge that she was free now, that she was now at the mercy of a man, this man, that she wasn't quite sure the decision she'd made would be any better than what she'd left.

And now, to make matters worse, the memories of his hands on her skin were coming back, crowding out the anxiety, the fear. Her body was reacting in an entirely inappropriate way, both for this conversation and for the place, and her breasts, threatening to break free of her unfastened bodice, were beginning to ache. She knew without looking that her nipples were swelling, pushing hard against the scratchy fabric. They remembered how skilled his hands had been, how gentle his mouth had felt. Pregnancy had made them twice as sensitive, unfortunately, and that sensitivity seemed to have traveled to every nerve end in her body.

Her husband.

She swallowed hard and turned away.

"You'll have to take that ridiculous thing off," Luke said, loosening his collar and clearing his throat. There was a different kind of tension now; Kemi knew without asking that her husband quite likely was remembering what she was remembering, although she could wager he was nowhere as uncomfortable.

"Kemi."

She shook her head.

"Talk to me," he said. "Get it out, whatever it is. It's not good for the health of the child otherwise."

She was too cold now, all of a sudden; the sweat on her exposed skin made her shiver.

"Kemi—"

"Why did you marry me, anyway?" Her voice was piteous and she hated it, but she had to know. "Why? You could easily have paid me off."

To her surprise he half laughed, somehow combining it with a rueful grunt. "You won't like the answer."

"Try me."

For a moment the only audible things were the air conditioner and the faint strains of Flavour, serenading his imaginary lover in a song on the car's sound system. Luke's driver thought it appropriate for newlyweds, apparently. If only he knew.

For the first time since she'd known him, Luke looked…uncertain. Exposed, and it was such a surprise it kept her silent, slowed her breathing, quelled the racing of her heart.

"I wanted," Luke said, "to take care of you."

Kemi felt a glow of pleasure, followed just as quickly by dismay. At first the words sparked a little beat of her heart; then, just as quickly, she felt it drop to her stomach. Tender feelings had not inspired this statement; this was Luke. It didn't matter how gentle he was with her in bed. He didn't have feelings for her and never would. Kemi might have been an innocent, but she was schooled enough in human emotion to see when it threatened to carry her away. If she allowed herself to think of Luke in any terms but business, she would be hurt, and badly. If she wanted to emerge from this marriage unscathed—

What if he falls in love with you?

Kemi drew in a breath. Of course that part of her that still believed in fairy tales would think that way. Just because she was a princess didn't mean she was headed for a happy ending with the man who'd come to rescue her.

Kemi blinked and looked up to see her husband peering curiously into her face. She forced a smile that covered crippling anxiety.

"I don't plan to be a liability," she said quickly.

Luke turned his head, looked at her in the darkness. "Pardon?"

"I'll do my best to be an asset to you. I don't want to be a burden. I'm not—I'm not a charity case, Luke. I might have been sheltered, but I have a lot to offer, too—"

She was babbling and was fully aware she sounded insane, but she couldn't seem to shut her mouth. Luke was staring at her with so much astonishment that it would have been funny in any other context. She dug her freshly manicured nails into her palm, trying to shut herself up.

"Did I ever in any way, shape or form, imply I considered you a liability?" Luke asked.

Now she felt more than a little ridiculous. "No," she said in a small voice. "You didn't, but—"

"I've never done anything I didn't want to do," he added. "Do you understand what I'm trying to say, Kemi?"

Her face felt as if it was on fire, now, and she was glad for the warm, muggy cover of night. "I—"

"You are—" and here Luke began ticking off his fingers "—a king's daughter. You are pregnant with my child. You've brought me increased social status and an immediate family—"

Kemi swallowed. She'd never felt more like a commodity in her life, although she supposed her father might agree with Luke.

"Don't underestimate your value, Kemi. Come on," Luke said briskly, and just like that, she realized the car had stopped. Luke gave her his coat to pull on over her dress, and in a flash, she was mounting the stairs to the jet, the portal to her new life.

The interior of the jet was a study in luxury. Rendered in soft shades of buttery gold and rich brown, it featured oversize pods with built-in workstations, plus carpet so deep that the heels of her mules sank into it. Soft music played over the speakers. Luke gave her a lightning-quick tour as two attendants milled about, making the cabin ready for takeoff. There was a sleeping area complete with a working shower, and a bed made with sheets and blankets so lush and thick her fingers lingered on them.

"This is your life now," her husband said simply. "It'll take you anywhere in the world you want to go."

They sat down and strapped in for takeoff, and when

the plane finally reached cruising altitude, they were free to move around the cabin. Luke motioned for her to join him in the sleeping cabin, pulled a curtain aside to reveal loungewear specifically for the seven-hour flight—sweats, dressing gowns, yoga wear, all in fabric so soft it would feel like nothing on the skin.

"I'll leave you alone," Luke said, then tilted his head. "Do you need help…?"

"No," Kemi said quickly, then blushed when Luke lifted his eyebrows. "I mean—maybe. I'm sorry—"

"If you apologize to me one more time, I'll leave you on the tarmac."

She supposed he was joking. "You have to acknowledge this is strange," she said, and shrugged his coat onto the bed before presenting her back to him. She could feel the air-conditioning on the bare skin of her back, and she wished, fleetingly, that she was wearing something more substantial under the dress than the flimsiest set of lace underwear ever. Not that it would move her husband, she thought a little bitterly. Sometimes she felt as if that night of passion had been a figment of her imagination.

She closed her eyes as Luke came up behind her, the warmth of his body radiating onto her skin. When she stood like this, when he could not see her face, it would be safe for a moment to close her eyes, indulge the slow roll of want she'd learned to expect. Not that she could tell him this. Her wants were not part of the bargain involved in this marriage of convenience.

Luke's fingers brushed the length of her spine—completely unnecessarily, she thought with a flush of something very much like anger.

"I'm not entirely sure," he said after a pause, "how, after a day of partying so hard, you can still smell so good."

What? Her cheeks were fairly burning now.

"At first I thought it was perfume," he said, and the husk that had entered his voice made her breath catch. "But no. It's you. It was the same at the lounge that night…"

The night they'd had sex, that one and only time. Kemi immediately felt a heaviness in her breasts, a tightening in her nipples. They remembered Luke, and how good he'd made her feel. They wanted his hands on her. Luke's slim fingers flicked open one hook at the small of her back, then another. Kemi gulped.

"Your skin is so warm," he said, almost idly, and she felt the dress give a little more. Three. Four. He'd reached the soft lace waistband of her underwear now, and his fingers skimmed the inside, just a whisper of contact.

"New?" he murmured, and his lips grazed her ear. When they made contact, there it was—that surge of molten heat burning right at her core, spreading outward. She wondered helplessly if it was different for women who were more experienced—married women, or women who had sex all the time. Was there a way to cap this, to react in any other way but this pulsating, aching want that burned a lighting-hot path from her breasts to between her legs? And as for Luke, who was he? What kind of a person treated her with such supreme indifference, then turned round with the next breath, proclaimed he wanted to protect her, and, currently, was stroking her skin with the backs of his fingers, as if—as if—

She twisted out of his grip and turned, facing him, groping impotently for the bodice of the dress. It was a wasted effort. It already sagged at her hips. She wrapped her arms around her chest instead, feeling incredibly foolish, but determined to speak.

"Are we going to have sex now?" she blurted out, then clapped a hand over her mouth. She couldn't believe she'd said that.

His brows lifted, and high. "If we were, probably not anymore."

Kemi felt her face grow hot, but she forged ahead. "I just need to know—" She paused, trying to find the words. "Is this—in name only? *Are* we having sex? Am I expected to make sure that you're satisfied in that area?"

"Kemi…"

"Will there be other women? Will you—" Kemi choked a little. "I don't know how this works. I don't know the rules."

Luke sighed. "Get dressed."

"What—"

"Get. Dressed," he repeated. "We're not having sex, and I think you can get out of your dress well enough now. We can talk when we get to the Seychelles."

Not ever, or not for the moment? Kemi scrambled into a long-sleeved cashmere shirt and matching palazzo pants, heart still thumping oddly. She draped a thin shawl over her shoulders, slipped her feet into delicate slippers with a designer logo Tobi certainly would have killed for and walked out into the main cabin, doing her best not to look at the bed she left behind her.

Luke was half-disgusted with his own behavior. The second he'd gotten her alone, putting his hands on her, and— why? He'd had no intention of trying to seduce his wife. He had no intention of doing anything except keeping an eye on her till she had her baby, then ferrying her off to whatever place she fancied most, leaving him to live the rest of life in peace.

The problem was his body was refusing to cooperate. One look at Kemi in that state of half undress, her arms barely able to contain the flesh they were trying very inadequately to cover…

What the hell was wrong with him? Even now, although

he wasn't as rock-hard as he'd been in the cabin, he was nowhere close to being in a state where he'd be able to think objectively.

The next hour was cordial, though it was strained. He bullied Kemi into eating something—he still wasn't happy with the lack of color in her face—and he showed her to the main sleeping cabin. He was relieved when she fell asleep, tucked soundly into her converted bed. She could not know it, but the day had been an incredible strain for him, too. He could feel tension tightening at the corners of his temples, threatening to spill over into a headache that he knew would cripple him if he allowed it.

Heaviness was creeping in as well, a blanket of melancholy that he recognized and even welcomed. This sadness had been his constant companion for years and was as familiar as a relative, or an old friend. This he knew how to navigate.

His feelings for his young wife were something else entirely.

Luke had danced, had smiled for photographs, had held Kemi close, had even kissed her when the occasion demanded. He had greeted her countless relatives and sat in a hard, uncomfortable chair beside the king and laughed and joked with her brothers and danced with her young nieces and nephews and made merry for what seemed like hours and hours. The exhaustion of the facade was stealing through his body now. He was numb, ready to lie down, strip off his finery and curl up in the dark until he felt normal again. The hundreds of people he had interacted with today would have no idea that he was as numb inside as a winter's evening. They would have no idea he felt nothing, and hadn't felt anything in years. People would go back to their homes to tell the story of the princess and the billionaire and laugh and smile and wish for such a Cinderella story for themselves.

They had no idea. No one ever had any idea. Pain was for him, and him alone, and if he never felt any sort of joy at anything again, it was nobody's business but his.

Yet the lovely young woman half curled up in her bed, only a few feet from him, stirred things inside him that he'd thought were long dormant. It wasn't about lust, or about sex—Luke had and could live without those. It was a fierce sense of protectiveness, of caring, of wanting to fold Kemi into his arms, to protect her from the world's ills.

She'd seen so much already. And he was her husband now. Unfortunately, he was possibly the most damaged person for the job.

Luke sighed inwardly and half turned over, staring out at the inky darkness of the night. He received word from his men on the ground that the house that they'd purchased in the Seychelles was ready to receive the two of them. He looked forward to it. His room would have a stout lock and a stocked minibar. He would be able to immerse himself in this darkness that was quickly creeping over all his extremities, just for one night, and then he would bury himself in work until the darkness was gone. It was how he'd managed for years, and nothing would change.

Kemi stirred and muttered in her sleep. He peered over at her. Her lovely face was troubled, even in sleep, and she threw out an arm, muttering something—

She was having a dream, and not necessarily a happy one.

As she stirred, she grew all the more agitated, and Luke sat up.

Her face was drawn in an expression of such vivid pain that his breath caught in his throat despite himself. The look on her face was one of sadness, one of pleading, one of regret. She whispered a fervent "no!" and then twisted sideways, shoving the fine down blanket to the floor.

"Kemi?" Luke asked, sitting bolt upright in his chair.

She did not hear him; she was too deeply entrenched in that world between waking and asleep, held fast by whatever the demons that disturbed her were telling her. She began to mutter things in Yoruba, but her distress was clear though the meaning was not. She threw out her hands, and the cry that escaped...

"Kemi!" Luke sprang to his feet and crossed the few feet between them, placed a hand on her arm. She was visibly shaking now, and the words she spoke were mingled with tension and grief. He shook her a little, and she moaned. He reached out and placed a hand on the side of her face.

"Wake up," he said, low and consistent. He did not want to shake her. She looked so fearful, and he did not want to add to her distress. "Kemi. You're having a bad dream. Can you hear me? It's Luke. Wake up."

Her eyelids fluttered as if they were reluctant to leave their place of slumber, but Kemi finally opened her eyes. They were cloudy with sleep and confusion, and she looked up at her husband. The fear in her eyes made him take a step back; she looked like a hunted animal.

"Kemi," he said, loudly this time, and clearly. "It's Luke."

Kemi drew away from him, pulling back as far as she could go, rubbing her arms against the goose flesh that had prickled up. "I—"

"You had a bad dream," Luke said.

She swallowed hard; he could see the motion going down the line of her throat.

"What were you dreaming about?"

Shame crossed her face. "I didn't mean to disturb you," she said. "It happens sometimes, but— Was I—was I screaming?"

"Do you usually scream?" He peered into her face hard, trying to read her expression.

A vivid flush crept over her face beneath the lovely brown tints of her skin. "Sometimes. Only when I'm— Oh, it doesn't matter. I'm so sorry I disturbed you."

Luke did not know what caused him to do it, but he sat down on the end of the bed. Kemi drew her legs in close as if to avoid contact with him, but he ignored this.

"Were you dreaming about the abduction?" he asked bluntly.

She looked down at her hands.

"Does it happen very often?"

"Almost every night," she said softly.

"Do you always wake up as terrified as this?"

She was silent for a long moment, and then she spoke. "The dreams happen when I'm deep in sleep, or when I'm very tired. Different things happen in them. Sometimes it's at that moment, that first moment when they pull the gun on me. Sometimes I'm in a crowd, and they're chasing me, and I'm trying to press through the bodies, and I know someone is calling me but I can't quite break to the edge of the crowd, where I know I'll be safe. Sometimes I see the men themselves, and their faces, and they hold me down, and they try to touch me—" Her voice broke.

Nausea roiled through Luke. "When you were kidnapped, did they—"

She shook her head quickly. "No, thank God. But they told me pretty much every minute that they could, if they wanted to. They rough handled me once or twice, and—" She swallowed, and hard. "I really don't want to talk about it."

They sat in silence for a moment, a silence only punctuated by Kemi's soft, irregular breathing.

Luke reached out without even knowing what he was doing and touched her face. Her skin was cool and clammy, covered with a thin layer of sweat. "So it's been like this for you since you were—"

"Sixteen." Kemi's fingers were wrapping nervously round the base of her braids, pulling tight until the lack of blood left her fingertips a dull white. "My sister and I sleep in the same room, and that helps. They gave me sleeping pills for a while, but that made it worse. It just made it harder to wake up when I was in the middle of one."

"Have you ever talked to anyone about these nightmares? Do you have panic attacks, or anything else?"

She lifted her shoulders. "I don't have panic attacks, although I am anxious sometimes in crowds or spaces where I haven't identified any exits, or I'm in the middle of strangers. I'm rarely alone—that helps."

They sat in silence for a long time, corrupted now only by the humming of the jet. "Have you ever talked to anyone about this?"

"Well, Father Sylvester said—"

"Is Father Sylvester a psychologist?" Irritation crept into his voice. He knew the penchant his people had, especially the more religious ones, for turning to religion instead of science, but the terror on this young woman's face was not something that could be banished by prayers or oil or lighting candles. He waited one long moment before he sighed and gestured. "Move over."

She stared up at him; her dark eyes went wide. "What are you—"

"I'm not your sister, but you are pregnant and you need to get some sleep," he said flatly. He stared at her until she, eyes still wide, scooted over, and he eased himself onto the bed beside her.

"They are meant to sleep two people, anyway, and I'll try my best not to snore," he said. "You need help, Kemi, and you will get it soon. But for tonight, if you need someone to sleep with you, I will."

The residual fear on her face had faded away to something else completely, something that was reluctance mingled with a softness that tugged somewhere deep in his chest, despite himself. "You don't have to—"

"Yes, I do," he replied immovably. "I said that I wanted to marry you to take care of you, and I will. I haven't always been the best at anticipating the needs of people, but I will try my best to anticipate yours. I meant what I said today in front of the priest, Kemi. We may have married for unorthodox reasons, but it is my intention to make sure you want for nothing."

Kemi said nothing, thank God, but her eyes blurred just a little, and she allowed her lashes to drop. Her only response was to slide beneath the covers on their airplane bed, and after a moment he did the same. They did not speak, not until the regularity of her inhales and exhales told him she was back to sleep.

Sleep was not to come as quickly to Luke, however. He was utterly aware of Kemi beside him, of the soft, sweet smell of lilies that hung over them both, of the warmth radiating from her silky skin. He would not touch her; this was not the time or the place. But he could not deny that feelings were stealing into places that he'd thought were long locked down.

He remembered the terror in her face, her soft moans, the way she'd twisted and tensed with pain. He could not offer her love, but he could help her overcome this, help her abandon the ghosts that had scarred her mind as well as her abductors had scarred her body. He could hire experts to take care of those psychological scars. He could take care of her, give her the life she'd been denied because of one mistake.

Perhaps, he thought wearily before drifting off to sleep himself, this would be the key to his redemption. He had destroyed his ex-wife's life; perhaps he could make it up by helping Kemi to build hers. He could not love her, but he could get her to a place where she finally could forgive and love herself.

Unfortunately, he was beyond repair. But he would not give up on her.

There it was again, that overwhelming feeling of security and safety that seemed to associate itself with Luke.

Kemi kept her eyes closed tightly until she was sure he was asleep, then half rolled over to look at his face. In the dim light of the cabin, it looked more handsome than ever, outlined gently with the shadows that filled sharp crevices and depths. She was tempted to reach out and touch his face, to run her fingers over the smooth planes as he'd done while cupping her cheek, but she held herself back. Sex was one thing; allowing herself to indulge in any sort of sentiment toward Luke was quite another.

She'd been quite impulsive enough already. And Luke had made it abundantly clear that this marriage was about mutual benefits to both of them, not anything that would ever resemble tenderness. If she was to guard her heart, she must begin now. She must not allow herself even a single thought that bordered on sentiment about this quiet, stern-faced man she had married.

I'm going to take care of you.

The words echoed in her mind nearly every time she looked at him. She believed him with all her heart, and that was where the danger lay.

Impulsiveness had gotten her kidnapped. It had gotten her *pregnant*. She could not risk her heart the way she'd risked her body those two times. A broken body could be repaired by a skillful surgeon; a broken heart was far harder to fix. And perhaps a broken heart lay beneath the impenetrable wall that was Luke Ibru.

Why else would he be so stoic, so silent?

Why the hell did she even want to find out? Why

couldn't she leave well enough *alone*? Curiosity had never brought her anything but pain.

Luke's eyes opened wide just at that second, and he grimaced, then hissed. Kemi screamed, loud enough to wake the dead, and sprang backward. She would have definitely ended up on the floor in a pile if Luke hadn't been as fast as he was. He reached out, gripped her wrist, hauled her back up to the bed.

He was laughing.

She'd never seen him laugh before, at least not with the glee of a teenage boy who'd managed to startle a girl. It brightened his eyes, changed the symmetry of his face. He looked younger. More vibrant. She was so arrested by this new image of her husband that she took a deep breath and quite forgot to be angry.

"You look scared to death," Luke said, sounding very pleased with himself.

"If that is how you comfort people who just had nightmares, I'd rather have you sleep where you were before!" Kemi huffed. She drew the blanket up to her breasts and sat bolt up in bed. "Really, Luke—"

There was something in his eyes other than amusement, something so fierce and possessive that it quite stole her breath. "I'm sorry about your nightmare," Luke said.

She squirmed a little. "It happens."

"As my wife, you have unrestricted access to every resource you need. When we get to the Seychelles, I'm going to have someone on the ground for you to talk to. A professional…"

Kemi's heart was beating so rapidly in her chest she placed a hand over it in an attempt to still it. "Luke, I don't expect—"

"And besides that, just tell me what you need, and it's yours. You haven't had anyone stick up for you all these years," Luke said emphatically. "I'm going to."

The words sat warm and full in Kemi's chest, engulfing her like an embrace. "Luke, I don't—"

"No, Kemi, listen to me," Luke said, gently. "You are far too young and the world is far too wonderful for you to be buried because of a simple mistake. You owe it to yourself. You owe it to yourself to do well, and to have every dream come true. What do you *want*?"

Kemi's mouth went dry. As a princess, and after what had happened to her, no one had ever asked her that question before. She licked her lips. "I'm not sure—"

"You don't have to answer me now, but you must want something. What is it? School? To live somewhere? To get involved with philanthropy? I have all the resources to make whatever you want your reality. You must give me your word that you will let me help you."

The urgency in his voice took Kemi aback completely. She did not know what she'd done to cause it, or to make him feel as if she was this much of a priority. They'd had one night of passion together, yes, and he'd shown up and taken her away from the palace, and from her father's oppression. Still, there was no reason for him to be so invested in her—no reason she could actively see.

"Why are you saying these things?" she asked, and she had to swallow to keep her voice from trembling. "We're having a child together Luke, but you could have access to that child without anything from me. It is your right. I would not keep the child from you. We're not in love, and we are not going to be. You don't have to feel so responsible for me—"

"You are my *wife*," Luke said insistently. "And I want you to be happy."

Kemi could very much be flattered, could be swept away by the timbre of his voice and the passion of his words, but she knew instinctively that they weren't for her. She sat up completely, allowing the blanket to slide down to her lap and crossing her arms over her chest. "Can I ask you something?"

"Go ahead."

Kemi licked her lips before speaking. "What happened to your ex-wife?" she asked. "Why did you two break up?"

The silence in the room, she thought, was dense enough to be measured.

Luke was looking at her, but he wasn't really seeing her, not at all. There was a distance in his eyes that she recognized. It reminded her of the way she sometimes tried to disassociate herself from her own memories, to step outside her own body, to look at herself as an observer instead of one who was actively reliving an experience.

"We had a son," he said. His voice had taken on the type of clipped quality one uses when one is relaying important but particularly painful information. "He died."

Kemi placed a hand over her mouth, feeling shock rush over her, ice-cold. "Oh my God—"

"It happened a long time ago, Kemi."

A long time ago? The man sitting before her was in his midthirties, she knew that. And unless he'd married as a teenager, a long time ago wasn't a timeline that made sense. "How long ago?"

"It doesn't matter," he said calmly.

Shame swept over her as she realized how insensitive her question must have sounded. "Luke, I am so, so very sorry. I had no idea. If I'd known—"

"There is nothing to be sorry about," Luke said crisply. "It happened. My wife and I were unable to resolve differences that came up soon after the loss of our son, and we separated. She has, quite fortunately as I mentioned before, found herself a new situation, and I have gone on myself to be quite successful. It's a part of my life that I don't care to relive, Kemi. I am telling you because it is your right as my wife to know the larger parts of my past.

And—" He paused, then looked down at his hands, at the slim gold band there, as if it was some foreign object he was still trying to become accustomed to.

"You lost a son," Kemi said softly. A brief shadow crossed her husband's face. It happened so quickly that she could have imagined it, but there was nothing, she thought, that could make one imagine this. "Was he sick? Was he—"

"Sickle cell," Luke said tightly, with all the wire-fine control of a general issuing orders.

Oh. Kemi bit her lip. The name of the genetic disease alone carried much weight. Luke took in the expression on her face and nodded his head.

"I'd rather not speak about it now," he said crisply. "We'll get this child tested, of course, and you as well."

Kemi swallowed hard and nodded her head. She had no idea if she was a carrier herself; her father had never brought it up. "Understood," she said softly. "But I do want you to know how very sorry I am for your loss."

Luke offered her a small smile. "That is very kind," he replied, but the smile didn't come close to reaching his eyes.

Emotions, unbidden, emotions that threatened to boil over, roiled through Kemi. She was shocked to find that she desperately wanted to close the distance between them, to wrap her arms around her husband's broad shoulders, until he drew her against his narrow frame the same way he had that magical night they'd met. But even if the forbidding look on his face did not prevent that, the alarm bells pealing in her head did.

She could not afford to get emotionally involved with Luke Ibru. She could not afford to want to peel back the layers that surely hid a darkness, a hurt that he wasn't saying. She recognized hurt, having experienced it so deeply and so palpably herself so many times. She knew exactly what it looked like, and more than that, she knew what it looked like when it was being hidden by a facade of respectability and stoicism.

There was no way she could help Luke. Not when she was so messed up herself, and not when helping him was dredging up feelings that she knew could lead to nowhere but heartbreak.

She lifted her chin. "Thank you for everything," she said, softly. "I will do my best, Luke, not to be a burden to you in any way."

A gleam of what might have been admiration entered her husband's eyes. "You are not a burden to me," he said. "And all I want you to do is to enjoy yourself, Kemi, and take advantage of this marriage to be the woman you want to become. I failed my first wife. I swear that I will not fail you."

CHAPTER EIGHT

WHEN LUKE AND Kemi exited the jet he'd chartered to the Seychelles, he immediately felt a sense of relief, a sense of lightness, combined with the melancholy that he knew would increase slowly as the days progressed. The Seychelles were beautiful—in fact, other than Nigeria, they were his favorite place in the world. But they held memories.

Years ago, a young Luke purchased a sprawling estate there for himself and his family, a way for them to get away from the bustle and the madness of Abuja and Lagos, and to have time together. His ex-wife, Ebi, had always loved the Seychelles. She always said a little dreamily that they reminded her of Eden, or some other paradise in a fairy book.

They had been a paradise then for both of them. Now, the place was a graveyard for memories that he knew would haunt him for the rest of his life. When he arrived at the large, gloomy airport he'd passed through so many times, Luke felt the familiar prickles of pain creeping up his spine to his head, tightening his temples.

None of this has power over you. Nothing *has power over you.*

At least his house was gone, sold to a businessman with a sprawling family who'd needed a summer home.

He'd finally managed to nag Kemi into choosing one of his suggestions, and now that they had arrived, he was pleased. And Kemi seemed pleased, too. Her eyes had widened with wonder as they left the airport, and he'd had the driver take his time so that she could peer out the window, stare out at the landscape as they drove through Victoria.

"It looks very much like Nigeria, but not," she'd exclaimed, and Luke knew exactly what she meant. The lushness of the land, the bright greenery that shrouded the roads, the muggy air…that was all familiar to them. But the Seychelles featured narrow gray paved roads that curved up and around hilly, rocky areas, and stone fences that hugged the side of the road, some new and painted bright, some so old and weather-beaten they blended with the greenery, seemed almost happenstance. Faded red roofs dotted the hills around them. The waters were clear as blue-tinged glass. The air with each breath whispered the promise of pleasure, of ease, of *rest*.

"Don't kill yourself leaning out the window," Luke scolded, pulling Kemi back to the seat of the Range Rover that had met them at the airport, but the joy on her face could not be blanketed by his usual dourness.

"It's *paradise*," she breathed, her eyes sparkling with excitement. The fatigue and fear from the flight were completely gone; her skin was dewy and velvet-soft, and she looked years younger. "Do we have to go to the house right away?"

"What would we do outside?" groused Luke.

"There are things to see. I Googled," she said, and lifted her chin. "The Sir Selwyn-Clarke Market—"

"No one calls it that. It's just the central market," Luke said, amused. "And it's on our way, I think. We can go, if you're so eager to buy dead octopus and rotting fish." There was something else that sparked deep in his chest when Kemi looked like this, so alive, so beautiful. It did not completely obliterate the heaviness within him, but it nudged at it, just enough to let a little light through.

"Do you know," she said, her face growing serious, "that aside from the Abuja trip, I hadn't been outside my father's compound in years, except under guard?"

He opened his mouth to reply, but she continued. "It's never more than an hour or two, and it's always connected to church, or something official. Something where I'm monitored, where security forces go ahead and behind, armed. This morning I woke up when we landed and realized that I could go out, that I could order a car, go shopping, go to the market, to a nightclub, even—"

"Even with the way it worked out the first time?"

Luke was surprised at the laughter that broke from her throat. It transformed her face into something so bright and animated that the pressure in his chest he'd begun to associate with her widened and tightened.

Mine.

The word came to him, soft as it was unbidden, and he swallowed. He could not think of Kemi in that way. He was far too damaged to possess any woman, especially one who'd been through what she had.

"At least I can't get pregnant this time," she said and smiled, splaying her hands over her belly. When would she start showing, he wondered? He couldn't remember what it'd been like with his first child. He had a sudden impulse to draw her in his arms the way he had already, to skim his palms over where she bloomed with new life. But he did not. Instead, he cleared his throat.

"*One* stop," he said, and she clapped her hands. "The central market?"

"The central market," she repeated, and he knew the look of pleasure on her face would stay with him for a long time. He fought it down with some effort. He could give her today; then he'd find enough to keep her busy.

He could not afford to be delighted with her company.

To go to the central market meant mingling with the hundreds that swarmed the enormous shopping center on foot beneath brightly colored umbrellas and stalls swathed in bright colors. The smells of spices, seafood and perfumes all mingled together, sometimes in perfect harmony, sometimes clashing horribly, but always interesting. They made their way slowly through the perimeter together, sans car or driver, with Luke to open doors and help Kemi down and carry the knobby packages and bags she filled as they proceeded. Mangoes, coconuts, plantain…she bought it all. Shopping, even for food, was definitely a weakness of Kemi's, and Luke was first astounded, then amused, then curious.

"Your father is a king," he jeered, watching his wife bury her neck in a pile of cheap amber necklaces. "You're buying the same things as eighteen-year-olds on a gap year."

"I like to shop," she said defensively, then smiled. She knew her face was shiny with perspiration and likely unflatteringly round beneath the broad-brimmed hat she'd purchased to protect her skin from the sun, but she didn't care. She was free for the first time in years, and the steady pressure of Luke's hand on her lower back made her insides curl pleasantly. She stood on her toes and kissed him on the cheek; he looked surprised, but not displeased.

"Thank you," she said simply.

He attempted one of his grouchier looks, but it didn't quite land, especially when Kemi nestled into his side and wrapped her arms round his waist, ignoring the damp, sticky heat. "Princess…"

"This has been my nicest outing in a very long time," she admitted.

"An open-air market? No need to flatter me," Luke jeered.

She slapped his arm gently. "No! I'm serious. My father was so paranoid about kidnappings that we only went to high-end boutiques, you know? Places that could be swept first, or that would open early or late..." Her voice trailed off as she became lost in memory. "We were never out in public, not really. This is—nice. It's different. And don't worry—I know this doesn't mean anything."

He relaxed marginally. "All my resources are at your disposal, Princess. Kemi—listen," he said and lowered his head so that he could look deep into her eyes. Suddenly it seemed very important that he tell her this, and tell her now. "Listen. I want you to create the life you want and let me help you make it."

"Luke—"

"I mean it." He paused. "Just because we're not...you have to come out of this with something."

"Something. Just not you," she said a little wryly, then cleared her throat and pulled away.

The sudden feeling of loss was as sharp as it was surprising, and he cleared his throat, licked lips that felt dry all of a sudden.

"You don't have to worry about me," she said after a long moment.

"Good." He kissed her on the forehead. "Let's get you home."

Home.

The soft gray stone villa Kemi had selected lay on the edge of a private beach and featured pieces that had been imported, bit by bit, from places around the world where the former owner had found fine and unique building materials. The house was not large, but every room was exquisite, lovingly honed, carefully curated. There was a huge garden dotted with stone benches, a maze of roses and other local flowers, and a fountain in the middle.

The house itself featured a massive kitchen, dining room and multiple sitting rooms for entertaining and for dining. Luke's favorite room was the library. He'd instructed the staff to line the walls with the biographies and military histories he loved to read, and soft, hand-braided rugs lent the tiled floor a little cheer.

Luke and Kemi were greeted by Kingsley, the housekeeper that Luke had sent ahead. He'd been the overseer at his previous home. The older man's face was bright with curiosity. Luke knew his staff must be buzzing about his marriage, but he wasn't going to give them the satisfaction of a full disclosure. Kingsley smiled and inclined his head to both.

"How are you, sir?" Kingsley asked. "And welcome, madam."

"Doing well, Kings." Luke swung the single bag he carried up on the porch, and the two men faced off. Kingsley was the only link to Luke's past in the Seychelles; after much consideration, Luke had kept him on. At least Kingsley would know the full context of his employer's odd behavior. He had been there that night, after all, the horrible night his infant son had gone into crisis, and he'd been the one to drive them to the hospital, as Luke had been completely incapacitated himself—

He fought the memory down with some effort.

"Will you be taking your meal in the dining room, sir?"

Luke shook his head. Food was of little interest to him. "No. You may go, Kings. I'll get something when I'm hungry. And there's enough food to feed half the island in the car… Kemi and I did a little shopping."

Kemi cleared her throat. There was a gleam in those soft brown eyes that could have been anything. "I actually wouldn't mind something, Kingsley. I'm pleased to meet you." She then rattled into a Yoruba greeting and extended her hand; Kingsley's face brightened with delight, and he took it, bowed in the traditional manner, then answered back in the same language.

"Should I leave you both alone?" Luke asked dryly.

Kingsley snapped back to attention. "Oh! Madam was asking me where I'm from," he said, looking more animated than he had in years, Luke thought with half amusement, half irritation. "I told her—"

"Never mind," Luke said crisply. "Kemi, why don't you let Kingsley show you around and then we'll eat?"

He said it more as a question than a statement, and he thought he saw Kemi stifling a smile.

"That would be lovely," she said, almost demurely.

"Very good, sir. I will take your bags up. Madam, you can come with me."

Luke nodded, unbuttoning the top two buttons of the dress shirt he'd worn for the flight over. He'd make sure their meal ended as quickly as possible, and—hopefully—get some time alone. Their afternoon together had been completely off script, as had been the fun he'd had. He'd enjoyed steering Kemi through the marketplace, enjoyed their banter, enjoyed the easy way she'd opened up. It was all very well and good to enjoy her company—he wanted her to be happy here, after all. But he had to watch the lines, the ones that would blur at the edges, shift from camaraderie into something deeper. Something that would require his heart and would hurt in the end.

He could not allow Kemi to become someone he wanted to hold on to, not when he had such a talent for losing what he loved.

Kemi was a princess, yes, but nothing about her upbringing had prepared her for the absolute splendor of the estate. In person, it looked far different from the photos she'd been given to choose from. The house was a four-story stone edifice that loomed tall and proud on beach-side acres of lush vegetation; the warmth of sunshine and the perfume of flowers tickled her nose, even indoors, and if she listened closely enough, she could hear the sea.

Kingsley droned on about architecture and the artists commissioned to custom-make tiles for the infinity pool that curved round the property like a moat, and the solar panels on the roof that conserved energy, and their celebrity neighbors, but Kemi was instantly lulled by the serene beauty of the place. Creamy tiles with just a hint of color, like a blush under skin, were cool beneath her bare feet. In every common area, glass windows stretched from floor to ceiling, and the sun streamed in through curtains of the light, translucent silk linen. Light and softness seemed to be the theme in the villa; even the hard edges were tempered by touches so delicate they made Kemi wonder. This exquisite house seemed so far from Luke's graveness, it was absolutely incongruous.

She thought about his ex-wife and what their home would have been like, then pushed down the thought. Luke had been frank enough about his past; it was their present that she should worry about, and what would become of them.

What did she want them to become? She had to admit the question had no answer as of yet. The only thing certain was the fact that she was finally free. Her life stretched in front of her, bright and full of promise, and an excitement she'd never allowed herself to feel before began to bubble deep in her chest.

Kingsley showed her to an enormous bedchamber, rendered in soft colors that reminded her of the beaches back home—blues and greens and silvers, and again, filled with plenty of light. The room was beautifully decorated but completely impersonal—it would take time to make it her own. There was no sign of Luke in the room, and she presumed he had his own apartments. Sleeping arrangements, she thought, her stomach turning a little, were not something they'd discussed, and perhaps her husband had made the decision for her already.

She washed quickly in the enormous cream-and-blue-tiled bathroom and dressed carefully in a diaphanous caftan of sea green that seemed to match her surroundings. Kingsley returned for her at the appointed time, then showed her to a dining room. It clearly was meant for intimate meals; there was a small, gold leaf–coated round table and chairs, and a steaming spread of all her favorites: fried rice and stewed meat, candy-sweet yellow plantain fried crisp round the edges, a virgin cocktail in a tall, slim tumbler.

The table was set for one. Her face burned, and she looked at Kingsley, who looked uncertain for the first time since they'd arrived.

"*Oga* is resting, Ma," he said and cleared his throat. "He asked me to tell you to go ahead, and he would see you in the morning."

Kemi sank wordlessly into her chair. All the exhilaration from seeing her new home had evaporated completely with Luke's disappearance. She had no right to be disappointed, she knew; this was no ordinary marriage.

Night came with rain, a tropical rain that softened the edges of the sky, turned the famed Mahe sunset into a smudgy gray. After Kingsley retired for the night, Kemi found herself quite alone. She was tired but not yet ready to go to bed. Aside from their night on the jet, this was the first time in years she'd sleep without Tobi's reassuring closeness there, in the room, and she was a little apprehensive, silly as it was. She was a grown woman, after all!

Perhaps in this new environment, the dreams would dissipate as well.

Kemi peered out into the darkness, then slipped barefoot out onto her bedroom's enormous balcony, dressed in a soft cream T-shirt, a holdover from her hen party, that reached midthigh. Despite the overhang and the netting on the balcony, the rain quickly misted on her skin and clothing, and she closed her eyes, welcoming the refreshing coolness. She could have walked through the house, but she still felt odd about that as well. For all she'd chosen it, it was Luke's home. She'd contributed nothing, except perhaps the life that sparked in her womb. She folded her hands over her tummy. She wasn't quite showing yet, and wouldn't for some time, but she did feel so very different. Fuller. Sensitive. More aware.

"Are you going to like the rain?" she whispered. It was the first time she'd talked to the little one growing within her. It felt odd, but she pushed on nevertheless. "I'm glad for it. The sound means we'll both get some sleep tonight."

A rustling noise behind her made her whirl round, alarmed, and her heart jammed up into her throat. "Who—?"

It was Luke.

He looked very different from the dapper businessman who'd accompanied her on the trip; lounge pants hung low on his hips, and a V-neck T-shirt in snowy white showed off a great deal of chest. Circles had darkened the skin under his eyes, and his mouth was drawn. Taut. He looked as tired as she felt.

"I'm sorry for scaring you," he said and peered through the doorway. "What are you doing out there? It's pouring."

"I was just getting some fresh air—I was trying to see the hills. You—" She paused. "You weren't at dinner, and—"

"No, I wasn't," he agreed. "Come in here."

Kemi did so, pausing to take off her wet slippers at the doorway. The dampened fabric of her shirt had it sticking to her skin; she realized a little uncomfortably that it was quite translucent now, as well, and the air-conditioning in the room…

Luke's eyes skimmed over her body with that odd possessive air he had, and she felt her skin flush.

"You're not showing yet," he remarked mildly, and Kemi's hands flew to her lower belly.

"I'm not sure when I will be," she admitted.

"The doctor will tell us tomorrow." He took a step closer, and Kemi's sensitive nose detected the unmistakable scent of whiskey. He was not slurring his words, however. "I just had a nightcap and wanted to offer you something but remembered you can't," he said, with one of those flashes of humor that came and went with him. "And I know you have nightmares," he added simply. "I didn't want you to wake up and find yourself alone in an empty house."

A little spark in her chest grew, blossomed to flame. "You came."

His face looked as if he regretted it already; a line of bone jutted out of his jaw. Kemi swallowed and stepped into the pool of light inside her bedroom.

"Thank you," she said simply.

Awareness was next, awareness that came from his closeness, from her state of undress, from the knowledge that she already knew how well their bodies fit together, from the fact that, yes, she was lonely, and had been for years, and her one-night stand with Luke had sparked longings in her that had long lain dormant.

"You're wet," he said, and his irises were dark as the warm, damp night, dilated against the whites. Kemi felt her stomach tighten to the border of pain; it was longing, a longing she didn't expect. She knew without looking that her nipples had hardened to the point of making her simple nightwear nearly obscene, and that it would do nothing to hide the shadow between her legs, either. She lifted her arms instinctively to cross them over her chest; then after the barest moment, she dropped them.

For some reason she didn't want to hide herself from him. Not tonight. There was some niggling part of her that wondered, if she did this, if he'd *react*—

"There's a little bit of a curve, just here," she said, placing a hand flat on her abdomen. "You can touch, if you want."

His coal-dark eyes flashed dangerously, and Kemi felt heat engulf her from head to toe. It was a dangerous invitation, and they both knew it. He crossed the distance between them, and his fingers closed on the hem of her T-shirt.

Kemi's breath quickened.

"This isn't what I came here for," he said gruffly.

"It wasn't why I asked you to touch me." She sounded a little breathless. It was not a lie—not really—but she had wanted him to draw close to her, and if this was to be the consequence—

"Tell me why," her husband said, "you want to have this baby. I've never really asked you that."

Oh. She swallowed, then bit her lip. Tobi had asked her the same question, too, and it had left her just as silent. Not because she didn't know the reason why, but because there was no way on God's green earth she could say it out loud to anyone. No. That would leave her even more exposed than she was now, near-naked and trying not to tremble.

"Luke—" she started, then faltered. Why would her heart betray her in this way, when she needed courage now most of all? She could not say the truth—that the heady, lust-soaked night in Abuja and Luke's gentleness with her

in his bed had given her an attachment she felt she had
no right to have. There was a longing to love in Kemi, so
much that it threatened to spill over sometimes, so hard
that it manifested in physical pain. Luke had awakened
that, and though she knew even then she'd never have
him, he'd given her a gift.

A baby. A child she could protect, could love uncon-
ditionally, could pour out that love on. But she could not
tell Luke any of this; instead she licked her lips.

"My mother was ill after having me," she said, and
her voice was soft. "It was a risk. She didn't die, but she
was always in poor health because of it. I lost her a few
years ago, but she did something meaningful. She gave
me life. She loved me. And when I was in a position to
do the same—"

Luke nodded, his expression veiled. His slim hands slid
over her hips, beneath the damp fabric of her T-shirt; it
was growing increasingly difficult to speak, but she managed, stuttering a little as those slow palms went round
to where her backside curved, a whisper-soft caress on
her skin. *Heat.* Every touch of his left a burning path.
"Luke—"

"Loving a child is like nothing else," he said, and his
hands stilled, and he suddenly looked so very sad that
her own throat filled. He reached out, cupped her face.
"You'll see."

She knew that the whiskey was likely responsible for
this sudden show of…whatever this was, but—well.

Perhaps it was an excuse for what they both wanted.
Kemi had never been needed, either, and the thought that
Luke might have come to her that night for that reason,
even subconsciously so—

"And what about you?" she asked. The words were a
little bit shaky; his hands had slid to her lower back, and
upward, and she'd never wanted her breasts touched more

in her life. *Kiss them. Suck them. Make me feel—* They were words she could not…was too shy to say.

"About me?" Yes. His hands had come round to cup the weight of her breasts in his palms. His thumb skittered over her pebble-hard nipple, and she swallowed a gasp.

"You will love the baby, too," she said, and even through the haze of lust her voice came through, clear and sure. "I know you will. You—you're a good man, Luke."

There was an intake of breath as if she'd hit him, and when she looked up his face was so forbidding she nearly stepped back. He looked absolutely haunted, for just a moment, and then he cleared his throat.

He did not acknowledge what she said, but he pushed up the hem of the thin T-shirt, where she was already bare and swollen, aching with need. His fingers danced between her thighs, and she shook her head.

"Kiss me first," she said, through lips that barely moved. Her husband's eyes could not grow any darker than they were already, but they deepened. In a moment they were transported back to that mad, magical night when they'd connected in the first place.

He slanted his mouth against hers, and she closed her eyes.

There it was, she thought, and tears sprang to her eyes at the unexpected tenderness of it. She tasted alcohol and warmth and wondered for one wild moment if perhaps this was wrong. But he cradled her face in his hands and kissed her mouth, her chin, her cheeks, where moisture slid from her lashes, and when he eased himself against the cradle of her thighs he fit so perfectly—

This was more than indulging in lust. That would have been hurried, frenetic, unskilled. This was slow, careful, a gentle slide of skin on skin, calm where she was agitated, sure where she was shy, teasing out what she wanted. He let his lips hover over the skin of her lower belly, breathing in the scent of her, kissing her there with the same tenderness as he did her mouth, holding her close as her body shuddered release once, twice.

"I feel like I've got butterflies inside," she said shakily, after, when he asked if she was all right. Then he laughed, transforming his face to something softer, younger.

"No nightmares tonight," he said, almost as an order, and she shook her head vigorously, loosening her braids from the high coil they'd been in for bed. She bit her lip hard, then sat up.

"I want," she began, but she couldn't finish the sentence. Instead she slid one leg over where he still strained for her, reached down to touch where he was smooth and hot. She could not look at him, but she did hear his intake of breath.

"Please," she said, and his hands slid beneath her hips, lifting her, helping her, and finally, *finally*—

She cried out as they came together, and his voice was little more than a gentle rumble in her ear. She could not make out the words, but she could feel the way his body tightened beneath hers, feel how perfectly they fitted together. He was patient with her, guiding her, holding her steady till she found her own rhythm, chased pleasure exactly the way she wanted it—

When she finally collapsed against the broad warmth of his chest, totally spent, his arms crept round her, and she fell into a deep and exhausted sleep.

CHAPTER NINE

THE NEXT MORNING, Luke slipped away from her bed in the early morning, when light was just beating the darkness back, and went back to his own room. He'd forgotten to turn on the air-conditioning before sleeping, and the heat was nearly overpowering; it had increased as the sun came up. It was oddly cleansing, although Luke felt drained and weak.

He took one of the water bottles that Kingsley had left on his nightstand, downed it and exited into the compound. He made his way back to the main house and over the cool, sweet-smelling carpet of grass to the mosaic-lined pool that surrounded the main house, almost like a moat in a castle. The freshwater pool had been scrubbed clean and filled with cool, clean water; it smelled strongly of chlorine. Luke shucked off his shirt and pants, then stood at the edge of the pool, flexing his arms for a moment before diving in.

The cool water was a shock to his system, and his head instantly cleared. He surfaced and floated on his back, looking up at the deep blue sky with its soft white dusting of clouds. He loved the sky here. It seemed to stretch into infinity, a near-otherworldly shade of sapphire blue, a perfect match for the water that lapped across his body.

He would swim around his house again and again, and he would eat food when Kingsley brought it to him, and he would sleep, and he would avoid Kemi, completely. Last night had been enough warning. Life had seen fit to, in a horribly ironic way, set him up with exactly what he'd lost. And it was terrifying.

There were so many things to be afraid of. The feelings for his new wife that budded, unbidden, every time he looked at her. The health of the child that was to come, and the fact that he might, as scarred by the past as he was, do nothing but fail both. He enjoyed the cool, slippery resistance of the water on his body, and he thought.

Happiness hadn't evaded him, not really. He'd avoided it, because there was always something there to snatch it away. Those first losses had nearly broken him. How much was a man to take before he said, *enough*?

Luke swam until his limbs were quite tired, then walked on the rubbery legs to the covered porch. He sank into the nearest chair and wiped himself down with the towel that had been left there, probably by Kingsley. It smelled faintly of lavender and lilies, bringing back yet another memory, one that was completely unrelated to his ex-wife or to their little infant son, resting in the All Saints' Anglican Cemetery only a few miles away. He remembered the softness of a warm female body, yielding to his while music played below them, and his own body throbbed with life. He remembered the tender way she'd touched him the night before, and the way she'd called him a good man. It'd melted him completely. Completely. It was disconcerting to find that the walls he'd erected so effectively had been risked with a single touch from his wife.

Kemi.

She had been so absolutely ready, so eager for him, despite her innocence. He had taken her virginity, despite the fact that he knew next to nothing about her. It had been a moment of impulse that was completely unlike him. His ex-wife had been his first; there were no promiscuous years in Luke's past. He had been raised by a stern and unyielding military father who had drilled his own values into his son, and besides, he and Ebi had fallen in love so early that it left him little time to indulge in many of the indiscretions his mates had. They had made fun of him because of his devotion to Ebi, but he hadn't cared. His heart, mind and soul had been solely for her. He'd made his fortune; they'd married. But his carelessness had killed their son, and he'd lost her as well as the child.

There would be no room for pursuing anybody else in a romantic sense, no matter how sweet Kemi had been, or how beautiful she was, or how much she'd trembled in his arms, or how naturally she fit there. She would have the baby; he would provide for them.

That was all he was capable of doing, and he reminded himself of it as he saw her approaching. She held a tray of the simple fare Luke usually enjoyed while in Seychelles: fresh locally baked bread, butter, fruit and cold meat sliced thin and sweet, and a pot of tea so strong he could smell it even without lifting the lid. Without looking at him, she set it down on a small table that waited poolside, then lowered herself into the nearest deck chair and folded her soft, small hands.

"That was rude, disappearing the way you did this morning," she said.

Despite himself, his breath caught. She wore another one of those thin, diaphanous dresses she seemed to favor; this one skimmed her full hips, and slits at the sides allowed for easy movement, as well as unfettered access to the legs beneath. His gaze skimmed down their smooth, gleaming lengths as she sat and tucked fabric around them; he couldn't help himself. When he looked back at her face, her eyes followed the beads of water sluicing down his abs to the waistband of his trunks, as if fascinated. He cleared his throat, and she blushed.

"I'm here because I don't want you to worry," she said and cleared her throat. "Yesterday—"

"I'm not worried," Luke said pleasantly, ignoring the thudding in his chest. This was fine. He'd eat this fine breakfast, ignore the new softness in his wife's eyes and have her busy with the things he had planned for her in no time at all.

First thing: he'd take care of that nightmare issue of hers. He could not sleep in her room night after night, after all. That certainly had been counterproductive. And far too dangerous. She was much too alluring, and he was too susceptible. If he thought her the kind of person who could have sex with no strings attached, it'd be different, but—

He closed his eyes briefly. Even the thought of his heart getting involved filled him with dread. The quicker Kemi was fixed, the faster he'd have his redemption, and she'd be free. And they'd deal with the nightmares tomorrow.

CHAPTER TEN

KEMI DIDN'T REALIZE she was seated with a therapist until the middle-aged woman in spectacles peered over them at her, a kind expression on her face. She had a laptop on the small table Kingsley wheeled into the main sitting room for her, and she smiled.

"I'm glad you agreed to see me today," she said, serenely. "I'm Agnes."

"Kemi," she replied, confused. She'd been treated to a bewildering series of appointments her first few days in the Seychelles; there was a doctor, a nutritionist, a yoga instructor, a man trained in self-defense... All showed up on a schedule handed to her each morning by Kingsley, and so far, she'd seen every single person meekly.

Luke hadn't shown up for a single appointment.

All Kingsley had said that morning was "the doctor is here, Ma," and she, assuming her to be a gynecologist, had assented. Now the woman was asking—

"Will you tell me why you're here, Kemi? What are your goals?"

"To have a baby?" Kemi said, confused.

The older woman's lips twitched, ever so slightly. "Your husband mentioned that you'd been having nightmares?"

Disbelief dragged Kemi's mouth open. "I'm sorry, are you a—"

"I'm here to talk. But only if you want me to," the woman said and smiled. "Congratulations on your baby."

Kemi took a deep breath. There were a number of things she could say at this point, none of which were useful. The woman was here to help her, after all. But, in the case of her husband—

It had rained the first three nights that Kemi was in the Seychelles with Luke, and she'd spent all three with him.

If one could call it that.

He slept in her room, yes, but as distantly as he possibly could, on a blue sofa moved discreetly in for that purpose. As soon as dawn softened the sky to gray, he crept from the room and was unreachable for the rest of the day. Absent. He sat in his study and pored over his work, and any attempt to invade his inner sanctum was met with polite but cool stares and kind but very brief answers. They left her stuttering, leaving the room, berating herself silently for her lack of backbone. The few times she tried to initiate a response, his head was bent to his computer, the set of his shoulders and head a direct message: *Stay away.*

At night, however, he showed up as if he'd been summoned. He climbed onto the sofa and lay there, quiet, until Kemi managed to still her pounding heart long enough to sleep. He never spoke more than a short "good night," and he never touched her. Kemi did not know whether to be disappointed or relieved. Their one night together—he obviously regretted it, and Kemi hated herself for the lack of backbone that kept her from opening her mouth, from demanding answers.

And after virtually ignoring her since their night together, Luke Ibru had the audacity to—

"Please excuse me one moment," she said simply, then whipped out her phone, texting Kingsley on his house line to bring in tea. That, if anything, would be enough to keep her new psychiatrist occupied until she dragged her reticent husband out of the shadows.

It perhaps wasn't the classiest approach to stand in the grand foyer of the villa and shout Luke's name until he showed himself, but Kemi was beyond caring at this point. He was Nigeria's top security chief; she knew there must be *something* in the house that was picking up her voice.

True to form, her husband showed up in minutes, his brow creasing. He wore a linen shirt that clung damply to his skin; he must have been swimming, she realized. "Is the baby all right?"

"Is the baby—" Funnily enough, in that moment she'd completely forgotten she was pregnant. She took a deep breath and licked her lips, then opened her mouth—

"Don't overheat yourself," Luke warned.

His utter lack of curiosity enraged her all the more. "Aren't you going to ask why I'm out here, screaming your name like a fishwife?"

He exhaled through his nose. "You're scheduled to see Agnes today, and if you haven't taken ill, I'm presuming something in the session upset you?"

Kemi just stared at him for a full moment. "You're unbelievable."

"I—"

"You've come to me every night—" Kemi's voice wavered "—since we've gotten here. Every night. You've watched over me. You made love to me once, then tried to act like it didn't happen. Aside from that, I haven't seen you at all. And then you foist me off onto a therapist, without my knowledge—"

"Psychotherapy is very beneficial, Kemi," Luke said with that exaggerated patience that made her want to punch him. "And prejudice against it is quite backward. I won't force you, of course, but I think it would be good for you. You're about to become a mother—isn't it essential you become the best you can be, for your child?"

"*Our* child," Kemi said through tight lips.

Luke waved a hand as if the distinction was of little matter, then stepped closer to her. He reached out, placed his fingers beneath her chin as if talking to a child.

"Listen to me," he said, and his voice was both soft and urgent. "You went through trauma. Get help, get healthy. There isn't anything worse than living under the burden of something that's unresolved. Let me help you start your life anew."

The irony of the statement made Kemi nearly reel. Could she call him hypocrite, or merely blind? Could he truly not see the ridiculousness of his own statement, a man preaching a mental health message, whereas he kept himself more tightly closed than a locked door?

Unless it's you. Luke had always made it abundantly clear that his responsibility to her extended because she was carrying his child. Perhaps it was ridiculous to expect anything more, to want more. But it was impossible for Kemi to separate the tenderness of that first night in her room from everything else. Night had bled into day, segued by the soft pink light of dawn, and Luke's gentle consideration had bled into her heart, despite her best efforts. Kemi was not yet cynical enough to be able to draw a line of demarcation that would last. They were like lines she'd drawn in the sand on Badagry's beaches as a child, lines that only a few passes of seawater would erase.

She wanted to know more about him, and she was willing to push for it. "You don't get to do this, not without opening up yourself. If you don't talk to me, I won't say a word to her."

Luke opened and closed his mouth, and for one thrilling moment, Kemi wondered if he would curse her. Instead he let out a breath, and his mouth twisted downward. "Since you insist—"

"I do." She straightened to her full height, set her jaw.

"Agnes isn't a stranger, Kemi—I've seen her myself," he said, and his voice was clipped. Clinical. Matter-of-fact. "My son died on this very island, four years ago, because of my negligence. No amount of therapy can change that fact. I am a sickle cell carrier, as you know, and so is— *was*—my ex-wife. I—we—planned to put off having children until we could safely complete an IVF cycle, which would ensure an embryo with no issues. We were careless while on vacation, and she became pregnant. She refused to consider terminating the child once the genetic results came back, and I became father to a sickler."

Kemi's breath was stuck somewhere in the vicinity of her throat. All she could do was fix her eyes on her husband's face, on the absolute lack of expression there. He looked like a person who was reciting lines he'd learned, or was reading from a teleprompter; nothing but his lips were moving. It was as if all the air had left the space, leaving nothing but the sound of his voice. He was intent on the shock factor, on blindsiding her with it, on stunning her into silence.

"There are treatments, yes, some very good ones, and some patients do very well. I poured a great deal of money into medicines, clinical trials—everything. But my son's case—he was just too weak, and the damage to his organs—" The sentence ended abruptly, as if there were no more words. "Have you ever witnessed a child in crisis?" he asked, and his voice was suddenly soft and yet with sharp undertones that seemed to cut more now. "It is one of the worst things in the world to witness. They *cry*, Kemi. They cry and they don't stop. Their bodies grow tense and they shake. You hold them, cradle them, and it doesn't matter—it hurts them more. Every touch hurts them, no matter how gentle. Imagine being a mother, and doing what comes naturally, and you're hurting your child."

Kemi swallowed hard against the ball of tears that was forming in her throat, but Luke wasn't even looking at her. He continued.

"Then you take them to hospital and watch the doctors pump them full of pain medication that's meant for middle-aged people having surgery. I had to watch it time and time again until my son finally, mercifully, died—"

"Luke," Kemi choked out.

"Oh, it was a mercy. No child should have to suffer that much." Luke paused. "Then his mother broke down. Understandably. She'd been strong for a very long time." Luke's face was ice-cold and hard, and Kemi suspected that he couldn't stop even if he tried. The worst thing about it was the tone of his voice. There was still absolutely no emotion there, although the words he said were terrible, awful, bringing up images that made her own body tense.

"She had a breakdown," Luke said, "a terrible one. And do you know what I did? I looked her in the eyes and I shut down. I couldn't help her. I couldn't even help myself. I'd promised at our wedding to be her partner in everything, to protect her, and to protect our family, and I couldn't—"

Kemi was weeping quietly by now, tears running silently down both her cheeks.

"I feel guiltier about that," he said after a long pause, "than I ever will about anything. You want me to open up, Kemi, to be something for you. I admire you for it. But there is simply nothing left within me to fix. I want you to get the help you need, and to be the extraordinary woman that you already are. But please, don't try to make this any more than it is. It will not work. I do not want it." He took a breath. "Are we done here? Agnes is waiting for you."

He didn't wait for a reply; a moment later, he strode from the room.

Kemi didn't move.

Her mind was solely on her husband, on the hard, unyielding line of his back as he left the room. She desperately wanted to chase him, even though she had no idea what she would say if she caught him.

Luke had wormed into her heart, along with his determination to make sure she was left with no scars from the way she'd been brought up aside from the visible ones. Now she understood why he was so determined for her not to blame herself for her abduction.

He shared some of that guilt himself, even though it was for different reasons.

The pain he must have endured—it was pain that he would not allow himself to let go of. Just like her, Luke felt as if he *deserved* his plight.

She now in an odd way felt better about the way he'd distanced himself from her. Grief and loss were a punch to the gut. They robbed people of their very existence, but they also made them incredibly self-centered, and in a way that would be nothing but detrimental to both them and the people around them.

Did Luke not think that he was worthy of love? The thought that he might not tightened her throat.

Had he consigned himself to a prison of his own making, as punishment for a crime that he still thought he was guilty of committing? How could one person bear that for so many years? And how could she help him realize that he held his own release? She, the wife who had been foisted upon him by an accidental pregnancy, a woman with absolutely no formal training, a woman who knew nothing about him up until this point?

She cared. Heaven help her, she cared. And she knew in that instant that what had blossomed in her heart during those quiet nights together was turning into something else entirely. Still—the look on his face—

Protect yourself.

It would be foolish to fall for Luke. More foolish than the impulse that had driven her to his bed in the first place. And yet, Kemi wanted to find a way to connect with him. Even if he would not—could not—be anything other than this to her, it would be a fitting way to repay him for what he'd done for her and ensure that the child she bore would have a father who wasn't afraid to love them.

After that disastrous meeting with Kemi, Luke felt closer to panic than he had in years. He had to forcibly hold it in, drawing air through his nose sharply. He attacked the work on his desk with violence. Kemi represented turmoil, a turmoil that had forced its way into his life with the night they'd shared, turmoil that only grew with each passing day. Kemi was light and softness where he was dark and sharp corners. He did not know how to make room for her in his life without dislodging himself completely.

And also, for the first time, he wondered if being utterly dislodged might not be so bad, after all. But the thought of stepping forward, the very idea that there might be something beyond the wall of grief he'd stayed hidden beneath all these years—

Luke swore under his breath, slammed his laptop shut. It was no use. The infinity pool beckoned, as did the decanter of whiskey in his room. And then, night would fall, and his wife—

He swore under his breath again, then started when a knock came to his door. "Enter," he called in a voice that was much calmer than he felt.

"It's me."

Of course it was her. Luke closed his eyes, briefly. "I'm working."

There was silence for a moment, and then the door creaked open. The door he hadn't locked, he thought irritably, and he stood just in time to see Kemi in the doorway. She was barefoot and wore one of the soft, filmy dresses he'd come to associate with her, one that just touched the floor round her feet.

Her face was carefully veiled, even though she smiled, and he only had a moment to realize he didn't like that at all before she spoke.

"Don't worry. I know it distresses you, and I'm not going to push what you said today any further. I just want to say that I'm sorry, Luke."

Pity. Specifically what he didn't want, but he'd blubbered like a fool this afternoon. He lifted his chin. "There's nothing to be sorry for."

"I know." There was a look of determination in her eyes, one that immediately set him on his guard.

"What?" he demanded, and to his surprise she laughed.

"Are you always this defensive?"

"I don't know what you mean."

She lifted her shoulders. "You move through this life with such a determination to be aloof. I understand now why that is, but…isn't that exhausting?"

Luke was silent. Yes, it was exhausting. But admitting that to Kemi would mean admitting it to himself, and that wasn't something he could afford to do.

She continued. "We're having a child together—" And here, her hand skimmed the soft curve of her belly, almost absentmindedly. His throat tightened; he'd touched her there once or twice during their nights together, dared to let himself imagine for a second what fatherhood might be like. But he hadn't told her, and he wouldn't. He could not.

Control was all he had left, and he could not lose that, too.

Kemi cleared her throat, and he realized he'd been staring off into the distance. "I'm sorry, please continue."

She smiled, and again his heartbeat leaped into his throat, because it brightened her eyes, softened her whole face.

"I'd like for us to be friends," she said. "We're going to be coparenting in a few months, if nothing else, and it's important. I promise that I won't… I won't push for anything else. Plus, you're helping me far beyond what you probably should—"

"You're my wife," Luke interrupted, and she shook her head.

"It doesn't matter. If we were…" Her voice trailed off. "If we were something, it would be different, but we're not. Friendship is the only thing I've got to offer you, and I'm determined to. You need one. And *I* need one."

Luke blinked. This was so absolutely unexpected he had no idea how to handle it.

"What would this entail, then?" he asked after a long moment.

She lifted her shoulders. "Whatever comes naturally. The only requirement is that you don't hide from me. Even if you don't want to see my face, tell me—don't *avoid* me. And we should spend some time together. We haven't left this house since we arrived—"

"We went to the central market the first day!"

"Yes, one unplanned trip." Kemi smiled again, but this time the light didn't reach her eyes. "And if you don't want to take me, I'll go myself. I've spent the past eight years virtually locked up, Luke. I know things are different now, but some things about this feel very much the same. You're trying to protect me from myself, just like my father did. And I'm *tired.*"

There was so much vehemence in her soft voice that Luke was startled. Memory took him back to the first night he'd seen her—so uninhibited, losing herself in the music, allowing herself the indulgence of happiness, just for a moment. It hadn't been her supple curves, or her lovely face, or the long, dark braids that framed it that had made her beautiful, that had caught his eye. It had been her spirit. And if in keeping her safe, he'd somehow surpass that—

Luke eased himself to his feet, and Kemi's brown eyes widened.

"Friends," he said guardedly and allowed his lips to tilt upward, ever so slightly. "And no more nights together, either. I think those may end up being more confusing than anything else."

An odd look crossed her face; he saw her color heighten, and she dropped her eyes. "I—"

"Your first experience with love shouldn't be with me," he said quietly. "And I'm not going to deceive myself into thinking that just because what we did was under the cover of darkness, it doesn't count. It was remiss of me."

The acknowledgment hung between them for a long moment; then Kemi nodded, and Luke drew in a breath. It was oddly cleansing, as if something had dissolved between them, some sort of barrier that had previously been unspoken.

"You can trust me, you know," Kemi said after a moment.

"It's not you I'm worried about," Luke said grimly. "Now go. And please, for goodness' sake, don't gallivant about the Seychelles by yourself. I'll arrange an escort for you when I'm not busy—you're not a prisoner here. And yes—tonight, we'll spend some time together."

"As friends," she said, and her mouth twitched.

"Right." Lord, what an odd word that was for him. Who

was the last person he'd called a friend, who cared about his plight? Jide didn't count; he saw the man maybe three times a year. The realization that he'd shut everyone out, withdrawn in his own pain—

How did one even come back from that? How did a person remedy something like that? He pressed his lips together, then realized Kemi was still staring at him, that softness back in her expression.

No.

He cleared his throat. "Two hours?" he compromised. "That'll give you some time to get ready, and me to wrap things up here."

Her delighted smile took his breath away, and he knew instinctively that it wasn't just about going out; it was about stepping outside with him. Which was terrifying but also warmed his insides in a way he couldn't deny.

CHAPTER ELEVEN

WHEN KEMI EMERGED from the main foyer of the house to see Luke, resplendent in a matching linen shorts set, his feet clad in a pair of surprisingly threadbare yet expensive canvas sneakers, she smiled.

"What?" he asked.

"The casual look suits you." Then she looked outside the open door, clapped her hands over her mouth—and began to laugh so hard that tears rolled down her cheeks.

Her husband's smile was inscrutable, but there was a glimmer of something in his eyes that had never been there before, and it warmed Kemi's heart to see it.

"What on earth is this?" she asked.

"If you insist on acting like a tourist, I thought you might fancy one of these," Luke said dryly. He crossed the first few feet to one of the bright blue technicolor buses famous on the island and tapped on the window. A thin man with a scraggly goatee nodded back at both of them.

"This is Thomas," Luke said. "He will be taking us to the beach, and to where we are going to hike. Don't get too excited about the bus—I can only take so much of this. Our usual car will meet us when we're coming back. You can muddy your boots until then, though."

Kemi took Luke's hand and allowed him to help her up the steps of the bus, then peered inside and began to laugh again. "Is this what you call muddying your boots? Luke Ibru's idea of roughing it?"

"There's only so much tourist trap behavior that I can stand. I wasn't about to get on an actual *bus*."

"But tourists don't take these buses, islanders do!"

"Do you want to stand here arguing about schematics all day, or are you ready to go?" Luke demanded. "We are very much on the clock."

Kemi laughed out loud again and proceeded to the middle of the public bus. The seats had been covered in some sort of soft upholstery that gleamed pale blue in the sunlight filtering in from the sparkling windows, and a minibar was installed snugly against three seats. It was the most ridiculous-looking thing she had ever seen. Luke sat down with a completely serious expression and opened the bar, reaching for a glass of mineral water.

"Drive on, Thomas," he said, and the bus lurched off with a groan and a rattle that made Luke wince.

"You are a dreadful snob, Luke," Kemi half scolded, half teased. "Haven't you ever taken the bus in Abuja?"

"Have you, king's daughter?" Luke asked acidly, but with no real malice.

"You know I haven't. But I would if I could." She paused and smiled as a memory overtook her. "My sister, Tobi, hailed an *okada* one day when we were at the market. I'm scared of motorcycles, but she thought it would be a grand adventure. The man took off so fast, and my feet were still on the ground… I hadn't mounted properly yet. Tobi screamed bloody murder, and he stopped a few feet away and almost fainted."

A smile flashed across Luke's face, a real one this time, and he leaned back with amusement. "I'm sure you miss your sister."

"Oh, very much. I would do anything to have her here right now."

"Do you think she'd like the bus?" he asked dryly.

"She would think what I think—that this is a slightly corny yet very sweet and funny gesture."

"Nice to know, but I don't care much what she thinks," Luke said and lifted his eyebrows. "I only care what my wife thinks at the moment. Would you prefer another mode of transport? The whole thing can be history in about five minutes."

Kemi shook her head vigorously and reached for the glass of mineral water he'd poured for her, still laughing. "Don't you dare. So far, this is the nicest day I've had in the longest time."

Luke cleared his throat, looking slightly embarrassed, then leaned back onto the seat, touching the soft cover with critical fingers. "I was an only child," he said. "It must be nice to have a sibling you're quite close to. Feel free to invite her at any time."

"Thank you," Kemi said, touched. "But I think I'd like to have you to myself for some time. After all, aren't we supposed to be on a honeymoon?"

To her surprise, Luke's mouth tilted upward into the fullest smile she'd seen on him in days. "One hell of a honeymoon," he said and rubbed his hands over his hair. He hadn't smoothed it into submission with the pomade that she normally smelled on him, and she found that she rather liked the riot of tiny coils standing up on his head. They made him look younger, less stern.

"Well, we're in a gorgeous location, we eat amazing food and we've alternated between having sex and fighting," Kemi said with a perfectly straight face. "Sounds like a honeymoon to me."

Luke's answering laughter was lost in the bumps and jostles as the vehicle lurched onto the main roads, and Kemi peered out of the glass windows, as bright and as delighted as she had been the day they'd arrived. She turned back to find his dark eyes resting on her face with more than a little curiosity.

"What?" she asked and tossed her braids back over her shoulder.

The vehicle bumped and jostled over the winding roads, the leafy green of the hills looming in the background.

"So what would your perfect honeymoon look like, as long as we're talking about it?"

He was trying, Kemi noted with some surprise. He was trying to engage her, trying to make conversation that didn't revolve around business, or future plans, or what they weren't. Kemi's lashes lowered. She didn't know why she suddenly felt so shy. Perhaps the intensity of his gaze had something to do with it.

"I never really thought about place, or time, or particulars," she said and leaned back into her seat. "It's always been more of a vibe, I think. I always imagined myself being somewhere with someone where I felt safe and able to rest. Enjoy each other's company."

"The Seychelles definitely evoke that feeling," Luke said after a pause. "I first fell in love with them as a place to get away from all the hustle and bustle of Nigeria. Compared to Lagos or Abuja or Port Harcourt, there really isn't much to do, but it's a place that facilitates relaxation so much. I had a house here before, on Eden Island."

Kemi was staring at him in intrigue; she didn't think that he would've ever opened up so much to her. Something about the bumpy roads and warmth of the sunshine streaming in and the sweet tartness of the sparkling water and fruit that he was sipping seemed to mellow Luke out, and his eyes drifted over her a bit lazily. "She loved it here. And so did the baby. My old estate is on another island, far away from the town. I had no desire to see anybody else while I was here, so that was another enticement to sell."

At his sudden foray into memory, Kemi found herself feeling more than a little despondent, something that surprised her. She blamed the pregnancy. But…if he was here the entire time, thinking about the family he lost, and she and her unborn child clearly didn't measure up, was this outing completely futile?

As if he'd read her mind, Luke fixed dark eyes on her face. They were calm and untroubled. "I'm telling you this because *friends* tell each other things," he said. "Don't think that I'm not having a good time. I will complain, I will be irritable, but… Kemi, this is nice. Thank you."

Kemi was surprised to feel tears springing to her eyes, and Luke was beside her in a flash, handing her soft tissues from a paper box, patting her on the knee. "Pregnancy," he said by way of explanation, and Kemi nodded, glad to have the excuse.

"I've been so emotional about everything lately," she explained and wiped her cheeks with the flat of her hand.

"Tell me what you're feeling, bodily," Luke said.

"Oh, a sensitivity to smell, mostly. I can't stand the smell of raw fish, but I still can't seem to get enough of it."

"Perhaps you're going to give birth to a mermaid," Luke said with a quirk of the lips.

"*Olorun maje,*" Kemi said and shuddered. She, like many Nigerians, did not take kindly to any mention of the beautiful, devious water spirits that supposedly caused so much mischief. She knew Luke was joking, but the familiar sugars from her childhood and years of sitting on the hard bench of St. Augustine's Church in her father's town had taken their toll. "No mermaids for me, please and thank you."

"They're supposed to be able to seduce any unsuspecting man that crosses their path," Luke said, a little teasingly. Kemi was beginning to feel a little dizzy from his closeness, and from the fact that the corner of his mouth was tilting up in the type of smile she had never before seen on his face, except perhaps on that first heady evening they'd spent together. "It makes me wonder how easily you managed to get me."

"Me I'm not a mermaid, oh," Kemi said teasingly, in dialect, and she shifted. The mood was much lighter now, although that familiar awareness she felt every time Luke was anywhere in her vicinity was building at that moment, increasing with every second. The bus hit a particularly sharp curve, and Kemi found herself pressed flush to her husband's side, warmth seeping into her skin. He held her close for the briefest of moments, then released her.

"Said the girl who lives by the sea," Luke murmured. His lips were precariously close to her ear, and Kemi closed her eyes. She was almost disappointed when his lips did not brush the soft skin there, and he moved back to his own seat.

"I'm glad you are doing well," Luke said, and the moment was over.

Kemi was left to think that despite her best intentions, this "friends" thing might be harder than she'd thought.

They took a long ride through the winding roads that snaked round the island, and the rises and falls of the hills and the sharp corners that made Kemi's heart leap to her throat. The Seychelles possessed a sort of tempered beauty with a wildness beneath it that manifested in the steep rocks, in the heavy trees, in the brightness of the sun. The island itself was relaxed, slow moving, a place for indulgence, for pleasure. She knew that somewhere through these roads there must be ordinary people, people going to work and coming home and falling in love and raising their families. But she did not see any of these things in these moments with Luke. He seemed determined to make her first official outing in the Seychelles one of unparalleled glamour.

First, they went to the beach, a massive stretch of sun-bleached white and blue tidily flanked by a massive resort where they needed passes to enter. It wasn't until Kemi remarked on the lack of people even on that gorgeous day that Luke admitted he'd arranged for them to have the whole place to themselves.

"That must've cost you a fortune," Kemi exclaimed.

"No, not really," Luke said. "People rent these beaches for private parties all the time. We're just having a very small one."

They waved goodbye to the bus and watched till it was swallowed by the dust of the road. Luke then produced a stout pair of hiking shoes for Kemi and slipped on a pair of his own.

"The hike is a little bit difficult," Luke said, eyeing her pleated palazzo pants dubiously. "Are you going to be able to do it? I thought it was a good idea, but now that I'm thinking about it—"

"I'll be fine," Kemi said with a smile.

"There's a helicopter set to fly us back once we are done. It would be no trouble to call it now."

"I'm not worried. I'm quite a sturdy girl, as you can tell," she said, slapping her hips. "And if I run into any trouble, I have a big, strong husband to lean on."

Luke smirked and flexed playfully, and Kemi found her eyes lingering on the long muscles rippling on his back, beneath the soft linen of his shirt. Yes, Luke would be able to assist her through anything, carry her if need be. His slimness was completely misleading; she'd been shocked, that first night, when she ran her hands over his body and found it as hard as finely hewn, polished stone...

Luke coughed, that little twitch lifting the corners of his mouth again, and Kemi found herself flushing. She adjusted the broad-brimmed hat she'd brought along so that it tipped a little over her face.

"Let's head out," she said airily.

Kemi was not disappointed by either the leisurely hike or the solitary beauty of the beach, not at all; Luke could see it in the way her eyes sparkled. The stretch of land was covered in a soft layer of powder-fine sand, with enormous sunbaked boulders sticking up invitingly, just waiting for beachgoers to scale them, to lie on them and imbibe the warmth of the sun. They stopped constantly, to sip water, for Luke to take her pulse bossily or force her to sip salty-sweet electrolyte water, to point something out for her to look at with his enormous binoculars. The water was blue tinged in some places and clear as glass in others, and swimmers could see their feet even in the deeper parts.

After one brief swim, Kemi's arm began to ache, and she was content to stay close to shore and sat in the ocean, smiling serenely as the clear, salty water lapped over her legs and belly. Luke swam out until the shore resembled a strip of pale white, then turned back. When he reached where Kemi was still sitting in the water, her legs pruning from the moisture, his muscles burned pleasantly.

"Are you having fun?" he asked. It was also surprising, finding how comfortable he felt. They did not say much to each other, but they seemed to move in perfect sync.

"I am, but I'm hungry." She offered a mock-petulant look, which made him laugh.

"Well, there's plenty for us to eat. Kingsley packed a hamper full. A couple of hampers, I think." They hadn't brought them on the hike, of course; Luke had arranged for food and water to be left for them on the island. "He's a famous overpacker. You're going to be so full you can't walk."

Kemi stood, brushing wet sand from her legs. "I'll show you how to build a fire if you want—we can warm up the grilled meat and fish that way."

"A fire?" He lifted his eyebrows.

"Yes, city boy, a fire," she teased. She kept him busy collecting bits of seaweed and driftwood as she dug a sizable pit, then built a little pile of tinder and set it to flame, blowing gently till it caught wood and burned brightly. Kemi rummaged through the well-stocked hamper and produced a roll of foil; she covered a pan and set their lunch on it.

"This is fun. We used to do this on the beach near my father's," she reminisced, and her eyes were at once as far away as they were soft. "It was one of the happier parts of my childhood, before the kidnapping."

They sat, shoulders almost touching, staring into the crackling flames. Behind them another set of Luke's hires for the day appeared as if out of nowhere, silently setting up a soft white tent with walls of thin gauze that fluttered in the wind. Inside they set up a table, chairs, coolers filled with food, silverware, plates and bowls, and took the rest of the food to be warmed at a tiny kerosene stove and laid out elegantly.

"You just thought of everything, didn't you," Kemi said, her voice low. She was not looking at Luke. She was staring into the fire again, and he wondered what she was thinking. Her face was very soft, and her eyes, low. At this close proximity, he could smell her, that sweet floral, combined with good clean sweat and ocean. It was unmistakably attractive.

Kemi drew a deep sigh and leaned her head down on his shoulder. The contact felt surprisingly natural, and it felt even more natural to wrap his arms around her, draw her close.

"Are you tired?" he asked. "Was a hike too much for you?"

"It definitely was a lot," she admitted, "but it feels good. I haven't had such vigorous exercise in a long time. My arms and legs are aching, but in a good way, you know? The way it does when you know you've accomplished something."

"You use your arm very effectively."

She smiled, then rubbed at the scarred skin. She'd have to rub the sunscreen into it or it would itch profusely later. "I was fortunate to regain strength over the years, although it still tires quickly."

He made a low sound of acknowledgment in his throat, and Kemi slowly turned her head. He suddenly had trouble breathing, being so close, looking into those dark, clear eyes. She wore no makeup today, and her braids were now tied back, but it only enabled him to see more of the loveliness of her face. He could not help but to reach out and cup her cheek in his palm.

Being close to her in this way, despite everything he had resolved not to do, felt as natural as breathing. Kemi inhaled softly, and he knew she felt it, too.

"I wish I could be what you want," he said, and he could hear the naked longing in his own voice. It was the first time he'd allowed it to bleed through since this utterly enchanting young woman had wandered into his life that magical evening, and saying it released something deep in his gut, something knotted tight, something he'd been holding firmly to for goodness knew how long.

"You can't be anything for me, or for anyone else, unless you're happy yourself." Kemi's face was drawn and sad. She reached for the hand on her face, brought it down to the slight warm curve of her belly. "Our child is waiting for you, Luke. And I want you to be able to give them all the love that they deserve."

Her words struck somewhere deep in his heart, in the tender void the loss of his son had left. His first instinct was to shrink back, to pull away, but for perhaps the first time, his internal battle was strong enough to pull him in the other direction.

"I don't know how much I'm capable of giving anymore," he said, and his voice was the one of the man he'd been, not the man he'd created.

"You are fully capable," Kemi said, and with so much conviction that he blinked. "You saw me that first night, and I felt drawn to you instantly, Luke. Safe with you. Whenever you touch me, it's just—right. And if you hadn't loved so hard in the first place, there would be nothing to shield now. You are fully capable. You're just—afraid."

You're just afraid. She was right, of course, and hearing it stated so baldly had him drawing in a sharp breath. "If you knew—"

"I'm not condemning you," Kemi said, and her voice was heavy with sadness. "I'm just saying that I understand why we can't—"

She swallowed, and they were left with a silence between them, punctuated only by the sounds of nature. Then Kemi spoke again.

"God willing, this baby will be strong and healthy," she whispered. "And I want you to love them with all the goodness you've already shown me."

"And you?" he asked with a husk in his voice. He knew it was incredibly unfair to ask such a question, especially when he'd told her so decisively he could do nothing for her. But here, on this white sand beach, away from the prying eyes of the world, in this little bubble of paradise they'd created for themselves for a few hours, he could say almost anything. And for once in his life, damn the consequences. Consider what it might mean to let go, to actually be happy. He did not wait for an answer; he removed his hand from her belly, from that tense, warm skin, leaned in and kissed her.

Happiness.

Luke suspected, in this soft haze of skin on skin and the time it took to get from breath to breath, kissing Kemi's soft lips in the light of the early afternoon, in one of the most beautiful places in the world, happiness might feel a lot like this moment. His hands didn't wander. This was a moment for tender exploration, not for the type of passion that had swept him away with her since the beginning. This was…gentle. Soft. The actions of a lover, not someone consumed by lust. He was worshipping, not plundering.

The soft moan she let out as a response was felt deep in his gut, but it was the soft exhalation of "no" against his lips that stopped him. He pulled back, reluctantly, breathing hard.

"I'm very sorry. Beaches will do that to you," he said gently.

Kemi did not speak, but her hand crept down to find his, and they linked them, foreheads pressed together, trying to get their bearings.

"Everyone deserves to be happy," she said after a long moment, as if she'd been trying to find the right words. "You deserve it, Luke."

No one had ever said those words to Luke before. Well, perhaps Jide, who knew everything about his past. But everyone who'd said that had known him before, before the demon that was grief had taken him over and turned him into something he did not recognize.

"I wouldn't even know where to start," he admitted, and his wife's arms crept round him.

"This is a start," she said, and the two of them rocked silently on that white sand beach until time faded into nothingness.

CHAPTER TWELVE

KEMI DIDN'T WANT the night to end.

It was everything she'd ever dreamed of, really. After separating from their embrace, hot and cold and shaky all at once, they were a little shy but got their bearings back. They roasted catfish and peeled pieces off with their fingers, blowing on them and laughing till it all was gone. They waded into water that was unimaginably warm and crystal-clear, then lay on the sand to dry. They sat under the massive canopy that had been erected for them, ate fresh fruit, watched the sun set. Then they headed into town, to one of the many nightclubs that dotted the city center.

There was more food, and dancing, and mocktails dripping with luscious island fruit. Luke's strong arm did not leave her waist all that night, and Kemi's pulse did not stop racing, not even when they were huddled close in the luxury helicopter that hovered over the islands as they flew home, dots of brilliant light in the city below. She hesitated just the slightest bit when they finally reached the door of their villa, and Luke's brow creased.

"Are you all right?" he asked, yawning.

She managed a smile. "It's stupid, but—I don't want to go inside. It's been so nice."

"It's three in the morning, Kemi."

"I know," she said, and the expression on her face must have been absolutely tragic, for Luke began to chuckle.

"Let's do this," he said, and he rubbed his hand over his head. His eyes were still bright, alert. "Balcony, fifteen minutes? We can have a cup of tea, chat and then *bed*. I insist."

She nodded, rapidly rinsed the salt and sand off her skin, and headed to the balcony, where Luke already waited, lounging on a deck chair, looking as fresh as he'd done that morning. He was staring down at the infinity pool glimmering in the moonlight below; his expression was thoughtful.

"Thank you for today," she said and smiled.

He grunted, but his face was calm. Pleasant.

"It was my first date, you know," she said, cheerfully, "and yes, I'm going to count it as a date, regardless of what we are or aren't."

"Is it?" His brows lifted to the limit. "Not even before—"

"I was *sixteen*. And my father is a king. A small king, but still a king."

"You didn't have a chance."

"Not in hell." She chuckled and lowered herself to the nearest deck chair, accepting the tea. It wasn't her usual dark Yorkshire blend; this was pale and smelled strongly of—

"Honey, pineapple juice, raspberry leaves," Luke said briskly, then took a sip from his own mug. "Raspberry tea is great for pregnancy."

"Oh." She took a small sip; warm, sweet brightness exploded on her tongue. She closed her eyes and leaned back. She was tired, but it was the kind of weariness that comes from enjoyment, from satisfaction, and warmth suffused every limb. "I'm going to sleep so well tonight."

"Good. That's the idea." His voice was brisk. Businesslike. Back to being the man she'd married. She felt curiously disappointed; she'd enjoyed the hint of warmth that their day in the sun had teased out. And now that she knew that man existed—and more, that he still wanted her—the memory of his gentle kisses on the beach turned her stomach inside out.

I bet you could get him if you tried.

The thought nearly made her choke on the tea in her mouth, and her eyes darted over to where her husband lay sprawled on his deck chair. His body was lean and taut beneath its cover of soft linen; his face was serious, dark and unreachable as the night.

She must have a very big impression of herself, thinking that she could—and the fact that she even wanted to—

Color was rushing up to her face now, and she lifted her mug to her lips to hide her confusion. If she did "get" Luke—did manage to break through that wall he'd erected so effectively around him—what would it be for? Would she gain something, something that she instinctively craved, something that she had no name for? Or would she be unleashing a storm that would break over her head?

She swallowed, then turned over on her side, peering at her husband.

He was asleep. His face had relaxed into something soft, with a hint of gentleness that made her throat tighten. The idea was there, and she knew it wouldn't go away. She could feel it in her chest, sparking, growing.

She'd always been aware on some level that she wanted Luke. She'd asked for his love for their child. But this—wanting to make him want her—

How would that even happen?

Perhaps if you showed him yourself, were honest about what you wanted—

She swallowed hard. Even the thought of being so vulnerable was terrifying. But she looked at Luke, and bit her lower lip, and knew, without even considering more, that she was going to try.

CHAPTER THIRTEEN

THE NEXT DAY did not bring a reprieve from thoughts of Luke, and her usual doctor's visit in the morning, a session with Agnes and a fast-paced hour of self-defense training did nothing to help. Afterward she stood in her room, facing the mirror, wiping sweat from her face and bare shoulders with damp scented towels Kingsley had left for her, trying hard to catch her breath. It was as if the physical activity had lit a flame within her, and thoughts of her husband stoked it, made it burn all the brighter. Her face, eyes and body had the lushness of a woman who had softened, ripened, was ready to be loved.

She closed her eyes, feeling a little dizzy. Desire came with a heady unexpectedness these days, and she understood for the first time why women were left so devastated by men who didn't want them. It was all-consuming, this feeling.

Luke.

Barefoot, she left her room and walked silently down the hall, the tile cool beneath her feet. She would go to him. He was in his study as he always was, she knew, and a part of her wanted him to see her like this, soft, vulnerable, flushed with want.

She was tired of hiding.

When she reached the study door, Kemi took a deep breath, steeled herself and pushed open the massive door to Luke's study.

"Do you want to hear what I've learned?"

Kemi. Of course.

He looked up, then his mouth went dry. His wife was dressed alluringly in a skintight pair of leggings and a sweat-dampened tank top. Her skin gleamed with perspiration; her eyes were bright.

He cleared his throat.

"Do you like your new instructor?"

"Very much."

He was surprised by a little flare of jealousy, more an irritant than anything else. "Good. He'll come twice a week until you're up to speed. Aside from the physical defense, you'll have weapons training, stealth, para-military—"

Her mouth tipped up a little. "How to give birth during a fight?"

Oh. He felt his cheeks heat a little, a reaction that surprised as well as discomfited him. "I forgot about that. We'll switch to more theoretical training in upcoming weeks."

Kemi lifted a hand to rub her shoulder, and he caught the gesture quickly. "Are you in pain?"

"Not really, just a little sore—"

"Your trainer didn't stretch you out?" He stood. "I told him about your arm."

"He did." She smiled a little. "And the arm wasn't a problem, not today—he worked around it, and it doesn't ache any more than usual. I think I'm just out of shape."

That was all Luke needed to know. "Come here."

She bit her lip and hesitated for only a fraction of a second before walking over. Assisted stretching was something Luke had done many a time during his stint in the army, or at the gym. As close as he was to her now, however, he realized this would be very different—and the moment he touched her, placing gentle hands on each side of her face, he knew his motives weren't entirely pure.

"Tell me if anything hurts or makes you uncomfortable," he said, looking her straight in the eye. Kemi was very good about hiding her nervousness in public, but even in only these few weeks with her, he'd gotten to know her tells. A clenched jaw. Her fingers squeezing the life out of her handbag. The flutter of her throat as she swallowed.

She wasn't like that with him. Every bit of her body was limpid and yielding, suffused with heat that he could feel through the thin workout clothes. The white tank was completely insufficient in containing her; her nipples were pressing against the cloth so vividly she might as well have been wearing nothing at all.

Kemi was swallowing now, and Luke fought back the urge to kiss the supple curve of her neck, to follow the movement as it descended. His nostrils flared; she smelled sweet and feminine and—

"Luke," she breathed.

He shook his head and applied gentle pressure on both sides of her neck.

"Quiet," he said a little more curtly than he'd intended, but she shook her head, stood on tiptoe and pressed her mouth hungrily to his.

The next few moments were filled with the hot wetness of her tongue sliding over his.

He could no longer resist her. It was futile to even try, he realized in a rush that came all at once. He'd kissed her on the beach with a tenderness born of their conversation; this was something much more elemental. Princess Kemi Obatola had slipped through his defenses, both emotional and physical; on the beach he'd kissed her in a bid to touch her heart, and now—

This was hopeless. He could not be around her without acting on his desires, and the fact that she so clearly wanted him did nothing to help matters.

"Luke, please," she whispered, angling her body against his, and that was all it took.

When he shoved his hand into her leggings, they both groaned. Her folds were slick, almost unbelievably so, and her body tightened and began to shake just from that brush of his fingers. He stilled them and she whimpered protest; he shook his head.

"Not yet," he gritted out.

"Why?"

"Because I want you naked," he said, and the lust in his voice had thickened it to something else, something he didn't even recognize. Kemi's eyes dilated in response. He made quick work of her sodden tank and bra, biting back a groan as her skin was bared to him; her head lolled back when he nosed that warm, fragrant place between her breasts.

"I'm so sweaty," she murmured in a voice that shook a little. "Luke—"

"You're perfect," he said, and he saw her bite her lip, hard, when his thumb went back and forth against her distended nipple.

"Luke."

"Do you like that?" he said soft against her other breast before drawing the nipple in his mouth. He tasted salt and sweetness and Kemi bucked beneath him and if she'd come, he didn't know or really care, because all that was on his mind was *tasting* her—

He had her leggings down in a moment, and his head down between her legs. Her tender flesh was swollen and pink and glistening with her arousal; he was gentle, exploring her, coaxing her to a shuddering climax while trying his best to ignore the throbbing in his own body.

He let his head rest against the softness of her inner thigh, listening to her rapid breath as it slowed, returned to normal. Then she shifted, turned; one leg was up, and she straddled him with more dexterity than he would have expected from a pregnant woman. He groaned as her heat came in contact with where he was aching, throbbing for her; she bit into the plumpness of her lower lip and ground her hips down, slowly.

"I want to," she whispered. "Please."

CHAPTER FOURTEEN

SHE FELT ODDLY VULNERABLE, straddling Luke in this most unlikely of places, so exposed, feeling so very awkward. He'd parted her with gentle fingers, teasing her with the tip of him where she strained to hold her hips aloft, and she bit her lip. This was literally the third time she was having sex ever, and the fact that she was so on display, flesh gleaming almost indecently under his office lights—

"Kemi."

She looked down at him, where she was reflected in liquid dark eyes. He ran his hand gently over the curve of her stomach. It was no more distended than it was when she'd indulged too much at the wrong time of the month, but he was looking at her with a tenderness that she'd never thought him capable of.

"It's all right, love," he said gently, and Kemi took a breath, stifled a little gasp, watched as he watched them come together.

She did not know whether he looked at her then; she closed her eyes tight and braced herself and began to move, her hips automatically circling, sinking deep into his. His fingers inched toward where she was swollen between her thighs, but she pushed him away. She was too sensitive there, and she wanted to maintain control over the pleasure she was giving him now. She felt his muscles grow taut beneath her thighs and his large, slim hands grip her hips hard enough to bruise, and she knew, instinctively, that he was close—

Kemi saw it in his face—the tightening and the release, even before she'd felt it in his body, loosening his grip on her hips. She let her own body relax and her head drop; her braids, falling forward, shrouded them in a little tent of scented hair.

Luke muttered something in a language she didn't understand; she started to move, to ease herself to the ground, wincing a little as he pulled out of her. It wasn't painful, not at all, but the loss of the connection and the sudden blast of cold air on her skin made her feel very aware, and a little lonely. She folded her arms over her breasts; Luke turned hazy eyes to her, let them flicker over the still-naked length of her body.

"I don't know why you bother," he said dryly. "You'll need much bigger hands, Princess."

For the first time the name sounded like an endearment rather than a mockery, and Kemi felt emboldened enough to sidle up to him, kiss him softly. When it was over, he sighed and drew her close.

"Thank you," she said after a beat.

"For what?"

"Everything you've done so far—"

"Please don't thank me after sex," he said crisply, even as his lips tipped up slightly.

"But it's so good," she said simply, and in that moment she was determined never to hide her feelings again. Regardless of what Luke said with his mouth, his actions spoke louder. And this was a man— Well. He'd taken her out of her father's home when she'd been unable to do it herself. He'd ensured she felt safe. And when he made love to her, he did it with the determination of someone who wants his partner to feel nothing but pleasure. Luke Ibru's actions were those of a man who had the capacity to love body, mind and soul, with complete dedication. With every encounter, Kemi's feelings for him deepened. And now—

She should be cautioning herself, slowing down, convincing herself not to love him. But it was already too late, wasn't it?

You love him. The realization cramped her lungs so tight she could barely breathe. She squeezed her eyes shut for the briefest of moments; she didn't want Luke to see what surely was burning bright in them.

"Luke," she said, and his eyes grew veiled. They should really get up, stretch, bathe; she wasn't sure where his sweat ended and hers began, but the intimacy of the moment was what she wanted.

My love.

"Kemi—"

"No. It's all right." And as she spoke, she knew it was. Kemi had never had much occasion to use her heart before, and it now felt so full there seemed no room for any negative feelings, regardless of what he did. "I know you don't love me."

He inhaled, his face troubled. "Kemi—"

She shook her head. She would not give him a chance to reject her, or to convince her this was infatuation born of a girl's first sexual experience, or gratitude, or any other logical theories he might come up with; she already knew it would crush her. "I won't expect it of you. I just want…" Her voice trailed off.

Luke was silent for a long moment, then he cleared his throat and rested his chin on the top of her head.

"You know I can't," he said.

Kemi ignored the dull ache that surfaced. "I know. But we're terrible at this friends bit, aren't we?"

Luke's eyes registered surprise. Then, to her surprise,

he began to laugh. It was rueful and a little self-mocking, but his body was relaxed when she nestled into him.

"There's something about you that makes it very hard to stick to my resolutions," he said softly, and his lips grazed hers. The soft, warm haven their bodies made together was lulling them both into something that felt not quite real, and Luke, for some reason, wasn't pushing her away. He seemed to want to indulge in this moment as much as she did, to make this evening perfect for her.

He shifted then, and when he spoke his voice was quiet, as if he'd read her mind. "I don't know what it is about you that makes me want to come back, even if it is impossible."

She swallowed hard. "What do you mean?"

He didn't reply, only toyed with the feathered ends of her braids, smoothing where he'd ruffled them. His face was dark and thoughtful, and the way he held her—could he possibly be considering that they might...that they possibly could—

Stop projecting what you want on him.

She took a breath, closed her eyes and opened them. Friends. That's all she'd promised him, the fact that his hands were still skimming her breasts and that heaviness was still building between her thighs notwithstanding. Whatever had shifted between them would remain unacknowledged.

"Will you have breakfast with me in the morning?" she asked, and her voice was soft. "Will you have to work?"

"I'll make the time." He yawned and rolled over and was gone, and Kemi smiled a little in the darkness.

"Is this your idea of a quiet breakfast?" Luke asked, brows raised to the limit. "I feel like I should have dressed up a bit more."

Kemi laughed, and even to him the sound was tremulous, a little nervous. "I—I went a little overboard, I guess."

Overboard was right. Everything in the main dining room was a perfect balance of refined elegance and restraint, combined with undeniable luxury. The table dressed in white linen groaned beneath the weight of silver chafing dishes filled with a bewildering variety of breakfast food—an English fry-up, *moin-moin*, yam with steam curling from its fluffy white insides, fried stew fragrant with onions and crayfish. Soft Afro jazz played from hidden speakers. Tiny white candles were scattered about, points of light in the rays of sun that filtered in from the white-curtained windows.

In the midst of all this splendor was Kemi herself, dressed in a lovely copper nude silk, feet bare and studded with tiny gold rings, her braids loose and flowing to her waist. She looked like a living incarnation of a goddess, someone meant to be worshipped, and when he looked at her, his throat tightened.

She was absolutely radiant.

Luke was discomfited to feel his heart skip a beat. Not a goddess—he was wrong in that. She was the sun here, beaming gentle, seductive rays that warmed his skin as well as his heart.

Since when had he been so sentimental? And how on earth had tender feelings for his wife managed to surface, to capture him so effectively? He'd fostered stony-faced indifference as his only weapon all these years from feeling anything, and the fact that this young woman could worm her way through after the briefest acquaintance possible…

It won't last, an ugly little voice whispered in his ear, and he shifted. *It never does. You're cursed. And you'll drag her down right along with you. You can't protect her. You can't protect that child—you can't protect anyone.*

And yet—fool, idiot that he was, he still wanted her. And that want spurred him to reach for her, draw her close.

"Thank you for breakfast, Princess," he said, and she trembled a little in his arms, then stilled.

Where was this lump in his throat coming from? He slid his hand upward, brushing over that sensitive spot on her neck that he'd kissed so many times, to cup her cheek. She closed her eyes and raised her chin to meet the caress.

She's blossomed, he thought. And he couldn't claim credit, not really. All he'd done was bring her out into the sunlight. He felt a now-familiar ache of desire, but it had evolved to something else; he desired to hold her. To be close.

It was a desire he could not indulge. Grief still took up so much space in his heart; he could not allow his wife to move into such cramped quarters. To have her, to let her in and then to lose her... His mind raced through the possibilities. Sickness. Death. Growing apart. He knew how easily they could happen, because all had happened to him in quick succession. He could not trust life to be kind to them, and he could not be sure his heart could withstand such disappointments a second time.

Distance.

Kemi sighed and burrowed her face in the crook of his neck, and he shifted, trying to keep his movements subtle as he moved away from her. He felt cold, bereft; it was coldness he felt deep inside him, not just because of the ocean breeze on his skin. He could not become used to the warmth of her skin, her voice, her nature.

He had to bring this back to their default. He cleared his throat and raised his chin.

"Your skin is warm," he said and frowned, glad for the distraction. It was damp, too, and the sheen on her skin was from perspiration, he realized, not just pregnancy. "Close the windows, Kemi, and turn on the air-conditioning. I understand aesthetics, but you must be careful not to overheat."

"It's hot outside, but I love the way the curtains move with the breeze," she admitted and moved to do as he said. Luke cleared his throat, forced some humor into his voice. Perhaps it would dislodge the lump that was growing in his throat.

"I've appreciated it, now turn on the air," he said dryly, and she smiled and went to close the windows. When they were seated at the table, he served her first, then dug into his food himself. "How are you feeling?"

"I'm well. Still tired, mostly, but I think that's my only symptom."

"Right." He frowned slightly. "How far along are you now?"

"Almost thirteen weeks." Her hand drifted down to her belly. Her waist had thickened a little, although she did not yet have the telltale curve that would herald her pregnancy to the world. "My stepmother says first babies sometimes don't show till the sixth month. This sounds wild, but I'm looking forward to having the bump—"

"Your first full scan should be coming up next week." Luke's eyes suddenly seemed very far away; he blinked, then eyed her abdomen as if it were radioactive. "You're not a carrier for sickle cell, we know that now, thank God, but there are other things."

Oh. The enthusiasm drained from her, and she swallowed and sat up. She hated it when Luke used that patronizing voice on her, but she took a breath and counted to five before answering. It wasn't about the testing; of course Luke wanted to be sure the child was all right. It was more about the fact that he'd so callously swept away the quiet, romantic haze they'd been in since yesterday. She cleared her throat.

"And if anything was wrong?"

Luke did not allow his face to move. "We'll cross that bridge when we get to it. There are options."

There are options. The words landed ice-cold in the pit of her stomach, and she placed her hands protectively over it. She knew the gesture was dramatic, as best, but she could not help it. "You only want this baby if it's perfect?"

"I do," he said coolly. "You have no idea what it means to have—"

She had no idea what he was going to say, for she stood to her feet, throwing her napkin down on her still-full plate.

He stared at her, openmouthed.

"You. Are. An. Ass," Kemi said, almost enjoying the look on his face as his voice registered.

"Excuse me—"

"Not only that, you're a *coward*," she said, voice strained by emotion. "You deliberately shifted the conversation the moment there was any hint of closeness, and you're back to being the cold person who came to propose to me in Nigeria. You wanted to put me back in my place, to remind me of precisely what we cannot be—"

"Kemi." There was warning in his voice now, but that only made Kemi angrier.

"My feelings for you aside—" oh, fantastic, she'd said it out loud "—we agreed to be friends. To coparent. You haven't been to a single doctor's appointment since I've gotten here, looked at a single report with me. I have no idea whether you're hoping for a boy or a girl, or what your tribe does for new babies, or what you think of by way of names, or whether you'll even be there when the baby is born. All you've managed to relay is that you want to *kill it* if it isn't up to standard—"

"Kemi!" He looked horrified at her accusation. "I never—"

"It's selfish, and it's mean. Your grief has made you cruel, Luke, and self-indulgent. And I cannot bear being in limbo any longer!"

Damn him. *Damn him*. And damn her for reacting so emotionally. She turned and ran from the room, half hoping that Luke would come after her.

He didn't.

A sensible woman would have gone to her bedroom, maybe cried a little, washed her face, come out and made an appointment with the doctor. But Kemi hadn't been very good at being sensible as of late, had she? And her lack of it had gotten her into this fix. She chewed her lip until it bled, then slipped her feet into the hiking shoes she'd worn with Luke only days ago, opened the door and left. They clashed horribly with her dress, but she didn't care at this point.

She needed air. And for the moment, there was none in her husband's house.

When she was outside the main gate of the house, past the gardens and the glimmering infinity pool, she blinked, slightly disoriented by the sunlight and the heat. Without one of Luke's swanky cars to take her, she had absolutely no concept of where to go, and only a few rupees in her purse. She lifted her chin and began to walk, lifting a hand to shield her eyes from the sun. Sunglasses would be fantastic, but she refused to go back into that oppressive house to look for any.

Instantly, her body knew exactly what it craved; powder-soft sand, clear blood-warm water, the smell of the sea, sun-warmed rocks. She could lie on them, close her eyes, allow the Seychelles sun to warm where her husband had left her cold. She needed quiet; she needed to be alone. Kemi knew how to fall in line; her father had bullied that into her. The fact that she was facing that with her husband, however—

It would be easier if she didn't feel so strongly for him, an intensity that she refused to name. If she admitted she was falling in love with her husband, heartbreak would not be far behind. She'd learned not to risk things physically anymore, but in the matter of her heart—

She picked up her pace, began to walk rapidly. There was a bus stop about a half mile down the road, and she had no idea when the buses came and went.

Finding the station was easy enough; navigating her way to where they'd been the day before was harder. She exchanged broken English with several passengers until she found one who gave her sketchy directions, and changed buses several times as well, getting lost a few times in the process. By the time she arrived at the resort and claimed a ticket to go onto the beach, adrenaline had infused her body down to her very fingertips.

She'd *done* it! For the first time in years, she was out on her own. It was terrifying. Thrilling. Intoxicating. Luke faded away in the headiness of it—and the biggest realization of all—

She wasn't afraid. Not anymore.

Kemi raised a hand to wipe at the sudden dampness on her cheeks. Part of her wished she could share this moment with Luke, but it was for her alone. It would not mean much to others; they might even ridicule her. But to her, this represented healing, and a knowledge that regardless of whatever happened in future between her and Luke, she would be all right. Her baby would be all right. They would be all right. She had no idea what the future held, but she did know that—

She rested her palms on her abdomen. She would not feel movement for many more weeks, according to the baby books. But she could feel the firmness there, the slight roundness of a belly that would soon expand. And she was *glad*.

"I'm glad you're here," she said, out loud to her child and she meant it. She didn't need Luke. She loved him—his strength, his protection, his gentle sternness. Losing them would hurt like hell. But she didn't need them.

She had everything she needed here inside her, a reserve of strength she'd always been too afraid to acknowledge. But she wasn't afraid anymore, and she'd call upon that strength for everything else she needed. She lifted her chin, fixed her eyes on the horizon. The walk to the spot she wanted to go to was far, but she knew exactly where it was. She'd buy water and some fresh fruit from the man on the beach there, and lie on the rocks, and wade in the water. She'd enjoy herself, and she'd go home, and then she'd deal with Luke.

For now, she would not think about him. She'd think about herself, for once, and all the possibilities that lay ahead, with or without Luke. Lagos. Seychelles. Abuja. America.

The world.

Luke's first hint that something was wrong came in the heat of late afternoon, when Kemi did not show up for her self-defense lesson. He knew she'd left, of course—no one left the premises without his knowledge, thanks to the security system he'd designed himself. And she'd left, no doubt upset by the turn their romantic breakfast had taken. Guilt crept in, soft but insistent, and he fought it back with every argument in his arsenal.

I was telling her the truth. And if she didn't like it—

Yes, he had told her truth, didn't he? But he'd told her in the most clinical way possible. He'd said it primarily to dim the light in her eyes that had been there since their night together, since that morning. He'd wanted to stop what was happening between them in its tracks. And he had. And she was gone.

By herself.

Wandering somewhere on an island she'd never been on before. The Seychelles were paradise, yes—and they were small and intimate, nothing like the sprawl of Abuja or Lagos. But she was vulnerable and inexperienced, and if something happened to frighten her, or if she wandered into one of the seedier bits—

Luke wouldn't have been much of a security chief without the techier aspects of his job leaking to his everyday life, and he knew exactly how to track her. The GPS on the mobile he'd given her could be switched off at will, and he pulled up the connected app.

He'd told her about the tracking element, of course; he'd intended it to be a source of comfort for a kidnapping victim. She hadn't turned it off, and he felt oddly reassured at that. He'd have been able to override it, naturally, but he was glad he didn't have to.

He watched the screen, riveted by the movements of the little purple dot on the app. She moved at a terrific clip for a bit—a bus, no doubt, or a taxi. The nonlinear route she took confused him for a bit, but her general direction became clear. She was headed to the beach. Their beach.

The last place where they'd been happy, together, before he'd wrecked it all this morning with his foolishness.

Luke didn't get a thing done. He watched the little dot move, as if mesmerized, thinking of the young woman it represented, her sweetness, her softness, how absolutely right she felt in his arms. On the beach yesterday, when he'd kissed her and nuzzled the sweet creaminess of her skin and inhaled the scent of her, lost in it, he'd felt more than protectiveness or lust. It was a sensation of drowning in the best possible way, of wanting to hold her tight enough not to know where his body ended and hers began.

That had been what had scared the hell out of him, not the baby's health. And now—he hadn't pushed her away. He knew Kemi. She'd be back. The question was what he'd do when she came.

You have to try. The answer came from deep inside, where the voice of the man he'd been lurked sometimes. He'd heard it more than once since he'd met Kemi; it had urged him to approach her in the first place, had surfaced in those first kisses, in the few times he'd opened up. And each time it grew a fraction louder, making him wonder if it was indeed possible to resurrect, to know what love was again—

You have to try. If nothing else, Kemi had been right—he'd been selfish. His grief, both natural and expected, had morphed into something utterly self-absorbed, a weapon to lash out at others. That wasn't him. That wasn't who he wanted to be.

Luke impatiently put his tablet away, stared at his desktop for a long moment, then took a breath as an idea came to him. He knew what he needed to share with her, and how he would share it.

His mind, however, was also fixed on that tiny purple dot. It moved slowly within one area, alongside the coast; she must be on the beach. A memory of how beautiful she'd looked there the day before made him swallow, re-open the app. He would not call Kemi; any apology he gave her would need to be in person. But he watched. And when the dot finally stopped moving, for ten minutes, twenty minutes, half an hour, three-quarters of an hour, one hour, ninety minutes—

His imagination attacked him with images that tumbled over one another with a rapidity that left him breathless. Kemi, attacked. Lost. Robbed. Lifeless—

Stop it. He was being more irrational than she was, and she was the pregnant one! He took a deep steadying breath, but the thought of that motionless dot made him pick up his pace.

If anything had happened to her— He closed his eyes. If he thought he couldn't forgive himself before, this might actually send him over the edge.

JENNIFER A. LEWIS

finally, out the thought of the women had decided this
cool up the house
I wonder, so I thought of the this I would want a top
of the child to much as a person make a man would unhappy
the ride was that was the nas

CHAPTER FIFTEEN

"HEAT EXHAUSTION," THE DOCTOR announced, dragging off her gloves with a flourish.

Exhaustion wasn't the word. Despite the IV of fluid that had just gone into her arm, Kemi felt more tired than she ever had in her life, and her head ached. She was very carefully turned away from Luke, who was hovering anxiously over the edge of her bed in the villa. His eyes were wild and anxious; he'd been muttering things about pregnant women who gallivanted about when they were supposed to be resting, but they both knew what this was about.

Luke had found her on the beach, exhausted from her hike, sitting immobile on one of the massive boulders and sweating profusely, too tired to even try and find one of the vendors who sold water and fruit. Their first excursion to the beach had been chartered, carefully planned, and she'd had a helicopter ride back. This morning she'd walked literal miles in the hot sun.

It could have been bad. It could have been very bad.

"Baby's doing beautifully. We need to take care of Mama just as much, okay?"

"Okay," Kemi said softly.

"Drink this," the doctor said, placing a large glass of cool water beside her, and dumping a packet of electrolytes into it. "You," she added, pursing her lips in Luke's direction, "you make sure she stays in bed. No phone, no computer. Just good old-fashioned movies. Only get up to use the bathroom, and this room stays cold. Understand?" With that admonition, the older woman collected her equipment and left. One pause became two, and two became a silence that had height, width, breadth, depth.

"Kemi," Luke said.

She concentrated on breathing. Hurt squeezed her lungs tight, and she knew if she spoke she'd cry, so she didn't.

"Kemi."

She turned on her side, focused on the enormous Kehinde Wiley that hung on the wall. It was a clever bit of decoration, she thought; the subject, a man with piercing dark eyes and high cheekbones, looked enough like Luke to be him without the pure narcissism of a self-portrait. A conversation piece. Luke had surrounded himself with them so effectively that no one ever got beyond the superficial. And though she had shared his bed, though she wore his ring on her hand...

"Kemi."

She didn't speak. Why should she? Instead, she tugged the blanket up over her bare skin. Luke sighed, then climbed into bed with her, still fully dressed. She smelled starch and lemon and pine and shoved him away from her.

"Your cologne is making me nauseous," she said, her voice sounding muffled even to her as she told the lie. He stilled, then sighed and was finally, finally gone. She thought she would cry, but she didn't. She was too tired to do anything except lie there, staring at the painting until the colors began to fade into each other and the wan light outside finally succumbed to night.

When Luke returned his body was warm, damp and completely bare except for a pair of shorts hanging from his narrow hips. He'd brought her another cool drink,

sweet with tonic water and chunks of fresh fruit, and
watched as she drank it before handing her a pile of photographs and climbing in next to her.

The photos were of a round-faced little boy with a head
full of dark hair. The boy was bright-eyed, laughing—and
a spitting version of Luke.

Again, he was trying. But this afternoon's disappearance had forced his hand. It wasn't *real*, and she needed
to stop digging. Kemi fought back her first impulse: to
sit up in the bed and demand, dramatically, that he tell
her everything, that he produce everything he'd held back
from her until this point. She shoved down her natural
curiosity and handed the photos back to him.

"He was beautiful," she said softly, and Luke's eyes
clouded a little. She dropped her own. "Thank you for
showing me."

"The anniversary of his death…" Again, he was forcing the words out, but at least they were coming. "It's tomorrow. I usually go to visit him in the morning—he's
buried not far from here."

What? Kemi felt a dull pain in her chest. The anniversary? Another thing he'd hidden from her until she'd run
away from him, had virtually forced his hand. She closed
her eyes, forced herself not to react emotionally; he would
not like that. She bade the tears pricking behind her eyelids to stop—at least till she could wipe them in private.
What kind of husband would not even let her in enough
to grieve with him? But she'd shouted at him enough already today. "I'm so sorry, Luke. I didn't know."

He was surprised at her lack of reaction; it flickered
across his face, along with uncertainty. "Are you all
right?"

"I'm very tired." The hand of dignity reached out
and steadied her, and she took a deep and shaky breath,
placed her hand on her abdomen. Luke's second child,

she vowed inwardly, would never know how dysfunctional their family was. She'd make sure of that. She was a married woman, and an independent one, with a passport and, unlike in her father's house, free will. She could have done anything she wanted after marrying Luke. Instead, she sat uselessly in his massive villa like the fool she was, waiting for him to love her.

Leave.

It was as if some spirit listening took her thoughts, spun them into the word, whispered it in her ear. There was nothing stopping her from going, even if she wanted to, today, but first—

"Luke," she said, and she swallowed hard before continuing; she did not want her voice to tremble, not this time. "I can't do this."

"Kemi—"

"And I'm keeping the baby, regardless of what happens." She stopped to steady her trembling lips, placed her hands on her belly. *My baby.* "I understand now, Luke. You don't have to worry about me anymore."

"Except I do." Pain flashed across Luke's face. "And I'm only going to say this once, so I need you to listen. My son died in my arms." It seemed he was trying hard not to slide into his usual clinical way of speaking; he closed his eyes, took a breath before he spoke. "It couldn't be helped—he was very ill. But you knew that already," he said, as if disgusted with himself for repeating it.

"Luke," Kemi said softly. He shook his head.

"It will keep coming up—again and again. It's never left me. It will spoil everything if I try. Do you understand?"

She did, and she nodded numbly.

"I want you to know that—" He swallowed. "You're beautiful, Kemi. You've got the kindest heart of any woman I've met, and I know that you're going to excel and be an exceptional mother."

"Luke—"

"No. No, Princess—" And then he kissed her, a short, hard kiss that forced her to pay attention. "I don't want you to think that you lack in any way," he said fiercely when both of them could breathe. "You deserve love, and you deserve it from a good person. After my son died, Kemi, I was a mess." He grimaced. "I was so immersed in my grief that I couldn't help Ebi with hers—in fact, I pushed her away. It was the cruelest thing I could have done to a person I professed to love, Kemi—"

He had to stop for a moment, and Kemi eased herself from his grip, moving backward.

"What are you saying?" she asked.

"I'm saying," he said, "that I'm incapable of loving you the way you need. And I'm not sure I've got the strength to fix it." She opened her mouth, but he shook his head, leaned in and focused on her face, intent, determined that she would not miss a single word. "I'm not sure— I'm in recovery, Kemi. I'm not even sure I'm recovering, really, not the way I'm supposed to. It's made me selfish, yes. And I think that might be part of why I've pushed you away so hard. If I bring you in now—if I bring in our child—I risk failing both of you. And I can't heal and know I'm hurting you at the same time, my love."

It was the first time he'd used such a specific term of endearment for her, and it sounded so *right* on his lips, as if it'd slipped out without his permission. She closed her eyes for a moment as if to savor it, then cleared her throat. "Luke—"

"Kemi, I'm not asking—"

"No, let me talk," she whispered, then sat up, allowing her blankets to pool in her lap. "Look at this, Luke," she insisted, pushing up the short sleeves of her lace nightgown to reveal the scarred flesh of her arm. "It was injured. And it was weak, for a long time. And it still aches sometimes. But I worked at it. It still can't do exactly what it did, but it's not—it's not useless. And you're damaged, Luke, but you aren't useless, either."

Something shone, hungry and dark, in Luke's brandy-dark eyes, and for a wild moment, she thought she'd gotten through to him. But he blinked and shook his head, and the moment was lost.

Kemi sank into the fat down pillows, feeling more tired than she had throughout the entire pregnancy. It was a tiredness born out of disappointment. She could not seem to make more than a superficial connection with this man who handled her body so tenderly in the dark, who successfully calmed her fears, who made her think that she could have an identity separate from the trauma that had followed her since she was a teenager.

Now she looked at him and wondered if in staying in the Seychelles, and staying with Luke, she hadn't set herself up for failure.

"What is it?" Luke said, and her mouth compressed. Of course he could read her mind.

"I don't want to stay with a man who will never love me," she said.

It was an odd relief to say it out loud, and for the first time, she felt in control of the situation. Luke might have financial and physical mastery over her, but her emotions were her own. If she were to supplement all this self-defense and her newfound freedom, she had to be honest with herself at every turn.

"I'd like to go to school," she said. "I'd like to go back and do my master's, starting in September, before the spring semester. I'd like to study cybersecurity, maybe, or engineering. I did really well in math and in the sciences when I was in secondary school and in my undergraduate."

"While pregnant?" Luke asked. His eyes had grown darker than they were normally. Unreadable.

"This is the twenty-first century, Luke," Kemi said. "And while I am incredibly grateful for everything that you've done for me so far, I can't be living in your house, under your control, not even having a chance to know the full truth about you or the way you live your life. I know we planned to divorce eventually. I am…grateful for the time we've spent together. It was kind of you. But if we are to live as strangers, I'd rather we live completely separately, from now."

"Do you really mean that?"

"I haven't got a choice," Kemi replied.

Luke made a noise low in his throat, and his hand skimmed down the small gulf of eiderdown quilt that sat between them. Kemi's cheeks began to burn as she remembered the last time they'd been here. Luke's head had been buried between her thighs, and he'd told her, lips muffled against her most intimate skin, that she had to watch him, to look at him. He said it in a low, raspy voice that was so gentle and yet so filthy that it made her flush to think about it, weeks after. Now, she pressed her thighs together and thought with a little despair that though she might manage to control her words and actions around him, she might never be able to control her body. And they'd only made love a handful of times. It really wasn't fair.

Luke tilted his dark head, and the moment was shattered. "Kemi," he murmured.

She couldn't bear it when he looked at her that way, with that odd mixture of guardedness and longing. "You don't want to know me," Kemi said, "and you've tried to keep me at arm's length since the day I so stupidly allowed you to take me to that hotel of yours. I wish that I'd stayed at home, where I belong."

"I wish you had, too," Luke said, and his voice was low. Regretful.

Hurt blossomed in the middle of Kemi's chest, but she refused to let it show on her face. Perhaps she'd picked up more than a thing or two from her husband. She raised her chin.

"I'd like to be in the air by tomorrow," Kemi said. All the emotion of their conversation had resulted in a dull, throbbing headache at her temples.

"All right."

They stood for a long moment, breaths steadying, and Luke wordlessly lifted his hand to hover over her belly.

"May I?" he whispered.

She swallowed hard, closed her eyes, nodded. *It's useless.* She knew it, and he knew it. It was the reason she allowed him to drop his head, to splay his fingers across her abdomen, to kiss his child goodbye, and finally, the way they both knew was coming, to kiss her softly, gently and in that damned tender way he had. He kissed her eyelids, her forehead, her cheeks and, finally, her mouth.

A fitting farewell, she thought, for the man she'd come to care for so deeply in such a short amount of time.

She'd married out of convenience, but she'd also married in hope that something beautiful could come from all this. There had been something about Luke that night she'd met him, some feeling of safety and tenderness; she'd followed it, trusting instinctively that it would lead to what just might fill that yawning emptiness that had been inside her all these years.

Use me, Luke had told her before they married. *Use me and take your freedom.*

It was time she took his advice.

CHAPTER SIXTEEN

A DAY LATER, Luke woke at dawn and placed his still wan-faced wife in a car that would take her to the airport. In an hour or two, her flight would be hurtling through the sky toward the rocky shores and sapphire-blue skies of Martha's Vineyard, and Luke, finally, would be left alone. It was as if all the light had been let out of the house, and the smell of lilies stubbornly clung to his bed, his clothing, the corridors, even his skin.

"Kings," he ordered. "Please monitor my wife's flight for me and text me when they're at cruising altitude." The older man nodded his assent. Normally Luke would do it himself, but today—

He ate a solitary breakfast and swam rapidly around the length of the infinity pool until his nerves were calmed, then, dressed in sober gray, he climbed into his car and left the estate.

The All Saints' cemetery lay at the edge of the city of Victoria, and this was where Patrick slept, peaceful and silent in his tiny coffin as the years went on. The end of April culminated in his birthday, and as he did every year, Luke visited his son on that day before flying back to Nigeria. As usual, he felt no pain, only a dull ache beneath his ribs that he knew would manifest into something sharper, later, when he was alone.

He reached the site a little earlier than he normally

did, his eyes pausing on the little clusters of mourners scattered here and there on sun-dried grass. He avoided looking at the ground; fresh cuts in the soil always made his stomach hurt. He didn't even know why he was here; it wasn't as if Patrick knew he was here.

Still... Luke had failed him spectacularly as a father. He couldn't neglect to do this one thing.

It was pure chance that he saw the small figure at the edge of the property, moving rapidly toward the gate. He knew it was Kemi immediately. She wore one of the light, fluttery dresses she favored, in a somber shade of brown, and her hair was pinned on top of her head.

What the hell?

Luke began to run. "Kemi!"

She hunched her shoulders together and began to move more rapidly, an impressive feat considering the heels she still insisted on wearing everywhere. He caught up with her in a few easy strides, reaching to grip her shoulders, spin her round.

Kemi's breathing was labored, and her skin was damp with exertion. "Let me *go*," she insisted furiously, yanking away from him.

"What the hell are you doing here?" Luke demanded. His heart was beating so wildly he wondered, panicked for a moment, if he'd be able to catch his breath. *"What are you doing here?"*

Her eyes were large and frightened in her face; Luke did not care. His entire body was tense with—with—

She's here. And his chest was filling, bursting with an emotion that he could only categorize as gladness. Kemi was *here*.

"You're supposed to be over the Indian Ocean," he whispered.

"Luke—"

"I don't understand." He didn't even sound like himself; his voice, even to him, was quiet. Broken. His heart was pounding so loudly it obliterated any other sound; he could feel emotions crossing his face in quick succession, as if they'd been torn from him, so violently it was impossible to hide them.

For the first time, standing here on the soft soil that held his son's remains, he didn't want to hide them. His wife's compassion had swept away his defenses with what seemed like a single stroke.

"Kemi," he said, and he could not say any more, for his voice cracked painfully.

Kemi was crying openly now, hands folded across her abdomen. She had blossomed in the past weeks, he noted distractedly. It was obvious to him, at least, that she was pregnant now, and the soft curve only added to her loveliness. He'd thought of her as lovely since the beginning, if he allowed himself to think about it. And now, for the first time, he found his mouth opening, not to chastise or to censor, but to say—

"I'm grateful," he said, and he could not steady his voice despite his best efforts. He'd never thanked her, had he? Not for her openness, not for her willingness to extend the hand of love and, when he'd rejected that, friendship? He remembered holding her close on the white sand beach, how perfectly they'd fit together, the warmth that had radiated off her skin. Life had seen fit to give him something beautiful in Kemi, and he'd been so self-absorbed he'd pushed it away. But Kemi—she'd always been selfless, hadn't she?

Kemi broke into his thoughts when she inhaled noisily, shook her head. The movement loosened the long braids atop her head, but she did not seem to notice when they slipped down, one by one, to her shoulders. She held out her hands; they were filled with tiny white roses and African violets of the deepest hue of purple he'd ever seen. Even crushed to her chest, they gave off a heady, vibrant scent.

"Take them," she choked.

"Kemi—"

"They're for Patrick. You told me yesterday. And I couldn't just leave you here by yourself, not after everything you'd done for me. I was angry, and it was cruel. I'm so sorry. I promise I'll leave tomorrow, and—" She took a shuddering breath. "Luke—"

"Why would you care so much?" Luke managed through numb lips, then stepped forward. His anger was fading into something else entirely, and he woodenly extracted a handkerchief from his inner pocket and dabbed at her face with it. She sighed a little when he touched her, closed her eyes and rested her forehead against his.

"You know I love you," she whispered. "I'm not ashamed of that, and I'm not going to take it back."

The knot that had been growing in his chest since he'd sent her away drew a little bit tighter. "Kemi—"

"I feel pain when I think of Patrick, because I know how much it hurts you. I know how much you miss him. I know you blame yourself for his death, and I know there are no words for that." She was nuzzling his face now, and Luke could not answer, because the lump was rising in his throat, so hard and so fast that he just might—

"You know—" And here, she hesitated. "I never thought I'd be able to forgive the men that kidnapped me, that ruined my life, but I did—because forgiveness is a gift. It's got nothing to do with the other person—it's giving ourselves a chance to let go. And you need to forgive yourself, Luke. Please—even if I never see you again—"

Forgive yourself.

The words pierced the haze of pain that clouded Luke's senses, wrapped soft and tenderly around them. When was the last time he'd allowed himself softness, or empathy, or love? He'd pushed away all expressions of sympathy so quickly, never allowed them to land, because—

"I don't deserve it," he said, and his voice sounded foreign even to him. It was rough with the kind of emotion he'd had no idea he was capable of anymore, an emotion that Kemi seemed to drag out of him without trying. She'd done it the first time he'd seen her, both of them so absolutely out of place in that smoky nightclub, and had that night that had drawn them together so inexorably and produced the child whose heart beat beneath Kemi's now.

"Stop it."

"No, I don't." The words were building in his throat, a tsunami that threatened to overflow, unless he managed to stop it—

The cheek against hers was rough and stubbly, but it was the sudden wetness there that surprised her. And then Luke was cradling her with such a mixture of softness and strength that she couldn't move, even if she wanted to.

"Princess," he whispered, and it was an endearment, a question, a plea. "*Princess.*"

She lifted her arms round his neck, pressed so close she was no longer sure where he ended and she began. This feeling had always characterized their encounters, but this was the first time it had ever felt so—

"Won't you talk to me?" she said, cupping his face in her hands, and then, yards away from where his son was buried, he did.

"She wasn't supposed to get pregnant," he said. He was trying for his usual dispassionate tone, but the anxiety that came through tightened her throat and started a new stinging in her eyes. "We were sloppy. We were supposed to go for IVF, but I was sloppy, and she—"

"Luke. I know." He'd said all this before, but she suspected he needed to say it again, the same way she'd relived the trauma of her own kidnapping, over and over, until the memory no longer held power over her. His heart was beating so fast, and the hands that clutched her so clammy, that she was afraid for him, but he kept speaking, faster and faster, as if some force were compelling him not to stop.

"He had it *bad*. He had the best treatments, of course, but the crises, they were the worst, Kemi. He'd just shrink into this little ball of nothing—his arms and legs would tense up, so hard they looked like they might break if you tried to loosen them—"

Kemi pressed a hand to her mouth.

"I was almost relieved when he died, Kemi. *Relieved.* The last crisis was that bad—" Luke broke off then, and she'd never seen such a ravaged expression on a man's face before. He stopped as if he knew he'd said too much, then he took a full step back.

"I'm sorry," Kemi said simply. Whatever Luke had done to clean her face a moment ago had been completely obliterated by fresh tears; she looked at him now through that watery film. He was visibly trying to calm himself; she wanted to shout for him not to do so, not to retreat back into himself. Now that she'd seen Luke for who, for what he really was—

He wasn't incapable of love. No—instead, he'd loved too much. And she had no idea how to help him, except—

She moved forward quickly, wrapped her arms round his middle, and for once he didn't push her away. Instead, he drew her close.

"It's not that I don't want you to be happy," he said, and for the first time, humility leached through into his voice. "I don't know how to get past all this. I don't know how to talk about it—"

"You just did, to me."

"Right." He laughed, a short, ragged sound. "But the

process is going to be ugly, Kemi. It's been ugly. I've been selfish enough already with people I've cared for. It's better this way—"

"To be alone?"

"Would you prefer to stay with me with no guarantees, Kemi? That's no way to live. You'll survive without me. You already have." His face grew fierce. "Have you any idea how proud I am of you? You should be proud of yourself."

Kemi had no words to say; she lifted her hands to her mouth instead. Luke bent, kissed her on the forehead, took a step back.

"Come on, Princess," he said, and his voice was oddly gentle. He also looked at her and, for the first time, smiled at her—truly smiled at her. It was as gentle as rays from the morning sun; it warmed Kemi from the inside out.

"Should we visit him together, then?" Kemi whispered.

He opened his mouth as if to protest, but then he nodded.

By the time they left the cemetery, Kemi's hand folded tight in his, she knew that Patrick had been short and scrawny, with brown eyes that took up his entire face, and a knobby head constantly covered with some kind of lump from climbing, crawling, running.

"I wish I could say he was absolutely adorable, but he wasn't," Luke said ruefully. "He was a terror. He got into everything, and he bit. But he was full of life and high spirits, and to see him so ill—"

"I understand," Kemi said softly, placing her hand on the back of his.

"I hope to God you never will," her husband said emphatically.

The two sat in a small open café close to the estate, sipping from a pot of fragrant tea, a plate of untouched sardine sandwiches between them. The table was so small and wobbly it necessitated their sitting very close together, foreheads almost touching. Luke's voice was more quiet and intimate than she'd ever heard it, and oddly enough, Kemi felt completely at peace. It was as if something had been purged from both of them that day; she had no idea where this would end up, but she'd missed a flight, Luke hadn't yet mentioned the missed flight and—

"What happens now?" she asked out loud.

Luke did not look surprised; he looked a little rueful and still quite sad, but he was not hiding anything from her. Not anymore. There was a quiet regard for her in his eyes that made her skin warm. It was more than the lust that had characterized their early encounters. He saw her, valued her and wasn't afraid of her seeing him. Not anymore.

The question was: Would that be enough to sustain them in a marriage that they'd already decided needed to end?

Luke's voice broke into her thoughts. "I don't know what happens next. But I'd like us to go home."

Home.

Could he mean it? Could the word have expanded in his mind to include her, include the small family that they could be?

Even after everything that had happened, she was too afraid to ask. She eased herself to her feet and followed him to the waiting car.

CHAPTER SEVENTEEN

LUKE FELT FAR too wrung-out to even want sex, talk less of perform that evening, but he wanted his wife, and desperately. She shed her day dress and washed and came to him, smelling sweetly of eucalyptus and mint, to their darkened room. When she was in his arms, he sighed, then slipped a hand over the rounded curve of her lower belly. He wanted to explore her in this quiet, loving way, with no other expectations.

Let me hold you.

There was silence in their cool, darkened room, and when he finally spoke—

"I should probably talk to someone."

She shifted in his arms a little, tipped up her chin. When his lips met hers in the dark, she sighed a little. "Agnes?"

He winced. He wasn't thrilled by the idea, but at least she knew all his history. "Most likely."

In the darkness, he felt his wife sit up, and he reached for her, depending on smell, warmth, her sweet essence to guide him in the cool, dark room. It was shocking, how addictive she'd become in the past few weeks, how necessary. And yet he'd tried to send her away.

"I can't promise that we'll work," he said. As he spoke his arms encircled her waist, skipped her breasts, came to rest on her hips. Her bare skin on his felt like heaven. "But I want to—"

"You want to?"

Love you. Be with you. Luke swallowed hard, then bent and spoke the words against the cool shell of her ear. If he spoke them too loudly, perhaps whatever misfortune had followed him in love would hear and snatch her away from him again.

"If I get into this," he said, "and something happens—"

"It won't."

"You're more arrogant than I am if you actually believe that," Luke said dryly. His hand skimmed over her belly, cupped it, and she took in a breath.

"I'm terrified," he said after the briefest of moments. There. He'd admitted it. "And I do love you, Kemi. But—"

"I'm terrified, too," Kemi replied, just as quietly. "But I love you enough to give it to you as a gift, whether you return it or not. And that has nothing to do with whatever may happen down the line."

The words brought that prickliness to the back of his throat again, and Luke fought it down with all his might. Once was quite enough for one day. He cleared his throat. He knew the biggest battle was yet to come; it would be in the form of waking up the next morning, realizing exactly what he'd done and not running as far and as fast as he could.

It's a gift. And Kemi had never asked him for anything before, except himself. Was loving her enough to push his fears back into the shadows? Her love radiated from her so strongly he felt it whenever they were together; he saw it burning from her eyes. The feeling of being loved was slipping past his defenses, one by one. It did not demand that he resolve them; it simply was there, and that—that—

Kemi sighed in his arms, and he realized belatedly that

she'd fallen fast asleep. He laughed out loud for a moment, then settled down beside her.

It's going to be all right.

For the first time in years, he thought it—and he let himself believe it. Just for that moment. The rest would take time, but if he kept on believing it for one more moment, and the one after that—

Perhaps it would be all right, after all.

Perhaps.

When Kemi woke the next morning, Luke was beside her, the hard planes of his body curved around her protectively. His dark eyes were half-open. When she blinked and half sat up, he offered her a smile that was more uncertain than anything she'd ever seen on his face before.

"Good morning," he said gently, and she felt a flutter deep in her stomach that at first she attributed to her very handsome husband, but then it was there again, as if a coven of butterflies had chosen to make her abdomen home. She froze; Luke caught the look on her face and frowned. "What?"

"I think the baby moved," she gasped.

"What? Really?" His hand immediately moved to cover the lower part of her abdomen. Of course he couldn't feel anything—he wouldn't be able to for months. "That's impossible. It's too early."

"Perhaps." She laughed. Maybe it was the baby. Maybe it was just the butterflies of a mother overcome by joy, but she didn't care, for Luke's hand was under her gown, fingers splaying over the bare skin of her belly.

"Hey, little one," he whispered, and Kemi actually felt her heart swell. She dropped her own fingers to cover Luke's, right over where their son turned comfortably in his warm space. She saw Luke's eyes flutter shut; when he murmured something under his breath, she asked what it was.

"Prayer for health and safety," Luke said, and he reached up, pressed his lips to the back of her hand.

"I didn't know you were religious."

"I'm not," Luke said dryly, "but I'm not taking any risks this time around."

EPILOGUE

CHOOSE JOY, LUKE said to himself and straightened up, arranging the soft folds of his dull gold *agbada* over his shoulders. Kemi sat to the right of him, body still a little swollen from her recent childbirth. Her eyes were fatigued beneath layers of makeup; her smile was a little unsteady. Soon the main part of the naming ceremony would be over and she would be able to go inside their massive bedchamber in their Abujan apartment, hand the baby over to his Auntie Tobi, who sat at a table of honor, bursting with pride, and sleep.

"Only a little while," he whispered, bending and allowing his lips to brush her ear. She shivered a little, and a tremor went through him as well. He tried his best to hold back, to act toward his wife in moderation; he was as addicted to her now as he'd been to grief only a few months ago. He would soon learn balance; it would temper in time. But for now...

"Enjoy your love," Agnes had said in their first counseling session together, a smile on her face. "Enjoy each other. Revel in the good days. Comfort each other on the bad. And create a life you want to live together, free of your past."

And now—exactly seven days ago, Kemi had given birth to Ayodele Ibru. *His son.*

Joy has come home, the little boy's name meant. And

it was true. The little bundle in his wife's arms now represented so much: joy, as his name was. Freedom to love again. And not a replacement of what he'd had, but a tribute to new life, to what was to come. And many, many more years with Kemi, whom he loved—and delighted in discovering more about—every day. She'd blossomed during her pregnancy—enrolled in school, started work with his development team on a security app for a growing network of Abujan women and glowed with life. Strength. Purpose.

Yes, joy had come for both of them. They'd chosen it. And he knew the future held only better things for himself, his princess and his royal son.

* * * * *

RETURN OF
THE OUTBACK
BILLIONAIRE

KELLY HUNTER

MILLS & BOON

'Some rise by sin, and some by virtue fall'
—William Shakespeare, *Measure for Measure*

PROLOGUE

THE RED RIVER GUM floorboards in the ballroom gleamed with the shine of fresh beeswax polish and the soft glow cast by dozens of antique wall sconces. Every set of doors along the generous expanse of wall to the west stood open to the veranda beyond, even if doing so would provide scant protection from the night moths drawn towards the light. The rest of the homestead at the heart of Jeddah Creek station had been dusted, buffed and made to look like the expensive Victorian-era folly it was. Whoever had thought to bring white wrought-iron features and open verandas into the middle of a red desert landscape bloated with dust, drought and a fiercely relentless sun had been quite mad. That or English and dreaming of the world they'd left behind.

Judah Blake often wondered how long it had taken his English ancestors to realise people dreamed so very differently here.

He'd been back a little over a week, and if he still found going through an open door or eating whatever he felt like whenever he felt like it a challenge, he liked to think he kept those challenges to himself. He'd been born and raised on Jeddah Creek station; he knew this harsh land and all its wonders. He'd conquer being back here soon enough.

His eighteen-year-old brother, Reid, had been the one to suggest some kind of party to celebrate Judah's return. Judah had been the one to turn his brother's modest suggestion into a society ball. He'd needed to know just how much damage his imprisonment had done to his family's standing, and what better way than to send out invitations to a big charity ball and see who showed up?

He'd spared no expense—no one would ever complain of his hospitality. Whatever a guest wanted to drink, they would find it here. The food had been flown in alongside catering staff and musicians. A small army of cleaners, tradesmen and a couple of event co-ordinators had spent the week preparing the homestead to receive guests. Stock hands had spent days setting out a parking area for all the private planes and helicopters those guests would arrive in. Not all the guests would be wealthy. Some would arrive in little outback helicopters more suited to mustering cattle than providing luxury transport. Some would bring the family Cessna, the outback equivalent of a family car. Jeddah Creek station ran straight across the border between Queensland and the Northern Territory and was a nightmare to get to by road.

And yet, out of the several hundred invitations he'd sent out at short notice, only a handful had been declined.

He could blame some of that willingness to accommodate him on his family name. His father had been a member of the English aristocracy—a lowly baron who had married the daughter of a viscount and fled to Australia to escape the sanctimonious superiority of her relatives. But his parents were dead, one after the other, these past six months, and Judah was *the* Blake now, with all the fealty it entailed.

He could blame some of the attendance on the fact that he'd been blessed with a handsome face, wasn't yet thirty, and wasn't yet married. And he was rich—Old Money rich, even if his recently deceased father had burned through most of it. He also had thirty billion dollars' worth of New Money, courtesy of two cryptocurrency investments he'd made at just the right time. He'd tried to keep that windfall quiet, but in the rarefied world of one-percenters there were always some who made it their business to know which way the money flowed.

And that, above all, was why so many people had chosen to show their faces here tonight. With thirty billion dollars sitting in his back pocket, it apparently really *was* going to be that easy for the same people who'd ignored him for more than seven years to step up now, forgive him his sins and welcome him back into the fold.

Amazing how many of them had already been in contact on account of investment possibilities that might be of interest to him. Good causes, all. Could only help him restore his tarnished reputation, they'd implied, and he'd smiled fierce and flat and told them he looked forward to catching up with them soon.

They had no idea what kind of man he'd become. *He* had no idea what kind of man he would be now that he was out and blessed with more wealth than he knew what to do with and so many open doors.

All he knew was that he wanted everything back the way it was. His parents alive. His soul not yet stained by what it took to get along in a cage, but it was too late for that. Nor was he ever likely to will his parents back to life.

Retrieving the parts of Jeddah Creek station his father had sold off, though…that was something he *could* set right. His birthright and his solace. *His* land, not Bridie Starr's.

'Don't do anything rash once you get out,' the visiting psych expert had said in the days before his release.

As if Judah hadn't spent the past seven years and then some learning to control his every thought and feeling.

'Avoid split-second decisions.'

Guess the doc had never had an inmate with a shiv heading towards him, fast and furtive.

'Give yourself time to adjust.'

This sounded like halfway good advice.

'Your reading of people will be off. Give others the benefit of the doubt.'

Like hell he would.

Bridie Starr had taken temporary possession of land that belonged to him and the fix was very simple—nothing rash about it.

He wanted it back.

CHAPTER ONE

'Do you know what you're going to wear?'

'I haven't decided yet.' Bridie Starr stared despondently at the lemon meringue pie Gert had whipped up seemingly out of nowhere and wondered, not for the first time, where the other woman had learned to cook. Not around here, that was for sure. Here being the channel country of central Australia, and far, far away from any kind of crowd. Bridie had been born and raised here on Devil's Kiss station. Gert hailed from Barcoo, a few hundred kilometres to the south. Neither place tended to grow master chefs.

Gert arrived at Bridie's homestead for three days every fortnight and made the place bright with beeswax, laughter, shared cooking and conversation, before heading next door to Jeddah Creek station to do the same for the Blakes. A two-day stint with the Conrads to the north, and then Gert would return to her home and set up to make the trip all over again.

Gert was the glue that kept people around here connected.

'I'm not sure I even want to go to the Blakes' ball,' Bridie confessed.

'Can't say I'm surprised.'

And why should she be? Bridie's shut-in tendencies weren't exactly a secret.

'But you have to go,' the older woman continued briskly. 'People will be looking to you to see what you'll do now that Judah's back. It'd be cruel to act as if you're scared of him.'

'I'm not scared of him.' And she didn't want to be cruel. 'It's just…why did he have to go and throw a society ball, of all things? Out here?'

Gert's thin lips stretched into a smile. 'Used to be a time when fancy balls were all the rage at Jeddah Creek station, you're just too young to remember them. They put on at least one a season and all the fancy types would be there. The things we got up to…' The older woman sounded positively wistful. 'Your mother loved them. She and your father used to dance all night long, and they were good at it.'

Bridie's mother had left the world not long after Bridie had set foot in it. Gert was the only person who ever talked freely about her.

Her father never spoke of his wife at all.

Okay, so her mother had loved dancing and balls. Maybe Bridie could learn to love them too. She'd already RSVP'd that she and her father would be there. No way could they stay away after everything Judah had done for her. And she had to be presentable, which wouldn't be hard, what with a closet full of rarely worn designer clothes at her fingertips, all of them tailored just for her. Granted, they were half a dozen years out of date, but haute couture never really dated. All the age of a piece did was show other people for how long someone had been obscenely wealthy.

Bridie didn't consider her wealth obscene, but once upon a time she'd modelled such clothes and sometimes she'd been allowed to keep them. She'd been a rising star with the face of an angel and a body on the cusp of womanhood. She'd had absolutely no clue about the predators roaming the glittering, crazy world of high-fashion modelling.

Her awakening had been a hard one.

'What did people used to wear to these balls? Full formal?'

'Absolutely.'

'Breast medals and sashes and things? Gloves for the women?'

'No to the medals and sashes, yes to the family rings and jewels, sometimes gloves,' answered Gert. 'Landed gentry and all that. Sometimes it's subtle, but it does show.'

Bridie blew out a frustrated breath as she tried to mentally turn Judah next door into Lord Judah Blake, peer of the realm, bona fide English aristocracy. 'Right, then. Gown time. She pushed a hand through the thick waves of summer-wheat-coloured hair, liberally sprinkled with darker shades of brown, and vowed yet again to get a proper haircut before the ball.

'He phoned this morning wanting to speak to you.'

'Judah?' She'd been dodging his calls all week.

'So ring him back.'

She nodded, knowing full well that returning his call would take more guts than she had. At least at the ball they'd be surrounded by people and the conversation wouldn't get too personal too fast. Ease into things slowly was her motto.

'You're not going to call him back, are you?' stated Gert flatly.

'No. But I will be at the ball, dressed to impress, and I *will* speak with him then and welcome him home and shower him with gratitude and whatever else I need to do. Trust me, Gert, I have a plan.'

'Good girl,' soothed the older woman. 'Have some pie.'

Something was up. Gert never let anyone at the lemon meringue pie before it was cool, but she cut Bridie a slice and watched with barely contained disapproval as the warm filling oozed all over the plate.

'Now.' The older woman's steely gaze could have skewered a razorback at a hundred paces. 'Let's get this sorted, sweet petal.'

Sweet petal… Oh, this was bad. Worse than when Bridie had used the giant Limoges vase that used to sit at the end of the hallway as a frisbee target…and nailed it.

'What are you going to wear?'

Judah watched from his vantage point at one end of the ground-floor veranda as his guests spilled out of the crowded ballroom and into the night to speak in glowing terms of the landscape they'd flown over to get here and the beauty of the old two-storey Victorian house in the middle of nowhere.

'Jeddah Creek station, what a magnificent place.'

'Judah, you're looking so well.'

And for the truly brave, *'I miss your parents and I'm sorry for your loss.'*

His brother was somewhere inside, ten years younger and almost a stranger. Reid had been running Jeddah Creek in the four-month gap between their father passing and Judah getting home, and he'd done a good job.

The boy—man—had a strong network of school friends, all freshly graduated and most of them taking a break year before stepping into whatever their families had planned for them. Plenty of Reid's friends were here tonight and he hoped to hell they could hold their liquor because he wasn't exactly policing them. Maybe he should have a word with the exorbitantly priced bar staff the event co-ordinators had insisted on hiring. Let them know that monitoring the alcohol intake of his guests, young and old, was their job, not his.

And then Reid stepped into place at his side, his blue eyes bright and searching.

'She's not here yet. She promised she'd come,' said Reid by way of greeting.

'Who?'

'Bridie.'

There was only one Bridie in Judah's universe and he'd been trying to set up a meeting with her for days. So far, she hadn't even had the courtesy to return his calls. 'Maybe she had a pressing engagement elsewhere.'

'Not Bridie. She's practically a shut-in. Wouldn't leave Devil's Kiss station for years after the incident, and even now she has to work her way up to going out.'

'Then perhaps she's working her way up to it.' The thought of Bridie not making the most of her freedom didn't sit well with him. Stubborn tendrils of anger flickered to life inside him. He'd sacrificed his freedom in service to her. The least she could have done was make the most of her opportunities.

'I know she was worried about how everyone might gossip about her and you,' continued Reid. 'She wasn't looking forward to that part.'

Boo-hoo.

'She's a photographer now,' Reid said next.

He knew.

'Landscapes mostly, of around here. I took her up in the mustering helicopter a month or so back. We ended up taking the door off and rigging up a harness so she could lean out and take aerial shots. I haven't seen them yet, but she said they turned out real good.'

They had.

Resentment curled, a low buzz in the pit of his stomach, and all because his teenage brother was what? Friends with Bridie Starr? Her confidant?

Why hadn't she returned any of his calls?

Bridie was in between him and his brother in age. Twenty-three now, no clueless girl. Would he even recognise her? Of all the photos sent to him these past seven plus years, not one had been of her.

'See that your friends don't drink too much tonight. The last thing we need is an incident.'

'I know. They know. There won't be one.'

How could his teenage brother be so very sure?

Reid seemed to read his mind, and smiled, fierce and swift and just that little bit familiar. 'Your reputation precedes you, man. They'll behave.'

'Does it cause you trouble? My reputation?'

Reid shrugged. 'Not out here.'

'What about when you were at school?'

Another shrug. 'Saved me the trouble of being friends with fair-weather people. That's what Dad used to say.' He squinted towards the east. 'This could be them. Dunno why I expected them to come in the long way around when it's so much quicker to cut across country.'

Judah waited as the thin spiral of dust on the horizon turned into a plume, and a dusty once-white ute came into view. Hard to know what he was feeling, with his emotions locked down so tight, but now was not the time to lose the iron control he'd spent so many years developing.

So what if curiosity was killing him?

So what if the thought of her being a hermit made him seethe?

He could still use that information against her if she didn't bend to his will and sell him back his land. And why wouldn't she sell? She'd done nothing with the land she now owned. It was just sitting there waiting to be reclaimed.

By him.

After all. She owed him.

It took fifteen more minutes before Tom Starr and his daughter walked up the front steps of the homestead and stopped in front of him, and if Judah had thought Bridie astonishingly beautiful before, it was nothing compared to the looks she possessed now. She had a mouth made for crushing, wide-set eyes the colour of cognac, and hair every colour of brown he could imagine—from sun-bleached streaks of honey-gold to burnished bronze shot through with the deepest mahogany. Natural colours, all of them; her hair had been the same wild woodland riot when she was a child.

She still possessed the body of a dancer, all fine bones and elegance, and she carried herself like one too. Her slip of a dress covered her from neck to knee and was a deep twilight blue. No sleeves, no jewellery. Her only accessory was a little black purse that she clutched in front of her body with both hands, her knuckles almost white.

She could barely even look at him.

'Thank you for coming.' His rusty manners had been getting such a workout tonight.

She glanced up, startled, and he found himself enmeshed. Falling into memories he didn't want in his head, and as for allowing them to surface, no. Just no.

'Wouldn't—' She had to stop to clear her throat. 'Wouldn't have missed it. Thank you for inviting us.'

Such pretty lies.

He wanted to reach for the tension knots in his neck. He wanted to reach out and see if her hair felt as silky as it looked.

He wanted to possess this woman who had never been his, who he barely knew but for the fantasies about her that he'd woven in his head. He wanted his father back, an explanation for all the photos she'd sent him month after month, and above all he wanted to know why she'd bought into his birthright. Did she honestly believe he wouldn't be back to claim it?

But what he really wanted—needed—was time out away from her so he could claw back the composure he'd lost the moment she'd locked eyes with him. 'Reid, why don't you show Bridie where she can freshen up and then get her a drink and a plate of food?' Babysit, he might as well have said, but Reid seemed up for the role and Bridie looked grateful.

He watched them go, remembering that at sixteen she'd walked the catwalks of Paris and graced the cover of *Vogue* magazine.

It still showed.

And then he dragged his gaze away from her retreating figure and prepared to greet her father. 'Tomas.'

'Welcome home,' offered the older man. 'I'm sorry your parents aren't here to greet you.'

'So am I.' He'd never once imagined when he went away that they'd be dead before he returned. 'Maybe you can tell me what happened to my father's business acumen and why he died practically bankrupt.' And why no one had told Judah, and why Tomas had been helping Reid out on the farm in every way he could.

'You sure you want to talk about this here?' Tom Starr didn't look as if he wanted to discuss much at all. 'We could set up a meeting.'

'Been trying to set up a meeting with your daughter all week, Tom. No one's answering and I'm all out of patience.'

The older man looked puzzled. 'Why call Bridie? She doesn't know anything about your father's business dealings.'

But it hadn't been Tom Starr's name on those property deeds, it had been Bridie's. 'What happened to my father?' At least he could get some information from the older man. 'Before he died he let go of things he'd treasured all his life. Cattle bloodlines. Family jewels. *Land.*'

Judah watched as the older man seemed to age another decade before his eyes.

'Grief.' The older man swallowed hard. 'Grief and anger at the way you were treated swallowed your father whole. After you were convicted, your father drank more. So did I and more often than not we drank together. I had plenty of shame to drown and he had a son who'd protected the defenceless and paid an unfair price for it. Your father kept telling me his fancy lawyers would find grounds for appeal, and I just kept on praying it'd happen, but it never did.'

Grounds for appeal. What a joke. As for parole, that concept hadn't worked for him either.

Maybe it had something to do with his swagger.

'A couple of years back I made the mistake of telling your father I was the one who pulled the trigger,' Tom offered gruffly.

Judah stiffened. 'We had a deal. We *swore* that would stay between you and me. No one else.' They'd done it to protect Bridie. So a child would have her only parent at her side to help pick up the pieces of her life. 'You *swore*.'

A man was only as good as his word.

'I thought it would help if he knew you were a hero twice over.'

Some hero. More like a fool. 'Did it?'

'No. He turned even more bitter and twice as uncaring.'

'So who else did you tell? Does Bridie know you pulled that trigger?'

'No one. No one else knows what happened that night. I—after that I thought about it, but—no.'

Why not? He was itching for a fight and he didn't know why. Why did his father get burdened with the truth and not Bridie as well? She was an adult now, wasn't she? No longer that terrified broken child.

'Protect Bridie,' the older man offered weakly. 'She'd take it hard if she knew.'

Protect Bridie. It was the reason he'd shouldered the blame in the first place, all the way to lockup. He'd arrogantly thought his sentence wouldn't be a long one. He'd had the best lawyers money could buy and virtue on his side. He'd never dreamed he'd spend years imprisoned for his supposed sins or that both his parents would be dead before he got out. More fool him.

Protect the innocent children.

How could that be *wrong*?

'My father had hardly any money left when he died. He'd sold off land. You were his friend—or tried to be. What happened?'

'He started playing poker. It was something to do other than stew, I guess. He tried to get me interested, but I'm a lousy poker player and the buy-in was out of my league. Turns out your father wasn't much of a poker player either. I bailed him out of debt a couple of times. I took out a mortgage, but in the end I didn't have any more to give without losing Devil's Kiss. I know he got more money from somewhere, but it wasn't from me.'

There was a ring of truth to the older man's words. 'How much did you give him?'

'None of your business, lad. Give means give. I'm not asking for it back.'

'And you have no idea why your daughter's name is on some of the title deeds for Jeddah Creek station?'

Silence greeted him. A depth of shock that couldn't be feigned. 'I don't know anything about that.'

Interesting.

'Look, I can't say how Bridie got her name on those deeds,' said Tom. 'But at a guess, I'd say she bought them off your father because he had gambling debts to pay that he didn't want your mother to know about. Bridie's not worldly. She doesn't crave power or money or fame, but she does—or did—have money saved from her model-ling days and inheritance money from her mother. She doesn't have friends, but she has a good heart, and she owes you, we both do, so please, when you ask her why she holds those deeds hear her out.'

'I would if she'd return my calls.' Hard to believe Tom didn't know about those.

'I know you've left messages for her. I urged her to answer you, but Bridie can take a while to commit to doing things. Fear can paralyse her. And I know people think I mollycoddle her, and maybe I do, but she didn't come back from that night ride whole, Judah, none of us did, and it's been a long road back to even halfway nor-mal for her. She's doing her best here tonight, and she's doing it for you, so don't—'

'Don't what? Turn on her? Take my anger out on her?

Why would I do that when I've spent more than seven years *helping you protect her*?'

'I was going to say judge,' the older man said wearily. 'You're angry because helping us—protecting her—has cost you too much, and I get that. God knows I can never repay you. But don't judge my daughter the way you have every right to judge me.' The other man met his gaze dead on. 'She doesn't have a deceitful bone in her body. You'll see.'

Bridie couldn't seem to stop her hands from shaking. She'd clasped them behind her back in an effort to stop the tremors, but that move exposed the boyish contours of her chest to the gaze of others and she didn't like that either. She'd tried folding her arms in front of her and wrapping her fingers around her upper arms, but that came off as utterly defensive, she knew, and that simply wouldn't do. Holding a drink of any kind was out of the question. Holding someone else's hand might have grounded her but she hadn't done that since her early childhood when she'd held her father's hand or her aunt's hand, or Gert's.

The couple standing next to her started up a conversation about the country they'd flown over to get here, and Bridie joined in, sharing a little local knowledge, and learning in turn that they were from Sydney and the parents of one of Reid's friends. She was then able to talk about Reid's flying lessons and pilot's licence and how they occasionally mustered stock these days using drones rather than helicopters. Reid could fly those too, and so could she.

In ten minutes, she made more small talk than she'd made in six months, but her hands had stopped shaking and her stance didn't feel quite so rigid. She felt almost relaxed. As if she really could mix in with an unknown group of people and do it well.

And then the string group started up and Judah took to the dance floor with a woman old enough to be his grandmother and wealthy enough to wear rings on every finger and pearls at her neck and not give a toss about whether it looked overdone.

The couple beside her took their leave and headed for the dance floor too, such courtly manners for the middle of nowhere, and she wondered whether Reid was up for making a welcome home speech to his brother and whether she'd be called on to say something too. Was that the kind of welcome home she should be considering? Some grand public gesture to cement her allegiance to the man who'd saved her life?

There was no water on the drinks tray a waiter dangled in front of her so she took a champagne and wet her lips and tried not to look like a wallflower in her Givenchy dress and Jimmy Choo shoes, both of them dragged from the bowels of her wardrobe. She'd worn her hair long and had cut bangs into it just before she'd come. Bangs to frame her face and shield her eyes. Eyes she could feel widening as Judah returned his dance partner to the side of an elderly gentleman and locked gazes with her.

His lips tilted into a half-smile as he headed towards her and there was nowhere to run. He didn't ask to take the glass from her hand, he just took it and set it on a nearby table and held out his hand.

'Dance with me.'

It wasn't a question.

She took his hand, hers cold, his warm, and pretended she was back on the catwalks of Paris with all eyes upon her, assessing the clothes and the vision of a celebrated

designer. She'd liked modelling beautiful clothes once
upon a time. She'd loved strutting her stuff on the catwalk, fluid and assured, pretending she was a dancer or
Audrey Hepburn or Coco Chanel. Pretending she was
someone special. That particular flight of fantasy got
her to the dance floor, small mercies, only now she had
another problem as Judah turned towards her and put
his palm to her waist.

'I can't waltz,' she whispered, panicked. For all that
Gert said her father had been quite the dancer in his day,
he'd certainly never taken the time to teach his daughter
that particular skill. 'I never learned.'

'Then we'll sway from side to side like half the other
couples on the floor. I don't care.' He drew her in and
the scent of eucalyptus and something altogether mas-
culine drifted with him. 'Put your hand on my upper
arm.' He kept gentle hold of her other hand and she did
as suggested, and his arm was warm too, beneath the
fine fabric of his suit.

She squeezed just a little bit and he raised a wicked
eyebrow in return. She was used to wiry men with plenty
of muscle and not a lot of fat to be going on with, but
Judah was built to a whole different level. 'What have
they been feeding you?'

'Slop.'

He probably wasn't joking. 'Sorry, I—stupid comment. The food tonight is excellent.'

'You haven't eaten any.'

How did he know? 'Well, it looks good.'

'So do you.' Words that made his lips curl in a whole
different way from before, and if that was a smile, heaven
help him. 'But you already know that.'

'I do know that. I dressed up in my best because I
wanted to make sure I honoured your welcome home

party by looking as put together as I can.' She followed his dance lead, stepping slowly side to side, and fixed her gaze over his shoulder.

He added a slow turn to their swaying. 'I liked the photos you sent.'

One a month, every month, since he'd gone away. She felt his gaze on her face but refused to look at him. 'The first ones weren't very good.'

She could feel his shrug. 'They were to me.'

'I almost stopped sending them. You never wrote back.'

'What would you have had me say?'

And there was another question she had no answer to, but the music kept playing and their feet kept moving and maybe they didn't need to say anything. She'd shown her face and accepted his command to dance—as if she'd had a choice—and she felt as if she held lightning and thunder in her arms. Why wouldn't she feel that way? He was her ultimate protector and he'd paid mightily for taking on that role, sacrificing his freedom so she could survive hers.

'You haven't answered any of my calls,' he said.

'I…know.'

'Too busy or too afraid of me?'

Another question she didn't know how to answer without throwing every vulnerability she owned at his feet for him to tread on. She spared him a glance. Those eyes…some kind of mossy green, ringed with such a dark navy-grey around the edges. She'd always thought him fierce on account of those eyes. A force to be reckoned with and a perfect match for wild Jeddah Creek station.

He'd killed a man who'd been stalking her. Pulled her bound and shaking from the cramped, pitch-black car boot she'd been trapped in and delivered her safely into the arms of her father. He'd been locked away because of it, and she owed him her truth.

'At first I was afraid of everything and everyone. Shadows made me jump. Other people made me cringe. I could barely leave my room. And then one day my father yelled at me from the other side of my bedroom door. He said, "Judah's the one sitting in a prison room staring at the walls, Bridie, not you. How do you think he'd feel about squandering his freedom on someone who's refusing to live?"'

'Smart man, your father.'

She couldn't look away from him. 'A week later I went to the kitchen for breakfast. A few weeks after that I made it to the back door and stepped out onto the veranda. I took a picture and sent it to you.' She'd kept right on sending them. 'For seven years, six months and two days I've thought of you sacrificing your freedom for my life. It made me step out of my comfort zone and keep on walking. So, am I afraid of you? No. But I have been using you for years as a cattle prod to help me face my fears. My feelings for you are complicated.'

'I'll say,' he muttered, after a very long stretch of silence.

She had nothing more to say. Nothing to do except fidget beneath that watchful, wary gaze.

'What are you going to do now you've lost your cattle prod?'

'Do you always ask such difficult questions?'

He shrugged. 'I don't usually ask personal questions at all. Like you said, whatever is between us is complicated.'

She looked around the glittering ballroom filled with Australia's beautiful and wealthy and wondered if any of them walked with fear as a constant companion, like her. Or which of them had broken the law and paid the price, like Judah, and how hard they'd had to fight to come back from that. 'I'm glad you're back. I didn't answer your calls because I wanted to tell you in person. *Thank you* in person for saving me.'

She felt the tension in him rather than saw it. A simmering waiting quality that burned. A heavy-lidded gaze that banked hard, but not before she'd seen the sudden flame of sexual interest in his eyes. Oh, she'd seen that before, but not from him, never from him.

And she might not be afraid of him, but she *was* afraid of what could happen to a man with too much pent-up desire and not nearly enough self-control. They lost their minds and let fantasy rule. They saw only what they wanted to.

And then Judah loosened his hold and stepped back, and suddenly she could breathe again, even if her hands were too clammy and her body too hot.

'My father sold you land in the last year of his life. Yes or no?'

'Yes.' She'd been dreading this part of the conversation. 'It's complicated. The money didn't always go directly to him. Sometimes I paid bills for him instead.'

'You mean gambling debts.'

'I didn't ask. But, yes, probably.'

'I want that land back. Whatever you paid, I'll pay it. More, if that's what you want.'

'No, you don't understand.'

'Double the price you paid. I want it back.'

'Judah, you don't understand. It's not for sale. You can—'

'Everyone, if I may have your attention.' His voice rang out across the ballroom, stopping music and movement and turning all eyes towards them. His arm at her waist was a band of steel, keeping her in place, but why? What was he doing?

'First, I'd like to welcome you all here tonight. I appreciate the time and trouble so many of you have taken to get here. Welcome to Jeddah Creek station. I hope you find the hospitality and the connections you make here tonight to your liking.'

A waiter approached them with a tray full of drinks and he took one and passed it to her before collecting another for himself. 'Secondly, I'd like to introduce one particular woman to you all. A woman whose name you will have no doubt heard in connection with mine even if you haven't met her personally. A woman of rare compassion and resilience. Someone who has seen the darkest actions mankind has to offer and yet somehow manages to retain her sanity and goodness.'

He couldn't possibly be talking about her.

'Someone who inspired me to look outward rather than in, at a time when all I could see were concrete walls and prison bars. A pioneering soul, with a vision for merging two great farming families and two iconic properties to allow for more conservation projects and forward management of the land we hold so dear. Ladies and gentlemen, please raise your glasses to Bridie Starr.' He smiled down at her, all shark. 'My future wife.'

Say *what*, now?

Wife? What wife? Had he lost his mind while in prison? A little bit of insanity to accompany that very impressive, very fine physique?

'Smile,' he ordered softly, as the guests applauded, and showed her how to do it. 'People will take one look at you and think we're not serious.' He touched the rim of his glass to hers. Just that little bit lower than the rim of her glass, to be precise, and wasn't that supposed to indicate some measure of respect? 'To us.'

'What us?' she hissed behind the cover of golden bubbles. 'What exactly do you think you're doing?'

'Getting my land back.'

'By *marrying* me?' She laughed. She couldn't help it. She was still laughing as she lifted the glass to her lips and proceeded to drain it. Moments later a waiter had whisked it away and they were dancing again, her mind a whirl and her body following along behind. 'Can you be *any* more insulting?'

'You refused to sell. What did you think I would do?'

'Oh, I don't know. You could have waited two more seconds and *listened* to what I had to say. You could have easily done that, but no, straight to blackmail and coercion and *marriage*? Are you *nuts*?' She stepped in close, super aware of all the people beginning to move around them as she raised her lips to his ear. 'The only reason I bought the land in the first place was because I didn't want your father selling it to anyone else. I kept it safe from harm so I could return it to you, because I *owe* you.' She took a deep breath and let the true depth of her anger show. 'I was two seconds away from *giving it to you*. You utter *idiot*.'

CHAPTER TWO

IF JUDAH HAD learned anything in lockup it was to never back down, even if you had just picked the wrong fight. That mindset had got him through more than seven years of prison politics alive and relatively unscathed. Whether it would get him through the rest of this dance remained to be seen.

'We don't have to stay engaged for long,' he tried, and she trod on his toe with the point of a scissor-tipped stiletto. 'Ow.'

'You're absolutely right.' Her eyes glowed like cognac. 'Five minutes should do it.'

But he couldn't break their engagement five minutes after announcing it. He had a reputation to protect. Status that relied on money, hype and his willingness to kill to protect the innocent. Foolishness could never be part of that mix. 'One month, and I'll make it worth your while. Diamonds. A carat a day.'

'And now he thinks I can be bought...'

Everyone has a price.

'I'll pay triple whatever you paid for my land in the first place.'

'Really not motivated by money...'

What was she motivated by? Had she mentioned anything he could use? Anything at all? 'Ah, but think of the privacy you can buy with it. I hear the Conrad place might be coming on the market soon.' The Conrads were their current neighbours to her north.

She eyed him sharply. 'Who told you that?'

'The Conrads. Look, the only reason I went with the marriage plan in the first place was because I never dreamed you'd be so stup—'

'*Do* keep going,' she murmured dulcetly. 'Dig that hole deep.'

'I never dreamed you'd be so *generous* as to *give* the land back.' Where was the grift in that? The jockeying for every tiny advantage? 'You realise all this could have been avoided if you'd taken my calls?' Ouch. Ow! So much for fancy butter-soft-leather dress shoes. 'Do you know how sharp your shoes are?'

Although not as sharp as her tongue.

In prison, he'd been Mr No Feelings at All.

Ten minutes after clapping eyes on Bridie and a tsunami of emotions was threatening to overwhelm him. Anger, desire, yearning, embarrassment, frustration and more desire—all of it itching to escape him no matter how many other people here tonight would see and use his weakness against him.

For years and years and far too many *years* he'd been waiting for the day when he could come home to Jeddah Creek and put his life back together and build on the legacy his family had left him. He'd make his parents and his brother proud. He'd restore the family name he'd dragged through the dust. He'd become a philanthropic force to be reckoned with.

Instead, here he was, ten days out and about and making an utter fool of himself.

'Don't do anything rash. Avoid split-second decisions.'

Too late for that.

'Give others the benefit of the doubt.'

Missed that one too, even with Tom Starr's blatant plea to do just that.

All he'd sensed was her resistance to selling the land that should have been his and he'd been back in the prison yard, fighting to win.

How could he be so stupid as to let her get under his skin?

It was too hot in this ballroom full of expensively dressed predators.

And what was this wave of cold sweeping over him like nothing he'd felt before? Not when he'd stood before the court, waiting for his sentence to be handed down. Not when he'd tried to stem a dead man's wounds and bathed his hands in blood.

He didn't realise he'd stopped moving until Bridie stepped from his arm and tugged at his hand.

'Come on,' she muttered. 'We've danced enough.'

And then they were leaving the dance floor and heading for the nearest exit, and he did not have control—couldn't even breathe for the iron band around his chest. All he could do was hold on and hope she knew where she was going.

'Blake.'

Devlin Conrad stood in their way, his wife Judith at his side, and both of them were beaming.

'Please, may we be the first to congratulate you on your engagement?' said Judith. 'What a wonderful union. It makes so much sense. And your land-care initiative is music to our ears.' She glanced towards her husband. 'If you added our property into that mix, just imagine what you could do.'

Devlin Conrad nodded. 'We should talk about that.'

He could only nod.

'Are you looking to sell?' asked Bridie.

'Yes, but not to just anyone. To you both. To make our run part of your vision.'

'Done.' How he squeezed the word out he'd never know. But it took the last of his air.

'Yes,' said Bridie quickly. 'We'll be in touch. So sorry, excuse us, we forgot the ring.'

She led him to the veranda and then to the left, around the corner, trying the handle on every door. He'd never noticed before how evenly spaced they were and how much they reminded him of institutional corridors.

At last she found an unlocked door and pulled him in, shutting the door behind them and pushing him against the wall with a surprisingly firm hand. They were in the old stone laundry and the only light came from the slatted shutters high above the door, and with the dark, enclosed space came a fresh panic that had nothing and everything to do with being a fool.

'Breathe,' she demanded, and he would. Soon.

Just as soon as he got out of this cell.

'You're having a panic attack.'

This time it was his turn to lead her through an interior door and into a long lit hallway. Was he blue yet from all the breathing he wasn't doing?

He needed space.

Space and quiet and no people tracking his weakness and waiting for a chance to come at him.

The formal sitting room was at the end of the hall, with its dark jarrah wainscoting and parquetry floor, its pressed tin ceiling and deep blue walls and expanse enough to swing a cow. It also housed several of the most uncomfortable Jacobean needlepoint armchairs in the world, a couple of ancestral portraits and a dusty collection of stuffed hawks.

It was still better than the little concrete laundry.

This time Bridie had the forethought to switch on the light beside the door. Her action lit a naked globe hanging from a long cord in the far corner of the room. There were other switches, other light sources in the room. That one had been left in place to please historians.

'Shall I shut the door or leave it open?' she asked.

'Leave it.' He didn't close doors these days, not one in all the time he'd been home.

'Still not breathing,' she reminded him, and he vowed to get right on that. Might as well hang onto the back of a chair while he was at it, in the interest of staying upright.

Breathe, you scum.

Can't you even do that right?

Breathe.

Bridie walked around the edges of the room, turning table lamps and feature lights on until it was lit up like some kind of mad night at the museum, and he tracked her every step.

There'd been no stuffed birds in prison. Heaven knew it was an odd thought to be having, but he held to it and somehow it reassured him. Breathing resumed. Bridie kept paying him no attention.

'Who's the stuffed hawk collector?' she wanted to know.

'My great-grandfather. The one in the portrait over the fireplace.' The one who'd come to Australia but had never ever managed to call Jeddah Creek station home. A failure, they'd called him. Too pampered for the outback. Soft in the head.

But he *had* stayed the course and built the family wealth for the next generation of Blakes to inherit. Only with his burial back in England had he finally returned home.

Bridie continued her leisurely lap of the room and

stopped in front of the portrait. 'It says here his name was Edward. Very noble.'

'It wasn't a panic attack.'

She stood there looking like an angel in the glow of a butter-yellow lamp as she turned to study a John Constable painting of the English countryside. 'I used to get them a lot,' she said quietly. 'Panic attacks. I thought I recognised the signs. Not that it matters—I needed to get away from the crowd before I had a meltdown too.'

'It wasn't a meltdown.'

''Course not.' She slanted him a look from beneath impossibly long lashes and he promptly lost what little breath he'd managed to scrape together. 'I needed to leave the ballroom. I thought I was serving your needs as well.'

His need was blindingly clear.

This wasn't a prison yard. Bridie hadn't been looking to screw him over. She'd had no beef with him at all, although she probably did *now*. He needed to apologise.

'I'm sorry.' Those words came easier than expected. 'I overreacted when you said you weren't selling the land. I didn't let you finish. I didn't listen and I put you in a bad position.'

He shoved his hands in his pockets and stared at a stuffed goshawk, with its delicately striped breast feathers and sharp yellow eyes.

How a dead bird's glare could shame him into wanting to be a better man he did not know, but that was exactly what it was doing. Or maybe it was the undeniable goodness of the woman who stood quietly in the shadows. Giving him space. Doing her level best to see to his needs.

'I can make another public statement later this evening and break the engagement,' he offered. 'You don't have to be there. People can think what they want.'

Another rash, split-second decision.

Just what he needed.

Bridie trailed her fingers lightly across the carvings on the back of a chair. 'What about the Conrads' offer?'

He'd barely registered that. But he did want their land and he hoped to hell they'd still be interested in selling it to him once he'd called the engagement off.

'I mean, it's not as if you don't have the money,' she continued quietly. 'But they mostly seemed interested in selling it not just to you but to *us*.'

There was that.

'I'd like to hear about your conservation plans too,' she murmured.

He stared.

'And I'm thinking that if we stayed engaged for a while we could both save some face. You could buy the Conrad place, and I could have a fiancé for when I'm in Sydney next. That'd be good.'

She was doing a better job than he was of planning their way out of this mess. 'What's in Sydney?'

'A gallery exhibition of some of my landscape photographs. Part of the agreement is that I be there in person on opening night. You could come too and be my...' Her words tailed off as if she didn't know how to finish that sentence.

'Cattle prod?' he offered.

'That too. You can be my notorious muse if you like. I'm sure the gallery's publicist would be thrilled.'

'When's it on?' He hadn't left Jeddah Station since leaving the correctional centre. Given tonight's performance in public, that was probably a good thing. Was he ready for Sydney? He didn't know. But if he didn't go he'd never know. 'When's your exhibition?'

'Two weeks this coming Thursday. The gallery is at The Rocks and I'm staying at the Ocean View, near the bridge. I'll book another room for you; we wouldn't have to share.'

The thought of sharing a room with her brought forth a whole new set of problems he didn't want to admit to. 'I can do that.' His need to negotiate and control what was happening took hold. 'In return we commit to one month's fake engagement.'

'There's more.'

'More gallery openings?'

'More that I want from you in return for committing to this fake engagement.'

He spread his hands and waited.

She took a deep breath. 'Reid's been talking about building some eco lodges up on the ridges between Jeddah Creek and Devil's Kiss. He wants to bring tourists in. Give them a taste of red dirt and endless skies. Helicopter rides. Quad bike tours. I hate the idea but if it's going to happen, I want to be part of it. Financial investment, a voice when it comes to what type of tourists to target, the lot. It's not that I don't trust Reid, but he's young—'

'And you're not?'

'And enthusiastic,' she continued doggedly. 'And you're talking about putting strangers on my doorstep, and privacy and safety is a huge concern for me. I want a say in how it's done.'

He had no idea what she was talking about. His little brother hadn't yet seen fit to mention those plans. 'I can't promise anything without Reid's input.'

'He looks up to you. He'll follow your lead.'

Judah sincerely hoped not. 'If he does agree to involve

you, we can announce the deal when we break our engagement. Better as business partners and so on. And
for that I want three months' worth of fake engagement
to you.' Having a temporary fiancée might even help
bring others on board with his not-for-profit conservation trust plans. Investors loved a settled man.

'Agreed.'

For someone so seemingly fragile, she certainly knew
how to combat coercion, intimidation and fake engagement announcements. She was making him feel like an
amateur.

'Breathing back to normal now? That band around
your chest loosening up? Chills gone?'

How did she—? Goddamn panic attack symptoms.
'Yes.'

'Great, because Reid and my father are standing in the
doorway and I think they want a word with us.'

Great. Just great. How much had they heard?

He turned, squared his shoulders, and prepared for
the worst.

'Interesting announcement,' said Reid. 'A little warning would have been good.'

'Spur of the moment,' he offered. *Give* him his land
back after buying it fair and square. Who *did* that?

'We'd been talking about land mergers and conservation options and business deals and when the Conrads
started talking about selling we might have got a little
carried away,' said Bridie.

Reid ran a hand across the back of his neck as if working out the kinks. 'So is your engagement like a fake one
to get people on board, or some kind of business merger,
or are we talking the real thing?'

'It's real enough,' said Judah and stared his brother
and her father down. 'Any objections?'

'I'm good.' Reid shared a glance with Tom. 'I'm also going to go find sane people to drink with now. And, uh, good luck.'

Reid left. Tom stayed. The older man looked from one of them to the other and back again, finally settling his shuttered gaze on Judah. 'She'll forgive you anything. You should know this.'

'No, Dad, not anything,' corrected Bridie. 'But I don't think Judah's beyond repair. You don't think he's beyond repair either—you've praised him often enough over the years, remember?'

And why shouldn't he have Tom Starr's approval? Judah wanted to roar.

That night…that crazy, bloated clusterfest of a night that had branded Judah a killer and Tom a grateful father still haunted them all. Would they ever be free of it?

Until this moment he hadn't truly understood that the answer was *no*. The lie at the heart of it would never let him and Tom Starr go. 'Good to know I'm not *beyond repair*.'

'Hey, no, wait. Repair was my word,' Bridie said hurriedly. 'And definitely the wrong word. Dad, I know the engagement announcement surprised you and you want answers. And I'm not going to insult your intelligence by claiming it wasn't a bit spur of the moment. It's probably not going to last, but while we're on a roll why not explore what we might be able to do conservation-wise if we were to combine Jeddah Creek, Devil's Kiss and Talulah Sky? Think about it.'

'If he hurts you—'

'Dad, I'm not sixteen any more. I'm not so naive I can't see the make of a person or whether they're out to harm me. I'm not being taken advantage of. I'm not doing anything I don't want to do, and Judah's not out to harm me.'

Judah and her father locked gazes.

They both knew what happened to people who chose to harm Bridie.

'Let me know when you want to leave,' said Tom. 'I'm ready whenever you are.'

'Half an hour,' she said.

'Half an hour,' echoed her father and left, as if he couldn't stand watching them a moment longer.

'How are you tracking?' she asked when they were alone again, and the honest answer was not well. He kept waiting for retaliation and instead he got fragile little Bridie doing her best to soothe him, humour him and, heaven help them all, *protect* him.

This was not how his world should be.

'Getting there,' he muttered. What else could he say? *Take me back to lockup where I know how the world works?*

He crossed to a painting of wolfhounds racing across a field of green and lifted the painting from its hook to reveal a safe—one of several in the house, but this one housed some of the family's older, finer jewels. Or, given his father's gambling habit, maybe it now held the paste equivalent.

'You need a ring. Come and look.' He gestured her over and opened velvet box after velvet box of jewellery. The diamond and emerald tennis bracelet looked sparkly enough and he opened the clasp. 'Give me your wrist.'

Bridie held out her wrist and he fastened it and thought of the zip ties they used on prisoners and hoped to hell she didn't feel similarly tied down. At least her wrists weren't bound together. 'My grandmother had a diamond and emerald ring that should be in here somewhere. The emerald is the centre stone with two diamonds either side and she had slender hands like you.'

A dozen different rings of various shapes and sizes later, he found the one he was looking for and eased it from its snowy velvet cradle.

There was something timeless about it. The emerald a rich and vivid green that held its own against the diamonds that flanked it, all of it set in filigree white gold.

'Oh, wow,' she said. 'Art deco.'

'Yes or no?'

'Oh, yes.'

She held out her hand. He slid the ring on her finger and it fit as if it had been made for her.

She watched it sparkle for a time and then nodded. 'Beautiful. I'll give it back when we're done.'

'Keep it. When we finish up you should keep it.'

She looked startled. 'I couldn't. It's a family ring, isn't it?'

Why was she so surprised by his generosity when hers had humbled and shamed him? 'And now it's yours.'

Their re-entry into the ballroom brought on a torrent of congratulations and well wishes.

What would he do next, people with bright smiles wanted to know, and then didn't know what to do when he said give back to his community, restore his family name and preserve the land in his care.

Congratulations on your engagement, they said. What a fairy-tale ending for you both.

Let me know when you want to do business, they said, as if he were a goose fat with golden eggs.

Bridie too had to weather a swollen river of effusive comments.

'Look at you, all grown up and so beautiful.' That

seemed to be the general verdict and she wore the comment awkwardly.

'I can't help the way I look,' she murmured to him after one such comment. 'It's not exactly a skill.'

'What a catch you've made,' others said to her in his presence. 'A lord of the realm, fiercely protective and money to burn. Lucky *you*.'

Her hands had begun to shake again.

Maybe it was his turn to rescue her. 'Time's up,' he told her. 'Let's find your father and get you out of here.'

She didn't protest. She did lean over and press her lips to the edge of his mouth in farewell, and it would have taken only the tiniest turn of his head to light a fire he'd have no hope of ever putting out.

'Talk soon,' she said, and he gave the tiniest nod because her scent was in the air and words were beyond him again. 'I want to know which photos of mine you liked best. Make me a pile and once all your visitors have gone I'll show you where I took every one of them. A welcome home trip.'

'You'd do that?'

'Of course I will.' She stood too close. It had been so long since he'd held a woman in his arms, any woman, let alone one who could make his head swim. His control was stretched so very thin. 'It's just kindness.'

Judah returned to his guests and followed his original plan for the evening to make himself available. He drank sparingly and listened to business plans and politicking. He took note of relationships and the levers that sustained them. He filed away every last sniff of information he collected and made no promises whatsoever when it came to what he intended to do with his money. He was back in touch with the movers and shakers of this world and he fully intended to carve out his place in it, but it would be on his terms, not theirs. By the end of the evening the smarter ones had figured as much, and the rest…they'd learn.

When the party wound down and people went back to their luxury planes and had their pilots take them away, or slept in their planes, or stayed on in his guest rooms, Judah took a farm ute and headed north, away from all the people, until he reached a stand of old red river gums with their distinctive bark peeling back to a smooth and ghostly white.

He spread out his swag in the bed of the ute, with the tailgate down and the vast sky above. Thin mattress, canvas cover, and a pillow so soft he could hardly bear the comparison to the prison lump he was used to. He wondered if his brother would suggest he get therapy if he made this his bed for the foreseeable future.

No walls. Just stars.

No other people breathing, snoring or weeping. He'd swapped those sounds for the thrumming of riverbank insects going about their business.

This place. Photo number sixty-two of the eighty-eight photos Bridie had sent to him over the years—he'd memorised each one before carefully handing them back across the desk to be put with the rest of the belongings he'd been stripped of.

She had no idea how much her photos had meant to him, those monthly reminders of who he was and where he belonged.

He'd had no idea how closely they might have documented her steps these past years. From the safety of her back door to the edge of the veranda. From the old Hills Hoist hung with freshly washed clothes to the edge of the house paddock and the windmill and water trough.

Such familiar things, each one set just that little bit further from her homestead.

He wasn't the only one to have lost years of freedom because of the actions of a thwarted madman—he knew that now.

In his absence, she'd built him up to be someone he wasn't, but he'd done exactly the same to her. They needed to move past that if they wanted to be business and land conservation partners. He'd agreed to that, heaven help him. Same way he'd agreed to be her fiancé for the next three months. He who had no business whatsoever being around someone so delicate and beautiful. Someone who could unravel him just by looking in his direction. Someone who could make him forget where he was with the touch of her hand.

He missed intimacy so much and she was right there... ready to forgive him anything. Thinking of him as some kind of hero—and what a joke that was, even if thinking of himself as a hero had made his incarceration that much easier to bear. Protector of the innocent, no matter the cost. Honourable to the end. A man of his word.

A *good* man.

Until tonight, when he'd ripped that myth apart.

Forcing an unwanted engagement on Bridie. Lying about it to his brother and her father and everyone else in order to save face and belatedly offer Bridie what protection he could. Pledging to buy Conrad land under false pretences. Wanting to take Bridie's sweet, parting kiss and turn it into an inferno.

Not exactly a good man any more, was he?

'Don't do anything rash. Avoid split-second decisions.'

'Give yourself time to adjust.'

'Give others the benefit of the doubt.'

He'd done *none* of that and Bridie had paid the price with an engagement she couldn't possibly want. He'd allowed Bridie to protect *him* when he'd fallen apart, and that couldn't happen again. He needed to undo all the tics he'd learned in prison and figure out who he was and who he wanted to be, and above all keep his desire for Bridie's touch to himself and *not* take advantage of her goodwill and sweet nature and sense of obligation.

Pull yourself together, Judah, don't be a disgrace.
Be a better man.
Rather than be ashamed.

CHAPTER THREE

'WHERE'VE YOU BEEN?'

Judah halted at the question his brother threw at him from his position behind the kitchen counter. A large cooktop and a couple of ovens lined the wall behind his brother, with a cool room at one end and a regular fridge at the other. Odd, how such a seemingly innocent question might grate on a man who'd been forced to account for every minute of his day for such a long time. Or maybe not so odd at all.

'Because I made a heap of breakfast for the guys before they left and I saved you some. So what'll it be?' his brother continued, oblivious to Judah's scowl. 'The works? Bacon, sausages, tomato, scrambled eggs, toast. Or there's the veggo option of bruschetta. I didn't make that one. Nico's training to be a chef.'

'And Nico is…?'

'A friend from school. Trent Nicholson. Good man.'

He should probably stop thinking of his brother and all his friends as boys. He should also stop being so quick to take offence. Soon would be good. Making some kind of decision about what to eat for breakfast would be good too. *Any time now, slowpoke, you can do it.* He doubted the prison psych's advice to take his time when making decisions applied to something as simple as food choice. 'I'll take the second one.'

'Coffee too?'

'You're speaking my language.'

Reid beamed and set about getting the fancy machine to produce liquid heaven, and Judah finally forgave him that very first 'where've you been?'. 'You said your friends have already gone?' The city caterers were still around, he'd seen them on his way in, but they too were scheduled to leave by lunchtime. Solitude again.

'Yeah. Couple of them could have stayed on, but I didn't know how you'd feel about that. You were pretty clear about wanting everyone gone by this morning.'

'That didn't include your school friends. This is your home too.' Clearly, they had some work to do when it came to communicating wants and needs.

Reid slung food and coffee in front of him and Judah pulled up a stool and tucked in, still silently marvelling at the taste of good food. Not to mention he now had unlimited access to all kinds of kitchen utensils that could so easily be shaped into shivs. Not that he needed to shape anything into a shiv, given that a row of kitchen knives was right there behind his brother, stuck to a magnetic strip on the wall.

His brother followed Judah's gaze. 'You keep looking at them. Why?'

Probably not a good idea to mention that he was counting them. Again. And that he counted them every time he walked into the room to make sure they were all still there.

'They can go in a drawer if you like.'

'Then I'd have to open the drawer to count them and that'd be worse.'

Reid had his mouth open and his fork loaded but everything stopped at Judah's gravelly confession.

'I see,' he offered quietly, and then slowly filled his mouth with food.

Judah tried to see any trace of his freckle-faced eleven-year-old brother in the quiet eighteen-year-old stranger sitting across from him and could find none. Reid was whipcord lean, tanned and a recent haircut had gone some way towards taming his thick, wavy brown hair. His blue eyes were still as bright as Judah remembered, except laughter had been replaced by a wariness usually reserved for freshwater crocs.

'I expect it'll take a while for you to adapt,' his little brother said carefully. 'I had some calls from a social worker before you got out. She gave me a bit of a run-down on what to expect.'

'What did she tell you?'

'Are you feeling angry, frustrated and depressed yet?'

'Not yet.'

'Good start.' Reid nodded encouragingly, and for some reason Judah wanted to laugh. 'Anything changed so much you barely recognise it?'

'Apart from you? No.'

'Do you feel overwhelmed?'

Last night didn't count. 'No.'

'Any negative influences I should know about?'

'I had a run-in with a horsefly yesterday and won. I'll try not to hang around them too often.'

'Good luck with that out here. Any addictions?'

'Not yet. And I doubt I'm going to become addicted to your breakfast conversation.'

'Har har. I'm checking in with you like they told me to. Guess you pass the test.' Reid nodded his approval. 'You want to come flying with me today? I can show you the new access road and set of yards we put in up near Pepper Tree Ridge.'

'You could.'

'We could pick Bridie up on the way. She likes it up there.'

Why wouldn't Reid and Bridie get together every now and then and have formed a friendship born of common ground and neighbourliness? Why did he scowl at the thought of it? 'I'd rather we didn't include Bridie. Not today.'

'Trouble in engagement land already?'

'No.' How much should he confess? But the thought of looking like a weakling idiot in front of his brother didn't sit well with him. He was the *older* brother, dammit. 'But it's not exactly a traditional engagement and I like a bit of distance.'

'I'll say,' muttered Reid and narrowed his gaze. 'Do you blame her?'

'For what?'

'For getting kidnapped and you having to sully your soul and kill a man in order to get her back?' Reid had a frown on his face.

'Do I blame Bridie for my sullied soul? No.' He didn't *have* a sullied soul. Not yet, and he aimed to keep it that way.

For the first five years of his incarceration he'd stuck steadfastly to the idea that it was nothing more than his *duty* to protect the weakest link in his world. Damn right he could still look at himself in the mirror and know he'd done the right thing.

His resolve had faltered somewhere around the seven-year mark when his mother died.

When his father had followed not two months later, passing so swiftly they hadn't even been able to arrange prison leave for Judah to say goodbye, Judah's resolve had faltered some more.

He'd missed so much. Left his parents alone out here, then left Reid to fend for himself. Reid, who for these past six months had been in charge of thirty-odd thousand square kilometres of some of the most dangerous and inhospitable grazing land in Australia. A property Reid didn't even have a claim to because Judah as first-born son had inherited the lot. But not one scrap of that was Bridie's doing or Bridie's fault. 'I don't blame Bridie for any of that. My actions, my responsibility.'

'Hero.'

'In your dreams.'

'Yep. Big hero.'

'You keep thinking like that and I'll only disappoint you. I don't want to disappoint you, Reid. I want to get to know you and for you to know me.'

A sentiment that silenced his brother completely.

'Bridie mentioned last night about you wanting to build tourist lodges up on the ridges,' Judah continued carefully. 'Care to share?'

His brother nodded, his eyes brightening. 'I want to build a couple of luxury eco-tourism lodges up above river bend. Fly-in fly-out, a minimum five-day package, with fishing, sunset cookouts, stargazing, sunrise wellness yoga or something, I don't know, and day trips out to Carper's Ridge. This is my home and I love it, but it's lonely, and that won't change unless we change it, you know?'

'Or you could move to where the people are.'

Reid held his gaze. 'Is that what you want me to do? Go? Firstborn takes all when it comes to land, I know that. And I can set down elsewhere if you want me gone. But you asked me what I want, so I'm telling you. I want to stay here. I want to fly interesting people around and find out how this place inspires them. I want a home of my own, one day, on Jeddah Creek land or nearby, and if you buy the Conrad place, maybe I could go there. Eventually or something.'

'Definitely.'

'Yes!' Reid flung his arms in the air and did a lap of the kitchen island, every inch the teenager. 'Yes! My hero.' Reid came at him from behind, wrapping his long arms around him and kissing him on the side of the head. Whatever discomfort with physical contact Judah had with people, Reid clearly hadn't inherited it.

'Don't make me lunge for the kitchen knives, man,' Judah protested. 'Get off me.'

'I love you.' Hug. 'My brother the land baron.' Kiss.

'Okay, that's enough.'

'Mate, we need to work on your people skills,' said Reid, returning to his side of the counter, thank God. He was like an overgrown puppy. 'But apart from you buying all the land, and me wanting in on that deal in any way I can, what do you think of my eco-tourism idea?'

'Would you like a silent, cashed-up brother for a partner?'

'Hell, yes.'

'What about a concerned neighbour for a partner? One who wants a say in how things will be run?'

'Tom?'

'Bridie.'

Reid frowned and scratched his head. 'Bridie wouldn't be silent.'

His take as well. 'Correct. But if we're going to have a tourist area we need a development plan. Set limits that won't be crossed and have happy neighbours, Bridie in particular, and make sure she doesn't feel threatened by you bringing strangers onto their land.'

'You're protecting her,' said Reid with a sigh.

'Would you prefer I didn't?'

'No.' Reid scratched his hair and left a peacock's ruffle in the dark mess. 'Or yes. Maybe I want her to push on more than she does.' He shrugged. 'Maybe we can do three lodges. One for your use, one for mine, one for Bridie and her photography. She could run courses. Teach.'

'Or maybe she won't be into that at all,' Judah warned. 'But you could ask.'

Reid nodded. 'Or you could.'

'Silent partner, remember?'

'Not so silent now though, are you?'

'Set a business up to serve a need and it'll grow. And, yeah.' He'd been thinking about conservation management plans for years and he liked where his brother's head was at. 'Maybe not so silent after all.'

Bridie couldn't quite comprehend what her father was saying. Possibly because he was saying very little.

'I'm heading off for a while.' That had been his first sentence, swiftly followed by, 'Don't expect me back any time soon.'

'But where are you going?' She followed him out to his twin cab as he tossed an old-fashioned suitcase in the back. The vehicle was old enough to need new shock absorbers and back brakes and probably a couple of tyres. Serviceable enough when driving around the ten thousand or so square miles they called Devil's Kiss, but beyond that he was pushing his luck.

'But where are you going?' she asked again when he didn't respond.

'Might go and see your aunt for a while.'

'In the Kimberleys?' Because that was where Aunt Beth lived, and as well as needing a reliable vehicle to get there, even a one-way trip was likely to take days. Her father had never once left her here alone for days. 'Is she sick?'

He shrugged, squirrelly and unable to meet her gaze.

'Are *you* sick?' Although, if he was, surely he'd be heading east for medical care rather than west.

'No. I just need to get away from here for a while. Maybe a long while.'

And then he pulled her close, kissed her cheek, muttered, 'Take care of yourself, love,' and was gone in a cloud of dust that would linger for half an hour before settling.

She stood alone, hands on hips, in front of the white wooden homestead, a few carefully tended gum trees flanking it, and watched him go with a sinking feeling she hadn't felt in years.

Not as if he were leaving her unprotected.

She was a perfectly healthy twenty-three-year-old, born and raised on Devil's Kiss remote cattle station and perfectly comfortable around spiders, snakes, reptiles, feral pigs and uncivilised bulls. She knew every bit of this land and the people on it.

Curtis and his elderly partner, Maria, lived in the station-hand house—retired now and living rent free in exchange for the safety of their company and a few odd jobs here and there.

Jake and Cobb were salaried cattlemen and they and their wives and children lived in newer cottages further north and closer to town. She could call on them at any time if anything that she couldn't do needed doing.

She had Gert for three days every fortnight, and Gert

even had a room in the house. It wasn't as if Bridie was being abandoned in the middle of nowhere.

Shucking her boots at the door—because why undo all of Gert's hard work?—she stepped into the kitchen area of the grand old homestead that glittered like a shimmery jewel in a desert of burnt umber. It was a one-storey house, not nearly as big as the Blake place, but similarly Victorian flavoured. It had a corrugated-iron roof and wraparound verandas framed by elaborate wrought-iron lacework. Stone walls kept the inside of the house reasonably cool and the windows and abundance of French doors leading onto the verandas let in light, but not sunshine, and that too helped to keep the scorching heat at bay. Nothing ever kept the dust out.

Gert looked up as Bridie entered, the screen door clicking shut behind her. 'All good?'

'Hard to say. Dad just lit out for parts unknown like his tail was on fire. And I don't know when he'll return. I don't understand. He seemed fine last night. Even after the engagement announcement.'

'About that...' Gert had been at the ball. 'Bit of a surprise.'

'Mm. More of a business arrangement than anything else.'

'Will we be seeing him here today?'

'Judah?' She had no idea when she'd be seeing him again. 'Er...not that I know of. Deals to cut, guests to farewell, that kind of thing.' She assumed...

'You should see if he wants to come over. I'm making ginger snaps.'

'I don't share your ginger snaps with just anyone.'

'Not even your fiancé?'

'Maybe if he asks nicely. Anyway, I'm heading for the darkroom. If anyone phones, come and get me.'

'You mean if your fiancé phones?'

'Or Reid.' Reid might want to talk with her about the way she was trying to shoehorn in on his tourism plans. 'Or Dad.' Just in case he saw fit to tell her what was wrong. 'But if anyone from the gallery calls, I'm not here. I'm out getting that final shot and it absolutely will be with them before opening night.'

Gert snorted and flapped her hand in Bridie's direction. 'Go.'

Bridie usually found developing film and pictures the old-fashioned way cathartic, but not today. Today her spacious darkroom reminded her of the lengths to which her father had gone to make it not remind her of the car boot she'd been bundled into during her abduction.

They'd fitted an old sitting room out with a revolving no-light no-lock door, and red LED strip lights. They'd covered windows and built benches and hung clothes lines for photos to hang from. These days her set-up was as good as any commercial darkroom in the city. Not that there were many of those left, given the advances in digital photography and automatic printing.

Thing was, she loved watching an image appear, ghostly at first, and then more certain, except today she wasn't feeling very certain about anything.

Why had her father left Devil's Kiss so suddenly? Had Judah's reappearance dredged up too many ugly memories for him? He'd never say that, of course. Keep going, move on, no need to obsess.

She and her father had each been given ten free psych sessions after the event, courtesy of some government programme or other, and surely there was nothing left to talk about or even think about after that?

Facts were facts. Her father and Judah had been driving farm utes and between them had railroaded Laurence Levit and his zippy little sports car straight off the beaten track and into the superfine red dirt. Laurence's car, with her in the boot, had bumped over shrubbery and swerved hard before coming to a stop, bogged to the axels, and no amount of revving had done anything but dig them deeper.

Car doors had slammed. Bridie had started kicking and hadn't heard much, but she had heard the shot. Then Judah had been there, reaching for her, his face pale and shocked. A rufus red moon had hung low in the sky, silvery light glinting off the blade of the knife he'd used to cut the tape that had bound her hands and feet. She'd clung to him like a burr and his arms around her had been like bands of warm steel and he'd smelled like sweat and fear.

Her father hadn't tried to save Laurence at all, but Judah had tended the fallen man once he'd handed her off to her father. His efforts after the fact had earned him a charge of manslaughter rather than murder. He'd been just twenty, younger than she was now. Twenty and imprisoned on her account, and she'd always had a hard time finding the justice in that, but there was no point dwelling on it.

Move on, said her father, who'd been wholly uncomfortable in Judah's presence last night, and who'd taken off this morning for places unknown.

Bridie's big, beautifully appointed darkroom, which she usually took so much pleasure in, wasn't working for her today. Not when memories held sway. Better to be out and about, searching for that elusive final photograph for her exhibition—the one that would link all the rest of them. She already knew what needed to be in that shot. Fear. Foreboding. Freedom. Wonder.

All she had to do was look through the lens and find them.

'Change of plans, Gert. I'm heading out to take some shots and I'll be back before you leave.' Bridie sailed through the kitchen and ducked into the wet room for her boots and hat. 'Wish me luck.'

Two days later, with the weather radar promising late-afternoon thunderstorms if they were lucky, Judah finally paid her a visit. Gert was at Judah's now and her father still hadn't called, and if the sight of Judah strong and stern and unmistakably present made her unaccountably happy, probably best not to mention it.

'Greetings, fiancé of mine. How's it going?' she asked, aiming for breezy and doing a fair job of it if his almost smile was any indication.

'Not bad.'

She loved the rumble in his voice and the way he stood at the bottom of the steps, boots planted firmly in the dirt and his jeans clinging to strong legs. His cotton shirt had seen better days and the sleeves had been rolled up to expose corded forearms and prominent veins. He wore a black felt hat that dipped at the front, pinched at the top and sat level at the sides. He looked so quintessentially of the outback that it put her at ease. No matter where life had taken him, he'd grown up here, he knew this place the same way she did and there was comfort in that, and security. 'If only your wheeling, dealing billionaire buddies could see you now. What brings you by?'

'Gert said your father was away.'

'Yup.'

'For how long?'

'He didn't say.'

'I've been trying to get hold of him.' Judah studied

her from beneath the brim of his hat and she wished she
could see his eyes a little more clearly.

'Join the club. But if he's heading for Broome, he's
likely well out of range.'

'What's in Broome?'

'My aunt.' The same aunt who'd travelled with Bridie
to Paris all those years ago, both of them so totally out
of their league they'd been easy pickings for a predator
like Laurence. He'd been Bridie's modelling agent, and
her aunt Bethany had never stood a chance against his
calculated seduction. It had made his obsessive control
over Bridie's career all the more insidious. His growing
need to possess Bridie in every way possible had kicked
in some time after that.

'How is Beth?'

'She blames herself for bringing Laurence into our
lives and not realising how dangerous he was. She went
into exile after the kidnapping. My father says she's too
ashamed to show her face here.'

Judah frowned. 'That's cracked.'

'I know. I miss her hugs.' But he wasn't here to get
the low-down on her dysfunctional family. 'Have you
asked Reid about me joining you guys in the eco-tourism business?'

He nodded.

'And?'

'You're in.'

'Yes!'

'But it's growing as we put together a mission statement and growth goals.'

Say what now? 'Meaning?'

'I want to roll Reid's project into some broader, stra-
tegic land preservation plans I have for the area. Buy the

Conrad place. See if your father will turn over some of Devil's Kiss land to the project.'

Mr Moneybags and clever along with it. How many times would she have to shift her take on this man, now that he was home? 'I'm about to head out and try and get some shots of the storm front coming in. Want to fill me in while I'm doing that?'

He looked towards the darkening sky. 'You want to be out in that?'

She so did. 'By my calculations it's going to break over the eastern channel plain. I aim to be just east of Pike's river crossing when it does.'

'And your father's not here to know if you'll return. I'll come.'

A blessing for protective neighbours. 'I'll drive.'

Five minutes later they were on their way, heading out in her Land Rover, and she tried not to obsess too much about how good Judah smelled. Some kind of body wash or soap with a hint of woody musk. Expensive. Totally wasted on cattle, but definitely not wasted on her.

'Can I photograph you today?' And before he could say no or ask why: 'From a distance and for dramatic impact and perspective. You against the storm.' A fitting end to a set of photos that had always been about him, whether he knew it or not. 'A visual reminder for me that you're back where you belong and maybe now we can all move on.'

He looked out of the window and didn't answer, and she didn't push. He hadn't said no, and that meant he was thinking about it. If he at some point put himself in her camera's way she'd have her answer and they wouldn't need to talk about it ever again.

'Tell me about this exhibition of yours,' he said, and she had no problem at all with that request. 'Twenty of

my best photos, printed and framed and about to be hung
by professional curators in a light-filled gallery in fancy-
pants Sydney. I need one more, and I'm fretting because
I don't have it. The home run. The closer.'

'And this storm's going to give it to you?'

'Maybe.'

Already the sky was darkening to the west, the red
dirt beginning to glow with that peculiar Armageddon
light. Every contrast more vivid for not being bleached
away by a relentless sun. Oncoming clouds, light at the
edges and deepest grey in the middle, heavy with the
promise of life-giving rain and the not-so-subtle threat
of utter carnage.

Best not to get caught out in these fast-moving
cloudbursts or they could be bogged for days, but she'd
checked the wind direction earlier and figured they'd be
able to stay just south of it.

Assuming the wind didn't change.

She headed off track and they cut across the loose dirt
and scrub until she reached a shallow river crossing that
the vehicle made short work of. She pulled up on a wave
of dirt not long afterwards. From here the ground undu-
lated to the north and west and flattened to the east and,
with the right light and the right lens, subtle panorama
contrasts could be found.

Set-up only took a few minutes. Tripod and cameras,
lenses and light meter and Judah watching in silence, his
very fine butt planted on the bonnet of her ride, knees
bent and his boot heels hooked over the bottom rung of
the bull bar.

'Storm's that way,' he rumbled when she snuck one
too many glances in his direction.

'There's a food basket in the back if you're hungry.'
She'd hit the fridge hard after he'd said he would join

her. Double brie, quince paste and fancy crackers, she had 'em. Anzacs with wattle seed. Dark chocolate with raisins. Leftover ham sandwiches with real butter and Gert's magic relish. She had it all. A honeymoon basket, she'd thought with horror as she packed it, and had thrown in a couple of tins of baked beans and a round of salami in case they got stuck and also so that it wouldn't be a honeymoon basket any more. 'Drinks are in the esky.'

'Are you practising for when the lodges are built and you're bringing city photographers out here?'

'Yes. That's what I'm doing.'

Not trying to honeymoon him at all.

She'd made him grin and wasn't that a pretty sight? Her fingers itched for a camera even as she turned her back on him and bent to put her eye to the nearest camera and tripod. She wanted to play around with the zoom on this one. Heading back to her kit, she fished out a thin wire presser that would allow her to take a shot without pressing any buttons on the camera itself and creating movement she didn't want.

'You have a lot of gear.'

More than she needed, true. She'd once thought that taking the perfect shot was all about the gear, but experience had taught her differently. 'I don't need half of it. I have my favourite cameras and lenses and I know how to get the best out of them. Live and learn.'

She could feel him looking at her. The weight of his gaze skittered down her spine, but she refused to turn around. 'I kind of do better if I think of life as a learning curve. Mistakes are part of it.'

She took a few shots, fine-tuned the set-up, and then hauled the picnic basket onto the bonnet next to him, fished out a ham sandwich and waited for the storm. It might not pass this way. She might have misjudged it.

But she didn't think so.

Several minutes later Judah dug into the picnic basket too and she waited for some snide remark about her food choices.

Instead, he looked utterly lost for a split second before muttering, 'All right, I am here for this,' and digging in.

He ate as if he'd been underfed for years and she ate up that vulnerability in him because it made him less perfect in her eyes, more human.

And then the world turned amber and the storm clouds rolled in.

She got to work as he packed away the picnic, always aware of him but focused on capturing the landscape in front of her.

When he sauntered out in it, welcoming the rain that raced across the plain towards them, she photographed him. The strength in his silhouette and the acceptance of the storm as he stretched out his arms and received the opening lash of stinging rain. Violence. Renewal. Nothing was fixed, least of all him, but he was her focus. Judah Blake, killer and saviour, his hat in hand and his face tilted skywards. Vulnerable and mighty.

Back in this place that had built him.

It was a spur-of-the-moment thought that made her set her cameras to take continuous shots so she could join him, taking his hand and drawing him into a dance more elemental by far than the one they'd shared at the ball. They spun and they stomped and tears filled her eyes and she let them because they'd mingle with raindrops and wash away and who would know the difference?

'You're here,' she yelled, as lightning lit the sky and

thunder rumbled and the rain pelted against them. 'I'm so glad you're here.'

And then he pulled her towards him, kissed her, and Bridie's careful, considered world exploded. When the debris cleared there was only rain and Judah, bringing her to life in ways she'd only ever dared to imagine.

Whatever he had to give, she could take it and it wasn't because of some nebulous sense of obligation for all that he had done. She wanted him.

He was back where he belonged, and she wanted him and that was all.

With a ruthlessness born of necessity, she drew him in.

CHAPTER FOUR

JUDAH HAD NEVER spun out of control so fast or slaked his need with such ruthlessness as he did now. Any gentleness he'd ever owned was gone, washed clear away as he framed her face with his hands, the better to devour her.

Bridie's hands were restless, trapped little fluttering sparrows at his chest, his waist, restless until she burrowed beneath his shirt and found skin.

He pulled her closer, his hardness impossible to conceal against her softness. His hands slid lower, lifting, positioning, unable to stop himself from thrusting against her.

Let me in.

She stilled. She tried to speak, or sigh, or maybe it was a protest, and that last thought was enough to douse him more thoroughly than any storm ever could. She didn't want this.

She didn't want him.

He wrenched his lips from hers and buried his face against her neck, nowhere near ready to let go of her and back away, but he had to.

'I'm sorry,' he grated.

'Hm?' She wove her fingers through his hair, keeping him there as she burrowed in closer.

He had no finesse. To rut against her much longer and

that would be him gone, spent and sticky in his jeans—worse if he managed to get her out of her jeans because then there'd be nothing to halt his reckless, greedy descent into animal behaviour. Judah cursed and put his hands to Bridie's hips, put some air between them, the better to get his brain to start functioning.

Her gaze met his, glazed, confused. 'Why are we stopping? This is perfect. You're perfect.'

What a thing to say to a man like him. 'You don't even know me.'

She stepped back, eyes narrowing, and her hands went to her hips. 'I could get to know you. We could get to know each other and then maybe we could do more of the kissing.'

'It wouldn't stop at kissing.'

'So? I wouldn't want it to.'

'You don't know me.'

'But I'd like to.'

He tried again to make her see reason. To understand his position. 'You won't like what you find.'

'How do you know?'

'After what I did to you at the ball, how could you *not* know?'

She looked at him a good long while, mindless of the pelting rain, and then took a careful step back. 'You're too hard on yourself, Judah. But if you don't want what I'm offering, I can't make you take it. We can just call it a spur-of-the-moment kiss. Forget it ever happened.'

'Let's do that.' He'd spent too many years thinking of this woman as fragile and terrified and young. And maybe she'd grown in years but she had no experience with someone as greedy for touch as him. As unstable as him. Seven long years and counting, and he didn't trust himself to be the kind of lover she needed. 'Trust me, it's for the best.'

He tilted his face to the sky and let the stinging rain pellets wash him clean of his burning desire to get naked and dirty with a woman too pure for him to sully. 'Please. We're not doing this.'

Had she touched him again his resolve might have broken, but she turned away and trudged back to her cameras, and he could only hope those canvas covers she'd set up over the camera bodies had done enough to protect them from the downpour.

By the time he came back in and Bridie had packed up, the storm had passed and red mud caked his boots. She passed him a towel in silence, not quite meeting his gaze, and he gruffly thanked her.

He couldn't have felt any worse.

'Are you ready to leave?' she asked quietly.

Note to self: never reject a woman's advances without having your own ride home.

The drive back took three times as long on account of the rain, but they didn't get bogged and eventually they pulled up alongside his truck. Bridie's hair had started to dry in loose curls to frame her face. Such a perfect profile to go with her long lashes and flawless skin. No wonder the modelling world had gone all in for her. No wonder the predators had come circling.

He made a hasty exit and then turned back towards her—simultaneously glad to be out of the car and shamed by his mishandling of the afternoon. 'Look, Bridie, you're very beautiful.'

She had a fierce glare. 'Tell me something I don't know.'

'I haven't had sex in nearly eight years and my self-control is hanging by a thread. I don't want your gratitude, your pity or to hurt you, so it's best I stay away from you. See out this farce of an engagement and then leave you be. Do no harm. Savvy?'

'Got it. You're too big, bad and dangerous for innocent little me.' She stomped towards her homestead and he figured that was it, but then she turned and fixed him with a soggy kitten glare. 'Does anyone actually believe that's who you are?'

'You'd better believe it,' he yelled, because seriously. 'Shouldn't you be *thanking* me?'

'For being a tool? Why does that need praise?'

'For my restraint!'

For stopping when he did, so as not to overwhelm her? For *protecting* her? Again, because apparently it was his lot in life to get screwed over for love of protecting Miss Bridie Starr, bane of his existence.

I'm not depressed, he could tell Reid when he got back to the house.

I'm peeling out of my skin for want of a woman I dare not touch.

Apparently, I'm also an idiot.

Bridie spent the rest of the day seething, developing film, and coming to the bald realisation that she'd somehow just taken some of the best photos of her life. Danger. Foreboding. Homecoming. Pleasure.

The cameras she'd set up to take a shot every thirty seconds had caught those moments of them together and they were more beautiful than she could ever have imagined, and she couldn't ever show them to Judah, or anyone else, because he'd turned her down.

For reasons that made no sense.

'Complete and utter idiot,' she muttered the following morning as she dumped a tea bag into a huge mug and switched the jug on to boil some water. Because she'd had glorious love-soaked dreams all last night and she most certainly had not let the memory of yesterday's kisses go. *Hell, no.*

'Are you talking about my brother?' a voice wanted to know, from somewhere over near the doorway, and there stood Reid, hat in hand and hair unruly. 'Because he's also a surly bastard.'

'What are you doing here?'

'I came to talk business. I'm also here to check up on you and see if your father's home yet.'

And that was another reason for her foul mood. 'I haven't heard from him.'

'Have you spoken to your aunt?'

'Not since the trial,' she muttered darkly. 'And before you ask, I never cut her off. I love my aunt, even if she's *another* complete and utter moron. She blames herself for being taken in by a monster who courted her to get to me, and she's too ashamed to speak to me. I phoned. I wrote. I *begged* her to come see me. To forgive herself because I sure as hell didn't hold her responsible for someone else's insanity. Fat lot of good it did.'

'Er...right.'

'How come I didn't hear your helicopter?'

'I came on the dirt bike.'

She hadn't heard that either. Existing in a world of her own, her father would have said had he been around. Which he wasn't. *Stubborn old goat.* 'And you're also here on business, you said?'

'Yep. Tourist lodge business. What are your thoughts on retractable roofs and floor-to-ceiling glass windows?'

Bridie blinked.

'So that someone who, say, doesn't like feeling

hemmed in and doesn't like sleeping indoors, doesn't have to sleep in a swag in the back of his ute every night.'

Reid sent her a beseeching look, inviting her to buy into his problems, but she didn't want to because she knew exactly where Reid's problems led. 'Judah?'

'Yep.'

Right.

'I just want to make it easier for him to get his life back, you know?' Reid continued. 'He's not always… coping. And it's the little stuff.'

Judah didn't exactly appear to be coping all that well with the big stuff either—if impromptu wanton kisses followed by a hasty retreat could be classified as such. Or maybe she was the only needy wanton person around here. 'What's not to love about disappearing ceilings and walls? Turn all the lights on and bring every insect for six kilometres around for a feed.'

'Okay, so my plans might need work,' Reid conceded. 'Wanna help?'

Two hours passed as they sketched cabin design after cabin design and talked about how best to accommodate eccentric guests with all sorts of needs. Reid's enthusiasm was contagious, and Bridie's interest in putting lodges on the ridges became real. She *wanted* this project to succeed. Two hours and three arguments later, they had a cabin layout they both liked. Bridie sat back, pleased with their progress. 'I'm on board with this.'

'Don't sound so shocked.'

'But I *am* shocked. I want these eco-tourism plans to work. I want to bring people here.'

Reid grinned and punched a fist in the air. 'I knew it! And you're going to be a world-famous photographer soon. That's a given.'

She put her palms to her face and rubbed as butterflies

found a home in her stomach at the thought of the final picture she'd chosen for the exhibition. 'I'm going to try.' The words came out muffled. 'What if the media fixates on my past, instead of my work? Drags me through the mud, and Judah too? And by extension, you.' She lowered her hands. Her fears came from a place of experience. 'You were probably too young to remember the way the press treated the story.'

'I was at boarding school. Believe me, I remember.' Oh. 'Sorry.'

'Not your fault, but you're right when it comes to not wanting to stir up that hornet's nest.' Reid picked up a pencil and began to number the cabin plans. 'I want to protect my big mean-dog brother. He's not nearly as tough and indestructible as he thinks he is. I thought your father would be here to help me.'

But her father wasn't here. 'How can I help?'

'Judah wants to talk about putting some Jeddah Creek, Conrad's and Devil's Kiss land into a conservation trust. Get your father to give him a call so he can get moving on that.'

'What else? And by that I mean something that's vaguely within my control.'

'Maybe invite him around for breakfast or call him once a day or something, so he knows you're okay over here. Same way you and Tom used to tag-team me after Dad died. Just…check in once a day. He worries about you over here on your own, and so do I.'

'I'll group-text you both a photo every day.' Problem solved.

'He could use a friend.'

'Reid—' She shook her head, hoping he'd understand without her having to explain. 'My feelings for your brother are complicated. Friendship's a stretch. There's so much in the way of it.'

Physical attraction. Saviour status. Rejection...

'What if you try befriending him in Sydney? Do stuff together. Sightsee and all that. That could work.' Reid sounded so hopeful. 'But don't be surprised if he stays out all night. He does that. I think it's because he can't stand sleeping inside four walls.'

Maybe she could order a roll-out bed to put on a balcony. Or she could just walk with him through the city all night long, befriending him. Which would make her the grumpiest emerging landscape photographer ever. 'I will be a sphinx in the face of your brother's strange sleeping habits. No comment.'

'Thanks.'

She enjoyed watching Reid striding past his teen years and turning into a truly caring and responsible young man. 'That's if he decides to come to Sydney with me at all. He might not.'

'He said he would, didn't he? My brother keeps his word.'

'Yes, but maybe I shouldn't have pressed him to come with me in the first place.' She'd been thinking of her own challenges when it came to stepping out of her comfort zone. 'It honestly never occurred to me that Judah might have issues with those surroundings, and frankly it should have.' She needed to stop clinging to her Judah-as-Superman fantasy. It was self-indulgent at best and had the potential to be downright destructive.

'I'll go alone.' Gulp. 'That's fine. I'll give your brother a call and let him know I've had a change of plans. I can invent a girlfriend who's joining me or something. Give the man an out.'

'I didn't say to sideline him,' objected Reid. 'A change

of scenery might do him good. What's wrong with sticking to the current plan and being there for him, if he needs a friend?'

'Yeah, but...' Reid didn't know about the kissing.

'Don't make me pull the *You owe him compassion and understanding* card.' Reid looked utterly serious. 'Because I will.'

'Oh, that's harsh.'

Reid glared.

'Can we agree that I need to at least give him the option of not going with me to Sydney seeing as, by your own admission, he's not coping with the little things?'

Reluctantly, Reid agreed.

Bridie did phone Judah later that afternoon. Not much of a phone conversationalist, Judah, and Bridie was little better.

They did 'hey' and 'hope this isn't a bad time to call' before she got down to the business of giving him an out when it came to him joining her in Sydney. 'Hey, so I'm thinking of heading to Sydney a day earlier than planned, and that's probably not going to work for you, so maybe you might want to rethink joining me at all?'

'Is this about the kissing?'

'Ah, no? Not entirely. As in, I'm aware there'll be no kissing if you do come.'

'It's for your own good.'

Did he seriously believe what he was saying? She had a feeling he did. How did such a good man develop a mindset that he was no good at all? Had his years in prison damaged him beyond repair? 'Yes, well. Not sure I agree with you there, but moving on. You don't have to come.'

'Is your father meeting you there?'

'Er…' She still hadn't heard from him. 'I'm going to go with no.'

'He still hasn't been in touch,' he guessed flatly.

'No, and I'm worried about him, but that's a different conversation.'

'I can come to Sydney a day earlier with you. Not a problem.'

Oh. 'Even if it's awkward between us?'

'When is it not?'

The man had a point. 'Okay, well, thank you. Wednesday departure, then, and a Saturday return.' How had she managed to add another day to the trip rather than cutting him loose? *Good job, dimwit. Really good job.* 'It's really not a problem if I go alone. You saw me at the ball, navigating people with ease.' Slight stretch of the truth there. 'I am all prepped.'

'Good to hear, but I'm still coming with you.' She could hear the iron in his voice. 'I gave you my word.'

CHAPTER FIVE

SYDNEY HARBOUR GLITTERED like the jewel it was as the plane banked hard, allowing Bridie a bird's eye view of the bridge, the Opera House, the skyscrapers and the roofscapes of the suburbs beyond. She and Judah had flown first-class commercial from Cairns, picking up the final leg of an inbound plane's international flight, and from the moment she'd boarded, Bridie had been having a champagne experience.

And her pleasure might just be contagious, given Judah's wry grin every time food or beverages were offered.

She'd opted for an easy-travel fabric—synthetic, lightweight, no crush—and the draping neckline of her shirt likely plunged a little too low, and her shoes were once again sky-high, but she'd added a scarf in every imaginable shade of blue and draped it just so, and she was surviving the nakedly admiring glances strangers kept giving her with surprising nonchalance.

Pretty woman. She'd owned that label once and made a career of it. It had brought Laurence into her life, but it had also opened her up to the world beyond Devil's Kiss, and that world had once been her oyster. Maybe it could be again.

All she needed was confidence enough to seize it. Blazing confidence.

Except for those moments when she kept fiddling with

the bracelet Judah had given her, or twisting her engagement ring around and rubbing at the stones with the pad of her thumb and hoping to hell those pretty stones didn't fall out on her watch. Maybe if she sat on her hands... that might help, but then Judah would probably ask if she was scared of flying and she would have to either nod and lie or confess to their 'engagement' bothering her more than she wanted to admit.

He was all easy control, with a coiled energy simmering beneath that mighty fine skin, and if she could just duplicate that combination, borrow some of his armour for the weekend, that would be great. Shake off the nervous tension that not even two glasses of very fine champagne could dim.

There would be a car and a driver waiting to take them to the hotel once they landed. She'd brought two pictures with her for delivery to the gallery, all bubble-wrapped and boxed, so as to stay undamaged during the trip. The curator had seen the images already and immediately wanted to hang both—a move Bridie had yet to give the go-ahead. Judah hadn't seen them, and if she wanted to use them in the exhibition, he needed to.

Not that he was truly recognisable. More of an outline bitten by rain, but it was him.

There was such a thing as permission, and she didn't have it and that was a problem.

Just ask him.

'Judah?'

He looked up from the newspaper he'd been reading, eyes like flint.

She chickened out at the last moment. 'Would you like to swap seats? The view's really good.'

'Keep looking,' he murmured. 'You're the landscape photographer.'

And there was her cue. 'Sometimes I take pictures of people. People in landscapes. Sometimes they turn out really good. Good enough to exhibit.'

He knew exactly what she was talking about, she'd stake her life on it. But he made no comment at all as he turned his attention back to the newspaper.

'If art is a journey, then you're part of my journey and your freedom is the finish line when it comes to my current body of work,' she continued doggedly.

'Do what you want with the photos you took,' he muttered, without looking up.

'I'd like you to see the one I have in mind for the exhibition,' she pressed. 'You're in it. You're facing away from the camera, but it's you.'

'If you think it's good enough for the exhibition then it is. I don't need to see it.'

'Do I have your permission to show it?'

He nodded curtly.

'Can I get that in writing? Not that I don't trust you to keep your word, but the gallery needs the surety.'

'I'll sign their form.'

'Thank you. Would you like to see the photo?' She had it on her phone. 'There's another one too, but I'm not as sure about that one. I'd really like you to look.'

'I'll see it on the night, won't I?'

'Yes, but…' He looked up, pinning her with his gaze. 'Okay, right. It'll be a happy surprise.'

Stop fussing, Bridie. He's said yes. What more do you want?

Apart from everything he was willing to give.

The hotel was everything a majestically placed five-star branded establishment should be, with the manager, a majestic example of understated yet reverential welcome, greeting them himself. 'Mr Blake, of course. And Miss Starr. You'll be occupying the Bridge Suite.'

This was news to Bridie, and she glanced at Judah for confirmation.

'It's bigger,' he said.

'Yes, indeed,' said the manager. 'Four hundred square metres of premium living space, with two bedrooms, living and dining areas, spa, stunning harbour views from floor-to-ceiling windows, a substantial terrace area and twenty-four-hour concierge.'

'Looking forward to it,' she said faintly. Guess being a gazillionaire opened up all sorts of doors, walls, windows and so on.

'Is there somewhere your artwork needs to go?' the fellow asked, and yes, yes, there was.

'I'm expecting someone from the Bridge West Gallery to collect it this afternoon.'

'But of course, Miss Starr. And will you be keeping it with you until then?'

'Thank you, yes.'

'I shall inform you when they arrive. We have the work of some of their artists here in the hotel, although the Bridge Suite, from memory, currently houses a small Olsen and a Noonan.'

She knew one of those names. 'Lovely.'

'They are of course available for purchase.'

'Of course.'

A porter materialised beside them. 'Andrew, please see Mr Blake, Miss Starr and their belongings to the Bridge Suite,' the manager said.

Andrew nodded and a few minutes later saw them settled into the most luxurious apartment Bridie had ever been in. 'How much is all this costing?'

'No idea,' said Judah from the terrace area. 'But it's on me.'

'But I said *I'd* pay. I was the one who invited you here.'

He shrugged, smiled, and suddenly looked inexplicably amused. 'What's a Noonan?'

'No idea.' But suddenly the amazing view of one of the most famous harbours in the world glittered that little bit brighter. There was so much movement out on the water, what with all the ferries and the boats motoring along and a deep rolling swell beneath them. So many people over near the Opera House, walking, eating at the restaurants that dotted the quay. That stunning view, and the utter indulgence of the spa room and the rest of the suite, almost drew her attention away from Judah, who'd ditched his business blazer and tie but kept the immaculate white shirt beneath. He was busy rolling up his sleeves, and, sure, the harbour view was amazing but nothing could compete with corded forearms, broad palms and long, strong fingers at work.

Maybe his bare chest could compete.

The muscles of his back.

What if he had a bath and then stood up to sluice down, facing the window? She could be watching from the doorway. Voyeurism had never been so appealing.

'Something wrong with my arms?'

Was that a rumble in his voice or a purr?

'Not that I can see.' Nope, all good. She refused to be embarrassed because she'd been caught ogling him. Time to check out the other view. White sails, blue skies, the play of light reflecting off skyscraper walls and windows. So busy. Was she ready for all that?

There was no rush, was there? She had time to catch the breath Judah had stolen.

They settled in while a maid unpacked their clothes into separate wardrobes in different rooms. The person from the gallery came to collect her work, and left her with the promise that the collection would be hanging in the gallery from midday tomorrow, and if she wanted to drop by earlier and introduce herself to the staff she was most welcome to. Mr Blake was also most welcome, and had needed no introduction. The gallery guy knew who he was and stood ready to fawn all over him at the slightest encouragement.

Judah didn't give it.

She had the unsettling feeling he was almost as uncomfortable with their fancy hotel suite as she was.

'Okay, famous person,' she said when they left. 'I'm for walking across the bridge and past Luna Park and ending up at Wendy Whiteley's secret garden. It's been years since I was a proper shut-in. I'm willing to find out just how far I've come. Want to join me?'

She turned from that beautiful view to find him watching her through narrowed eyes.

'Okay, make that please come with me. Yes, I'd be using you as a crutch. You're spectacular in that role, by the way. I've never felt so safe. But if you walk with me today, what's to say that tomorrow I won't walk to the gallery on my own? And back? With a detour through the shopping area at The Rocks. I could stop for a snack all by myself in the most crowded coffee shop I can find.'

'You could do that today,' he said drily.

'I could.' She tried to inject a little surety into that statement. 'I might need to work my way up to "I will", hence my invitation. I'm crowd-challenged, not stupid.'

He smiled as if he couldn't help it, and it was a wondrous thing, watching this man relax into his skin.

'I guess I could be of use,' he said, and there was that

purr again. Did he know he could send goosebumps dancing beneath her skin at the sound of it? Or that he was making her want to offer herself up to him all over again and to hell with being a virgin? She could go out and get rid of that here in the city and be right back in time to accommodate him. In her dreams this was entirely possible.

In reality, she'd never do such a thing, so if anything was going to change in order for them to get together it would have to be him. Not that she was trying to pressure him, because she wasn't. Kisses were out, friendship was in. Their fake engagement was nothing more than her being willing to wear a pretty ring.

They walked the bridge. They found Wendy's garden with its towering fig trees and magical view of the bridge. They caught a water taxi back and it took them beneath the bridge and deposited them at Circular Quay just as dusk turned the light that particular shade of purple. She itched for her camera, but she'd made a conscious decision not to bring it with her, the better to simply observe.

Not once had she felt threatened by her surroundings or other people.

Judah too seemed to take the city in his stride. He didn't have a lot to say, or maybe his body language spoke for him. Walking relaxed him, or being out in the open did. He hadn't like being cooped up, no matter how enormous the hotel suite. The restaurant they ended up at had an outdoor eating and bar area with a mighty harbour view. One drink turned into two as he asked her what a successful exhibition could do for her. What else she wanted to photograph. Where else in the world she wanted to go.

'Baby steps,' she replied. 'I'm all about getting this exhibition squared away, never mind what might come next.'

'Think big,' he urged. 'Go hard. Figure out your next steps now, before you need to take them.'

'Yet there I was offering myself to you in the rain and you were all no, no, I'm far too much for you to handle. You thought I should start small.'

His fingers stilled on the glassware in front of him. His gaze met hers, fierce fire banked by shadows.

'You give contradictory advice,' she continued. 'Just saying.'

No argument followed, just silence, tense and heavy.

'But I'm not dwelling on that. Much. Maybe a little bit. But I am willing to move on. Maybe we should give friendship a go.' Subtlety be damned.

'We could start by telling each other something only a friend would know.'

'Never eat from my plate,' he offered.

'Former model here. I barely eat from my plate, let alone someone else's. Thank you for sharing, though. Not your food, obviously, but your thoughts on sharing food.' Befriending a billionaire ex-con who had rejected you was hard. 'We're sharing a bottle of wine, though. Hurrah.'

'Now you,' he murmured. 'Spill.'

What was something about her only a friend would know? She barely had any friends beyond Gert. 'I have a night light in my bedroom. It's cunningly disguised as a power socket plug-in that shows where the door is, but it's a night light. I can't sleep without one.'

He didn't make fun of her. She gave him points for that.

'If I'm in a room I like to face the door,' he offered.

'What if there's more than one door? Like here?' The balcony eating area had several ways in and out.

'Then it's my back to the wall.'

Good thing they'd been able to accommodate him. 'None of the vehicles we own have boots. It's tray tops, twin cabs or Land Rovers. I'm very indulged.'

'That's all we have. They're practical.'

Something in common at last! 'Does this mean we're best buds now?'

'No.'

'But worth a try, right?' Was his sense of humour really that dry? Did he even have a sense of humour? Who would know?

He caught the eye of a hovering waiter and nodded for the bill before returning his attention to her. It settled on her like a weight she wanted to carry with her always. 'Definitely worth a try.' He waited a beat. 'I was angry with you when I heard you were a shut-in for a lot of years. I wanted you to soar so that my sacrifice was worth something.'

She didn't know what to say.

'I understand trauma a lot better now. Taking your time. Finding your way. Figuring out how to fit in. That's where I am right now. Inside.'

'I know.'

'That's why it's not a good idea for you to get too invested in me. I'll only let you down.'

'I know that's what you think.' She'd been there. She'd spent years in that place he was now. And she wept for him.

The bill came and they were out of there a couple of minutes later. The walk back to the hotel was downright romantic, given the artistry of the city lights and the lingering warmth of the day.

Silence helped.

The way they fell into step, shoulder to shoulder.

He didn't talk. Not even when they reached the hotel

and the lift doors opened and she stepped inside and he didn't.

'You're staying out for a while?' May as well make it easy for him.

'Yes.'

He didn't even try to come up with an excuse for not wanting to return to the rooms. This beautiful, broken man who refused to admit he was having a hard time fitting back into a world without bars. His dignity, pride, or even just his strongly developed sense of survival, wouldn't allow him to show weakness at all. And Bridie, forewarned, projected sphinx-like serenity. 'See you in the morning. I'm aiming for breakfast at eight in the suite. I'll save you a seat.'

'You do that.'

Not exactly a commitment to join her, was it? The lift doors began to close.

He stayed facing her even as he took a step back. 'Sleep well, Bridie. Give Noonan my regards.'

And then there was nothing but her reflection in mirrored metal doors.

CHAPTER SIX

IT WAS AFTER one in the morning, and Judah was heavy eyed and dreaming of sleep as the Manly ferry docked at Circular Quay and someone on the intercom told him and the cuddling young couple at the back of the ferry, and the old woman sitting inside the well-lit interior, to please alight and have a good night and that the next service would leave at five-thirty a.m.

Shame about the service stopping for the night, because he'd have ridden that ferry until dawn if he could have, and if that made him odd then so be it. Being out on the harbour soothed him. He'd missed the movement that came of travelling somewhere. That and horizons—he'd missed them too. After growing up in the outback, not being able to see a horizon every time he looked up or looked out had nearly broken him.

But he'd done it. Made it out, still young and fit and wealthy enough to live a life of riches and privilege others could only dream of. Viscount Blake, with a brother who worried about him and a beautiful woman who wanted his kisses, and, failing that, wanted to be his friend.

All told, he was a very lucky man.

He let the fifty-dollar note in his pocket drift to the floor as he passed the old woman on his way to the exit ramp. She had a trolley with her—one of those two-wheeled contraptions with a handle and a little seat—and a backpack as well. For reasons he couldn't quite pinpoint he figured she had nowhere to go. Ride the ferry, kill some time. Try not to give in to quiet desperation.

'Young man?'

He paused.

'You dropped your money.'

She had a look of steadfast honesty about her. As if it was all she had left and she wasn't giving it up without a fight. It was the same way he felt about his integrity. Other people could think what they liked about him, but *he* knew he was a man of principle.

'No, I didn't.' He picked it up and handed it to her, and helped her with her trolley as she tottered down the ferry ramp ahead of him.

'You're not from around here, are you?' she asked.

'No. And you? Where are you from?'

'Long story.' She had kind eyes and a twin suit with pearl buttons, this elderly woman with no home.

'Buy you a coffee over there if you have the time.' He nodded towards an all-night coffee house. 'I have time.'

By the time they parted, Mary—her name was Mary—had a room in a nearby hotel for a week, breakfast included, all the money he had on him, and his phone number. She'd worked as her late husband's bookkeeper all her life. Her husband had been a gambler, but she'd always had a roof over her head. Until he died and the creditors came calling.

'My accountant is looking for a bookkeeper,' he told her. 'You'd have to relocate to a small town in western Queensland and you might not like either the place or the work, but I can vouch for the people. If you're ever interested in taking a look, give me a call. I'll get you a plane ticket there and back so you can have an interview.'

'Sweet man, don't waste your money. I'm sixty-seven years old. Who's going to employ me?'

'Well, the accountant's seventy, so you still have a few years on him.'

She laughed and it was a hearty sound. He liked that. Other people's indifference to her plight hadn't yet broken her. 'I'll give it some thought. Thing is, I've lived in this city all my life. I don't know if I can change.'

'I understand.'

'You're a good man.'

'I want to be.'

By the time he reached his hotel on the harbour it was three a.m. and his hyper watchfulness had dimmed to a casual interest in his surroundings, made all the more possible by the lack of people.

He nodded to the night staff. Clocked their features and the names on their badges and headed for the suite. His room had a wall full of windows and a sliding door out onto the terrace, and maybe this was the moment he'd finally bed down inside a building rather than out.

The bed on offer looked softer than a cloud, all fluffy whites and soft greys with some navy stripes thrown in for variety. There was a feather and down quilt. Or maybe an even flasher just down model. Definitely no shortage of pillows. This was bedmaking at its finest, complete with turn-down service, slippers and a chocolate on his pillow, which he ate because it was there.

If this much bed wooing didn't fix him, nothing would.

He thought of homeless bookkeeper Mary and her fear of the unknown.

He thought about Bridie the shut-in and how far she'd come.

And shucked down to his boxer briefs and gave the bed a try.

Bridie woke early enough to catch the sunrise and this time she reached for her camera. She loved this time of day when the light still glowed softly and magic stirred the land. Judah lay sleeping on a recliner on the terrace. She didn't mean to wake him—she thought she was being stealthy and quiet—but when she turned back after getting her shots his eyes were open, even if shadowed by the forearm he'd flung across his face.

'I couldn't help myself. Look at that view.'

'What time is it?'

'Quarter to six.' Give or take.

He didn't groan, but it was close. A proper fiancée might have asked him what time he got in. A proper fiancée might have stayed out all night with him, but she was neither of those, although she did know full well that it had been after three before he got in. 'I ordered coffee from room service. Shall I order one for you? How do you take it?'

'However it comes.' Suddenly he was on his feet and stretching, and it was impossible not to look. He wore only boxers and there was not an inch of the man's body that hadn't been sculpted and honed to perfection.

'Let's try that again,' he rasped. 'Strong and black, no sugar and cream on the side.'

'I'm on it.' She left him on the terrace and called his order in, and if she snapped a couple of stealth photos of him out there enjoying the view for her own private collection, well, she would wrestle with her conscience later.

She so rarely got to photograph people—that part was true.

The novelty of it was making her take stealth photos of this man—a rationalisation so blatantly false she rolled her eyes and vowed to stop lying to herself.

He was beautiful.

Beautiful and dangerous and so utterly compelling that whenever she saw him she itched to capture a little piece of him to keep. A glance. The cut of his jaw. His stance. She wanted to memorise them.

Oh, hell. That was stalking behaviour.

Nausea crawled down her throat and threatened to return with bile. She found the shots and deleted them, conscience cleared, but the bitter aftertaste of obsessive behaviour still lingered. No one deserved to be the unwilling focus of someone else's obsession. She knew that better than anyone.

So when the coffees came and Judah entered the kitchen to get his, she studied him with a detached eye for detail and a determination to treat him with respect. 'I took a look at the clothes I packed last night—bear with me because I am going somewhere with this story...'

Maybe he hid a smile behind the rim of his coffee cup, and maybe he didn't, but somehow she could sense him unwinding into the space she'd left for him.

'And I'm heading out this morning to find new clothes to wear tonight. And because I wish to be friends with you, I'm not asking you to come with me and endure hours of boredom. You do you, I'll do me, and I'll be back after I've been to the gallery. I'm aiming for a late lunch up here in the suite, because I'll have had enough of people by then and I'll need to recharge before the exhibition opening.'

'Sounds like a plan.'

'I really would like for you to be there for me this evening,' she continued doggedly. 'I'm going to be nervous.' She was *already* nervous. 'But you don't need to be there if it's really not your thing.'

'In the eyes of the world you're my fiancée. It's your first show. I'll be there.'

'If I take your hand and squeeze, it'll mean I need to get out of there before I have a meltdown. And I know artists are known for being temperamental, fragile, or all ego, but I'd rather not be seen as any of those things.'

'Even if you are?'

She sipped her coffee and took strength from it. 'Yes, even if I am those things underneath. I don't want to show that vulnerability to the world. I think that's something you might understand and I'm asking for your help.'

'You'll get it.'

'Thank you.' She could ask for nothing more. 'Coffee's good.'

'Very.'

'I took pictures of you this morning when you were out on the terrace.'

'I know.'

'I deleted them.'

He said nothing.

'You dazzle me. You have such presence. All that coiled strength and power. I want to see how it works, break it down into understandable pieces, but I'm not a stalker and the thought that I'm beginning to act like one horrifies me. I won't ever take pictures of you again without asking your permission. I think that's important for both of us to understand. You have my word.'

'Okay.'

She could see his chest rise and fall beneath the thin cotton of the T-shirt he'd thrown on, along with sweatpants. 'You do realise I'm sharing a full basket of vulnerabilities with you here?'

'They weren't exactly hidden.'

Ouch, Judah. Ouch. 'You could reciprocate by revealing one of your many flaws. You might be scared of emus.' She loved it when he smiled, no matter how small. 'No?'

'No.'

'Razorbacks?' Those huge wild pigs were mean mothers.

'No.'

'Ghosts?'

'I'll give those their due,' he offered. 'I have a few.'

But he didn't name them and she didn't press. Why on earth had she mentioned ghosts to a man who had killed to protect her? And then lost both his parents less than a year ago, while in prison for his sin? 'They can dance with mine,' she muttered. 'They might even be the same ghosts. I bet you're afraid of mice.'

'In plague proportions? You betcha.'

See? They could have a meaningful, getting-to-know-you conversation if they tried. It took great patience and good coffee. And now she needed to retreat and leave him be, because she wasn't pushy or needy or utterly infatuated with him. She was Bridie Starr of Devil's Kiss station and life was full of joy and pain and growth and heartache and that was all just part of living. And dammit she wanted to live. 'So, I'll see you this evening?'

He nodded.

She turned away.

'Hey.' He'd waited until she was almost to her room. 'For what it's worth, you dazzle me too.'

By six o'clock that evening, Bridie's bravado seemed to have fled. Judah watched with growing concern as she refused a bite to eat and started pacing instead, pausing every now and then to look at the paintings on the wall and in doing so somehow make her silhouette look even smaller.

'How many people need to be at this opening for it to be a success?' he asked, and she wrapped her arms around her middle and looked blankly towards him.

He tried again. 'How many pictures do you need to sell for the exhibition to be a success?'

'I'm sure the gallery has a percentage in mind, but I don't know it. Sell-out show sounds good, though.'

He could help with her sell-out-show wish. He'd already secured one picture by calling through to the gallery this afternoon. He'd agreed that whatever picture of him she'd chosen to display could be part of her exhibition but hell if he was going to let it end up on someone else's wall. The gallery director had initially told him it wasn't for sale. Money had taken care of that objection. She'd promised not to sell the picture to anyone but him.

'Does this outfit look arty enough?'

She looked to him for an answer, but how would he know what arty looked like? Didn't arty people slink around in black trousers and turtlenecks? Or was that look owned by successful tech titans these days?

Bridie wore a vivid blue silk top streaked with grey and the burnt orangey brown of the channel country she called home. Sleeves to her elbows, the neckline as high and tight as one of his shirts. The top angled in towards her impossibly tiny waist and with it she wore severe grey trousers that flared at the bottom and didn't go anywhere near to covering lace-up black boots. It was a fashion look, as far as he could tell, and she wore it very well. 'Yes. You look fantastic.'

'Fantastically arty though?'

'Yes.' And he looked like a suit, because he only had a few looks and one of them was outback scruffy and another was prison rough and neither would do here. 'How did you get into modelling in the first place? Was it something you wanted?'

'Oh.' She looked momentarily surprised by his question. 'No. I didn't think about my looks at all much when I was growing up. I was just me and there was no one around much to see me anyway.'

'So how did you start?'

'I was in Melbourne with Aunt Beth for my fifteenth birthday and we'd gone to David Jones department store because she was going to buy me some make-up. That was her gift to me. It was the first time I'd ever seen those little make-up booths with women just standing around looking beautiful and waiting to make other people look beautiful too.' She smiled at the memory. 'Everything was so *glossy*. So there we were and this make-up lady had just given me smoky eyes and cheek-bones and then this beautifully dressed power woman rushed past and then backed right up and pointed at me and said, "*You*, come with me." It was fashion week. An hour later I was walking down the catwalk, filling in for a model who hadn't turned up. And that was that. Hello, modelling career, with my aunt as my manager.'

'Did you like it?'

'I loved the clothes, the make-up artists and hair stylists fussing over me, and the way I could sometimes barely recognise myself after they were done. Yeah. And then they took me off the catwalk and turned the camera on me and I got to see what great photographers could do with light and colour and settings and perspective and I was hooked. I wanted *that*, photography, only by that time Laurence was my manager and my aunt's lover and he didn't want that for me at all. He got more controlling. Started coming to every shoot. It only got creepier from there. I think he wanted a dress-up doll.'

Even after sitting at trial and hearing that Bridie had been beaten and kidnapped but not sexually abused, he hated thinking about what might have happened had Laurence not been stopped.

'Anyway. It cured me of wanting to be anyone's fantasy image ever again.' She crossed her arms in front of her and cupped her elbows.

He tilted his head, digesting her words. 'So how are you going to manage your public image and keep the crazies away this time around?'

'I'm kind of hoping that being engaged to Australia's most dangerous ex-con billionaire is going to do the trick. And I know it's wrong of me to put you in the position of having to protect me again but...' She looked away. 'You're the best there is.'

That right there was the reason there could never be anything between them. Her expectations were totally at odds with the screwed-up, shut-down mess of a man he was beneath all that protective saviour gloss she kept painting on him.

'Would you like a drink?' she asked next and gestured towards the mini bar. 'Something to help settle my nerves. Not champagne, that'd go straight to my head.'

'There's beer.'

'Perfect.'

'Okay.'

He fetched one for each of them and put music on. He watched her take the tiniest sip, not nearly enough to settle her nerves so he held out his hand and said, 'Dance with me,' because holding her in his arms and not putting any moves on her was clearly his torture method of choice and he figured it would keep her mind off the exhibition for a while.

His dancing hadn't improved since the ball and neither had hers, but they made do, in the shadow of one of the most famous bridges in the world and with a light show spinning across the Opera House sails.

'People are going to love your art,' he told her. 'You're going to charm them with your arty-looking self and talent until they beg for more.'

A dimple dotted her cheek when she smiled. 'I'll hold that thought close.'

'No problem. Seriously. Your photos are amazing. You've got this.'

They made it to the gallery with ten minutes to spare. The owner, Sara, greeted them with a relieved smile, plied them with alcohol and introduced them to the rest of the gallery staff. The gallery floor was grey concrete and the walls a severe kind of white that only gallery spaces could pull off. It pushed people's attention towards the art, he supposed, as, drink in hand, he turned his attention towards the photographs on the walls.

He recognised some of them because they were ones Bridie had sent him over the years, only the ones she'd sent him had been schoolbook size. These ones were larger, some of them much larger. The two panoramas on display, one below the other, ran the length of the wall.

Sara drew Bridie away, talking business Judah didn't need to know, so he planted himself in front of a red river gum tree he knew of old and studied the people who came through the door. Bridie would find him when she wanted to, and meanwhile the room began to fill. A wealthy couple to start with, a tourist, a student with a date he wanted to impress and maybe they were only there for the free food and drinks, but not all of them had free food in mind.

When one of the gallery staff discreetly enquired whether he was interested in purchasing the red river gum, because another guest was interested in buying it, he said no, and moved to plant himself in front of the next picture.

Bridie played the shy emerging artist to perfection as gallery owner, Sara, introduced her to various guests. Judah left them to it, watching from a distance and trying not to look too menacing. He'd just turned to study the pair of panoramas again when someone backed into him.

He turned. She turned, and flushed beet red to match her hair. Not a threat—though he checked his pockets to make sure that his wallet was still there. It was.

'I'm so sorry,' she began. 'I need a rear-vision mirror—oh!' Her eyes widened as her gaze reached his face. 'It's you.'

'Do I know you?' He didn't recognise her.

'No?' Now was the time for her to introduce herself, but she didn't. 'I mean, no, you don't know me and I don't know you, but you're the one in the picture.' She gestured towards a wide doorway leading towards another part of the gallery. 'In there.'

Judah raised his eyebrows. 'Ah.'

'It's very compelling.'

'Is it, now?' If he could get away without looking at it this evening, he would. Put simply, he didn't want to have to look at his mug in a photo and pretend he thought of it as art.

'My friends were joking that you couldn't possibly be real, but here you are.'

'Here I am.' *Save me. Save me now.*

'Such a shame it's already sold.'

To him, yes. It had better be. He looked for more red dots below the paintings in the room. Three sales out of nine paintings in the first half-hour. Clearly it was time to add more purchasing weight to the show. 'If you'll excuse me.'

He caught the eye of a gallery assistant who was at his side in an instant.

'May I help you, sir?'

'I want to buy the two panoramas over there.'

'Certainly.' Moments later, they too had red dots underneath them.

'How do I pay?'

'Ms Starr's instructions are that you don't pay. Whatever you want from the collection is yours.'

That wouldn't do at all. 'Do you know who I am?'

'Of course, Mr Blake, sir.' The man was unflappable. Judah swung between being righteously annoyed and reluctantly impressed by the man's intransigence. 'Whatever pieces you want here tonight are yours. Ms Starr's orders and already cleared with management.'

How generous. He didn't want any part of it. 'In that case, I believe you misunderstood my intentions. I'm buying the panoramas on behalf of Sirius Corp, not in a personal capacity, therefore Ms Starr's offer cannot apply.' Sirius Corp was the name of the company he'd formed with Reid and Bridie to build the eco retreats. 'If there's a third panorama on offer, I want that too.'

The man beamed with bright enthusiasm. 'There is

one other, and of course your purchase on behalf of another entity is a different matter altogether. If you'll excuse me, I'll see to the paperwork.'

Money. His family had always had it. Never before had he wielded it with such cynical understanding that success could be bought. Or at the very least, the impression of success could be bought.

He helped himself to a canapé—some kind of smoked salmon, cheese and chives in pastry option—and headed towards the wide doorway that would lead him deeper into the gallery.

He didn't see the photo at first. Not until he walked past the floating wall in the middle of the next room, but there was no avoiding it after that.

The picture took up at least half of the wall and he could all but feel the storm bearing down on him. True to her word, you couldn't see his face, but every line in his body screamed with a primal summons for nature to have a go at him: bring it on and don't make the mistake of thinking that taking him down was ever going to be easy.

Was this how he looked whenever a prison fight had been in the offing?

'Powerful, isn't it?' said a voice from beside him, and it was the gallery owner, whose name he now couldn't recall. 'But then, you're a very powerful man these days.'

'Is she going to let me have it?'

'Buy it? No. As I mentioned on the phone, it's not for sale. But it's yours for the taking, nonetheless. No one else gets to have it. Have you seen the other one?'

'What other one?'

'Turn around.'

He turned and this time he felt the impact of the picture like a punch to the gut.

All his fierce warrior majesty had morphed into boyish delight as he and Bridie danced in the soaking rain. Hand in hand, joyous and free—he looked so happy he couldn't stand to look at it for fear of that feeling being ripped from him.

He hated it.

He couldn't stop looking at it.

At Bridie, incandescently beautiful and tuned so finely towards the storm and to him, sharing her joy with him. Two seconds later she'd been sharing her body with him, swapping kisses, greedy hands on rain-slicked skin, tasting and taking. The memory played out while he stood there and stared. No thought for his current surroundings or the image he might be presenting when faced with his unshielded self.

He hated it.

He wanted it gone. 'Take it down.'

'But, Mr Blake... May I call you Judah?'

'No.'

'Mr Blake, I have no intention of bringing ladders and staff out and taking that picture down *now*. Let's talk again tomorrow.'

'Talk about what?'

It was a measure of his preoccupation with the photograph that he hadn't sensed Bridie's approach. She spoke lightly, with an undercurrent of anxiousness in her voice. Her eyes held the same wariness, along with a plea for him to be okay with her exposing them for all to see.

'You said there was a picture of me in the exhibition. You said nothing about hanging a picture of *us*.'

'I thought—'

'Wrong, Bridie. You thought wrong. I do *not* give my permission for you to show this here. I have not given my permission, do you understand?'

'Mr Blake—'

That was his name. He turned towards the gallery owner and made his position perfectly clear. 'Cover it up or take it down. Those are your choices.'

'Judah—'

'Bridie.' One word, with a world of warning behind it. 'I'm offering you a very simple solution, because I like to think I'm a very reasonable man.'

Her jaw firmed, as if she wanted to disagree with him. 'It's dust and rain and life and growth. It's joy. It's the best photo here.'

'It's *personal*.' Couldn't she see how vulnerable he looked? Didn't she realise how private that moment of welcome and renewal had been to him? How he'd let his guard down just once and let her—and only her—see his weakness? 'There is no other place on this earth that I can be me, except for out there. And you want me to share that with strangers?'

He couldn't.

She was asking too much.

'Mr Blake, Bridie, much as I love a good scandal, I really do recommend you set your differences aside for the next hour or two and concentrate on selling art. Red dot on the wall here, see? We can take this picture down tomorrow and when asked, I can say it's at the request of the buyer that it no longer be shown and that this is why collectors should come along to see new works on opening night. This particular piece is *not* part of any marketing material. It's not catalogued online. One night and gone, and for anyone here tonight it will be nothing but a faint memory. Unless we make a production out of removing it, and then it'll be a story.'

He hated it when other people sounded entirely reasonable and he still didn't want to agree with them.

'I'm taking silence as consent.' Gallery owner Sara smiled encouragingly at them both. 'Drinks all round. For this, I'll even break into my private stash. Anyone for a whisky?'

'Okay,' said Bridie swiftly, and come to think of it her face did look kind of pale beneath all her skilfully applied make-up.

He wondered if he looked thunderous. More like a storm about to break than the smiling man in the pictures.

Bridie turned to him. 'Judah, I'm sorry. I am. I never dreamed you'd react this way to a picture of us in the rain. I had no idea.'

Neither had he.

Don't do anything rash.'

'Avoid split-second decisions.'

'Give yourself time to adjust.'

Once again he'd done none of that and Bridie had paid the price. 'I'm sorry.' He was. 'I'm not a hero. I can't be that exposed.'

She glanced at the photograph and shook her head as if to clear it. 'I wish I could see what you see when you look at that photo. To me, it's everything I want home and happiness to be, and it's beautiful. You're beautiful like that. You're free.'

'Are there any more like it? From that day?'

'Many, many. The cameras took a photo every thirty seconds. It caught everything.' Her chest rose with the strength of the breath she took. 'You're welcome to see them. I can destroy them. I did ask.' Her eyes pleaded with him to agree with her. 'You *knew* you were standing in the frame.

'I'd never show them,' she added. 'And some of them crossed a line and became way too personal, I know that.

I just—I didn't think this one did. I did offer to show it to you on the plane. I *knew* I should have made you look.'

'My bad.' She was right. He'd agreed without knowing what he was agreeing to, and that was on him. 'Spur-of-the-moment reaction.' God knew he'd been warned about *them*. 'I'm coming good.'

He still couldn't bring himself to look at the photo again.

'And here we are.' Sara spared him an answer by way of shoving a silver tray with three crystal tumblers full of Scotch under their noses. 'All but one of the works have sold, and the night is still young. A toast.' She raised the last glass. 'To a remarkable new talent and a sell-out exhibition, I'm sure.'

'Really? All but one? Which one?'

Astonishment looked good on Bridie. Not quite as good as…what did she call it? His gaze skittered over the photo on the wall—the part with Bridie in it, whirling against the storm.

'Boots 'n Dust,' answered Sara. 'Bridie, darling, I'm being asked if you take commissions. Come and meet this wonderful couple from South Australia. I believe they own a grazing property down that way. Can you spare her, Mr Blake?'

'I can spare her.'

'You won't leave without me?' asked Bridie.

Why she still wanted him anywhere near her spoke volumes about her lack of alternatives. 'I won't leave without you. I might step outside though.' Let the lack of walls calm him. 'Text me when you want me to come back in.'

'I will.' She leaned up, her lips to his ear. 'I'm really sorry you don't like the photos but, please, please look at them again. Your superhero photo against the storm is stunning. *You're* stunning—all your inner strength and might. As for the one of us, the you in that pic is every bit as bold and beautiful as you are in the other one, and it's exactly what I want for you, whether I'm the one to share it with you or not.

'Happiness and joy, Judah. Because you deserve it.'

CHAPTER SEVEN

IT WAS HARD to feel like a successful landscape photographer when the man walking beside her was so tense and withdrawn. She should have stuck to landscapes, or at the very least forced Judah to look at the pictures she'd added to the exhibition at the last minute. She hadn't meant to hurt him. He probably hadn't meant to hurt her either, with his emphatic objection to the portrait of the two of them, but he had.

Their tentative friendship was withering away in the silence and she had no idea how to resurrect it.

'You're not coming in?' she asked as he stopped at the entrance to the hotel foyer.

'Not yet. Figured I'd walk for a bit.'

'Want some company?' It was a long shot, because every bone in his body suggested that, no, he damn well didn't.

He looked to her boots. 'In those shoes?'

'I have walking shoes upstairs.'

He shrugged, which could mean anything, but he stayed by her side as they returned to the suite, which was still as luxurious as they had left it, only now there was a bottle of champagne, a fruit basket, and chocolates on the dining table, along with a note congratulating her on her resounding opening-night success.

'From the gallery,' she murmured. 'I'll just go change my shoes.'

'Don't bother.'

Right, so he definitely wasn't interested in enduring any more of her company this evening. 'Okay, no. Didn't mean to intrude on the rest of your evening.'

'I meant that tiredness hit me like a hammer on the way up to the suite and what's not to like about the thought of opening a bottle of celebratory champagne and kicking back now that we're here?'

'Oh. Okay.' Four seasons in one day, that was him.

He reached for the bottle of champagne and made short work of opening it. 'Congratulations. You did it. Sold every painting.'

'And managed to hurt you in the process.' Might as well say it.

'I overreacted. Lashed out.'

'Again.' Because he'd done similar at the ball.

'Again.' He poured the champagne and left plenty of room for the bubbles to rise before topping off the glasses and handing one to her. 'I'm not proud of my behaviour.'

'Do you know why you do it?'

'I have a fair idea.'

She waited, and waited some more, and finally he spoke.

'I don't like being vulnerable. In prison…' He set his glass down on the table and looked her in the eye. 'In prison that's not on. You lock down hard and try to become as emotionless as you can. Nothing gets to you. No fear, no anger, no laughter. Nothing. Emotions are private. And now they're all coming out, all those feelings I don't know what to do with any more, and I feel exposed and it's dangerous. *I'm* dangerous when cornered. I need more control.'

She'd wanted him to reveal a few flaws, hadn't she?

Well, he'd just revealed a few monsters. 'And soon you *will* have more control, because you're honest with yourself and you're working on it. It's not a permanent character flaw. You're downright inspirational.'

'You need to get out more.'

'There's nothing wrong with my judgment.'

'I'm sorry,' he said simply. 'For my behaviour at the ball. For my appalling behaviour tonight. You deserve better.'

'Apology accepted.' He was so hard on himself. 'Please. Can't we just relax? Put on some music and take this party to the patio? You can stare out over the water and brood. I can close my eyes and pretend I'm back home dancing beneath the stars where no one can see me.'

'I see you.'

She turned away, suddenly shy about all but inviting him to look at her.

'You look at me, too,' he added.

How could she not? 'I know.'

'Have you ever had a lover before? Or is that too private a question to ask?'

'I'll answer you.' Honesty was important to her. 'No, I haven't.' Twenty-three-year-old virgin, that was her. 'And it's not because I've been waiting around for you to return. I mean, you were older when we were growing up and I might have had a tiny crush on you in my teens, but it wasn't a fixation. You were the hot older boy who lived next door. I think that's normal enough.'

He made a noise that could have meant agreement and she decided to take it as such.

'After you went to prison, my thoughts ran more along the lines that you were part of my world and I wanted you back in it where you belonged. It wasn't a romantic notion. More of a guilt-induced notion.' She put her glass down. She wasn't thirsty any more.

'You were a kid and you needed protection.' Those words were enough to make her look at him again. 'I don't blame you for what happened. Never have.'

A weight she never knew she carried rolled off her shoulders. 'Really?'

'Really. I don't blame your father or your aunt either, for allowing you to come into contact with a charming sociopath hell-bent on possession. Do you blame them?'

'Of course not.'

'Good. So lose the guilt and don't expect my forgiveness. No one made me do anything I didn't want to do, so there's nothing to forgive.'

'Thank you.' She steadied her thoughts. 'I'm grateful for your actions.'

'Don't be,' he said. 'It makes me question what you'll put up with from me.'

'I'm always going to be grateful to you for rescuing me, that's a given.' She turned and leaned against the railing, her hands lightly clasping it on either side of her and her back to the harbour view as she risked locking eyes with him again. 'I'm making good headway when it comes to not thinking of you as a superhero though.'

He laughed, open and honest, and she cherished the sound.

'Do you think we could press a reset button, you and me? Ignore the past. Forget the false engagement, and the way I exposed you tonight, and start over?' she asked.

'We can try.'

She turned to him and held out her hand. 'Hello. I'm Bridie. I'm not real good around people I don't know and

I've never had a man in my bed before, but you make me want to.'

He was laughing again. 'Don't lead with that.' But he took her hand in his and stole her breath away with that simple touch. 'I'm Judah. And I would love to take you to bed, but I currently don't trust my control. I can't promise to make your first time what a first time should be. I'm too…greedy.'

'For touch?' He still hadn't let go of her hand.

'For you.'

'I don't suppose you could keep me in mind and let me know when that control of yours returns?'

'I can do that.'

'Will you dance with me?' she murmured. 'I'm a terrible dancer, unless it's raining, and it's not raining, but moonlight and a beautiful harbour might improve my dancing too.'

'It would be my pleasure to see if it does.'

She held his hand as he led her to the centre of the terrace. She closed her eyes the better to feel him as he turned her into his arms. Those powerful thighs of his brushed against hers as they moved and the warmth of his palm settled in the small of her back and held her close. She dropped his hand but only in order to place both hands on his shoulders. His hands now encircled her waist. It was the school formal she'd never had.

She smiled at the innocence of it all and moments later felt his lips brush hers.

Okay, maybe she could open her eyes just a fraction, the better to see his reaction to the kissing.

He was close enough to see the thickness of his lashes and the faint frown between guarded eyes that held a question.

'There's that lack of control,' he murmured.

Oh. She wouldn't have put it like that. 'Can you do it again?' Three times now he'd smiled or laughed and meant it. She was on a roll. 'You know, if we did want to take this to the bedroom, I could always tie you up.' Would he beg her to release him? Would he strain against the ties that bound him? 'How many neck ties did you bring?'

'You want to go from virgin to dominatrix without passing go? That's nuts.' But his eyes flashed fire and the hands around her waist tightened, before deliberately, on his exhale of breath, making their way to her hips. 'Also, we've only just met.'

'I feel as if I've known you for longer,' she said. 'And I'd check in with you. A lot.' Not as if domination was her goal. 'You could direct me.'

Judah groaned.

Still not a no.

'There could be safe words. Traffic-light colours.'

'And cursing,' he muttered.

'Yes, all the curse words. Not a problem.' She smiled brightly.

'You have no idea what you're asking.'

'True.' But he kissed her again and she didn't think it was a no. She closed her eyes and surrendered to the moment as fire ripped through her veins.

'Do it.'

'What?' She hadn't *actually* been expecting a yes.

'Take my clothes off, tie me up, and use me. Let's see what you've got.'

Bridie felt her breath hitch at his gravelly challenge. 'Okay.'

'Okay.'

'Okay,' she echoed again. Now was not the time for rampant insecurity to make an appearance. She was Bridie Starr of Devil's Kiss station. A talented photographer who'd just held her first sell-out exhibition. An outback woman, bold and resilient—even if it had taken years to claw her way back to where she was today. She could do this. She could slide his jacket from his shoulders and let it fall. She could undo the buttons on his snow-white shirt. After that, she'd be covering new territory. She could improvise.

'You realise you're talking to yourself?' he asked.

'Oh. Did I say all that out loud?'

'Yeah.'

'Sorry about that. Then again…you'll be forewarned.' He smelled so good, so undeniably cologne-y and male that she couldn't resist putting her nose to the curve of his neck and breathing deeply of his scent and setting her lips to the skin below his ear. This was lovely—having free rein to indulge herself and experiment.

The shudder that ripped through him was encouraging.

'There are ties in my suitcase,' he offered.

'Show me.'

He removed his cufflinks on the way and she might have objected except that following him to his bedroom gave her the most wonderful opportunity to ogle the breadth of his back and the globes of his rear.

He found two ties and held them out to her with an air of challenge that was impossible to resist. She slid them around her neck, where they hung like a dressmaker's tape. She'd get around to using them, as promised. Soon.

First, she had a man to undress.

Bridie's thoroughness was killing him. Slowly, surely, as inevitable as sunset, she built a fire in him that threatened to become an inferno. She finished undoing the buttons of his shirt, and the brush of her fingers and knuckles almost had him coming out of his skin. She pressed a kiss to his chest as she slid the shirt to the floor, and then tilted her head up towards his.

'How am I doing?' Her voice only wobbled a little bit.

'Not bad.'

'Let me just strike *gives effusive praise* off your list of strengths.' But her hands kept exploring and her eyes shone with gentle humour and encouragement.

'Pretty good,' he offered in an effort to redeem himself.

'Funny man. May I kiss you?' Her lips brushed his, more tease than kiss. 'Please?'

'Yes.'

Her next kiss delved deeper, took longer and he couldn't help but take command of it. Showing her how to savour the sweetness, and by the time he'd done a thorough enough job, she'd opened his trousers and he was making tight little sounds of what could have been taken as protest but were far more aligned with surrender.

'Are you sure you want me to tie you? I mean…this is going pretty well.'

He stepped back, but only to take his trousers off, and she looked down and her eyes widened.

'Oh,' she murmured. 'Oh, boy.'

Virgin, his mind supplied helpfully. And he was definitely no boy.

'I should, er—or you should… I mean—' Flailing looked good on her. 'How does that even fit?'

'It fits.'

'Right. Of course. Of course it does. So if you just… lie on the bed and raise your arms and grab a couple of bars on the bedhead, I'll, wow, okay, that's a lot of muscle mass. How strong is a brass bedhead, do you think?'

He curled his hands around two rounded bedhead rails and figured them for hollow. 'I'll replace it if I have to.'

'How very reassuring.'

'Tie me up, Bridie. Do it now.' Before raging need got the better of him and he reached for her and forgot to be gentle. He wasn't even sure he knew how to be gentle these days. It was as if he had two settings: indifferent or destructive. The middle ground had deserted him.

She straddled him to do it, but instead of resting any weight on him she held herself a couple of inches above him. Suddenly his hands were on her hips, pulling her down against him before she could squeak. Silk panties, warm and slippery against his sensitised skin, meant he almost lost it.

Forget his overwhelming hunger for sex and how it might scare her. He needed in.

Needed to push aside her panties and sink into tight, willing warmth.

'No, you don't.' She reached for one of his wrists and slid a loop of fabric over his hand and pulled it tight and then raised his arm to the bedhead again. 'Co-operate,' she murmured, and he gave in to the urge to bury his face against the softness of her belly and surround himself with her scent.

'I am co-operating.' His voice was muffled but he trusted her to understand. He hadn't ripped her panties off, rolled her onto her back and buried himself inside her yet. How could she possibly think he wasn't co-operating?

She tied his other hand to the bedhead and smiled as she sat back and set the palms of her hands to his chest.

'Sit,' he urged. 'Make yourself comfortable.' He almost whimpered when she removed herself from the bed altogether, but it was only to raise her top over her head. 'Or that. Do that.'

Champagne-coloured lace underwear worked for him, no doubt, and for a moment he thought she'd get rid of that too and be as naked as him, but at the last minute she seemed to think better of it.

She was all long lines and slender curves and he wanted more.

This was torture.

'Music?' She made it happen, and then returned and knelt on the bed next to him as her gaze roved over him. 'May I touch you?'

Sometime this century would be good. 'Yes.'

She started at his fingertips, a slow, thorough investigation of every inch of him until she reached the planes and ridges of his stomach. Goosebumps followed in her wake and he closed his eyes and let his passion soar. He felt her hair brush his stomach before he felt her lips.

'Is this okay?'

'Don't stop.' *Never, ever stop.*

Eyes closed, he wasn't ready for the tentative lick she bestowed on the tip of his hard length. He should have strapped his feet to the bed too, because he'd follow that warm mouth to the ceiling if it meant he could have more of it. He clenched his hands around the ties that bound him and tried not to fill her mouth with more. Her pace, not his. Bridie in control.

By the time she'd explored every part of his erection with hands and mouth, his dignity had been shredded and the sounds coming out of him had more in common with beast than man.

'I'm not protected,' she murmured.

'Bathroom. Bottom drawer. Hotel supplies.' Bless them.

Her leaving the room gave him time to claw back slim threads of control.

'Large, Extra Large and Jumbo,' she murmured as she sank back down on the bed with a handful of condoms. 'I'm guessing now is not the time for social commentary on condom marketing?'

'So not the time.'

'Jumbo?'

'Yeah.' And even that would be a stretch. 'Roll it on me, sit on my stomach and lean towards me.' Would she do it? Take blunt direction from him?

Yes.

He tried to be gentle with her as he traced the contours of her bra with his lips. When he tongued a pebbled nipple and then closed his mouth over it and sucked gently, silk and all, she fed him more and caught her breath. *Yes.*

'More,' she whispered.

He'd have headed south, but Bridie wanted more kisses. This was why he was tied up and she was running this.

And then she dropped her panties and shed her bra and sat right back down with her soft folds caressing his length, and he dug his heels in and bucked. No need for anything to go in yet. 'Rock it, yes. Like that.'

He set up a slow rolling grind to help her find her way. He was already well on his way to insanity born of unutterable need as their kisses grew wilder and a storm rose within him. Bound, stripped bare, and aching for every little piece of her she was willing to give. So good. Beyond anything he'd ever experienced.

And then she changed the angle of her hips and he nudged her entrance and eased the very tip of him in. He all but howled his approval.

'Oh, you like that?'

Queen of understatement. She did it again, took him in hand and tested for fit, and he stilled on an upstroke, his teeth bared and his lips tight, so close to coming he could hardly bear it.

Had his hands been free... But they weren't and he was glad of it. 'More, Bridie, please. Just...use me.'

'I— It's...' She slid him a fraction further in and he met resistance.

'Perfect?' A man could hope.

'Daunting.'

'Give me your breasts again.' Maybe it'd help. This time he wasn't quite as careful. Laving became grazing, teasing turned to sucking. Bridie took more of him in and it was all he could do to stay still and not rear up and take what she seemed so determined to give.

It wasn't enough. She was hurting, not soaring. Curses left his lips as he pleaded for her to untie him so he could see to her pleasure, and his, but she refused him. His thrusting grew wilder and she stayed with him, getting looser, he thought, or maybe he only imagined she did. Her breathing grew ragged and she broke kisses in an effort to draw breath.

He came when she dug her nails into his chest. Nothing he could do about it other than dig his heels in and take his pleasure and strain and demand that she untie him.

Not until he softened inside her did she reach for the ties at his wrists. 'You bent the bedhead,' she said, but he barely heard her as he exploded into action, rolling her onto her back and getting his mouth between her legs, ravenous and apologetic for letting his pleasure come before hers.

He found her nub and set about driving her as insane as she'd so recently driven him. Inhibition had long ago left him as he set up a rough, pulsing rhythm, using his fingers to expose her and his mouth and tongue to bring her to completion. Satisfaction savaged him as she wove her hands through his hair, her eyes half hidden between generous lashes. He slid his hands beneath her buttocks, the better to position her, and figured he could stay there for ever.

She came on his tongue moments later, flooding him with sweetness, delighting him with her responsiveness.

He who hadn't held or been held in years allowed her to lead him back up the bed. 'You okay?' she asked. It nearly broke him. He didn't deserve such tenderness.

She checked his wrists and kissed the redness, a question in her eyes.

'It's nothing,' he said.

She tucked in beside him, with her head on his shoulder and her hand to his chest as if she belonged there, and he was powerless against her expectations. 'Are you okay?' he finally asked.

'I'm brilliant,' she murmured on the edge of sleep. 'Best night ever.'

So easy to please.

She'd wanted what he had to offer. She was happy with him, demons and all.

Wasn't that something?

CHAPTER EIGHT

BRIDIE WOKE THE next morning, tucked up against the hard, warm body of a sleeping man whose chest rose and fell in a slow, even rhythm. He'd turned into her at some point during the night, and how he could even breathe with her hair in his face was a miracle, but he managed it. She turned, little spoon to his big one, step one of her exit plan, and stared out through the floor-to-ceiling window at the sky, before closing her eyes and savouring the feel of skin against skin.

Morning could wait just that little bit longer, couldn't it?

Morning would mean conversation and explanation. Justification of actions that needed no justification and everything would become awkward again.

Her body ached in places it never had before, but she welcomed the feeling.

Welcome to sex, Bridie. Any complaints?

Not a one, except maybe her partner insisting he be tied up so he didn't get too rowdy for her. He hadn't. When she'd freed his hands he'd turned all that intense passion and power on her and sent her straight to heaven.

He hadn't left her during the night to go walking the streets or sleep under the night sky or whatever it was that he usually did. He'd stayed with her.

It was a heady, welcome thought given that her desire for him hadn't faded one little bit. She could go again. Her body was still stretched and moist for him. Unless... She teased her entrance with gentle fingers and felt no pain, but it was mighty damp, and when she saw her fingers they were red, and...

Oh.

Shower. Now.

Before Judah woke up and decided he'd split her in two.

She sprang from the bed and hightailed it to the bathroom and he let her go, not a word of protest and no physical restraint, and she didn't look back to see if she'd woken him. She was too busy being embarrassed.

Not until she'd washed away all evidence of last night's lovemaking did she lift her face to the spray. Was there a way to sneak back into bed with him after her hasty exit? A casual word or two: toilet break, now, where were we? Did she have the confidence for that?

Probably not.

She dressed and called for coffee and breakfast to be delivered. Same coffee orders as yesterday, full breakfast for two, and by the time it arrived and the concierge had arranged it on the table, Judah had appeared in the doorway.

'I ordered for us. Hope you don't mind.'

'I don't mind.'

He padded forward to take his coffee, his body honed for battle and his expression guarded. 'You left.'

'The bathroom was calling. Loudly.'

He studied her over the rim of his coffee cup. 'And you didn't return.'

'But I was just about to come in and try and wake you with the smell of good coffee.' There was that.

'Did I hurt you last night?'

He just wouldn't let it go. 'Physically, no. Though I'm a little sad that I've wasted so many years not having sex, because *damn*, Judah. I loved it.'

She had the pleasure of watching a slow blush steal across his cheeks. 'Oh, really?'

'Flat-out loved it.' Where were her manners? 'Thank you for the introduction. Although I'm sure I still have so much to learn.'

No offer to tutor her was forthcoming. But he did raise an eyebrow and hold her gaze.

She was Bridie from the bush and so many of its hazards didn't faze her. Surely she could continue her line of reasoning in the face of a raised eyebrow. 'You didn't overwhelm me. You could teach me. You could use hands.' Was that a flash of amusement in his eyes? Hard to tell, it was gone so quickly, leaving careful blankness in its wake. 'I'm sensing you have regrets.'

'Don't you?' he asked.

'Not one. Haven't you been listening?'

'You're in a hotel room with a man who made you tie him to the bed before he'd have sex with you. I'm wondering why you haven't fled.'

'Because it's you, and you had…reasons.' She waved a hand around to approximate those reasons. 'And I trust you.' Surely that was a good thing?

But he didn't seem to be similarly ecstatic about her confidence in him. Matter of fact, he looked downright uncomfortable. 'But I can take no for an answer, if it wasn't that good for you and you never want to do it again. Paradise lost and all that.' And on to breakfast before she fell apart in front of him. 'We have mushroom, bean sprout and three-cheese omelettes, bacon on the side, tropical fruits, yoghurt, and everything else on the menu that we don't usually have access to at home.' She lifted domes from plates as she spoke. 'Dig in.'

Maybe she'd done something right, because that was an invitation he didn't refuse and boy could he pack it away. She was more of a grazer, not all that food-focused, whereas he went for it to the extent that she wondered if he ever got full. He caught her watching, and she looked away, but not before he'd downed his utensils and pushed his plate aside with an abruptness that scraped along the tabletop and every nerve she owned.

She didn't know what to say. 'More coffee? I think it's a two-coffee kind of morning.'

His nod was enough to get her heading for the phone to order it. 'Anything else?'

'No.'

She didn't press. 'When's checkout?'

'Twelve.'

With their flight at five. They had all morning to fill in.

'Do you need to go back to the gallery this morning?' he asked.

Conversation initiated by him. She'd take it. 'Yes. Probably a good move to make sure the print you don't want on display comes home with us. Or goes home with you. Or me. Or whatever you want.' Was there any ground between them that wasn't treacherous? If there was, she hadn't found it yet. 'I do want to check out the button shop near the opal shop if I have the time.'

'Button shop,' he echoed. 'Because you need buttons?'

'No, I've just never been in a button shop before. Want to come along?'

'No.'

And why would he? He might have been sitting opposite her at the breakfast table, but every word, every look, spoke of a distance he wanted to maintain. Whatever they'd done together last night, however much his body had betrayed him, he seemed driven to regain control. And control was fine, he could have it, but did it really have to come with such distance between them?

'You're kind of remote this morning. I'm not sure what I was expecting.' But it wasn't this level of awkwardness. 'Hugs?' She was rewarded with a blank stare, but soldiered on regardless. Last night she'd asked for what she wanted and received it. The strategy bore repeating. 'Kisses?'

His gaze dropped to her fingers, her wedding-ring finger in particular, and he frowned.

Oh. The ring. Right. 'It's not as if I'm suddenly expecting our engagement to become real,' she sought to assure him. 'We still have a plan to end it, and I know it's not real and there'll come a time when…oh!' Man, she was so *stupid*. 'Last night at the gallery when we argued in public… Do you want to use it to set the scene for our break-up? Because that makes sense.' Of course it did. And here she was, begging for good-morning kisses.

The melon on her plate lost all appeal, nothing but slimy squares of food she doubted she'd be able to swallow. 'When do you want to do it? Today?' She reached for the engagement ring on her finger. Why was she even wearing it when she wasn't in public? It hadn't been genuinely given. Judah definitely didn't want to spend the rest of his days with her—he could barely manage a weekend. One night had been enough for him. A night out of time. No repeats. 'I'm sorry.' It wouldn't come off.

'Bridie—'

'It does come off, bear with. I don't want to damage it.' Her clammy hands and fumbling fingers weren't co-operating.

'*Bridie.*' She'd given him the perfect excuse to pull back, so why did he reach out to cover her hands and stop her from removing his ring? Why did her panic soothe him? Make him feel even more tuned into her than he had been last night? Did he feel better for knowing she was even more vulnerable than him? What kind of person did that make him?

The way out of this crazy engagement was right there in front of him. He had his land back and had paid Bridie fair market price for it. The Conrad place was his. He'd been there for her when she'd launched her new career. He'd made a mistake and had done his best to limit the fallout for them both. He could end this farce of an engagement here and now and *finish* this. Minimise the damage he was doing to her. So, why didn't he just let her take the ring off and give it back to him?

It wasn't chivalry that made him reach out and close his hand over hers. He just wanted that ring to stay right where it was. 'Stop,' he ordered gently. 'Let's not do that today. We'll get around to it eventually, and when we do we'll be ready with press statements, business goals in place and a story about how we make much better business partners than lovers.'

She stilled and searched his face as if testing his sincerity, so he gave it to her and to hell with the consequences.

'As for last night…' She bit her lip and let him continue. 'I didn't do right by you last night.'

'By all means, make it up to me.'

Her enthusiasm was so good for his ego. 'I intend to. What kind of jewellery do you like?'

'Are you going to buy your way out of a hole every time you think you don't measure up?'

Was that what he was doing? 'It's an option.'

'No, it's not.' She seemed adamant. 'Not with me. If you want to put last night behind us and never do it again, just say so. I'm tough. I can take it.'

So *not tough*. He remained terrified he would do something wrong by accident and break her. 'I do want to continue having sex with you. That's a given. But I'm also expecting you to give up on me eventually, and I don't blame you. Until then have at me.'

She sat back, eyes narrowed. What had he done now? No split-second decision-making here—he was thinking hard about how a relationship between them would eventually play out.

'No hard feelings,' he added.

'That's not the point, Judah. The point is to *have* all the feelings! You walked out here this morning and you've shut all yours back down!'

'Not all of them.' Frustration was riding him pretty hard at the moment. 'If you want an open, fun-loving guy who's in touch with his emotions, *that's not me*. It might never be me. *This* is the real me. Take a good long look.'

Who could blame her if she walked away?

She pulled her hand out from beneath his and aimed a smile at him that missed by a mile. 'You're such an ass. And if you think I'm ever going to give up on you, you don't know me. Lovers or not.'

They glared at one another across the table. Bridie was the first to break. 'I'm going button shopping.'

Buttons. This whole conversation had started with buttons. It was enough to make a zip man out of him. 'Let's meet for lunch. Fresh seafood. Outdoors.'

She stood. 'Is it a date or am I back to being your neighbour and fake fiancée again?'

'It's a date.'

'Good.'

She was almost to her bedroom door. 'Bridie—'

Make that through the bedroom door and out of sight. 'The sex was good. Better than good.' He'd damn near torn his hands from his wrists with the force of his ecstasy, and practically passed out afterwards. 'Thank you for putting up with me. For keeping us safe.'

Her head appeared from the other side of the doorframe, a riot of golden autumn curls and sparkly hoop earrings. Her eyes were guarded; he'd put that look there and that was a good thing. And then she smiled, and he could have sworn the sun came out. 'I loved it too.'

He was so screwed.

CHAPTER NINE

THE BUTTON SHOP Bridie ended up visiting supplied all the costume needs of major theatre groups in Sydney. Vintage buttons were especially amazing, Bridie had a sold-out exhibition on her hands and three landscape commission enquiries and the write-up on the show was headed for the weekend magazine of the national daily newspaper, courtesy of the 'palpable tension and dramatic history between two scions of the Australian outback community'.

'I can't control what photos will be used, but with a headline like that you can bet the story will make mention of the work Mr Blake wanted removed,' Sara had told her bluntly. 'I realise that won't go down well with him.'

'Can you ask them not to?'

'I can. You or Mr Blake might have better luck with that.'

Bridie didn't look forward to letting Judah know. 'You pulled the picture from the exhibition?'

The older woman nodded. 'Where would you like it sent. Also, framed or unframed?'

'I'll take it with me now, unframed. Thank you so much.'

'And is Mr Blake in…better spirits this morning?'

'Yes. He's quite recovered.'

'If you ever become worried for your safety, *call* me. Or come here to the gallery. I know the drill and I know it intimately. I can help you.'

Bridie blinked, taken aback. Did worldly, sophisticated Sara honestly believe that Judah would hurt her? On the strength of his behaviour last night? It hadn't been that bad, had it? 'Oh, wow, *no*. Sara, I appreciate your offer but you have it all wrong. I trust Judah with my life and for very good reason.'

'Of course, of course you do.' Sara's words flowed like redirected water. 'But my offer still stands. Call any time, and if you start talking about an imaginary exhibition in, say, London, I'll know you need help.'

'Okay.' What else could she say? 'Is this because of Judah's past? His reputation?'

'No, it's because I'm a woman of a certain age, with a lot of experience, and I lose nothing by mentioning that I am here for you if ever you need a safe place to be.' Sara gestured for Bridie to walk with her towards the office area. 'Now. Let's talk about booking you for another show.'

Judah was waiting for her when she stepped from the gallery. Only innate grace kept Bridie from stumbling down the stairs at the sight of him. 'Are you waiting for me?'

'Yes.'

'Because of this?' She held up the art tube containing the picture of them. 'Because it's right here.' She handed it to him without any more ceremony. 'The bad news is that the write-up in this weekend's paper is likely to mention it, and they're going to rake up our past connections as well as our present ones, which… I guess I expected that. Did you?'

'Of course.' He began to walk towards the quay, same direction as the hotel. 'But apart from that the write-up is good?'

'Sara thinks it will be.'

'Good. I have a water taxi ordered for half eleven. It'll take us to a restaurant the concierge recommended.'

But when they got to the hotel and he'd handed the picture tube over to be taken to the room, he steered her towards the tiny jewellery cubby to the left of the foyer. It had a three-strand pearl necklace and diamond and pearl earrings on a black dummy's bust in the window and was so beautifully lit that it looked like a renaissance painting. The pearls glowed with a magical lustre and the lack of anything resembling a price tag suggested that budget-conscious shoppers should keep on walking.

'C'mon in, I want your advice on something.' He opened the jewellery shop door and held it for her.

Was he buying something for himself?

'Mr Blake.' The gentleman behind the counter beamed.

Judah nodded. 'Martin. This is Miss Starr.'

'Enchanted.' The man reached below the counter and lifted up a velvet pad that contained three necklaces, clearly designed for women. Bridie looked to Judah.

'For you,' he said. 'A gift from me.'

She hadn't forgotten his earlier words about buying her jewellery because he felt he'd let her down somehow.

He hadn't.

His brutal honesty—in everything he said and did—was a gift in itself, forcing her to examine her own behaviour and immaturity. 'You don't have to. This weekend is already…' she shrugged a little helplessly '…gorgeous. Thought provoking. Revealing.'

'All the more reason for you to have something to remember it by. Take a look. I don't know your taste. You might not like any of them.'

But that wasn't the problem, because she loved all of them. The problem was the no-doubt astronomical and currently invisible price tags that accompanied the necklaces.

'I can't.' She backed up until she hit the door.

'A photo a month. A lifeline to home. You gave me that.' He nodded towards the counter. 'They don't even compare. Trinkets.'

'Beautiful, expensive trinkets,' she corrected as she met the salesman's long-suffering smile.

'Thank you, Miss Starr. Yes, yes, they are all beautiful and expensive, although I can't quite bring myself to call them trinkets—even if the customer is always right,' said Martin the despairing salesman, before regrouping. 'Take this one, for example: a triplet of perfectly graded natural white South Sea pearls with a nineteen-carat fire opal centrepiece set in platinum. A classic design.'

'Gorgeous.' She admired it from afar. 'Not exactly something you'd wear every day.'

'No indeed, Miss Starr. That one's a statement trinket.' He moved on to the next necklace, lifting it and letting it dangle from his fingers. '*This* one you could wear every day.'

Maybe if you were a queen. Or, nope, not even then. Bridie eyed the diamond and sapphire art deco pendant, before turning to look at Judah. 'Are you serious?'

'Do I not look serious?' He had a smile in his eyes that was hard to resist. 'I like the third one.'

It was a modern piece. A swirling landscape of white diamonds, black pearls, cerulean sapphires and pinky-orange-coloured stones that glowed with no less dazzle than the diamonds and sapphires. 'What are the pinkish stones?'

'Padparadscha sapphires, ethically mined, of course. Aren't they wonderful?'

'Stunning.' She leaned closer and the salesman mirrored her. 'But still not an everyday wearer.'

The man spread his hands, his expression helpless. 'Madam, we don't *do* everyday wearers.'

'She'll take that one,' said Judah, and to her, 'Today's a good day. Wear it to lunch.'

So she wore it to lunch and tossed her head and felt like a million dollars as she collected admiring gazes from nearby strangers. Maybe it was the pendant they were looking at. Maybe it was Judah, handsome sod with a watchful quality about him and a stare that encouraged people to mind their own business.

But even he couldn't resist the glitter of the harbour and a playful breeze, a cold beer at his fingertips and the freshest of seafood.

'I could do this more often,' she told him with a deep sense of satisfaction.

'Glad to hear it.'

'What about you? Enjoying yourself? Because you get all flinty eyed every so often.'

'Is that so?'

'Yeah. Seagulls giving you trouble?'

'More like some of your admirers don't know when to stop staring.'

Ah.

'Do you get that a lot?'

She nodded. 'And I've never enjoyed that kind of attention, but it's what you get with a face like mine. Beauty has its price. Or they could be trying to put a price on my absolutely stunning necklace.'

'Suits you,' he rumbled. 'Why have you stayed single when you could have any man you want?'

'Trust issues, I guess. Past trauma. Former shut-in. I might look like the prettiest doll in the shop but the hidden damage does run deep. And I live in the middle of nowhere—and like it.' She narrowed her gaze. 'I wasn't waiting for you, if that's what you're getting at. I thought I covered that last night.'

'You did.'

'And I know you're probably going to tire of me, because once you do adjust to life outside you'll shine so bright you'll leave me behind. But I'm aiming to enjoy you while I have you. I like you. I trust you. It's enough.' It had to be enough. He wasn't offering anything else and she was okay with that.

Mostly.

'Who else do you trust?' he asked.

'My father, Gert, Reid, my aunt—even though she thinks she failed me. That's five. Not bad. What about you? Who do you trust?'

He shrugged and lifted his beer to his lips.

'Anyone?' She waited for him to answer, but it was a long wait. 'Not even Reid?'

'He's young.'

'He's loyal,' she stressed. 'Give him a chance.' *And me,* she refrained from saying. *Give me a chance too. I'll do my best by you.*

But he didn't need that kind of pressure and neither did she. Maybe all they needed to do was take everything one moment at a time. 'I'm having fun. Are you having fun?'

'Maybe I am.'

'Oh, go on, say yes and make my day. I like where we're sitting, by the way. Both of us with our backs against the wall so we can see what's going on. In feng shui they call this the command position.'

'Is that so?'

'Yup. I'm a fount of useless information.'

'Good to know. How was the button shop?'

'Brilliant. Buttons have stories. I bought blue ones.'

'I can barely order from a menu, there's so much choice,' he offered after a moment. 'A button store would have blown my mind.'

From teasing to serious information in the space of a heartbeat. *Pay attention, Bridie, to what this man chooses to share.* 'Were you always like that with choices?' she asked carefully, and he shook his head.

'No. In prison they take choices away. Stay there long enough and *not* making choices becomes the norm.'

'But you're making all sorts of big business decisions. Huge, important ones with far-reaching consequences for conservation and land management. How does that fit?'

'That's something I've been thinking about since my teens and I've had plenty of time to fine-tune those dreams. There's money there to do it and making it happen is easy. There's no oysters versus bruschetta decision on the table.'

It didn't make sense to her, but it clearly made sense to him. 'I'd be impressed by your ability to compartmentalise except that eccentric billionaires are a dime a dozen.'

'We are not!'

'Maybe not,' she conceded with a grin. 'And thank you for telling me about your button issues. I like that you did.'

He looked oddly shy for a moment. 'You wanted to get to know me.'

'I still do. And when it comes to your land conservation plans, I want to help. I literally have tens of thousands of landscape and wildlife photos you can use in marketing or promo campaigns, and I'm up for taking more specific shots if you need them.'

'Just don't make me choose which ones.'

'I won't. Those decisions can be mine all mine.'

Look at us, she thought, all smiley and compatible. Take that, weekend headlines. What palpable tension and dramatic history between them? 'If I order the orange and almond cake and you order the sticky date pudding, I can try both of my favourite desserts on this menu. Not that I'm greedy and entitled, but I may just be an opportunist. Are you in?'

His smile came swiftly and, she liked to think, appreciatively. The shaking of his head suggested no, but then, 'Yeah,' he said. 'I'm in.'

By the time they arrived home that night a new understanding had sprung up between them.

No more pretending to be strong and invulnerable for either of them. Eccentricities were welcome—between them they had a fine selection—and upon request they would take a stab at explaining where they came from.

Trust didn't come easily to Bridie, but regardless of what had happened this weekend she still trusted him.

As for Judah's trust in her, Bridie figured he'd made some small headway with that this weekend, what with all she'd learned about him. They weren't friends—sorry, Reid, not a chance in hell, what with the sexy bondage times and the jewellery fit for a princess, not to mention all the button talk.

But they were something.

CHAPTER TEN

'WHAT HAVE YOU done to my brother?'

Reid stood on her veranda, hands on his hips and the dust from his buzzbox helicopter settling into every crack and crevice and on every surface it could find. 'How many times do I have to tell you?' she muttered sternly, and tried to look mean and ornery from her spot at the kitchen door. 'No helicopters in the home paddock. And what do you mean what have I done to your brother? I am his friend. I listen when he speaks, argue with him on occasion and try to keep up with the way he thinks.'

She'd also made it abundantly clear that he was welcome in her bed at any time, but so far he hadn't taken her up on that invitation.

'He's up at five every morning for push-ups and a workout, and then there's the daily meal menu—deviate from that at your peril—and then he has meetings until one, and every day he makes a point of grabbing me to watch the sun set and to tell me what he's been doing in as few words as possible. Yesterday his exact words were "I just bought a demo salt pond power plant to our west, and now I want all the land in between as well." Millions and millions of dollars' worth of deals, just like that.'

'Really not seeing your problem. Your brother's a powerhouse who now owns a powerhouse. Embrace it.'

'He still doesn't sleep in his bed.'

'Ah.' Sometimes he came to visit Bridie and told her all sorts of things about his hopes and dreams and what he wanted to achieve. Sometimes he took a stack of her print photos and took himself out to the veranda and laid them all out and then spent a good hour or more choosing his favourite.

She'd come to learn that it didn't really matter if there was something drastically wrong with the picture he chose. Celebration lay in the fact that he'd managed to choose one.

Sometimes he spent the night on the daybed on her veranda. But he spent it alone and come morning he'd be gone, with nothing to show that he'd ever been there in the first place, except that one time when a generous handful of paper daisies had appeared outside the French doors that led from the veranda to her bedroom.

If they now took pride of place in a cut crystal vase on the top of her bedroom chest of drawers, that was her business.

'Your brother's healing. He's finding himself and making up for lost time and doing a brilliant job of it. Be proud of him.'

Reid threw his hands up in surrender. 'You are so utterly gone on him.'

'Am not.'

'Are too. Last night he stripped the house of every item of green clothing, including mine, and now I can't find my best jacket.'

And he never would. 'The jacket is gone. Sacrificed to last night's bonfire. Something to do with never wanting to wear or see prison greens ever again.'

'It was my favourite jacket!'

'Have you tried wearing more pink?' She had. 'Or yellow? Or bright florals? Because you can probably influence your brother by colour alone, but don't tell him I said that. It's my secret weapon. Oh, and if you're looking for bath towels there's more coming. I ordered them this morning. Very colourful. Lots of spots and pretty patterns.'

'We already have a million bath towels,' Reid muttered as he stomped up the steps.

'Had,' she corrected. 'Apparently they were threadbare, or white gone grey, or something.' It really had been a magnificent bonfire. Very cathartic.

'Aargh!' Unlike his brother, Reid wasn't slow to let his emotions out. 'Why are you enabling him? I'll have no clothes left! There is eccentric and then there is Judah!'

There was some slight…more than slight…truth to Reid's words. 'Want some coffee? I have freshly baked Anzac biscuits for dunking?'

'I hope they're the size of dinner plates. I'm in a mood.'

'Yes. Yes, you are.' This earned her a teenage glare.

Reid was almost as at home in her kitchen as she was. She put the biscuits in front of him and turned to sort out the coffee. He'd straddle the bald blue chair with the fence paling backrest and scratch at the paint, the way he always did. The chair sat directly opposite the wood-fire stove that only got fired up in the deepest of winter nights. It didn't matter that fire so rarely burned in it. He was ready for it.

Judah wasn't the only eccentric Blake on the planet. Maybe it was a displaced Englishman thing.

'He's hired a home office assistant bookkeeper person, sight unseen,' said Reid as she put hot coffee in an oversized mug on the counter beside him. 'She's twenty-two, been in the foster care system since her father went to prison when she was ten, and she never finished school.' He pointed his Anzac biscuit in her direction. 'Let's hope she doesn't like wearing green.'

An office assistant? This was not altogether welcome news. 'Where's she going to live?'

'Shearer's quarters.'

'For how long?'

'Ask your colour censorship partner in crime. And while you're at it, remind him that his brother is not a kid and should be part of the hiring process next time, with a voice and a vote and a *say* in who gets to live in his back yard.'

'You're right. I'll tell him all that.' She didn't know what to think about another woman living out here and working closely with Judah. What if he came to like her? What if he sought out Bridie less?

'Whatever you're planning, I like it,' said Reid, watching her closely.

'I have no idea what you're talking about.' She schooled her expression into something a little less murderous.

'You don't fool me. You're shook too.'

'What is this shook? I'm good with change these days. Change is inevitable.'

'I'm glad you think so, because I'm going to Townsville this afternoon to collect our new employee. Want me to get anything for you while I'm there?'

Now that he mentioned it… 'Fresh pearl perch, a dozen rock oysters, black caviar, two lemons and a lettuce that doesn't need resuscitation.'

He stood up and swung the chair he'd been sitting on around the right way.

'If you can have it waiting for collection at hangar two, you've got it. Tell them to leave it in the cold room,' he said.

'I adore you.'

'I'm counting on it. Tell Judah I have one very nice, very olive-green woollen jumper left. Mum knitted it. When I wear it it's like a hug from someone who's just not there any more, do you know what I mean? I can't lose it. Can you make him understand that?'

'Why can't you tell him that?'

'Every time I mention the parents he shuts me down. He's not talking about them, which means I don't get to either.'

Her heart went out to him. Shades of her father, who never ever mentioned her mother because the pain was too vast. 'I'll tell him.' That was a promise. 'And I'll make him understand.'

Judah liked to think he stood still for no one, but the sight of Bridie lit by firelight demanded he halt and commit that vision to memory. Why else did he have so many bonfires at her place? He was running out of things to burn. Tonight, though…tonight she'd met him at her kitchen door in a pink slip of a dress that made him want to reach out and stroke every bit of her with reverent hands.

Reid had brought an esky full of fresh seafood back for Bridie, at Bridie's request, and Bridie had needed someone to eat it with. Reid was busy settling the new girl in, so Judah was it.

That was how Bridie had put the invitation to him, and apart from a slight curtness in her voice that he couldn't quite pin down to anything in particular, he'd taken her invitation at face value and rocked up showered, shaved, dressed for dinner and in a good mood.

Decision-making skills were coming back to him.

He didn't expect oysters, caviar and his choice of beer or champagne to be waiting for him inside the formal dining room of Starr homestead, but it was. Candlelight too and pressed tin ceiling painted duck-egg blue, with the walls a deeper blue altogether, wooden baseboards and an open fireplace up one end. Had it been winter, it might have been lit but at the moment it was stacked with wine. Photos of her parents and a pair of tall blue vases sat on the mantel. A spectacular black-and-white photo of channel country hung on the wall. He didn't need to ask in order to know that it was one of hers.

She'd gone to a lot of trouble to feed them this evening and, even if he didn't know why, he wasn't ungrateful.

He looked to the scarred oak dining table. Lots of glassware, lots of cutlery and, given his family history and schooling, he automatically knew what to do with every bit of it, no decision making required.

It wasn't until he pulled her chair out and saw her seated that he spotted the engagement ring and brace-let he'd given her months ago winking at him from the centre of the scarred oak dining room table. He took a deep breath and let it out slowly and hopefully silently as he took a vicelike grip on his composure. Don't jump to conclusions. *Don't* make snap decisions. No one went to this much trouble in order to break a fake engagement. Not that he had any experience with that. 'What's this?'

'*This* is a reckoning.' She swept a bare hand towards the table, urging him to sit. 'Either way, we're celebrating a productive few months and your outstanding re-entry into society.'

Pretty words and possibly true, but there was a pile

of his family jewels sitting on the table and he couldn't quite let that go. 'What kind of a reckoning?'

'A long overdue one, according to my libido. Sit, eat.' She leaned forward and lit a candelabra full of candles and snared him twice over with her beauty. He'd gained a lot of knowledge these past few weeks, months, plenty of it to do with his neighbour, friend and false fiancée, Bridie. She was resourceful and smart. Playful. Sneaky, even. Her father was still not home and she'd taken control of Devil's Kiss station with a sure and steady hand.

No doubt about it, Bridie Starr was an extraordinarily capable woman when on her home turf, and especially when she had a camera in her hand.

Time to pay attention.

'What do you want?' He asked more plainly. 'Because if you're looking for permission to show the pictures you took of me the other day, the answer is no. Hell no.' He'd been cleaning out a water trough for the cattle with his hat, and he'd taken his shirt off because why get that soaked too, and somehow he'd broken the water stopper while he was at it, which meant he was in there, boots and all with a fix, and by the end of it, he'd just laid back and closed his eyes and let the damn trough fill with him in it, his arms trailing over the edges and his wet hat back on his head.

'No,' he'd said when he'd heard her camera start clicking, but he hadn't really meant it and he'd been too content to move.

'But, Judah, *Man in Bath*,' she'd muttered and somehow managed to capitalise every word, and then she'd started *positioning* him.

He'd given her plenty of warning to put the camera down before dragging her in with him.

'I would *never* again put any of the pictures I take of

you out in the world for public viewing. Lesson learnt.' Her hand over her heart only served to highlight the necklace snugged against the gentle swell of her breasts. *His* necklace, the one he'd pressured her into accepting. He hadn't seen it on her since they'd left Sydney. What was it the sales guy had said? Not a daily wearer.

What use was it if she couldn't wear it whenever she wanted to?

His gaze slid to the sparkling little pile on the table and then away again. He reached for the champagne and at her nod filled her glass and then his. 'So what is it you want?'

'First, you owe your brother a new coat. You neglected to tell me it was his clothes we were burning last night.'

'Spur-of-the-moment decision. I'll buy him a new one. A better one.' Not green.

'He has a green woollen jumper. Your mother knitted it. He's very attached to it. Leave it alone.'

This time shame licked at him. 'I will.'

'Reid also wasn't impressed with your solo decision to bring a complete stranger into the home paddock, so to speak.'

'He's okay with it now, though.' Bridie gave him the look, one he'd recently interpreted to mean he needed to do more explaining. 'Bubbly, outgoing, down-to-earth girl.'

'Is that why you chose her? You've met her before?'

'Once or twice.'

'Don't make me beat more information out of you, Judah. Because I will.'

Her bluffing needed so much more work. 'She's the daughter of a guy I used to bunk with. I said I'd look her up when I got out and when I found her she was chipping cotton twelve hours a day, six days a week, doing the bookwork for a childcare centre in the evenings in exchange for childcare, and two weeks behind on her rent.'

'She has a kid?'

'A boy. He's nearly two. Last I saw, he'd fallen asleep on Reid's shoulder as Reid came out of the linen cupboard with a handful of baby blankets that used to be his.'

'Judah, Reid's a baby himself, especially in the world of relationships. What are you doing?'

'I'm bringing people into our lives because we need help and they might need a break, and we're building things. There's another woman heading this way next week. She's a sixty-seven-year-old bookkeeper I met on a ferry in Sydney, and if I don't trust my instincts now I never will. You willing to trust me, Bridie? They're both women. I wouldn't invite a man out here to stay before running it by you.'

'Then why not run the bringing of women out here past me too?'

'Because they're not as much of a threat to you? Being women and all?'

'Says who? Okay, I agree, it's unlikely they'd truss me up and stick me in a car boot, but there are other ways to pose a threat. They might not even know they're being threatening.'

'Threatening how?' He truly didn't get it.

Bridie squeezed lemon over her oysters and reached for the caviar spoon. 'You are so…so…irritating! And secretive. All I'm saying is would it kill you to share your plans before they hit me and Reid like a freight train?'

'That's not *all* you're saying.' He was still trying to get to the bottom of that. 'I know it's going to take a while to warm up to new faces around here, but we have plans and goals that you fully support. People with specialised skills are going to be coming in. I'm starting with these two—three—because I figured it might ease you in gently so you *can* get used to people coming and going. I thought it would help you as well as them.'

She stared at him with stormy eyes.

'In my defence, I extended one of those offers months ago and the other one weeks ago and neither of them took me up on it at the time. I'm not hiding information from you deliberately. I'm still figuring out the decision-making process and when it's an easy one I make the call because I can.' Did he really have to remind her about the buttons?

'I'm jealous.'

'You're—' He sat back. 'Of what?'

She smiled grimly. 'Jealous of a hardworking single mum who sounds like she could use a hand and who'll have daily access to you that I don't. You met a lady in Sydney who sounds like a treasure and you never said a word. You're entitled to a life of your own and I know that. It's just... I'm coming to the conclusion that I might be a little possessive. Of you. And that's not good because you should absolutely spread yourself around, doing good things for other people. It's nice. Unlike me.' She waved towards his plate of food, and then looked down at her own plate and stabbed an oyster with her fork in a way he was pretty sure no oyster had ever been stabbed before. 'These are fresh.'

'Whoa, wait. Back up.' He kind of liked the thought of her wanting to lay claim to him. No need to beat herself up about it though. He eyed her carefully. 'Can we at least agree that I have no sexual interest in these women and that you have nothing to worry about on that front?'

'No, because then I'd have to stop arguing before I've worked my way up to making my point.'

Good old logic. Not a big player in this conversation. 'By all means make your point.'

'You seek me out, you seem to like my company, and every time I ask if you want your ring back you say *not yet*. You let me see all your eccentricities and, sod knows, they're fascinating. You're fascinating.'

He wasn't exactly sure where she was going with this but surely she would get to the reason his ring wasn't on her finger soon. 'You're not finished yet, are you?'

'No. You also consistently ignore the fact that I'm dying of lust for you.'

He hadn't touched her since returning from Sydney. He'd wanted her to know what she was getting into if she was having thoughts about being with him. He'd buried lust beneath a mountain of work and had set about showing her all the negative traits he possessed. It was important before they started anything real that she knew the real him. He cleared his throat. 'Nothing wrong with lust. Shows you didn't hate what we did last time.'

'I'd like to do it again. With you. Pretty sure I made that clear. And I get that you don't want to sully me, or overwhelm me, or whatever it is you think you're going to do, but I'm a woman of experience now—'

He snorted.

'—and I'm losing hope.'

Four little words that shattered him more effectively than a crowbar to the head.

'I can't keep giving you this much of myself if you're not interested in taking this—us—any further.'

She had a knack for honest self-reflection that terrified him. And he hadn't been giving out scraps, he'd been lowering guards so deeply nailed into his psyche that they only moved a fraction at a time. 'I'm interested.' Understatement. The thought of losing whatever it was they had made him sweat. 'At the same time, I don't want to overwhelm or disappoint you.'

'But you don't disappoint me,' she said quietly from beneath a fall of lashes. 'I want another reset of our relationship. The Conrad land is yours now. You're making waves in the business world and society thinks you're golden. There's no reason to stay engaged unless we want to. My question is: do you want to?'

'Do you?'

'You first,' she said with a smile that didn't quite meet her eyes. 'I used up all my courage putting that ring on the table.'

Was she really saying she wanted to take him on for good, flaws and all? He wasn't quite ready to admit his fierce joy at that thought, even to himself, but he wanted that ring back on her finger and, timing wise, right now wasn't nearly soon enough.

'My reputation hinges on me being a reformed man,' he offered slowly, mind racing. 'I need to be seen as settled and steady. Combining Jeddah Creek and Devil's Kiss by way of marriage is a move my aristocratic ancestors would applaud. It's good business.'

'Not quite the reset I was imagining,' she murmured.

She deserved more, no doubt, but for all that his feelings for her ran deep—*you're in love with her,* a little voice whispered—she still figured him for a hero and he knew for a fact that he wasn't. The secret he'd held to for so many years, the one that had sent him to prison, clawed at him for release so that she could see him more fully, but he'd given his word and breaking it would have far-reaching and possibly legal consequences for all of them.

Hold your tongue. Give her what truth you can and make it enough. That was what he should be doing.

'I do want to marry you. I want that a lot, but I need you to be sure you know what you're getting into with me, and I don't think you do,' he told her baldly. 'That's my concern. You could still wear my ring while you figure it out.'

Her fingers rubbed at the spot where the ring currently wasn't. 'And would there be sex while I was figuring all this out? Because we haven't... Y'know...'

Oh, he knew. 'Again, I was giving you time to reassess.' And shore up his control. 'But if you need more to go on...'

'I do need more to go on.' They locked glances and she raised an elegant eyebrow in silent question. 'Your move.'

'Rest assured I'll be making one.'

'When?'

'Tonight.'

She changed the subject after that. Spoke about the latest set of plans for the eco cabins and how the indoor-outdoor spaces could become one with the help of sliding walls of glass that could swing out over a deck and either stay there to block the wind or slide seamlessly into the adjacent wall and disappear completely. Both the north-east and south-west walls had been tagged as slide-away. It'd be like living in a box without ends, but there were a few interior walls for privacy when needed, and a roof overhead...

The entire thing could be built in Brisbane, loaded in a container and trucked to the site and then put together in a day, by four labourers. If the cabins didn't stack up as promised, Judah figured the takeaway could be just as speedy.

The oysters were fresh and the caviar topped them off to perfection.

He helped her carry their empty plates to the kitchen once they'd devoured them. Two snappers sat ready for baking, covered in herbs and spices. 'What happens with these?'

'They're for the oven and I'm supposed to spoon the sauce over them every now and again while they're cooking. Easy as.'

She'd gone to a lot of trouble for him. 'Thank you for the wonderful meal.'

'Sometimes I want to try and impress you.'

'You always do.'

She got the food started and he wondered what she'd do if he leaned against the bench and held out his hand. Would she hesitate? Did she really understand what she would be getting into if she took him on for good?

'I have a question for you,' he began. 'It's about travel, English aristocracy and an ancestral home in the UK that needs a lot of work. On the upside, the money's now there to do all the work. If you marry me there'll be travel. Society connections to strengthen, or not, depending what kind of reception a murdering, ex-convict lord from the colonies is given.'

'Sounds horrific.'

'Yes. And you don't like to travel. I'm asking you to think hard about what marriage to me would mean. What would be required of you in order for me to fulfil my ancestral responsibilities. And I do plan to fulfil them.'

Her lips tightened. 'I'm not saying you couldn't find someone better for that role, because you definitely could. But it also sounds like someone should be there to guard your back, and who better than some scrappy little nobody that people will underestimate?'

'Not for long.' At a guess.

'What would your wife even be called?'

'You'd be Lady Bridie Blake, or Lady Blake, but it's only a prefix. A courtesy title. The barony would pass to our firstborn son. The only courtesy titles any of our other children could claim would be minor ones. Reid, for example, is The Honourable Reid Blake.'

'That's…pretty brutal on the younger kids in a family,' she murmured. 'And women.'

'Welcome to the peerage.'

'So, uh, children. Do you want to be a father?' she asked next.

'Yes.'

She made a small hum of approval. 'Daughters or sons?'

'Both. It'd help if they were legitimate.'

'Well, yes. I can see that.'

He held out his hand and her smile warmed his soul as she came to him willingly. He brushed her hair away from her face as gently as he could, marvelling at its softness and the warmth of her skin. 'Did you just agree to marry me and have my babies?'

'Our babies,' she corrected. 'And no, I haven't agreed to marry you yet, because you haven't asked me yet. Not properly.'

'Marry me.' He brushed his lips against hers and her eyes fluttered closed. An invitation to delve deeper and he took it. Salt on his tongue from the caviar, the sweetness of wine, and the innocent generosity of her every action. 'Say yes.'

She hummed in pleasure and set her hands to his waist. He could feel all his muscles clench as if he were ticklish and waiting for assault. But he wasn't ticklish, and the kisses continued. He let go of her hand and pulled her against him, soft heat to unbearable hardness.

She smiled through her kisses. 'You want me in your bed.'

'Never doubt it.'

'You can have me.'

'Still coming to terms with that. You haven't said yes to marrying me yet.'

She pulled back, out of his arms to check the food. 'You haven't said you love me yet. Or is that too much to ask?'

'It's not too much to ask.' But he still didn't know how to go about saying it.

'Let me guess,' she said drily. 'Love means making yourself vulnerable and that's hard for you.'

'Good guess.'

'Then I guess we'll just have to work on that. Can you hand me the plates from the warming oven?' she asked as she spooned sauce over steaming fish. He got her the plates, grateful for the reprieve, and she smiled her thanks. 'I hope you're hungry.'

'Famished.'

The tasty baked fish and accompanying greens, and the time it took to eat them, did nothing but ratchet up his tension. Was she going to wear his ring again or not? And how would he perform in bed? Would she want to tie him up again?

'Don't tie me up in bed this time,' he blurted, with absolutely no finesse.

She looked up from the delicate dissection of her fish. 'Okay.'

'Not that I—' He started again. 'I've been working on shoring up my self-control.'

'By yourself?' she teased.

'More or less.' She could think what she wanted and it'd probably be true. 'Those first few weeks at home... There were so many foods I hadn't tasted in years and I was a glutton for them, just shovelling it in. So many things I hadn't *done* in years and the need to do them rode me hard. And there you were. Willing.' He cleared his throat and took a sip of the very fine wine she'd served with this course. 'I had so little impulse control back then. I had freedom and no one was controlling my every move, and the curse of it all was that I could barely function. I wanted you and not in a good way. I wanted to *take*.' He shook his head. 'It wasn't right. You should have been scared of me.'

But she hadn't been.

'I have more control now. Over everything.' God, let it be true. 'Even with the occasional bonfire event.'

She lifted her glass and sipped, all effortless elegance and restraint. 'I know you do.'

'There's still a way to go.'

'I know that too.'

He refused dessert and then relented when he saw that she'd gone to the trouble of making lemon tart and had whipped cream to go with fat blackberries. They abandoned the formal dining room and Bridie served dessert on the veranda, and that, more than anything, calmed him.

He didn't know if he'd ever be much of an indoor person.

'Where do you go of a night to bed down when you don't stay here?' she asked.

'All over. Mostly the top of the escarpment if it isn't windy. River bend if I'm looking for extra shelter.'

'And you sleep in a swag?'

He nodded. Couple of rolls of latex mattress and bedclothes, all of it covered in a canvas outer and he was all set. 'Unless it's hot, and then I sleep *on* the swag in the bed of the truck.'

'What about the bugs?'

'I'm outback tough. There are no bugs.'

Bridie snorted at his utter bull.

'I wouldn't demand that of you,' he murmured, the thought of her flawless skin covered in bites not at all to his liking. 'I'm working my way in.'

'My bedroom has big screen doors out onto the veranda. You can't see the sky from the bed, but you could be outside in an instant. I'm inviting you in.'

He set his empty bowl down and waited with gentlemanly patience while she finished the last of her lemon dessert. They still hadn't finished the wine, but he'd long since stopped drinking it and Bridie's glass was still mostly full. Nothing they decided to do next could be blamed on alcohol.

He stood and held out his hand again, and she flowed into his embrace as if she belonged there. 'Where's your bedroom?'

He followed her to it and stepped into a world of lamp-lit linen and soft-looking pillows. Jarrah floorboards grounded the room and floor rugs added touches of silver, pink and saltbush-green. The big old four-poster bed looked so inviting with its fluffy pillows and pale blue bedspread and ivory sheets. Bridie's bedroom was classy, feminine and soothing. He loved it.

'Is this all right?' she asked, and he could tell she was waiting for him to bolt.

'It's you.'

'If I do anything wrong, you'll tell me, right?'

He had to laugh. 'That's my line.'

'See, I thought your line might have been *strip*.'

Oh, hell, yes. 'Good line. Great line. Inspired. Do that.'

She made a meal out of removing her clothes. The outer layer first, and whoever had designed her lingerie needed a medal, because it made his brain shut down completely. Lace, and plenty of it, cut just so to accentuate precisely how different her body was from his. So perfect. Practically untouchable.

'Hey.' She sought and held his gaze. 'It's only me.'

So not helping.

She reached for him with greedy hands and he responded in kind. He could be needy and greedy and reverent and tender all at the same time, couldn't he? He wanted to please. Willpower was everything. It had seen him through more than seven years of hell. Surely he could appreciate those itty-bitty scraps of lace she'd worn just for him without losing his mind?

'Just touch me,' she whispered. 'I *want* your hands on me. Any argument that I'm pure and virginal is rubbish now. I'm a woman of vast experience.'

No, she was the woman he couldn't resist. Not when she gave him so much encouragement. He toppled her onto that cloud of a bed and followed her down, the soft warmth of her skin intoxicating.

'Take a chance on me,' she murmured. 'I'm right here and I want everything you're prepared to give.'

Bridie felt the tremble in his fingers and the ragged tenderness of his hands on her skin, as she in turn took her fill. She couldn't get enough of the hard muscle that defined him, or the aching tenderness of his kisses. If this was his version of ruining her, being too much for her to handle, she could almost understand his logic.

He was absolutely ruining her for all other men.

He took forever to prepare her, with his fingers and his lips, and this time when he entered her, she welcomed him with laughing enthusiasm. Her laughter seemed to set something free in him, and he smiled as he set up a rhythm that had her shooting past the Milky Way and out into orbit within minutes.

Self-consciousness never stood a chance as she rode every pulsing, ecstasy-ridden moment, and just when she thought she couldn't go again, he snaked his hand between her legs and drew one last ripple from her as he found his own release.

She needed to tell the silent Judah with the heaving chest just how good that had been. Just as soon as she regained the power of speech.

It took a few minutes, but finally she had the voice for it. 'Judah?' She snugged up into him, leaving little room for daylight, and his arms came around her, the fingers of one of his hands twining through her hair to rest at the nape of her neck.

'Mmm?'

'Let's do that again.'

CHAPTER ELEVEN

Tom Starr definitely didn't want to talk to him, thought Judah grimly, as he left yet another message for the older man to call him. The couple of times Tom *had* responded to his questions, Bridie had been her father's spokesperson.

Yes, to putting a portion of Devil's Kiss station into the conservation trust Judah had set up.

Yes, to putting the payment for the land Bridie had purchased from Judah's father into the general Devil's Kiss business account.

Judah had hoped his blunt request for permission to marry Bridie would have got Tom to pick up or at least return the call, but no.

Nothing.

That was two weeks ago.

Even Reid had tried calling. Reid had a lot of time for Tom, because of how helpful Tom had been during that four months or so Reid had been alone out here—before Judah had returned.

That man—his father's friend, the one who'd helped Reid through those toughest of times, the one who'd pulled Bridie through her almost withdrawal from society—was a man Judah didn't know.

When he thought of Tom at all it was with a mixture

of frustration and anger, and deeply buried resentment that he didn't dare examine. That night... It had been two against one and Judah and Tom had been on home ground. They could have tackled Laurence, restrained him, neutered him on the spot... Between them they could have done *something* that didn't require ending the man. But Laurence Levit had burst from the car and charged them, and Tom, with his twenty-two-calibre shotgun that he'd used for years on the farm, hadn't hesitated and he sure as hell hadn't missed.

Judah didn't *blame* Tom for taking the shot. Not really. They'd all been running on fear and instinct.

But more and more, Judah railed against keeping secrets from Bridie. The woman who once more wore his engagement ring and who saw more of what lived inside him every day. Hopes and dreams. Struggles and failures. Hard-won success when it came to the simplest of decisions. She did more than simply encourage him. She believed in him.

He had *Notice of Intended Marriage* paperwork burning a hole in his desk drawer, and he wanted to move on that soon. *Just do it,* he thought. *Tell her you love her and that you've never been happier and just marry her and let the past stay buried in a vow of secrecy.*

Loving her didn't have to mean confiding in her, surely.

Even if he wanted to.

These days he didn't know what exactly it was that shook him from her bed in the dark hours of most mornings, but he tried to make it up to her. He'd taken to collecting wildflowers and greenery, whatever he could find, and returning with a fistful and either leaving them on her doorstep or bringing them with him to breakfast.

Bridie had clear run out of vases but her eyes would still light up every time he handed her a posy.

'Heard anything from your father?' he asked one morning after a night that had made him forget his own name and a morning spent watching the sun rise from the top of Devil's Peak. He was back on her veranda now with a coffee in hand, no sugar, and way too much cream.

'Yes.' Bridie sat in an old rocking chair wearing a stripy pink T-shirt and darker pink bed shorts, her hair in a messy bun and breakfast in hand; to Judah she'd never looked more beautiful. 'He bought an opal mine in Lightning Ridge, complete with underground home and a hole-in-the-wall shop front, and apparently he *does* mean hole in the wall. I don't know what's going on with him. He's too old to be having a midlife crisis and he hasn't said anything about meeting a woman, but what other reasons are there for his refusal to come home? He has no interest in the management of Devil's Kiss any more and I truly don't understand. This is his home. Why won't he come *home*?'

So Judah rang again, and this time Tom picked up.

'You're a hard man to reach.' Judah spoke first.

'And you're relentless,' grumbled the older man.

'Bridie's worried about you.'

''M fine.'

'Reid misses you too.' Might as well turn those screws.

'They have you now.'

Definitely not the answer he'd been expecting. 'You have a problem with me.' Statement, not question. 'Why? I've kept every promise I've ever made. Especially to you.'

'What do you want?' He could barely hear the older man.

'Permission to marry your daughter.'

'You don't need it.'

That wasn't the point. 'It's customary to ask for it.'

The other man said nothing.

Judah gritted his teeth before he spoke again. Bridie loved this man. Reid thought the world of him. 'You left. The minute I got home you left and I don't understand why. You have people here who love you and people contemplating big changes in their lives, and you're not here for them. Why not? What have I done wrong?'

'Nothing,' Tom rasped after long moments. 'But every time I look at you I feel ashamed at what I've put you through. The trial. Your sentence. The impact it had on your parents and your brother. On you. I'd go back in time and do things differently if I could, but I can't, and it pains me. It pains me to look at you and know in my heart what your generosity has cost you. I don't know how to make it up to you. So I try not to look at you at all.'

'Come home.' Judah didn't want Tom Starr exiled from the life he'd once loved. 'Take a look at what we're building here. Be a part of it again. And if your conscience is troubling you, we can sit down together, with Bridie, and tell her what really happened that night.'

Silence.

'Is that a no?'

'Why?' He could barely hear the other man. 'Why on earth would you want to do that?'

'Did *you* keep secrets from *your* wife?' Judah snapped, losing what little patience he had left. 'I don't *want* to marry your daughter and have to lie to her about that night for the rest of our lives,' he said, abandoning all pretence that he gave a damn about Tomas's conscience. He wanted his own conscience clear. He wanted Bridie to know what she was getting when she chose him. 'Is that really too much to ask?'

He blundered on. 'What if we sat her down and explained everything and that we did what we did to protect her? Surely she'd understand.' And be okay with a father who'd killed to protect her and a future husband who hadn't, but at least there'd be no more lies.

Tom Starr didn't reply.

'Can you at least think about it?'

'You gave me your word.'

'I know. And I've never broken it, even though you broke yours when you told my father what you did. But you could release me from my vow.' He couldn't see the other man to read his face. He had no idea what Tom Starr was thinking. There was just this sea of silence.

'We need to think about this.' There was a world of weariness in the older man's voice. 'If word ever got out I could go to prison. You could go *back* to prison. Is that what you want?'

'Word wouldn't get out because Bridie wouldn't tell anyone.'

'Are you sure about that? Because I'm not. Do you really think we should burden her with a secret she can never share without her whole world crumbling? *And* we'd be making her an accessory after the fact. Is telling her the truth really worth all that?'

The older man was right. He was being a fool. A romantic, idiotic fool. 'You're right.'

'I'm sorry, son, but I just don't see the sense in telling Bridie what happened that night and dragging her into the pit with us. You promised to protect her.'

'I know.'

'You gave me your word.'

'I'll keep it.'

'I know you will.' There was an ache in the older man's voice that he didn't know what to do with. An ache in his own heart because there was no way around this. Tom Starr was right and that was the end of it.

Their secret had to be kept.

Gert was baking and Bridie was stacking groceries; music was blaring and the sun had yet to sap the will to move. All in all, Bridie decided, life was good and she'd never deny it.

'Have you met the new people over at Jeddah Creek yet?' asked Gert.

'Yep.' A couple of times over, plenty long enough to form some opinions. 'Mary the bookkeeper is a sweet-heart, but she's kind of shocked by outback living. I don't know if she'll stay.'

'What about the young one?'

'Kaylee? She's a hoot. Big laugh, can-do attitude, tough as nails. And grateful, y'know? In that way that says she's seen a lot of rough road in her life. I have a feeling she'll stay—at least for a while. Her little guy's not even two yet. Cute kid. Judah and Reid are so pro-tective of him. You should see them.'

Gert snorted. 'Sounds about right. They have that ruling class serve-and-protect mentality, same as their grandfather did. And their father did too, before his lik-ing for a drink ruined him.'

'Yeah, maybe.' Bridie didn't know what bits of Gert's conversation she was agreeing with, but it probably didn't matter.

'You expecting visitors?' Gert asked next.

'Nope.'

'Because there's a line of dust heading in from the east and it's just turned into your driveway.'

The driveway was two kilometres long. Plenty of time for her and Gert to head on out to the veranda and wait. Eventually Bridie got a good enough look at the vehicle to figure out who it was. 'It's my father.'

'Huh,' huffed Gert and headed back inside. Bridie waited, and when her father pulled up and stepped from the cab, she unfolded her crossed arms and ran to greet him. His hug was as solidly comforting as it had always been. 'Hello, stranger.'

'Daughter.' He pulled back. 'You're looking bright.'

'It's all this newfound independence,' she countered drily. 'I've missed you, though.'

He looked uncomfortable. 'I needed to do a bit of thinking.'

'Finished yet?'

'Doubtful. Your aunt sent a present along for you. It's in the back.'

'You saw her? Is she well?'

He nodded. 'Got herself a good man who thinks the world of her.' His gaze didn't stray from Bridie's face. 'I hear you have one of those too.'

They headed into the kitchen, where Gert had coffee on and ginger nuts in the oven. Her father smiled. Gert didn't.

'Tomas Starr, is that you? I barely remember what you look like.'

'And a good day to you too, Gert.'

The older woman fixed him with a gimlet glare. 'Your room's not made up.'

'I can make a bed,' her father said easily.

'Are you back to stay?' Bridie asked, interrupting before war broke out.

Her father shrugged. 'For a while. Mainly to see if

you need anything and whether all the changes are working out.'

'They are.' She'd missed having him around. She wanted him back and for more than just a while. 'Opal miner now, huh? I would never have guessed.'

He dug in his pocket and pulled out two good-sized stones and handed one to her and one to Gert. 'It's a bit of fun.'

'Black opal.' Gert held hers up to the light. 'Tom Starr, you canny ass.'

'Plenty more where that came from,' he offered. 'You're both welcome to join me next time I head down that way.'

'Do I get to keep this opal?' asked Gert.

'Yes, it's for you. Thanks for keeping an eye on Bridie while I was gone.'

'Next time you take off for parts unknown, check in more,' Gert scolded. 'Your daughter worries about you. Those Blake boys have been worried about you too, especially Reid. He looks up to you. You encouraged that and now you've let him down.'

'He has Judah now,' her father countered.

Gert glared at him. 'And you don't think Judah could have used your support too? Tomas Starr, I never took you for such a fool.'

'Live and learn, Gert,' her father said quietly as he hooked his leg around a kitchen stool and took a seat. 'Live and learn.'

Gert headed off to the Blakes' at noon—nothing disrupted her schedule if she could help it, not even the return of the prodigal father. Bridie welcomed the privacy; she had so much to tell her father, from the success of her exhibitions to the photography job she'd agreed to in South Australia that meant she'd be away for a week, staying on a property that had a huge woolshed with a heritage and history she found fascinating. She wanted to tell him she'd sold the season's steers for an excellent price, but had resisted culling any of the main herd when buyers had asked for more meat of any kind. The Devil's Kiss stockmen would have known which animals to cull, no question, but it was traditionally her father's role and she hadn't wanted to overstep.

She waited until after dinner when their bellies were full of home-grown steak, jacket potatoes, asparagus and sweetcorn, and her father had settled into his favourite rocking chair on the veranda, before she broached more personal topics.

'Judah's been trying to reach you.'

'He did.' Her father's eyes were darkly shadowed.

'He asked me for your hand in marriage. He's old-fashioned that way.'

'Did you give him your blessing?'

'We talked.'

Bridie's blood ran cold. Never in a million years had she thought her father would hold Judah's past against him. 'He's a good man, Dad. The best. And I am so… so in love with him.'

'He puts me to shame.' Her father looked away, out over the home paddock and on to the horizon. He took a deep breath. 'What do you remember about the night that bastard took you?'

She shook her head. She hated remembering any of it. 'Laurence came to the door and I let him in. Offered him a coffee. He'd come all this way to clear the air between us, he said, and no one else was here.'

'After that,' her father ordered gruffly.

'I told him I wasn't going back to modelling. It wasn't

what he wanted to hear. He grabbed me. I struggled. He hit me. I passed out. I remember coming to, bound and gagged in the boot of a car. I remember you and Judah rescuing me and Levit bleeding out in the dirt.'

Her father nodded. 'And on the surface that's exactly what happened. Never forget, Bridie girl, that I love you. That I did everything in my power to protect you. And that Judah went way beyond what could be expected of any man to protect you too.'

'I know this already.'

But her father shook his head, leaned forward and brought the rocker to a halt. He stared at the weathered wooden floorboards as if they were the most fascinating things he'd ever seen. 'No, you don't. Not everything. We kept something from you.'

'What do you mean?'

'Judah didn't kill the bastard who kidnapped you, Bridie. I did.'

Don't do anything rash. Bridie used the words as a mantra during her drive to Jeddah Creek homestead. Don't act out. *Listen* to what Judah had to say. And all the while, with every red dust kilometre, the foundations of her world crumbled. Her father was a killer and a liar who'd sold his soul to protect her. And Judah…not a killer, but still a liar who'd paid a huge price for his deception. How could he have chosen to do that for her and her father? She didn't understand.

Bridie checked her speed as she approached the main house. There was a child living in the shearer's quarters these days and other new people about and it wouldn't do to run over them. She parked next to Gert's truck and took the stairs two at a time, only to almost bump into Reid, who looked to be on his way out.

'Whoa, steady Freddie.' He sidestepped her just in time. 'Judah around?'

'In his office.' Judah had turned the sitting room next to the library into his office. It had French doors leading onto the veranda and Bridie didn't bother going through the house to get there.

Judah looked up from his seat behind the desk as she entered, a smile crinkling his eyes. 'Just in time,' he said. 'The cabin plans are in.'

But she didn't want to pour over building plans with him. 'I've just been speaking with my father.'

'Gert said he was back.' He lifted an eyebrow. 'Bearing opals.'

Bridie didn't want to talk about little coloured stones. 'He said you'd asked for his permission to marry me.'

'I did.'

Judah sat back in his chair, everything about him easy and welcoming, except for those watchful, wary eyes.

'You want to know what else he told me?' She couldn't keep the rage out of her voice and it seemed useless to even try.

'That he refused to give it?'

She hadn't known *that*. Apparently she didn't know a lot of things that happened around here. 'He told me what happened that night, Judah. What really happened.'

She'd never seen a person shut down so fast. Any openness in his beautiful strong face disappeared like spilt water in a sandy desert. 'What do you mean?'

'What do you *think* I mean?' she cried. 'Did my father kill Laurence Levit, or did you? Because my father just told me he did it!'

Not by a blink did Judah betray any discomfort. 'I've

said all I'm ever going to say about that. I was convicted and I've done my time. Move on.'

'But my father—'

'Is mistaken.'

'Well, one of you is lying! And I'm inclined to believe him.'

Judah shrugged.

'Judah, please. *Talk* to me.'

'And accomplish what? Shall I make you complicit in a possible cover-up that took place years ago? Should I break the oath I might have made to your father to take the details of that night to my grave? What if I didn't shoot Levit? Do you want to see me up on perjury charges and your father locked up? Is that it?'

'No, I—'

'Then *stop* asking questions. Your father is a deluded old man. Don't believe him.'

But she did believe her father's startling words. That was the problem. 'But why would you *do* such a thing? Why would a young man with *everything* going for him—money, status, a loving family, good looks and good health—why would he choose to be locked up for something he didn't do? Will you at least offer me a theoretical answer to that question?' If Judah wasn't going to confirm a damn thing, could they at least play pretend while she got to the bottom of everyone's actions? 'Can't you open up to me just a little?' she pleaded. 'Because I don't understand. I just don't get it.'

'Is he of the ruling class?' Judah steepled his fingers and held her gaze, looking every inch the aristocrat. 'Or, y'know what? Scrap that. Maybe he'd simply been raised to serve and protect those in his care—the old, the frail, the *children*.'

'But if my father was the one who took the shot, why didn't he say so at the time? They might have gone easy on him. Easier than they went on you.'

'And who would have taken you in? Who would have cared for you the way your father did? Who would have had the love and the patience to help put you back together again? Your aunt? She was already struggling with her own issues. You don't have any other family. Your father was it. Who better to love and protect you than him? What if your father and that foolish young man made a split-second decision to protect you? And then did so.'

She had no answer for him. 'I'm not a child any more.'

'I know that.'

'You can tell me the truth.'

'Good, then hear this.' He spread his hands. 'I love you. And I'll protect you with my last breath, don't ever doubt it. This is me protecting you.'

Not exactly how she'd imagined his first declaration of love for her would go.

He watched as she twisted her engagement ring around and around. 'Are you going to keep that on?'

She didn't know. She was so *angry* with him. For stepping up to take the blame for something he didn't do. For defending his action as the right thing to do, never mind what it had cost him. For protecting her still. 'I'm so sorry,' she whispered.

'You're not to blame. You owe me nothing. And if you're going to take that ring off, *for God's sake just do it*!' He looked more rattled than she'd ever seen him, and she'd seen him rattled a lot. He ran an unsteady hand through his hair. 'I can't stand to watch you playing with it. That's my heart you're holding in your hands.'

His outburst jolted her some way towards recognising how hard this conversation must be for him too. 'You have to stop protecting me,' she defended weakly, even as she clasped her hands behind her back. No fiddling with the ring. Just a vicelike grip of one hand over the tennis bracelet on her wrist.

He glared at her with stormy eyes. 'I will *never* not protect you.'

'Truth is important,' she said next. 'Especially in a marriage.'

'How important?' His gaze didn't leave hers. 'If your father says he pulled that trigger I'll call him a crazy old coot and a liar to his face. If I'm not measuring up to some ideal you have in your head about what you want in a man and truth in marriage, walk away. Run. Because this is who I am.'

'I—' If she believed her father—and she did—she also had to believe that the two most important people in her life had been lying to her all along. Judah was *still* lying to her. 'I'm so confused.'

'It's really pretty simple from where I'm standing. You either understand where I'm coming from or you don't.'

She was confused and shattered. Judah was lying about who pulled that trigger. She knew he was lying. He *knew* she knew he was lying. But he wouldn't stop. 'I need time. I don't know what to think.'

He rose from his chair and headed for the interior door that led to a hallway inside the house. 'Let me know what you decide.'

'Wait!'

He stopped.

'You said you love me.' She hadn't imagined that, had she?

'I do.' He started walking towards the door again. 'It doesn't mean you have to love me back. That's not how it works.'

Moments later he was gone.

CHAPTER TWELVE

BRIDIE DROVE HOME, half expecting her father to have taken off again, but he met her at the door, no questions on his tongue but his eyes awhirl with them. She didn't know what to say to him, she really didn't.

'Judah says you're a lying old coot,' she offered finally. Might as well start at the top. 'So let's make ourselves a cup of tea and figure out where to go from here.'

She let the motions soothe her as she filled the teapot with leaves from the little tin canister that had sat on the kitchen shelf forever. Her father took his black and strong. She took hers with milk and liked it weaker, so she made sure she took first pour. And all the time she marshalled her thoughts and arguments so that the two most important people in her life would remain in her life. 'Let's take it out to the veranda.'

He picked up his cup and she followed him out, unsurprised when he chose the northern veranda with its relentlessly bright light that reached deep into the veranda and sometimes hit the windows. It had the best views, unmarred by garden trees. It was red dirt and spinifex as far as the eye could see, with very little variation in topography. Their most brutal view, in many ways. There wasn't a scrap of civilisation in it.

She sat down beside him on the veranda ledge and

nudged his shoulder with hers. They both sipped deeply of the tea.

'I've missed this,' he murmured.

'You didn't have to leave.'

'Needed to get my head on straight,' he said, and she thought about that. About what Judah's return might have done to him. Judah could reject the notion all he liked but he'd done so much for them. So much more than anyone could have asked of him. And all Judah had asked of them was to let it go and move forward.

'Thing is,' she continued doggedly, 'me, you, Aunt Beth—we can all blame ourselves for the decisions that led us to that moment.' She took her father's calloused hand, with the knuckles just starting to thicken with arthritis, and held on tight. 'I should never have chosen modelling and brought Laurence Levit into our lives. Aunt Beth should have known better than to be taken in by him, but she had barely more experience with predatory men than I did. You could have come to Paris with us and pegged him as a bad one or maybe you wouldn't have, who knows? Point is, he got hold of us and then kept on coming. The law didn't stop him. Those AVOs we had out against him meant nothing out here. Can we agree on that? That Laurence Levit wasn't stopped by ordinary means?'

Her father's hand tightened around hers, a squeeze to show he was listening. 'We can.'

'So whatever happened, happened. And one way or another we owe Judah more than we can ever say. Can we agree on that too?'

'Yes.'

She took a deep breath and exhaled noisily. 'The only payment Judah wants is for us to look forward rather than back, and I am on board with that. I can understand you not being in the same place, and that feelings of guilt or shame or the need for penance might be eating at you, but I want you to know that in my eyes you are both heroes. Laurence crossed a line when he took me. All the character witnesses they put on the stand, all those people who said he was an upstanding man, they didn't look into his eyes and see their own death staring back at them. I did, and it was me or him, Dad. Me or him. I'm glad you chose me.'

Her father squeezed her hand and then carefully let it go, but Bridie wasn't finished yet.

'Judah's adamant he did the deed and he knows I don't believe him, but he won't tell the truth. He's protecting us. Even if I'd rather he didn't this time around.'

'He's a man of his word,' her father muttered with far more complacency than Bridie thought was warranted. 'But look on the bright side, at least now you know the truth, even if he never confirms it. No more secrets between you two. A clean slate before marriage. That's a good thing, so I'm told.'

Wait. 'Did you know Judah was never going to rat you out?'

Her father shrugged. 'Might've.'

Holy—

'That's…' She had no words.

'Inspired?'

More like brutally self-serving. 'You left him to hang. Again.'

'I knew he loved you and wanted to marry you. I knew he could never tell you what really happened, no matter how much he wanted to. Not if he wanted to protect you from knowing too much. But if *I* told you, he could still deny it and we'd all be protected. And you'd know what he wanted you to know but could never tell you.'

'That's insane.'

'It worked.'

Heaven help her it had, but not without cost. She remembered Judah's stricken face and furious outburst when she'd been twisting her engagement ring around and around. When she'd been doing her damnedest to understand his position. 'You took a huge risk, playing us like that.'

'It worked.' He looked towards the horizon. To the harsh land that set a person against relying on others to fix their problems. 'No secrets between you now. Be happy. Reach out for all the happiness you can hold and never take it for granted.'

'Promise me you'll stay a part of our lives,' she pressed.

Her father offered up the ghost of a smile. 'I've got opal seams to find.'

'Then promise me you'll visit often and remember on a daily basis how much I love you and want you in my life.'

'Judah might prefer otherwise. What did he call me? A lying old coot?'

'Well, you are,' she felt compelled to point out. He was also her father. The same father who'd given her the time and space in which to heal from her ordeal. The one who'd helped her live her best life.

Bridie leaned her head against the veranda post. 'I didn't handle my confrontation with Judah very well. I got all caught up in truth-telling and couldn't see the bigger picture.' *Breathe in, breathe out and try not to panic.* 'It's possible he thinks I'm going to dump him.'

Her father lowered his cup. 'Are you?'

'No.' A world of no. 'I'm going to marry him and protect him and cherish him as best I can, and he's never going to think I don't love him for being the man he is. Not for a second. Not even a fraction of a second.'

'Best get on that.'

'I will.'

Bridie had a plan. Granted, it would take the assistance of several other people in order for her to pull it off, but the end result was going to show Judah exactly how much she cherished him and all that he was.

Her first call was to Reid, and he offered no quarter, speaking before she'd even said a word. 'What have you done to my brother? He's been working like a demon all morning to distract himself from thinking your engagement is off.'

'It's not off.'

'Mind telling him that? In person? Soon? As in, I will come and get you in the helicopter right now.'

'That's the spirit.' Might as well go with the flow. 'Tell him I love him like crazy and that the engagement is very much on. Tell him that I'm putting together an apology surprise for him and that you'll pick him up an hour before sunset for a helicopter joyride with me at the end of it. That's all you need to say. Can you do that?'

'Better coming from you.'

'Apart from that, which I will see to, trust me, I need your helicopter and your services as a pilot for the rest of the day. I'll pay triple the going rate. And sheets. I need every sheet you've got that's not already on a bed.'

'Sheets,' he echoed doubtfully.

'For when I run out of rocks and fallen branches. Oh, and do you have any toilet paper?'

'No way am I giving up my share of the toilet paper. You've gotta be family for that.'

'Bring it anyway,' she urged.

'You're sounding a little bit mad today. Are you aware of this?' He really was a sweet and mostly biddable man.

'I am mad. I'm mad at myself for letting your brother doubt his worth for a second.'

'I'm going to put you on speaker phone now because Judah's just walked in, and you're going to put him out of his misery by telling him that.'

'Wait! Will you help me? It'll be worth it, I promise. I'm aiming to create a truly memorable moment.'

'Speaker phone. Now.'

'Wait!' But she didn't think Reid had been open to influence on this particular issue. 'Judah?'

'Bridie,' he replied evenly.

Right, so…speakerphone. 'I'm, uh, hi!' So not ready to confront him yet.

Silence.

Bridie closed her eyes, took a deep breath and began. 'So, yesterday was tough to navigate. Lots of new and surprising information to think about, you know?' She rushed on without waiting for more astonishingly loud silence. 'But I don't want to call off our engagement. You are without question the finest man I know. I want to marry you, cheer for you, laugh with you and cherish all the little pieces that make you who you are. I still want that for us.'

No one spoke.

Bridie cringed, wishing she could see how her words were being received. 'Do you—is that what you want?'

She heard a heavy sigh, but wasn't sure whose it was. 'Did someone just huff?'

'That was me,' confessed Reid. 'I'm trying to get my white-knuckled, tongue-tied brother to say something at this very special moment in time but he's not responding to my cues.'

And then Judah spoke. 'Bridie, you don't have to do this. You don't owe me a damn thing.'

'Wait!' yelped Reid. 'What?' There was the sound of a scuffle and muffled words she couldn't quite hear and then Reid in her ear again. 'Sorry I interrupted. My brother hasn't quite finished speaking yet.'

She waited. And waited.

And held her breath and *waited*.

'I'm yours.' Rough-cut words that sounded as if Judah had carved them out of his heart just for her. 'Yes, that's what I want. So much.'

'Great. That's perfect. *You're* perfect.' Even if he wasn't one for fancy words. She could be the fancy-word provider. Not a problem. 'Will you join me for an hour before sunset? And probably after the sun sets too? I want to spoil you to make up for my...confusion... yesterday.'

'No need,' Judah rumbled. 'It's forgotten.'

'No, it's not, even though we'll never mention it again. Will you please let Reid bring you to me this afternoon, no questions asked?'

'Yes.'

Yes! She punched the air with her fist. 'See you then. Oh, and, Reid?'

'My rotor blades are at your service, future favourite sister-in-law.'

'I'm really glad I get a little brother out of this deal too.' And not just because she really needed his help if she had any hope of pulling her rapidly forming plans together in a day. 'How soon can you get here? I have so much for you to do.'

Reid found Judah in his office shortly after five that afternoon. Judah studied his brother, looking for clues as to what he'd been up to, but Reid's aviator sunglasses hid his eyes and nothing else about him looked any different than it had this morning. Well-worn jeans, loose T-shirt, work boots, ready grin. Reid had been back twice throughout the afternoon to refuel, so he'd sure as hell been covering some ground in his compact two-seater helicopter.

'Ready to go find your intended?'

Reid had taken to all but bouncing up and down on the balls of his feet. Nervous energy was a new look for Reid and instantly made Judah even more suspicious about what the afternoon held in store. 'Am I going to like this surprise?'

'God, I hope so,' muttered Reid. 'If you don't, I'm thinking of relocating to Canada for a recovery holiday. Got your wallet?'

'What for?' Who needed a wallet around here?

'ID in case we crash. I've been reading up on my aviation rules.'

His brother's words were almost believable. Only not.

'Just bring your wallet.' Reid spread his arms out imploringly. One of his forearms had an ugly red scrape on it that Judah was pretty sure hadn't been there this morning. 'C'mon, I've been humouring Bridie all afternoon and it was a very tough gig. Is it too much to ask that you take your wallet out of your desk drawer and shove it in your back pocket?'

'Testy.' But he did as his brother asked, and Reid's smile reappeared.

'How about a shirt with a collar?' Reid suggested next and Judah eyed him narrowly.

'Why?'

'Have I mentioned the amount of *effort* I've expended this afternoon on your behalf? Not to mention the effort

Bridie's put in. Last I saw her she was absolutely filthy, headed for a shower and obsessing about whether she had anything suitable to wear. Silk was mentioned, along with whether she had time to wash and dry her hair and do anything with it. I have never run away faster, but out of the goodness of my very kind heart I'm sharing this information with you in case you want to go and change your shirt.'

So Judah went to the adjacent walk-in cupboard and changed his shirt. 'Anything else?'

'Decent boots. Not work boots.'

'Is this a formal dinner situation?' Because he'd been expecting something a little more casual. Picnic from the back of her Land Rover somewhere out on the plains while the sun went down.

'I am sworn to secrecy. But if we don't get cracking we're going to be late. Sunset waits for no man.'

It wasn't until they were walking to the helicopter that Judah spoke again. 'Where are we going?'

'Up.'

'Can you be any more specific?'

'Nope.'

Reid flew helicopters with the confidence only youth and long hours in the seat could bring. Mustering would see them flying low and darting about, but this time he took them high and smooth and put them on a north-east course towards river bend. Not so far to go, then, and he wondered why Bridie hadn't simply asked him to drive there. But Reid overshot the mark, so maybe river bend wasn't their destination at all. Reid then confused him twice over by swinging them around to approach the river again, this time with the sun behind them.

And then he saw it: a word spelled out on the ground

with a combination of rocks, dead branches and some kind of white material.

The word was STRENGTH.

'I'm working from a script here, so let me get it right,' Reid told him through their headset two-ways. 'This is what Bridie sees in you. A man of strength. I see it too.'

Before Judah could comment, Reid swung the helicopter around in a show-off move and headed west.

Another word waited for them in the channel country, and it was as if a demented fairy had scoured the land for as many moveable rocks as they could find.

COURAGE was the word.

'This too,' said Reid, and circled it twice before taking them north.

'There's more?'

'Better believe it. Which is the point of this whole exercise. That you come to believe what she sees in you. Good thing she ran out of fabric.'

The next word said HONOUR.

'I like that one for you,' said Reid. 'I think it's my favourite.'

The next word was RESILIENCE, and it had been shaped out of some kind of heavy-duty canvas, pinned down by tent pegs and rocks.

'That one nearly did her in,' said tour guide Reid, while Judah sat there awash in words and none of them his. 'I had to help her with it because she was nowhere near done when I came to pick her up. Too many letters, man, way too many letters and not enough rocks in the world. Try PEP, I said. What about GRIT? I didn't do badly in my English exams, I had suggestions, but no. It had to be RESILIENCE. There's not a scrap of tarpaulin left in her shed.' Reid paused. 'Or ours.'

The next word was HOPE.

'She says a man without hope can't begin to imagine the future the way you do. Or work so hard to make it happen the way you do. Can't say I disagree with her. She had more words—it was a very long list, but there's only one more.'

'Good.' Because they were doing him in.

The last word was JOY.

'Joy?' he asked gruffly. 'Me? Now I'm sure she needs glasses.'

'Yeah.' Reid laughed. 'I queried that one too, but she swears there's a lifetime of it in store for you if you'll take her on. I'm to give you this now.' Reid handed him a white envelope. 'To read.'

In the envelope was a sheet of office paperwork, and words printed in a fancy font inviting him to the wedding of Miss Bridie Elizabeth Starr and Lord Judah Leopold Blake.

Date: Today
Time: Sunset
RSVP: Landing means I Do

'I'm your best man if that's what you want,' said Reid. 'And there's a wedding party waiting for you just over those trees. Gert is matron of honour and Tomas is the FOB—that's father of the bride—and he'll be giving Bridie away. I am bang up on wedding abbreviations after today. Old Ernie reckons he can legitimately marry you as long as you have some ID. I think he's dreaming, but what do I know?'

'Take us down.'

But Reid didn't take them down. Instead he flew over the clump of trees to reveal a pathway of rocks that led to a small group of people. Bridie stood out like a beacon in a slim white gown with tiny shoulder straps and the rest of it pretty much fell straight to the ground. Her riot of hair had been pulled away from her face and styled instead to cascade down her back. She held a posy stuffed haphazardly with desert flowers, the kind he'd taken to finding for her after a night beneath the stars.

'Reid. *Take us down.*'

'Those are the words I wanted to hear. Right after *Yes, oh, wise, hardworking and patient brother, I want you to be my best man.*'

'I want you to be my best man.'

'What happened to wise, hardworking and patient? You can't hog *all* the good words.'

'Reid, that woman down there is my North Star, my refuge and my soul. Get me down there before she changes her mind.'

'They're landing,' said Gert, and Bridie's heart soared.

Proving her love for Judah by springing a surprise wedding on him had seemed like a good idea at the time, but as everything came together, with Reid dropping her back at the homestead before flitting off to collect Gert, and then Ernie, and finally Judah, second thoughts had taken hold. What if Judah didn't want to marry her yet? What if he did want to marry her but wanted a different kind of wedding altogether? One that took a year or two to plan and involved many aristocratic guests? Maybe his inherited title meant he had to follow lots of rules before it was official?

Not that he was necessarily one for rules. He had his own unwavering code of honour and she loved him all the more for it.

She took a deep breath. In, out. In, out. While a brilliant afternoon sun gently kissed the horizon.

'It's normal to be a little bit nervous,' said Gert. 'And usually, it's the man standing here waiting for his bride.'

'Yay for equality,' offered Bridie weakly. She hadn't really thought this part of the afternoon through. Standing there scouring the sky and waiting for him to show had been *excruciating*.

She took a deep breath and exhaled noisily. She *had* given him the chance to simply fly away. Give him the invitation when you're on the last word, she'd told Reid. And then take him wherever he wants to go.

She'd had no plan B for if he didn't arrive, other than painfully, publicly falling to pieces. Why was it taking Reid so damn long to land the helicopter?

'Turn around and let me fuss over you,' said Gert, taking charge. The older woman's concerned blue gaze met hers as she tucked a strand of Bridie's hair behind her ear. 'You look so beautiful. So very ready to make that man happy, and there's no one who deserves happiness more than him.'

'I know.' She blew out another breath. Heaven knew what she'd be like in childbirth. Probably hyperventilating all over the place. 'I've got this.' She took Gert's hand and placed it over her racing heart. 'See?'

'Relax, child. He's here.'

She was never not going to associate the sound of the helicopter powering down with this moment. 'Is he heading our way?'

The older woman nodded and squeezed Bridie's hand before letting go. 'Tomas, you stand over here next to Ernie and I'll stand here, and all Judah and Reid have to do when they get here is step into place.'

Which they did.

Judah turned towards her, outback strong in dusty

boots, well-worn jeans, collared shirt with the sleeves rolled up and eyes that searched her face. 'Hey.'

'Hey.' Forget butterflies in her stomach. She croaked like a frog.

'Beautiful sunset,' he said next, and Reid elbowed him in the ribs.

'North Star,' Reid muttered around a fit of totally fake coughing.

Judah jostled him back, his gaze not leaving her face. 'And still nowhere near as incredible as you,' he added quietly. 'Are you ready to take on the world with me?'

'I'm ready.' So very ready to love this man for ever.

So Ernie married them.

EPILOGUE

JUDAH WATCHED FROM his vantage point at one end of the ground-floor veranda as his guests spilled out of the crowded ballroom and into the night. Jeddah Creek station glowed with the care that only endless money and strong vision could bring. Planes were parked wing to wing in the outer home paddock and tents had sprung up beside the planes that didn't have sleeping quarters built in. Last year's welcome home ball had only whetted people's appetite for another taste of Judah Blake, philanthropist, and the vast land protection initiatives he spearheaded.

A warm and playful breeze whipped at the wraps and the hair of the ladies present and the stars in the sky that he never took for granted drew gasps from the city folk not used to such a generous display.

This past year had been a rewarding one. Almost as if every mad idea for a better future he'd ever had in the past nine years was being acted out in front of him. Money, so much money available for his projects. Remote area cabins that were architectural marvels. Scientific research projects. Channel country preservation. His brilliant, talented, beautiful wife...

Bridie was inside the ballroom somewhere, but chances were she'd find him soon enough. She still wasn't one for big crowds, and her growing status as an artist made her nervous at times, but she was his fiercest defender and she was in there tonight talking paint colours with his godmother, Eleanor. Bridie wasn't just his North Star. She was all the stars in the sky.

He checked his clothes. White shirt cuffs with a quarter inch showing below the sleeve of his suit. His father's watch, and his grandfather's before that, partly visible when he extended his hand. Such things mattered to some of the people he was courting here tonight.

Bridie wore a pale blue gown tonight, her shoulders bare, a fitted bodice and a sleek fall of silk starting somewhere around her waist and finishing at the floor. A stunning blue opal, outlined in silver filigree, hung from a ribbon around her neck, her father's work. Bridie had already fielded a number of questions about the piece and had gleefully turned them towards her father, especially the single ladies of good nature and mature age. Tomas, who epitomised the rugged, wary outback loner, had suffered the first few ladies with dogged, near-mute politeness, which only seemed to make the ladies try even harder to put him at ease.

Tomas had last been seen fleeing from the ballroom, with Bridie's delighted laughter lingering in his wake.

Bridie laughed a lot these days and Judah never tired of the sound.

And then there was her beauty. Call him biased, but these days her considerable physical beauty seemed somehow lit from within. Contentment, she called it. *Or maybe it's wonder,* she'd once said to him. So many new experiences had come her way this past year and she seemed determined to approach every one of them with wonder and gratitude.

Approaches like that were contagious, no question, given that he'd recently started doing the same.

It was all too easy to be grateful for the life he was living now.

'Your wife has requested your presence at her side,' said Reid, sliding into place beside him. Reid was a hair taller than Judah these days and broader across the shoulders. Responsibility sat more easily on those shoulders, and with it came an easy confidence his brother had more than earned.

If Judah was the visionary and dealmaker of the trio, then Reid was the project manager with the people skills to make it happen. Bridie was their media manager with full control over visual promotional material and how and where it was displayed.

Sometimes, when he was feeling especially smug, Judah thought that together the three of them could change the world.

'She still with Lady Eleanor?'

Reid nodded.

'Have you persuaded your school friend to come and chef for us yet?'

'He says he can give us six months. I'm holding out for twelve so that he's here when the visiting astrophysicists arrive. Have you seen their list of dietary requirements? Talk about special.'

'Double what you're offering him.'

'I love spending your money. Consider it done.' Reid smiled cheerfully. 'Shouldn't you be on your way to rescue your North Star, your refuge and your soul?'

He was never going to live that down.

He was, however, moving towards the ballroom door.

He found her to one side of the dance floor, his godmother nowhere in sight. She watched him walk towards her with a smile she just didn't give anyone else. He tried to figure out what was different about the ones she saved for him but so far he hadn't been able to.

Hooked him every time.

'Dance with me,' he said when he reached her and held out his hand, and she slid hers into it, warm and utterly sure of her welcome.

And why wouldn't she be? She had him wrapped around her little finger.

'I'd like the photographer here tonight to take some photos of us dancing,' she said. 'That okay by you?'

'What for?'

'Private use only. You, me, the family photo album. They'd come after the brilliant ones of our first kiss and the blurry ones Reid took of our wedding.'

She'd kept her promise about always asking before taking pictures of him. He'd never quite got over how exposed he'd felt when looking at a picture of himself, never mind that he carried one small, well-creased picture of them kissing in the rain in his wallet. Every time he looked at it, he was transported back to the purest moment of freedom he'd ever felt.

He also knew how much Bridie regretted not having a single decent photo of their wedding. Didn't matter to him so much.

He'd memorised every moment. 'Okay.'

She nodded and sent a thumbs up to someone off to the side, presumably the photographer, and then he turned her in his arms and put a hand to the back of her waist.

They still hadn't learned how to dance properly. Maybe by their sixtieth wedding anniversary they'd have done this often enough to tear up the dance floor with their prowess.

'Something funny?' she murmured.

'Just thinking of our future.'

'Oh? And how's it looking?'

'Our sixtieth wedding anniversary's going to be a cracker.'

'Slow down. We have so many moments to look forward to before that.' She slid her hand from his shoulder, down his arm to his wrist, and brought his hand around to her front, placing his palm against her belly. 'You know how we started giving birth control a miss?'

His heart stopped. His feet stopped.

Everything stopped.

Her fingers sliding effortlessly into the spaces between his, caressing her belly, and he tried to speak but he didn't have the words and probably never would have words for this.

'Judah?' she asked uncertainly. 'Breathe. Breathing would be good.'

Breathing could wait. He closed his eyes and used the hand not already cradling their baby to tilt her face towards his. His eyes closed as her lips met his and he didn't care that they were in a public place and that every man, woman and dog could see his tumbling, vulnerable steps towards parenthood. Let them see.

He wasn't backing away from this moment of purest love and worship between him and Bridie for any reason. He was hers.

She broke the kiss, which had deepened considerably. 'Judah, we're in public.'

'Don't care.'

'We're being photographed.'

No flying ducks given. The smile wouldn't leave his face. He was going to be a family man. 'I'd like many children.'

'*So* getting ahead of yourself there on the baby front.'

'How about the kissing front?'

She kissed him again and he lifted her off the ground and whirled her around and she laughed and flung her head back, her hair cascading down her back and over his arms. There was nothing he would do differently when it came to all the decisions that had led him to this moment. Not one single thing.

'I'm so happy,' she said when he finally let her feet touch the ground again. 'You're breathing again.'

He was. Go, him.

'There will be no photos of the actual birth,' she warned, but she fair glowed with happiness. 'I'm beginning to comprehend what it means to be utterly exposed.'

'Not even for the family album?'

She was wavering. He could tell. 'I'll let you know.' She tried for ladylike primness, failed miserably, and he loved her all the more for it.

'Your call, North Star,' he rumbled as they started dancing again. 'But I'm thinking there'll be photos in that album.'

* * * * *

COMING SOON!

We really hope you enjoyed reading this book.
If you're looking for more romance, be sure to
head to the shops when new books are
available on

Thursday 14th
April

To see which titles are coming soon, please visit

millsandboon.co.uk/nextmonth

MILLS & BOON

MILLS & BOON®

Coming next month

CROWNING HIS LOST PRINCESS
Caitlin Crews

"I don't understand this…sitting around in pretty rooms and *talking*," Delaney seethed at him, her blue eyes shooting sparks when they met his. "I like to be outside. I like dirt under my feet. I like a day that ends with me having to scrub soil out from beneath my fingernails."

She glared at the walls as if they had betrayed her.

Then at him, as if he was doing so even now.

For a moment he almost felt as if he had—but that was ridiculous.

"When you are recognized as the true Crown Princess of Ile d'Montagne, the whole island will be your garden," he told her. Trying to soothe her. He wanted to lift a hand to his own chest and massage the brand that wasn't there, but *soothing* was for others, not him. He ignored the too-hot sensation. "You can work in the dirt of your ancestors to your heart's content."

Delaney shot a look at him, pure blue fire. "Even if I did agree to do such a crazy thing, you still wouldn't get what you want. It doesn't matter what blood is in my veins. I am a farm girl, born and bred. I will never look the part of the Princess you imagine. Never."

She sounded almost as final as he had, but Cayetano allowed himself a smile, because that wasn't a flat refusal. It sounded more like a *maybe* to him.

He could work with *maybe*.

In point of fact, he couldn't wait.

He rose then. And he made his way toward her, watching the way her eyes widened. The way her lips parted. There was an unmistakable flush on her cheeks as he drew near, and he could see her pulse beat at her neck.

Cayetano was the warlord of these mountains and would soon enough be the King of this island. And he had been prepared to ignore the fire in him, the fever. The ways he wanted her that had intruded into his work, his sleep. But here and now, he granted himself permission to want this woman. *His* woman. Because he could see that she wanted him.

With that and her *maybe,* he knew he'd already won.

"Let me worry about how you look," he said as he came to a stop before her, enjoying the way she had to look up to hold his gaze. It made her seem softer. He could see the hectic need all over her, matching his own. "There is something far more interesting for you to concentrate on."

Delaney made a noise of frustration. "The barbaric nature of ancient laws and customs?"

"Or this."

And then Cayetano followed the urge that had been with him since he'd seen her standing in a dirt-filled yard with a battered kerchief on her head and kissed her.

He expected her to be sweet. He expected to enjoy himself.

He expected to want her all the more, to tempt his own feverish need with a little taste of her.

But he was totally unprepared for the punch of it. Of a simple kiss—a kiss to show her there was more here than righting old wrongs and reclaiming lost thrones. A kiss to share a little bit of the fire that had been burning in him since he'd first laid eyes on her.

It was a blaze and it took him over.

It was a dark, drugging heat.

It was a mad blaze of passion.

It was a delirium—and he wanted more.

Continue reading
CROWNING HIS LOST PRINCESS
Caitlin Crews

Available next month
www.millsandboon.co.uk

Copyright ©2022 by Caitlin Crews

MILLS & BOON

THE HEART OF ROMANCE

A ROMANCE FOR EVERY READER

MODERN
Prepare to be swept off your feet by sophisticated, sexy and seductive heroes, in some of the world's most glamourous and romantic locations, where power and passion collide.

HISTORICAL
Escape with historical heroes from time gone by. Whether your passion is for wicked Regency Rakes, muscled Vikings or rugged Highlanders, awake the romance of the past.

MEDICAL
Set your pulse racing with dedicated, delectable doctors in the high-pressure world of medicine, where emotions run high and passion, comfort and love are the best medicine.

True Love
Celebrate true love with tender stories of heartfelt romance, from the rush of falling in love to the joy a new baby can bring, and a focus on the emotional heart of a relationship.

Desire
Indulge in secrets and scandal, intense drama and plenty of sizzling hot action with powerful and passionate heroes who have it all: wealth, status, good looks…everything but the right woman.

HEROES
Experience all the excitement of a gripping thriller, with an intense romance at its heart. Resourceful, true-to-life women and strong, fearless men face danger and desire - a killer combination!

To see which titles are coming soon, please visit
millsandboon.co.uk/nextmonth

LET'S TALK
Romance

For exclusive extracts, competitions and special offers, find us online:

f facebook.com/millsandboon

🐦 @MillsandBoon

📷 @MillsandBoonUK

Get in touch on 01413 063232

For all the latest titles coming soon, visit
millsandboon.co.uk/nextmonth

MILLS & BOON
A ROMANCE FOR EVERY READER

- **FREE** delivery direct to your door

- **EXCLUSIVE** offers every month

- **SAVE** up to 25% on pre-paid subscriptions

SUBSCRIBE AND SAVE

millsandboon.co.uk/Subscribe

WANT EVEN MORE
ROMANCE?
SUBSCRIBE AND SAVE TODAY!

'Mills & Boon books; the perfect way to escape for an hour or so.'

MISS W. DYER

'Excellent service, promptly delivered and very good subscription choices.'

MISS A. PEARSON

'You get fantastic special offers and the chance to get books before they hit the shops.'

MRS V. HALL

Visit millsandboon.co.uk/Subscribe
and save on brand new books.

JOIN THE
MILLS & BOON
BOOKCLUB

* **FREE** delivery direct to your door

* **EXCLUSIVE** offers every month

* **EXCITING** rewards programme

50% OFF
YOUR FIRST
PARCEL

Join today at
millsandboon.co.uk/subscribe

JOIN US ON SOCIAL MEDIA!

Stay up to date with our latest releases, author news and gossip, special offers and discounts, and all the behind-the-scenes action from Mills & Boon...

 millsandboon

 millsandboonuk

 millsandboon

It might just be true love...

GET YOUR ROMANCE FIX!

MILLS & BOON
— *blog* —

Get the latest romance news, exclusive author interviews, story extracts and much more!

blog.millsandboon.co.uk

MILLS & BOON
Desire

Indulge in secrets and scandal, intense drama and plenty of sizzling hot action with powerful and passionate heroes who have it all: wealth, status, good looks…everything but the right woman.

Four Desire stories published every month, find them all at:

millsandboon.co.uk

MILLS & BOON

HEROES

At Your Service

Experience all the excitement of a
gripping thriller, with an intense romance
at its heart. Resourceful, true-to-life
women and strong, fearless men face
danger and desire - a killer combination!

Eight Heroes stories published every month, find them all at:

millsandboon.co.uk